ROBERT RADCLIFFE

THE BRIDGE

HEAD OF ZEUS

First published in the UK in 2019 by Head of Zeus Ltd
This paperback edition published in the UK in 2019 by Head of Zeus Ltd

9 7 5 3 1 2 4 6 8

A catalogue record for this book is available from
the British Library.

ISBN (PB): 9781784973926
ISBN (E): 9781784973896

Typeset by Divaddict Publishing Solutions Ltd

Printed and bound in Great Britain by
CPI Group (UK) Ltd, Croydon CR0 4YY

Head of Zeus Ltd
First Floor East
5–8 Hardwick Street
London EC1R 4RG

WWW.HEADOFZEUS.COM

For Kate

CHAPTER 1

A little further and he came to another village, barely a ramshackle cluster of cottages and barns clinging to a hillside. He mopped his brow, squinting up at a brassy noon sun, then entered, following narrow cobbled alleyways to a tiny piazza with a stone water trough and a whitewashed chapel bearing the legend 'San Felice'. He sat, filling his water bottle from the trough and massaging his ankle. A rooster crowed, nearby sheep stirred in a pen, and somewhere a dog started barking, but the piazza was empty of human life. Fled the area, he guessed, gazing around, or simply hiding indoors fearful of strangers, as in every village he visited. Pulling the crumpled photo from his pocket, he rose wearily from the trough and approached the nearest door.

Twenty minutes later and having gained nothing but hostile stares and head shakes, he knocked on a door in a narrow alleyway, to have it opened by a grey-haired woman of about forty.

'*Scusi, signora,*' he began in his accented Italian, but after the merest hesitation she swung the door in his face. Instinctively his boot jerked forward, wedging the door ajar, for in that moment's hesitation, that fractional hiatus, he glimpsed something he'd not seen all day. Recognition. Of the face in the photo. And the fact that she was now cursing him furiously and shouldering the door and kicking at his foot like a madwoman told him for certain she knew who it was.

'Stop!' he pleaded. '*Cessare! Finire!*'

'*Tedesco* murderer!'

'*Tedesco?* Me? No! I'm—'

'You're Gestapo, I can smell it!'

'No, *signora*, you're wrong, I'm— Ow! That's my bad foot!'

'Then get it out of my door!'

'No, but listen…'

A gun barrel appeared in the gap, a British one, he noted, Lee Enfield, old but well oiled. Then the wooden stock, gripped firmly in two large and hairy hands.

'Step back,' a gruff voice ordered. 'Right now, or I shoot you dead.'

He wrenched his boot free and stood obediently back, hands raised. Mad kicking women were one thing, menacing husbands with rifles quite another. The door opened wider and a middle-aged man appeared from the shadows, dark and swarthy, hefting the gun in the crook of his arm.

'Who are you?'

'Not what you think, *signore*, I assure you!'

'Then what?'

'I'm… Well, I'm a friend.'

It took another ten tense minutes to convince them, and in that time the rifle never left his chest for a second. Using his pigeon Italian and the photo, and the other documents he'd been given as bona fides, and electing wisely not to inflame the situation further by offering the bribe money he'd also been issued with, he recited his story, answered their questions and explained his mission, repeatedly and unwaveringly, until finally they looked at one another and exchanged a dubious nod.

'Very well,' the man warned grimly, 'but if you're lying, and the slightest harm comes to anyone up there...'

'I'm not, and it won't, I assure you.'

'But if it does, I will hunt you down and kill you like a dog.'

They gave him water to drink, an onion to chew on, vague pointing directions, and sent him on his way. The path was long, steeply uphill, and in the warm spring sunshine he was soon breathless and sweating once more. His foot too became troublesome and he paused frequently to rest it, gazing up towards the distant hills for signs of human habitation. None appeared until after nearly an hour, when the path began to level on to a narrow plateau, and became pockmarked with farmyard jumble: rusting buckets, coils of wire, an ox plough. Then a badly painted sign appeared warning strangers to keep away, and suddenly two hunting dogs on chains leaped up from the grass, furiously pulling on their tethers and snarling like wolves. He gave them a wide berth, left the path and struck out in a wide arc which took him into dank chestnut woods smelling of leaf mould and humming with flies. At one point he closed to the forest's edge to glimpse a huge bull penned in a field. It tossed its head and stamped and snorted, and he knew he must be drawing near. Sure enough, ascending further on to a higher plain, the trees began to thin at last, bordering a sloping field of freshly sown maize. To one side, a second field had been newly marked out, and the coarse soil roughly turned ready for working. In it a man laboured, bent over, painstakingly clearing stones into piles by hand. Dressed in simple farmer's garb of serge trousers cinched with string, a collarless white shirt, corduroy waistcoat and cap, he moved slowly and looked much slighter and older than he should. Then he stood up to stretch his back and, doffing the cap to dab his brow, tilted his face to the sky, head cocked, as though listening.

And then there was no doubt at all.

My name is Lance Corporal Harry Reginald Boulter and this report is written by me April 27 1944. My birthday is March 12th 1915 so I am 29 years old. I live at 58 Oakley Road, Huntingdon, I am married to Janice Rose Boulter, we have no children. I first joined the army in 1938 as a private in 1st Battalion Royal Berkshires based in Reading under Col. Dempsey. In 1939 the battalion went to France with the BEF and fought at Dunkirk where we had bad casualties, but was rescued on 3rd June 1940 and returned by ship to Folkestone. After that we was stood down so I applied to join a special services unit and after being accepted in the autumn of 1940 was sent to 11 Special Air Service Battalion where I trained as a paratrooper at Ringway Airport near Manchester. A while after that we heard of a special op that was asking for volunteers and so I put my name forward without thinking. A while later I was interviewed by Major Tag Pritchard who was i/c the op which was to blow up an aqueduct in Italy. After the interview I learned I had been accepted and met the others in the team which was called X Troop including section leaders Capt Daly and Capt Lea and Lt Deane-Drummond who was intelligence officer. There was seven officers in all and forty or so ORs I believe including a number of sappers from the Royal Engineers plus two interpreters one called Picchi and one called Trickey. Picchi I heard later was executed by the Italians. Anyway we flew in for the mission which was called Operation Colossus

4

on Feb 10 1941 but unfortunately I broke my ankle when I landed and so played little part in the mission which was partly successful, the aqueduct being blown at one end but not completely destroyed. Anyway our orders was then to march sixty miles cross country and get picked up at the coast but there was no way I could do it, so was left behind. Maj Pritchard I want to testify was very nice about it but said that orders was orders and we all knew any injured got left behind. Private Trickey I want to testify was specially kind, he offered to help me but Maj Pritchard said no and I agreed as I would only hold everyone up. Private Trickey did promise to get a note to my wife Jan which he did I learned much later for which we are both very grateful. Anyway the others all left and I stayed behind at the aqueduct. Next morning Italian soldiers arrived in strength and though I fought them off best I could, I soon ran out of ammo and had to surrender. After a spell in hospital during which my ankle was badly set I eventually was sent to Sulmona POW camp where I met the rest of X Troop who had all been captured before they reached the rendezvous. We stayed at Sulmona POW camp two and a half years until September '43 when the Italian army surrendered. During that time Private Alf Parker and Lt Deane-Drummond escaped separately and I believe made it home. Anyway a few days after the Italian surrender we got up for roll call and found the guards had all run off and the gates left open so we just walked out. We all split up then, some stayed put to wait for the Allies to arrive, some went north to the Italian ports, while I decided to head south and make for our lines. This took some months and I had some adventures on the way, sleeping rough and living with partisans, I even went on a couple of raids with them, anyway I spent most of last winter living in a hay loft in a village near Chieti. Then when spring came I headed south again, until I could hear gunfire and artillery getting nearer, eventually sneaking across into Canadian held Allied lines near Trivento. This ends my report.

The officer slowly lowered the page.

'That's, ah, that's certainly quite a story, Lance Corporal.'

'God's truth, every word.'

'Hmm.' Holding it between finger and thumb like a discarded tissue, he turned the sheet over, examining its creases and stains. 'Which unit did you say you were in?'

'X Troop.'

'X...'

Boulter rolled his eyes. 'X Troop, 11 Special Air Service Battalion, 2 Commando. It's written right there!'

'I've never heard of such a thing.'

'That's not my problem!'

'Actually it is.' The officer shot him a warning glance.

Boulter slumped back, arms folded, waiting while the man reread his story. Yet again. The latest man that is, the third or fourth at least, after the Canadian perimeter guard, then the Canadian red-cap, then the Canadian major, then a blindingly stupid captain of the Irish Guards, then this one – a chinless wonder of a second lieutenant, about twenty years old by the looks of him and straight from Oxbridge into the Intelligence Corps. Smartly turned out, Boulter couldn't help noticing, with shirt and tie beneath a battledress jacket adorned with unit flashes and divisional insignia. How things had changed in the British army, he mused, in his three years away from it. Then again maybe not. Still the same old officer bullshit. Ducking suddenly, he glanced up as two Spitfires thundered overhead, heading west towards Monte Cassino. In seconds

6

they were gone, and the thunder faded to a hum. Still waiting, he looked around the tent, a typical army canvas-sided affair, with flaps for a door, a camping cot, table and chair for furnishings. And an armed red-cap standing outside.

'Am I under arrest?'

The lieutenant folded the sheet and, taking out cigarettes, offered them across the little table. 'Not at all.'

Boulter lit one then pocketed the pack. 'Then what?'

'You're under *guard*, for your own protection as well as ours.'

'What's that supposed to mean?'

'It means there are all sorts of people wandering the countryside hereabouts, hundreds probably, and many find their way through to our lines. Some, like you, are escaped British POWs, or say they are. But some are deserters, some fifth columnists, and a few, unquestionably, are enemy agents posing as British POWs.'

'Are you calling me a bloody deserter!'

'No, Corporal, it's just that we need to be absolutely sure whom we're talking to.'

'You're talking to me, Harry Boulter, you have my word on it.'

'And I believe you. But unfortunately we must verify it, through the proper channels, London, your former regiment, your, ah, special ops unit, and so on. Which could take a day or two.'

'But I've been here three days already!'

'I know. So to speed things up, I'm asking you to tell it to me again.'

'Tell you what?'

'Everything. From when you joined up, to when you arrived here three days ago. Every last detail. With dates, places and names. Especially names, as many as you can remember. We'll then type it all up into a proper statement, send it off, and have you on a ship home in no time.'

'And how bloody long is all that going to take?'

'Shouldn't take more than a couple of weeks.'

But it wasn't a couple of weeks. Just two days later the lieutenant was back, ducking under the flap, waving papers and gabbling excitedly about friends in high places.

'What friends?' Boulter asked incredulously.

'I can't say. But high enough to get you an air ticket home.'

'What?'

'It's true. Forget weeks rolling round a troopship getting torpedoed by U-boats. They're going to fly you home in a Dakota.'

'Who's they?'

'I told you, I can't say!'

'Strewth! What's a Dakota?'

'The height of luxury and comfort. Fast, too; it'll have you home in a day...'

Boulter shook his head. 'Blimey.'

'... just as soon as you complete a little job for them.'

As casually as possible, Theo replaced the cap on his head and bent once more to the task of sorting rocks from the tilth. He was being observed, of that he was now certain. First warning had been the distant barking of the dogs. Then had come the telltale roar from Bruno the bull a while later. Finally the glimpse of movement at the edge of the woods confirmed his worst suspicion. What he could not be sure of was how many were watching, and more importantly who. But it didn't matter, his carelessness had allowed strangers on to the farm and that was unforgivable. Now he must correct the situation.

Deeply ingrained procedures from half-remembered training courses came to him; instinct did the rest. First essential was to lead his quarry away. Straightening slowly once more he rubbed his back as though in pain, then began to wander across the field, unbuttoning his trouser fly as he went, all the while monitoring the movement in the trees. Just one person, he soon sensed, was following inexpertly along. So much the simpler. Entering the woods a hundred yards ahead of the man, he broke immediately into a sprint, bending double and moving swiftly along the rat runs and deer tracks that criss-crossed the forest floor. In just a few minutes he was behind his prey and moving stealthily forward, stooping momentarily to gather a fallen branch. Vaguely he wondered what should follow next; he only knew that protecting Rosa and the twins transcended all other considerations. Soon he could hear his man tramping breathlessly through the trees. A minute more and he could see him.

It was swiftly over.

Running forward and leaping up, he smashed into the man's back using his whole body's weight. The man sprawled forward with a shocked grunt; Theo was astride him in a second, and in another had the branch braced across his neck.

'Who are you?' he demanded quietly in Italian. The man sputtered and choked. 'Answer me now.'

'Jesus Christ, Trick!' Boulter gasped. 'It's me, for God's sake. It's Harry!'

They walked back down to the farm together.

'You're limping,' Theo remarked. 'Did I hurt you?'

'Yes, you bloody lunatic!' Harry grinned. 'No, it's the ankle. Never set proper. Plays me up sometimes.'

'Sorry to hear that.'

'Can't be helped.'

They arrived at the cottage and Rosa appeared, casting sidelong glances and suspicious scowls until Theo introduced Harry as a 'safe friend'. Then the twins came up, first Vittorio, nodding and grinning shyly, and finally Francesca, who accepted Harry's hand with a frosty nod, then turned away, as if already sensing what was coming.

'She seems a bit anti,' Harry murmured.

'They've learned to be cautious.'

He carried chairs out into the late-afternoon sun, Rosa brought wine and olives and the two men seated themselves in the dusty yard among the ducks and chickens.

'Lovely spot, Trick.' Harry gazed around.

'Yes it is.'

'Been here long?'

'A few months.'

'Farming and that.'

'That's right. Who sent you, Harry?'

'Intelligence bods back in Blighty. Top brass too. I'm to bring you home.'

'Did they say why?'

'You're wanted, I suppose.'

'Was there a message?'

'No, just that they want you back and, er, and that your dad's sick. Dying, in fact. He's asking for you.'

'Oh.'

'Sorry and that.'

Victor. The father he never knew. Who'd disowned him even before he was born. The only message he'd received was the letter in Cairo. Written nearly a year ago and asking for money. Now he was asking for his son.

There had to be more. There was always more. 'How did you find me?'

'Wasn't easy. Been traipsing around these villages for two days. Eventually got to the one down the hill here, San what's-it-called...'

'Felice.'

'That's the one. Banged on doors until I finally found someone who knew you. They pointed me here. Although not until they nearly shot me first.'

Theo nodded. 'Salvatore, and his wife. Good people. But I meant, how did you know where to look?'

'Intelligence bods knew you were in the district, but not exactly where. They also knew you'd never agree to come with someone you didn't know. Not voluntarily that is.'

'I haven't agreed.'

'Oh, er, well... anyway, then I popped up with my report, your name was on it, intelligence sprog at Trivento sent it off to London and suddenly it's all hands to the pumps. They're flying us home in a Dakota, you know!'

Rosa appeared, stooping to refill their glasses.

'What if I say no?'

'Ah, well...' Harry gulped wine. 'That possibility was discussed. Strictly speaking it'd be desertion, wouldn't it? So they'd just send someone else, red-caps or whatever, to arrest you and bring you home anyway. By force if necessary.'

'I'm done with it, Harry.'

'Done with what?'

'War. The fighting and the killing. I'll not do it any more.'

'Ah. Perhaps you could ask—'

'*Dovresti partire,*' Rosa murmured quietly.

Theo shook his head.

'He's asking you to leave, isn't he? And you should.'

'No.'

'Yes. It's time, Teo.'

'I can't.'

'You must. You spend your days with your mind in the clouds. At night you cry out in pain and terror. You hide here with us misfits, haunted by your devils, between the horror of your past and fear for your future. This is no way to exist.'

'I can't, Rosa. Please don't make me.'

'God knows I hate to, and the twins will be heartbroken, but you must. It is the only way for you to heal.'

'No...'

'And you must think also of your *fidanzata*. Perhaps there is news of her. Clara, Teo. Perhaps she is waiting for you as we speak.'

The sun was setting, fingers of dusty shadow creeping across the yard. Around them the spring air was already growing cold.

'Can I come back?' Tears gleamed on his cheek. 'Can I come back if...'

She stooped and kissed his head. 'Of course, northern boy. This is your home.'

CHAPTER 2

John Frost entered the briefing room, a converted milking shed to one side of the main house, and made for his usual seat near the back. Familiar faces nodded in greeting while everyone shuffled to arrange themselves in priority order, like schoolboys at assembly. Lowly battalion commanders like him at the rear, brigade staff further forward, then the division prefects and their lackeys, and finally the crème de la crème, 'Corps', who sat at the front, relaxed and chatty as they waited for the head boy to appear. Everyone, he noticed, was sporting red berets, airborne wings and insignia.

'From little acorns, eh?' his neighbour said with a nudge.

Frost nodded. 'Indeed.' 1st Airborne Corps, newly raised, two full divisions comprising six brigades, twenty battalions, or some fifteen thousand men-at-arms, all recruited, trained, equipped and ready to go. From scratch, in less than four years. It was scarcely believable, he mused, and a far cry from the days of Hardwick Hall and hiding in the bushes to grab recruits for a single battalion. Craning his neck, he glimpsed a tall figure sitting in front and recognized Richard 'Windy' Gale, his old boss from Hardwick Hall, now promoted to command the new 6th Airborne Division. As he watched, Gale turned, waved and signalled he wanted to meet later.

And leading this mighty force? As if on cue a side door opened and to raucous applause a familiar moustachioed figure entered, tripped lightly up steps on to a dais and strode to the front. Lieutenant General Frederick Browning DSO. 'Boy' Browning, founding father of the airborne corps, the man who had overseen its formation, encouraged its development, nurtured its growth and secured its future as a mainstay of the Allied offensive. He'd even designed its uniform. No wonder he was popular. Grinning broadly, he brandished a newspaper.

'We're official, chaps!' he shouted, to another round of cheering.

Frost leaned to his neighbour. 'What's that?'

'In *The Times*. 1st Airborne Corps. Officially announced today.'

'Must have missed it.'

'Nor does it end here!' Browning tapped the newspaper. 'In just a short time we'll be raising history's first airborne *army*!'

More applause, albeit less strident, for everyone knew what he was alluding to. Much promised, much delayed, much agonized over, the long-awaited invasion of northern Europe was finally nigh. D-Day – though the word was never spoken – was coming. And thanks to Boy Browning, 1st Airborne Corps, everyone also knew, would be playing a vital role.

Or half of it would.

Frost listened while the briefing proper got under way. It was the fourth he'd attended in as many weeks, sitting there in that noxious-smelling barn beside the Wiltshire mansion that served as Browning's HQ. And while his excitement over the coming invasion mounted with each briefing, so too did a nagging worry that his battalion might miss it. Each week he heard Browning and his staff describe the extraordinary magnitude of the preparations: two full army groups comprising five corps to be landed on beaches in northern France, airborne troops by the thousands to be dropped inland to secure the beach-heads, scores of individual targets, objectives and missions with code names like Tuxedo, Swordhilt and Skyscraper to accomplish. And that was just the first twenty-four hours. The timing, the complexity, the sheer scale of the plan was as bewildering as it was awesome.

'Unfortunately, Operation Wastage has been called off,' Browning announced to collective sighs from around the room. Frost too could only shake his head. To his counting, at least six ops had been proposed for his division as part of the invasion, only to be scrapped again. This latest one, Wastage, was a plan to drop 1st Airborne Division, including his 2nd Battalion, directly on to the invasion beaches in support of the seaborne troops. Frost had never liked the idea – one tiny error by the pilots and the entire division would end up in the sea, there certainly to drown. Yet the cancellation represented another disappointment for his battalion, which still had no role.

'It's frustrating, I know,' Browning consoled them, 'but don't worry, we've earmarked you 1st Div chaps for something equally important.'

Frost detected movement along his row and, leaning forward, saw a clerk waving a note at him. Handing it to the nearest man, the note began making its way along the line. Meanwhile, Browning was still talking.

'It's called Operation Quicksilver, and though it might appear inconsequential at first, let me assure you nothing could be further from the truth.'

His neighbour handed him the note. He opened and read it, allowed himself a nod, then folded it into a pocket.

Operation Quicksilver, it soon became clear, was little more than a diversion. A sham, a non-existent mission that would never happen. According to Browning, an entire fake army was being 'assembled' in Kent and Sussex, involving thousands of reservists and Home Guard extras, cardboard aeroplanes, inflatable tanks, dummy landing craft and vast fields of empty tents. This fictional force, called 1st US Army Group, had proper insignia and shoulder flashes, a general staff, and even a real commander, the American George Patton who was regularly photographed visiting his 'troops'. The idea was based on a previous fake army, the 12th, which a year earlier had successfully fooled Hitler into thinking the invasion of southern Europe would be through Greece rather than Italy. This time he'd think the invasion of France was planned for the Calais region, and so position his forces in the wrong area. At least that was the hope. 1st Airborne Division, as part of the deception, was to go to Kent and train for a massed parachute drop into Calais. A drop that would never happen.

After the briefing, Frost went in search of Gale.

'Johnny.' Gale pumped his hand. 'How are you?'

'I'm well thank you, sir. If a little brassed off.'

'Ah. Yes. And I do understand. But you mustn't worry, your boys are sure to get their chance.'

'It feels like we're being sidelined.'

'You're not. Monty wants you in reserve, that's all. In case of contingencies. Of which there are sure to be many.' Gale nodded at a heavyset figure standing to one side. 'You should speak to your new boss, Johnny. He's a good man.'

'General Urquhart? He's not even a paratrooper!'

'Roy's a fast learner. Get to know him. He'll do fine.'

Frost glanced around. The room was steadily emptying, attendees filing out while orderly staff collected unused notes, wiped blackboards and scoured the floor for dropped scraps of paper. Secrecy, everyone was constantly reminded, was of paramount importance. 'Can't you tell me anything?'

Gale sighed. '6th Airborne Division's going in a few hours ahead of the main force, Johnny, that's definite. While Roy and 1st Div is being held in reserve. I'm sorry but there it is. And that's all I can say.'

'As I feared.' Frost nodded glumly. Then forced a smile. 'You're going in ahead of the main force?'

'That's right.'

'So you might be the first Allied general into France.'

'I fully intend to be.'

'Good for you, sir.'

'Which brings me to another matter.'

'Oh?'

'An operation. Part of our brief. A *coup de main*. Another bridge, small team, company size, airborne of course, I'm to oversee it.'

'I'll do it!'

'Sorry, Johnny.' Gale patted his shoulder. 'Browning's already earmarked a company from the Ox and Bucks. They're training for it as we speak.'

'Then...'

'The thing is, it's an intelligence-led op, French Resistance and so on. And there's a chap in your battalion who has detailed knowledge of the target, and is also known to the locals. We need him on the team.'

'Ah.'

'Name of Trickey. Apparently he's been on SOE ops in Italy

17

the last few months but is due back any day. I need you to contact me the minute he reports in.'

Frost patted his pockets, withdrew the note and handed it to Gale. 'He already has.' He sighed. 'He got back this morning.'

The Dakota had deposited Theo on a breezy airfield south of Grantham. While the other passengers gathered their bags and dispersed, he and Harry waited on the tarmac beneath blustery skies, dazzled by the iridescence of the grass, and sniffing the Lincolnshire air like homecoming hounds.

'Wow.' Boulter gazed around. 'Would you look at that!'

'How long has it been, Harry?'

'Three years, two months and twenty-something days.'

'That's a long time. Janice will be pleased to see you.'

'I bloody hope so, I'm as hard as a chocolate frog.'

'I... Pardon?'

'Never mind. What about you, Trick? How long you been away?'

He thought back. Clumping down a gangplank in Algiers. November 1942. Another lifetime ago. 'About a year and a half. It seems longer.'

'Got a girl waiting?'

A Jeep appeared, raced across the apron towards them and squealed to a halt. 'Lieutenant Trickey?' the driver asked.

Harry jerked his thumb. 'That'd be him.'

'Actually I'm not—'

'Right-oh! Hop in please, sir. I'm to take you straight to 2nd Battalion HQ.'

Theo hefted his rucksack. 'What about Harry?'

'Who's Harry?'

'Me,' Harry replied. 'The man who brought Lieutenant Trickey home.'

'The 2 Commando bloke, now attached to 1st Battalion?'

'I suppose so.'

'They're based in Melton Mowbray. Bus stop outside. Cheerio!' He crashed gears, let the clutch out and sped off.

Twenty minutes later he turned the Jeep on to a gravel driveway and pulled up outside an imposing stately home. 'Stoke Rochford. Brigade HQ. Dead posh. 2nd Battalion's on the third floor.'

Theo plodded up a curving oak stairway, found the door, knocked and entered.

'Wait!'

An officer, a major, was standing with his back to the door, head lowered in concentration, gripping an upturned umbrella for a golf club. As Theo watched, he took careful aim and putted a ball across the carpet towards a cup.

'Missed, bugger it!' He turned. 'Your fault!'

'Sorry, sir.' Theo dropped his rucksack and made to salute, but the officer was striding forward.

'You must be Trickey.' They shook. 'Been expecting you.'

He was Digby Tatham-Warter, he explained, a recent addition to 2nd Battalion, and the new commander of A Company.

'Call me Digby, everyone does.'

'A Company? But where's Major Lonsdale?'

'Posted to 11th Battalion as second-in-command, lucky bugger.'

Colonel Frost was at a Corps briefing in Wiltshire, Digby added, offering Theo a chair, while the new battalion second-in-command, Wallis, was also away. As seemingly was everyone.

'Most of the boys are home for a long weekend. We've been twiddling our thumbs rather, weeks now, lots of training, lots of promised ops that never happen, it's all getting a bit tiresome.' He lowered his voice. 'Affecting morale too. The lads keep getting in trouble, going AWOL, fights in the pub, failing to come back after leave, that sort of thing.'

'Captain Timothy?' Theo asked. 'He was in A Company.'

'Tim got promoted and transferred to 1st Battalion.'

'Major Ross then. Commanding C Company.'

'Ross was captured, didn't you know?' Theo shook his head. 'In Italy, after Primosole, got snatched messing about behind enemy lines. He's in a German POW camp somewhere, causing mayhem no doubt. Vic Dover heads up C Company now. Sound chap. D'you know him?'

'Not really.' Lonsdale gone, Timothy gone, Ross gone, and so many others before and since. 'Is anyone left? From Tunisia, I mean.'

'Not sure. Oh, but Doug Crawley's back. He fought in Tunisia. Did you know him?'

A tar-black night, creeping down from Sidi Bou with Euan Charteris and the others. Then the nightmare walk to Medjez. Crawley, blinded by a shell, was led by the arm for two days to safety. By Dickie Spender.

'Yes I knew him. He was wounded.'

'Fit as a fiddle now. He leads B Company. And Padre Egan's still here – can't get rid of the old bugger!'

Theo nodded, overwhelmed suddenly by icy waves of memories. Memories that weren't his, but belonged to someone else. He shifted uncomfortably in the chair. His 'uniform' consisted of a second-hand battledress reeking of camphor and his old LRDG boots. No beret, no insignia, no lanyard, no lieutenant's pip; he wasn't even wearing his dog tags. He glanced down at his hands, cracked and calloused from Rosa's fields. They belonged all right, they were real, together with the other cracks and calluses he carried. But this room? This man? This battalion of strangers…

'Colonel Frost,' he said quietly.

'Won't be back until Monday.'

'I need to speak to him.'

'I'll see he's informed.' Digby was studying him, his expression an easy smile. 'He asked to be told as soon as you landed.'

'Good.'

'In the meantime, you're to go home and get some rest. Transport's laid on, travel warrant for the trains, some petty cash and so on.'

'Thank you.'

'We could stop by stores too, if you like, and fix you a proper uniform.'

'I don't want it.'

'As you prefer.' Digby made to rise. 'Then I'll see you downstairs.'

'It's not necessary.'

'It'd be a pleasure.' He picked up his umbrella, resting it on his shoulder like a rifle, then followed Theo down to the hall. There their boots rang on flagstones, dust motes drifted from a chandelier, and through the open doorway the Jeep could be seen waiting beneath gathering clouds.

'He thinks very highly of you, you know. Frost does.'

'I think highly of him.'

'He told me something of your record, with the battalion and, er, some of the other stuff too.'

'Did he?'

21

'He says you've done more than should be asked of any man.'

By the time he reached Kingston heavy rain was falling. Trudging along Burton Street in his soaked and stinking battledress, he could only but reflect on another wet afternoon, six years earlier, when he and his mother Carla, wearily humping their baggage, had first arrived in London so full of hope and expectation. Only to have their expectations dashed to the pavement, and their only hope the kindness of a stranger.

This time there was less kindness. No effusive welcome, no shrieks of delight, no pinching of his cheeks or ruffling of his hair. Eleni Popodopoulos, looking older and slighter than he recalled, opened the door, sank to her knees and burst into tears.

'Eleni! My God, Eleni, what is it?' He stooped to her.

She swatted him away, one arm over her eyes like a child.

'Eleni, are you ill?'

'Is heart.'

'Your heart? Here, let me help you.' He raised her up and began leading her through the door. But she broke free and started flailing at him with her fists, pummelling his chest as though battering down a door.

'Bad, bad, you BAD!'

'Eleni, stop! What is it?'

'You break my heart!'

'What?'

'I thought you bloody DEAD!'

He led her, sobbing, into the kitchen, sat her at the table and gave her water, then ransacked cupboards until he found the ancient bottle of ouzo she kept for special occasions. He poured, she drank, and gradually her sobs subsided to hiccups and sighs.

'I thought you dead,' she sniffed. 'So long and no letter, no nothing.'

'I'm sorry.' But he'd written letters, surely. Passed messages, sent radio signals, left word. People received them, handed them on. People *knew*. Lewis. The intelligence officer in Albanella. He'd contacted Massingham to confirm his bona fides with London. And Yale in Cairo. He'd told him to put his affairs in order and write last-minute mail. And he had, hadn't he?

'I believed it. You dead. We all believe. Mostly.'

'I really am sorry, Eleni.' He looked at her. 'Believed what?'

'The telegram.'

'What telegram? And what do you mean, *all*?'

'All! Me. You mama; new husband Abercrumble.' She shrugged. 'Vic too. And little girl, wha's a name, Nancy, and her mama.'

'You know about Vic?'

'Course. Long time. At leas' I have suspicious long time, but no proof. Then he got sick an' make contact. Trying to find you. He in the hospital, you know. Bad way.'

'Yes, I heard. What about Mama?'

Eleni sipped ouzo. 'She know too. But say nothing.'

'And Nancy? How long have you known about her?'

'A year abouts. I write you long letter, did you not get?'

Egypt again, Yale and the cancelled OCTU. A bundle of mail, including one from Eleni, and some mention of a little urchin. Hesitantly, accompanied by sniffs and trumpet blasts on her handkerchief, the details came out, trickling

23

on to the table like pieces of a puzzle, culminating in a telegram, delivered to Carla, apparently, by the lodger, Brown.

'Brown! Paper salesman chappie, remember? Though I know he not selling no paper, it bloody obvious, all that coming and goings. Anyway, you mama come home one day, this before she marry Abercrumble, and Brown, he standing here in hallway saying postman just brought telegram from War Office.'

'What did it say?'

Her eyes narrowed in recollection. '*Regret Acting Lieutenant T. V. Trickey missing presumed dead in action Italy.*'

'Nothing more?'

'Nothing.'

'When was this?'

'I don' know. Before Christmas.'

Theo shook his head. November, or was it December. Salo. An attic bedroom. A chair by a window. Pinpricks of light dancing on the black waters of Lake Garda like fireflies in a forest. *We arranged a few things*, Rommel had said. Like transfer to a prison he would never arrive at. Or another man's identity papers in an overcoat pocket. *Your future is in your hands.*

'And... my mother?'

'Pah! She say she never believe no bloody telegrams, stuff in pocket and never mention no more. But I think part of her believe.'

'I see.'

'You mus' telephone her, Teo, right away. I have number.'

'I will.' He hesitated. 'Yes I will, of course, but is she... Are they, you know, happy, she and Nicholas Abercrombie?

24

Before the telegram, that is. Obviously. What I mean is, is she happily married?'

Eleni shrugged. 'S'pose. I never hardly see her no more. Got money, that's for sure. They live damn nice place near Regent Park in West End. I been once, dead posh, bloody nice carpet.'

'That's, well... it's good that she's provided for.'

'She provided all right. She important lady now, Teo, the Partito Sudtirolese thing is grown damn big, with many important support. She have tea with lord this and lady muck, she has meeting with government ministers and chinwag royal personages.'

He nodded, staring at the table.

'Why? What's a matter?'

'Did she ever... talk about me? When she was still living here, I mean?'

Eleni sighed. 'She's changed, Teo, from scrawny slip who turn up at my door. Yes, she always proud, always determined girl. And yes I know she love you very much.' She slid her hand over his. 'But she changed, lovely boy. She different. She forget important things, like who she is. And important people. Like us.'

'I have been away a long time.'

'Yes but I not forget!' She squeezed his hand. 'Never once! All this time, I never forget, an' never stop thinking about you.'

He looked up; her eyes were filling again, her hand tightly clasping his. Then she was stifling a sob, and this time, when he rose from the chair and put his arms round her, and held her, and felt the shudder of her shoulders and the wetness of her tears on his neck, this time she made no attempt to push him away.

'No more, Teo,' she sobbed. 'Please no more this bloody war. I can't bear lose you again.'

'No more war, Eleni. That I can promise.'

'Thank God.' She clung on a while longer, sniffing and sighing; then came a muffled cough. 'These clothes stink something terrible, you know.'

'Yes. Sorry.'

'I clean them for you. Like I used to.'

'No. We'll burn them.'

The telephone rang.

'I leave it.'

They left it but it rang on and on. 'I better go damn thing.' She rose from the table. 'Might be lodger and I need the business. Or maybe is you mama even.'

But a minute later she was back. 'It for you!'

'But how...'

'God know, you only been here five minute. Some woman, sound posh, say her name Mrs Simpson at international research something. She say it urgent.'

The next day, a Friday, he met his parents. Both of them, together, for the first time in his life. It was his idea and at his insistence. Having spoken to Carla the previous evening – who sounded suitably delighted by his call – he told her she was to meet him at Vic's hospital at eleven the next day. At which she sounded less overjoyed.

'But why, Theo dearest? What possible good can this do?'

His reply was in Ladin. 'Because you owe me this, Mother. And I will not take no for an answer.'

Victor was at Hammersmith Hospital, which confusingly was not in Hammersmith but East Acton, next door ironically to the famous London prison, Wormwood Scrubs. Theo, breathless and flustered, arrived late, while Carla, to her credit, was already outside the hospital's imposing entrance, nervously clutching a handbag and dressed in linen suit, hat and gloves. He barely recognized her in the smart attire, her face made-up and her raven-black hair fashionably coiffed. Their embrace was warm if wary.

'But what on earth are you wearing?' she said, standing him back.

He looked down at himself. Too-large flannels and jacket courtesy of Mr Brown's wardrobe, a grey shirt discarded by another lodger, and Salvation Army plimsolls.

'I have no clothes at the moment...'

'No, but I mean why not in uniform? You look so smart.'

'No more uniforms, Mother. Shall we go up?'

Vic was in a men's ward on the second floor. Passing down between the beds, he almost walked past a shrunken figure lying on one, then heard a discreet cough behind and saw Carla had stopped.

'Father?'

'Bugger me,' Vic croaked. 'Here's a turn-up for the books!' He forced a toothy grin, but a moment later, his gaze switching between them, his face crumpled and he collapsed into a fit of noisy weeping. Exchanging awkward glances, the two pulled up chairs and waited for the spasm to pass.

'Is enough now, Victor,' Carla said sternly. 'You make yourself ill.'

'I *am* bloody ill!' he choked. More phlegm-filled sobbing followed, while neighbouring patients looked on in embarrassment. Finally he subsided to sniffing. 'Sorry. Don't know what came over me.'

'Have some water.' Theo poured a glass.

'Thanks, son. It's the emotion and that. Seeing you both like this, all of a sudden.'

'We understand.'

'You look very nice, Carla. Dead fetching.'

'Thank you. But I am married now, Victor, remember.'

'Course. Only saying.' He sniffed. 'So the, um, annulment thing went through?'

'Yes. It appears the marriage may not have been legal in the first place. In any case it is now annulled.'

'Good. I mean, I'm glad, for you. And what's-his-name.'

'Nicholas, Victor. You know his name.'

'Nicholas, yes.' He sipped water. 'Anders. You look good too. If a bit scruffy.'

Carla rolled her eyes. 'You can't even say *his* name correct.'

'I bloody can! Anders Joseph Thadeus something something *Victor* Trickey!'

'Wrong! It's *Andreas*, Victor. My God, can't you get—'

'Stop!'

They stopped.

'I did not bring you here to argue.'

'No,' Vic agreed sheepishly. 'Sorry.'

'I sorry too, dearest. But why *are* we here?'

'Because I wanted—'

'Bloody hell, it's the last rites! You've come to pay your respects!'

'No! I brought Mother here because I wanted to hear what happened.'

'What happened?'

'Between the two of you. In Bolzano. And Innsbruck. I want to know the truth about my birth, and childhood. About how you met, fell in love, got married, and then became separated. I want to hear an account that you

28

both agree on. Like an official record, or like a... a report.'

'A report?'

'But why?'

'Because it is my right. My birthright.'

So they told him. Reluctantly at first, and grudgingly, then with growing straightforwardness and then interest, humour, and even mild affection as the memories returned.

'Your mother, Anders' – Vic wagged a bony finger – 'best skier I ever met.'

'I beat you, Victor, didn't I?'

'That you did, fair and square.'

And though the events were over twenty years old, he heard surprisingly little disagreement over details, and as they described them he found he could clearly picture his young parents, and he saw how Carla's tone softened when she spoke of her family, and how Vic's eyes twinkled as he recalled his younger self, so full of pluck and wit.

'That bloody baptism party with your family! I was scared out of my life!'

'Yes, but it didn't show. Everyone thought you were most dashing.'

'Your grandad. What an amazing bloke. Mind you, I couldn't understand a word he said.'

Then, as the dénouement neared, with its tale of deceit and abandonment, he sensed Carla's resentment looming, and Vic's discomfiture, and so concluded the 'report' before it could turn rancorous.

'And when did you meet again?' he asked. 'Here in London, I mean.'

'Six months ago.'

'When the cancer come,' Vic added.

'Yes. You see I had learned, earlier, that Victor might not be dead.'

'When?'

She stifled a cough. 'I can't remember. Anyway, much later I met Nicholas and we wanted to get married and by then I had learned that Victor was definitely alive, but ill and in hospital.'

'How?'

Carla blinked. 'Eleni told me. So I came to see him. Once.'

'For the divorce,' Vic said.

'It was not a divorce, Victor, it was an annulment. On the grounds that there was never any *consumazione* of the marriage. Afterwards, that is.'

'More's the pity!'

'Victor! In any case it seem the marriage was not all legal, because the British legation in Bolzano didn't have correct authority, and anyway the papers are long gone.'

As they prepared to leave, Vic grabbed Theo's hand and asked for a few minutes alone. Carla waited downstairs.

'What was that?' she asked when he appeared.

'Financial matters.'

'Ha! Even on his deathbed he thinks only of money.'

'No, Mama, it is not like that.' They walked out on to Du Cane Road, smoky and grime-laden from passing traffic. Waiting at the kerb, he recalled a letter from Vic amid the bundle Yale had given him in Cairo. It had made no mention that he was ill or dying, but did ask for money. Theo had thrown it away in disgust. Wrongly, he now realized. 'He wants to make provision for his daughter. He wants me to be her guardian.'

★

He caught buses from Wood Lane to Baker Street, arriving shortly after one. Grant's office had moved again, this time to larger premises across the road, and it took him another ten confusing minutes to find it. SOE had clearly expanded since his last visit, now occupying several buildings in the street, with more offices in outlying locations. Nor was it as inconspicuous as it should be: 'This stop for spy central!' the bus conductor announced cheerfully as Theo jumped off.

'Yes, it's getting beyond a joke.' Grant cleared files and papers from a chair. His new office was bigger, and even had a carpeted sitting area with gas fire, but was as cluttered as ever. 'Can you believe, somebody turned up last week asking for the saboteurs' shop! Tourists too, they really think Sherlock Holmes lives here.'

Theo sat while Grant fussed. Nervous and dishevelled as usual, with bloodshot eyes and cigarettes burning in two ashtrays, he seemed more stressed than ever. More volatile and fragile too, as though years of grinding subterfuge had worn him brittle. For Theo's own part, sitting there in his borrowed civilian persona, and waiting impassively to impart his news, he found that he felt ready and prepared.

He wasn't.

'I'm really very glad to see you.' Grant finally slumped into a chair. 'Safe and well that is, Theo. Really glad.'

'Thank you.'

'You turning up has caused quite a stir, you know.'

'So I gather.'

'Tons of folk wanting to get hold of you.' He flicked through notes. 'Your battalion commander for one, then there's the divisional commander of 6th Airborne, then some infantry major called Howard, then the debriefers from Italian section, and various intelligence minions at SHAEF...'

'SHAEF?'

'Supreme Headquarters Allied Expeditionary Force. That's top-drawer stuff, Theo.' He thumbed the notes. 'And there are others…'

'They may have to wait.'

'Let them!' He drew on his cigarette, eyeing Theo through the smoke. 'How are you? Really.'

'Well enough, sir.'

'I thought I'd lost you.'

'Yes.'

'No, really, when that sigint came through in December, I thought you were dead.' He ground out the cigarette. 'And a very bad day that was.'

'Sigint?'

'Signals intelligence. A German radio intercept.'

'What did it say?'

Grant shrugged. 'That you were dead.'

'Who sent it?'

'Hard to say. All it said, in code of course, was that the British spy Theodor Trickey died under questioning at HQ Army Group B Salo Italy. We assumed it was a message from one Gestapo office to another.'

'So you notified my next of kin.'

'We had no reason to disbelieve it. Unfortunately.'

'No.'

'You had surrendered yourself in Naples, that much we knew. We worked out you'd been shipped north for questioning. After that nothing. For weeks. We could only fear the worst. Then came the intercept.'

'What's Brown to do with this?'

'Sorry?'

'Brown. Who is he?'

Grant lit another cigarette. 'He's a recruiting sergeant. And...'

'Yes?'

'Well, he's what we call a parish priest. He looks after our people, pastoral care, their families and so on. Keeps them informed, makes sure they're all right. Especially when things go wrong.'

'Does that happen often?'

Grant blew smoke. 'More and more, it seems.'

'I'm leaving, sir. You realize that.'

'Leaving?'

'The army. The war.' He glanced around. 'All this.'

'Really.' Grant pushed his chair back and walked to the window. 'That would be a great pity, Theo, so close to the end.'

'Sorry.'

'Especially as we have a job for you. An important one. It's from Churchill himself. In France.'

'France?'

'Yes. When the invasion happens he wants all the Resistance cells in France to rise up together, to cause maximum disruption to the enemy all at the same time. We're dropping our best operatives in to lead them. It's called Jedburgh, and you're on the list. It's the main reason we got you home.'

'I'm sorry.'

'This war, everything you've lived through these years. Don't you want to see it through? Now we're at the end?'

'No. I can't.'

'I see.' Grant stared through the window. 'There are practical implications, you know. You are a serving officer. It would be a form of desertion.'

'I don't care. They can put me in prison.'

'Something of a family tradition.'

Theo said nothing.

'I understand how you feel,' Grant murmured.

'No you don't.'

'I FUCKING DO!' He swung round, eyes glaring, a fleck of spittle on his chin. 'How bloody dare you! You think this is easy? You think I just sit here sending people off without a care? Without feeling? Without fearing for them every minute of the day?'

'Have you ever killed a man in cold blood?'

'That was your enemy! You're supposed to kill them. I've done worse.'

'Worse?'

'I've killed *friends*, Trickey! Allies. People on our side. People I like and respect and admire. People like you. I've sent them on ops knowing for certain that some of them were going to their deaths. You think killing a Jerry's bad, you try living with that!'

A door slammed somewhere, and car horns blared down in the street. Grant slumped back into his chair and turned his face to the ceiling, eyes closed as though sleeping. His left hand was trembling, Theo noted, while his cigarette stub burned unnoticed in the other.

'I'm sorry,' Theo repeated quietly. 'But it doesn't change anything.'

'I didn't expect it to,' Grant murmured thickly.

'You guessed?'

'I have known you a long time, Theo.'

'Yes. And I've given my word. Made... promises.'

'How convenient.' He lowered his gaze. 'How did you get out, by the way?'

'Pardon?'

'Out. You were in the custody of the Gestapo, which can't have been much fun. Then you weren't; you were living on a farm in Campania. So how did you escape?'

Rommel. It all made sense now. A place at his grandfather's prison as Andreas Ladurner. Or a stranger's identity in an overcoat pocket. *Make your decision, Junge.* Then a brief message to the Gestapo saying he was dead, and that was that.

Grant's cigarette packet was empty. He began plundering desk drawers until he found another, shook one on to the desk and lit up again. 'Do you remember the first time we met?'

'Yes. It was after I got back from France. In June nineteen forty. The day I got sacked from the East Surreys.'

'Indeed. You told me something very interesting that day, you know. You said he'd told you it was vital each of us knows which side we're on.'

'Who did?'

'Come on, Theo! We both know who we're talking about.'

'Rommel.'

'Yes, Rommel. Did you make a deal with him in Salo?'

'No.'

'You sure about that?'

'Yes.'

He held Theo's gaze. 'That's another pity.'

'Why?'

'Because there have been… developments, in that regard.'

'What developments?'

Grant shrugged. 'Doesn't matter any more, does it?' He picked up his telephone. 'Could you ask Section Officer Atkins to come in now please, Mrs Simpson. And to bring the file.'

Theo stirred uneasily. 'Who's that?'

'There is more than one way to fight a war, you know, Theo.'

'What do you mean?'

'Well, look at me!' He brushed ash from his lapel. 'I wear a uniform. I even have a gun, somewhere… I've never fired it though. Not in anger, not once. Yet I bet any money that I put in more hours fighting Jerry in a week than a whole platoon of infantrymen. From right here, in this room.'

A knock came, and a woman in her thirties entered wearing the uniform of the Women's Auxiliary Air Force.

'Ah, Vera, thank you for joining us. This is the young man I told you about. Theo Trickey, may I introduce Section Officer Vera Atkins.'

Theo stood, self-consciously straightening his borrowed clothes. 'Hello.'

Dark eyes bored into his. 'How do you do,' Atkins replied, without smiling.

'Vera virtually runs SOE-F. The F standing for France, of course. We thought, before you leave us, that it was only fair and proper we update you on the situation regarding a, er, friend of yours.'

Theo felt a chill on his neck. 'What friend?'

'Sit down, Lieutenant,' Atkins said quietly. 'It's about Clare Taylor.'

The wedding reception was the very next day, in a community hall five minutes from Burton Street. He'd found the invitation among a bundle of abandoned mail Eleni had thrown in a drawer. 'Dear Theodorable, we do hope you can make it, love Susanna and Albert. PS bring a bottle!' He'd stared blankly at the invitation then remembered her letter in Cairo. 'Next

36

spring probably April or May,' she'd written. 'I hope theres no hard feelings and your happy for us.'

He was deeply reluctant, but Eleni said he must go, as sitting around fretting was no way to entertain his eight-year-old half sister. The preparations took all day. First he visited the gentleman's outfitters in Station Road and bought new clothes, including shirts, jacket and tie. Next Eleni led him to another shop where, after much agonizing, he chose a girl's dress with matching cardigan. Thence to the shoe shop where he bought pairs for them both, trusting to Eleni's judgement that the size was right, and to the electrical shop where he bought a new electric kettle in a box. 'Top-notch present!' Eleni declared. Then he had to trek across London to collect his ward. And though the arrangements had been agreed by telephone, her mother Vi seemed put out at being excluded, and he wondered if she might yet refuse permission. But the new clothes – and the biscuits and flowers he brought her – garnered her grudging consent. 'Just make sure she's back in good time.' After that they had to trek back to Kingston, stopping halfway at Nancy's insistence for lemonade and a bun at a café in Victoria. So by the time they arrived at the reception they were late and the party already in full swing. He had a sudden attack of nerves, and for minutes he hesitated, pacing the street outside, listening to the laughter and singing, confused and fearful of what lay within. Finally, before he could delay further, a small hand grasped his and led him firmly through the door.

The room was packed, and noisy, and dimly lit, and thick with cigarette smoke. Bunting hung from the ceiling; a painted banner read: 'Congratulations Bert & Susi'. Trestles laden with crates of beer and plates of food lined one wall; in a corner somebody thumped out tunes on a piano, while in another a pile of presents lay on a table. Children darted in and out; somewhere a baby cried lustily.

'Theodorable!' Susanna rushed up, pink-cheeked and perspiring, and embraced him warmly. 'My God, it's good to see you. Have you lost weight? Is that a present? Oh, and who's this adorable little girl?'

'Hello, Susanna. Congratulations. On getting married. This is for you. It's a kettle; you plug it in. This is my younger sister, Nancy.'

'My God, yes! Hello, Nancy, you came round to my house. Remember, Theo?'

'I... Yes, I do.'

'What a gorgeous dress, Nancy! I say, would you like some cake? And there's a children's table over here with games and jelly.'

Before he knew it Nancy had left him with a cheery wave and he was alone in a room full of faces he hadn't seen in five years. Some came up and spoke, shouting at him beerily above the din; Albert Fitch clapped him on the shoulder; older men shook him firmly by the hand; one girl he couldn't recall sidled up, kissed him warmly on the lips, then turned away without a word.

But it was all just babble, and meaningless, and irrelevant. For Clare Taylor was missing and that eclipsed everything. And the sickening realization of it, the implications and the shock were like a fist to the stomach, driving the air from his chest and making him giddy with panic. It might signify nothing, the woman Atkins had said. Two weeks late calling in wasn't unusual. It could simply be equipment failure, or difficulties finding somewhere safe to radio. Or she might deliberately be keeping a low profile, or even gone to ground, which was standard procedure if things got too 'hot'.

38

'Anything's possible,' Atkins had conceded. 'Several girls have been compromised of late. But it's too soon to panic.'

'But what can we do?' he had pleaded.

'Get to her, ideally, and get her out. Before the enemy do.'

An older woman swam into view, a little drunkenly, and told him Kenny was fine and living in a POW camp near Bremen.

'Oh, well, that is good news, Mrs Rollings.'

'I'll give you his address if you like.'

'Yes, please, and also pass him my best wishes.'

Then Nancy appeared, her cheeks smeared with jelly.

'Hello, Nancy, are you having a nice time?'

'Ooh yes, they got streamers!' she said excitedly. 'And Vimto. Come and see!'

'I will, in just a moment.'

'Hello, Theo.'

A man, mid thirties, moustache, vaguely familiar, tall, wearing a coat and trilby, had slid unnoticed through the entrance. 'Your landlady said I'd find you here.' He surveyed the room with a half-smile. 'Looks like quite a party.'

'Colonel? Colonel Frost?'

'I was passing, thought I'd drop in and see you.'

'Passing?' It was the first time, Theo realized, he'd ever seen Frost in civilian clothes. He looked completely different.

'Well, no, not passing exactly. I heard from Digby you wanted to see me.'

'Oh. I... Yes. I wanted to tell you. In person, that is...'

'That you're packing it in. Yes, I know.'

'You do? And you're not angry?'

'Good heavens, no! I'm going to miss you, of course. We all are. But I completely understand, especially after everything you've been through.'

They paused, watching in bemusement as a conga lurched noisily by.

'Remember Sedjenane? That day on the hill?'

Theo nodded. 'With the ammunition mules. Yes, I do.'

'Your best work, if you don't mind me saying. And I'm not talking about the mules. And Depienne of course. Oh, and that blasted bridge at Primosole, with what's-his-name, that artillery-spotter chap?'

'Vere Hodge.'

'Hodge, yes. Saved the day pretty much, the two of you. And even back at Bruneval with that boffin Charlie Cox. We'd never have succeeded if you hadn't been there to hold his hand.'

Across the room Nancy and Susanna were dancing together. Spotting Theo, Nancy broke off to wave.

He waved back. 'It was quite a mission.'

'Bloody right. They all were. And terrific work, as I say.'

'Thank you.'

'And do you know, throughout practically all of them…'

'What?'

'You were as good as unarmed.'

CHAPTER 3

A week or so after the Rommel exhumation episode, Erik and I are taking lunch in the *Revier* bedsit when Corporal Prien suddenly bursts through the door.

'Russkies are across the Oder!' he gabbles.

Erik and I exchange glances. Slightly unsure as to the significance of this, we nevertheless don't want to appear uninformed. Accurate news, as opposed to rumour, speculation or propaganda, is hard to come by, here as anywhere in Germany. But Prien has a radio, and is a serving soldier with military contacts, and has been growing more cooperative of late, compliant even, as the war draws towards its inevitable close. So we have no reason to disbelieve him.

'We are aware of this, of course,' Erik replies dismissively. 'Thank you, Corporal, that will be all.'

Prien stiffens to attention, turns and departs. Which rather sums up the shifting balance of power in Ulm in April 1945. The war is lost, Nazism finished, freedom and democracy in the ascendant. We know it, Prien knows it, the general population knows it, only the deluded or deranged like our commandant Vorst are in denial. But the one unknown – and it's a big one – is who'll get here first. The western Allies or the Russians.

'Where's the Oder?' I mutter as the door shuts. Conjuring

41

my silk escape map from a pocket we smooth it over the table. Erik soon picks out the river and traces it with a finger. 'Polish border, here, it runs from Stettin on the Baltic roughly south before heading east into Poland. But God, look, it's less than a hundred miles from Berlin!'

'Still a long way from here, though.'

'Yes, but if Berlin falls, Russia wins and that's it. Drapes!'

'I think you mean curtains.'

'What?'

'Curtains. It's theatrical— Oh, never mind.'

'Where did that officer chap Brandt say the Yanks were?'

'Wiesbaden.' I jab at the map. 'On the Rhine. He implied they were stuck.'

'Well he would, wouldn't he!'

'Not necessarily. He has no reason to lie.'

'Of course he has, he's a Nazi! Anyway they'll be attacking along a broad front, won't they? Hundreds of miles wide probably, and advancing all the time. They could be anywhere.'

'Well, they'd better get on with it or we'll all be learning Russian.'

We stare at the map. The truth is we don't know, and conjecture is fruitless no matter how engrossing. At the end of the day Ulm is a minor southern city of little importance, and far down anyone's list of priorities, so all we can do is sit tight, be as patient as possible and get on with the job.

Which is changing, subtly, even if we barely notice it. Erik and I bicker our way through the days like an old married couple. We still tend to our in-patients, hold daily sick parades, visit outlying clinics and do what we can for the destitutes at the drop-in. We're still denied our liberty, locked in at night, fed scraps for rations and abused by Vorst and other die-hards we meet. We are still prisoners. But if the day-to-day practicalities of our imprisonment seem to change little, some things are definitely different. Attitudes. Like Prien snapping to attention, for instance.

After a lunch of hoarded Spam on bread made from sawdust, I have two clinics to attend: the ball-bearing factory at Böfingen and a textiles mill on the north side of town. Here the prisoners, mostly women, fashion German army blankets and uniforms from fabric shipped in from the east, but upon arrival I find the factory idle, the women lounging in the sunshine and the guards standing about looking perplexed.

'What's going on?' I ask a foreman.

'No fabric.' He shrugs. 'Haven't had a shipment in days.'

And when I question the women they confirm it.

'Look.' One of them produces a sample. 'The quality's so poor you can poke your finger through it.'

Another smirks. 'It's the same with the uniform fabric. And we only put half-stitches in, so they fall apart in a week!'

'We sow lice eggs into the seams too,' adds a third. 'Give the Boche bastards something to scratch about!'

Fighting talk. Lethally dangerous talk, in fact, under normal circumstances. But the circumstances aren't normal, they're changing, this further evidenced by a very short line at sick parade, as though getting ill is an irrelevance now. And as I attend to them and listen to their chatter, I realize what's happening. These women may be sick and starving, they may be bullied, berated and beaten – and worse – but they can sense the winds of change blowing. And they're preparing to hoist sail.

The Böfingen plant's similar, but more menacing. Here the German security presence is marked and aggressive. For the first time in weeks my papers are carefully scrutinized, and my bag and clothes searched before I'm allowed in. And

43

sick parade takes place at gunpoint. Yet the patients, mostly long-serving French POWs, are recklessly defiant, slouching about flicking hateful glances at the guards, ignoring orders and instructions, and muttering murderous oaths under their breaths.

'I hope you're not planning anything rash,' I say to one. 'It would be a tragedy if anyone got hurt. So close to *victoire*, I mean.'

'The only ones getting hurt will be these *connards*!' he replies threateningly.

And traipsing back to the tram stop, I come across an incredible sight. The Böfingen road bypasses Ulm to the east and I have to cross it. There, walking along, heads hanging, silent, muffled up in threadbare coats and scarves like a column of weary tramps, are German soldiers. Not many, but a steady trickle.

'*Woher kommst du?*' I ask one. 'Where have you come from? And where are you going?' But he just shakes his head.

Then I have to queue for the tram back into town. These no longer run as efficiently as they used to, because of staff shortages and damage from bombings. There aren't the engineers to service the rolling stock any more either. So Trudi tells me. A tram finally clanks into view and we all climb aboard. She's not on it, and I find I'm both disappointed and relieved at this. I've seen her once or twice since the visit to her mother's, but our rapport seems to have changed too, like the textiles women or the ball-bearing workers and their guards. Something in the dynamic has shifted, upsetting what was already finely balanced. We both feel it, I sense, but neither knows what to do about it. 'What did you expect?' Erik scolds when I broach the matter. 'It was pointless and ill advised from the start!' I can only nod blankly in reply.

Back in town it's my turn at drop-in. Ulm central these days is unrecognizable from the trim little city I arrived in back in January. Apart from the sooty finger of the minster spire still poking stubbornly skyward, virtually nothing stands undamaged. Masonry shards and broken glass crunch underfoot as I pick my way through the maze of cratered streets, smashed buildings and smoke-blackened rubble. Small fires still smoulder here and there, while a burst main gushes water down the road like a stream in spate. Few clear-up parties are in evidence either, and those that are seem half-hearted in their efforts. As though it's all a waste of time.

I follow the railway until I arrive at the chapel. As usual there's a line of people waiting outside. Starving, sick, destitute, their homes bombed to oblivion, their lives shattered and their menfolk gone, these are the true victims of this conflict, the by-product, the pitiful human dregs. Yet still living somehow, these ones at least, while upwards of a million German civilians, rumour has it, are dead.

Two women helpers are waiting, hefting shopping baskets and cardboard boxes.

'What have we here?' I ask.

'Blankets, a few tins and more old toys. Someone left them on the step.'

The Rommel family again, I presume, remembering I have an appointment later. I unlock the door and push inside, sniffing the musty air. Despite some dampness the place looks almost presentable, certainly more like a community hall than an exploded chapel. The roof and windows are now weatherproof, the floor cleared and cleaned; some enterprising soul spliced us into the mains electricity, giving lighting and power to a donated electric urn. And apart from the wood stove, and the rows of pews serving as a waiting area, there's an assortment of other furniture, scraps of carpet, a wind-up gramophone, toys and games for the children and a plentiful supply of books, magazines and newspapers to read. I can't help feeling rather proud of the place whenever I come here; it's ours, Erik's and mine, we caused it to be, a tiny illicit ark bobbing on an ocean of destruction. In one corner a curtained-off area serves as our office and clinic; I head towards it, dump my bag and coat, fire up Mahler on the gramophone, and the Lucie Rommel Centre for the destitute is open for business.

Half an hour passes, and the place is soon bustling. The stove burns, a soup of sorts brews in the urn, the gramophone squawks, homeless neighbours sit in pews exchanging gossip, while excited children charge about howling like Messerschmitts. I'm in the cubicle dressing the ulcerated leg of an elderly man when one of the women helpers appears round the curtain.

'Excuse me, *Herr Doktor*. May I ask you something?'

'Of course.'

'We wondered if we might open every day. Rather than just twice a week.'

'It's a nice idea, but Doctor Henning and I can only get here twice a week.'

'We realize that. But we could still open, as a place for people to come.'

'And hold clinics on the days we're here? Yes, it's certainly a thought. Let me speak to Erik about it.'

'Thank you, *Herr Doktor*. Oh, and there's a man to see you from the *Gemeinde*.'

I'm rather startled at this. The *Gemeinde*, as my German understands it, translates as the 'municipality'. Officialdom, in other words, something Erik and I try to avoid, as far as the drop-in goes. I peek round the curtain and see a man in his fifties wearing a rumpled suit, spectacles and homburg. He seems to be looking round with great interest, and even as I watch produces a notebook and jots something down.

'May I help you?' I enquire warily.

'You are Henning?'

'No, the other one. Garland.'

'Ah, the British captain. Even better.'

'And you are?'

'My name is Adenauer, I'm from the *Bürgermeister*'s office.'

'I see.'

He shakes my hand. 'I'm the *Bürgermeister*'s stand-in.'

'So where's the *Bürgermeister*?'

'There isn't one. The chair has been vacant since 1942.'

'Oh. And where's his office?'

'Marktplatz. But it was destroyed in December. Then it was in the museum. Which was destroyed in February. Now it's in my house, although we're hoping to move to the library. Once the roof's repaired.'

'Right. I see. Listen, I'm very sorry, Herr, um…'

'Adenauer.'

'Adenauer, yes, I'm sorry, but I'm not sure I understand.'

'The war is due to end.'

'Indeed.'

'And the Allies will prevail.'

'Without a doubt.'

'So we must make provision.'

'Provision.'

'Yes. The city of Ulm is undefended. The garrison has withdrawn, the senior military presence is unreliable or absent, the police are old men and severely under-staffed.

47

Local government structures barely exist. There is great fear and uncertainty among the population, particularly over what will happen when the Allies arrive. Law and order is already starting to break down.'

'Is it?'

'Which leaves you.'

'Me.'

'As the titular governing authority in the city.'

'The what!'

'You are the most senior Allied representative in Ulm. We wish only that the transfer of authority goes smoothly and peacefully. The city therefore looks to you to ensure this.'

'But—'

'And to ensure the protection of its people.'

Erwin Rommel left Italy to take up his new post in late 1943. Before departing he held a farewell dinner at his new home in Herrlingen for some of his old retinue, one of whom I learn was Gerhardt Brandt, who was applying for a transfer to his staff. At that dinner, Rommel, in reflective mood, spoke gloomily of his posting, which, even dressed up as a special assignment or *Führerauftrag* to save face, was clearly a demotion. 'I am no longer a soldier, but an inspector,' he joked dryly. More darkly he talked of his views on the war, and of the German leadership, including Adolf Hitler. 'Our brave soldiers are dying by the tens of thousands at the hands of incompetents and fantasists,' he said. 'Our efforts now should be about preventing the annihilation of Germany and its people.'

'How, sir?' a guest asked, surprised at his candour.

Rommel shrugged. 'End it. Before it is too late.'

Then next morning he went to work, and in true Rommel fashion attacked his new role with zeal and thoroughness. His brief was to inspect and report on Germany's countermeasures against the expected Allied invasion of northern Europe, specifically the much-touted Atlantic Wall defence system. This 'wall' formed the main component of the Reich's defences, supposedly forming a continuous and unassailable barrier along northern Europe's shores, all the way from Norway to the Bay of Biscay.

But it didn't, and what he found worried him greatly. Firstly the 'wall' wasn't a wall at all, but a random series of unconnected fortifications most of which weren't finished. Indeed, many had barely been begun, and several key ones existed only on paper. A few, he acknowledged, like those in the Channel Islands, or the Loire, or the Raversijde complex in Belgium, were complete, and impressive, featuring massive sea-facing guns and networks of emplacements, trenches and tunnels linked by sophisticated communications systems. But these were the exceptions, and it was soon all too clear that glaring gaps and vulnerabilities existed along the entire length, including several stretches with no defences at all.

Within days he was firing off reports to High Command, begging at the same time for the authority to take charge of the situation himself. Alarmed at the news, Berlin swiftly granted this permission and he immediately set to work, journeying hundreds of miles a day, castigating, chivvying and cajoling as he went, visiting every piece of coastline from Bergen to Bordeaux, revising plans, issuing deadlines, berating contractors, diverting materials and manpower, and galvanizing everyone from field commanders to lowly labourers with his infectious drive and urgency. He also visited the many military units tasked with manning these defences. Some he noted were crack troops of high calibre, but many were poor-quality conscripts from Eastern Europe, Russia and even from France. Regardless of this, his message to them was always the same: you must drive the enemy back into the sea at all costs. Let them ashore and we're finished.

He did his best, earnestly and tirelessly, but knew that completing the work was impossible; there simply wasn't the time, manpower or resources. Maximum effort therefore, he urged, should be concentrated on those areas at highest risk, northern France in other words, specifically the Channel coast from Calais to Brittany. Berlin concurred and by mid spring 1944 attention was further focusing on the Pas de Calais region, with Calais itself considered the most probable target for invasion. Calais was a large port, readily resupplied by sea and air. It was situated close to the border with Belgium, only a short march into the Low Countries and thence into Germany, obviating the need for long supply lines. It offered the shortest sea crossing for the Allied troop carriers, and short flights for their supporting aircraft. Finally, all the intelligence suggested Calais, with suspicious build-ups of British and American forces in Kent, fleets of invasion barges hiding in rivers and creeks, and intercepted signals about German troop numbers in the Calais area.

Rommel supported the Calais assessment, but only partly. His theory, which he circulated widely, was that the Allies would mount two invasions: a diversionary one somewhere in Normandy, followed by the main one around Calais. And the key to defeating both, he argued, was crushing the first one before it could take hold. 'Bloody their noses on the beaches of Normandy,' he wrote, 'and they'll think twice about landing in Calais!' All that was needed to achieve this, he went on, were improvements to the Atlantic Wall defences in both areas, sufficient forces to mount a proper defence, and the imaginative deployment of those troops such that they were ready to rush into action wherever the alarm sounded.

That and someone competent to manage it all.

Hitler, capricious as ever, and impressed as so often before by Rommel's strategic vision, as well as his tireless efforts, was inclined to agree with his old protégé, and so suddenly in April, to the fury of his competitors, Rommel found himself commanding Army Group B, and charged with the defence of northern France. Delighted to be a soldier again, he nevertheless knew the task was daunting. With the Eastern Front sucking up vast quantities of resources, and a second front halfway up Italy expending yet more, he was now expected to open a third front with whatever spares Berlin saw fit to allocate. And time was desperately short. Guessing he had barely weeks to prepare, he moved into a chateau south of Rouen, set up his headquarters and went to work.

Staff would record his efforts as prodigious, a return to the Rommel of old, of Gazala and Tobruk, and of the 1940 conquest of France. He was everywhere at once, backwards and forwards along the lines, visiting every emplacement, every battery, every unit, every last man, encouraging, questioning, exhorting and inspiring. Where he found weakness he strengthened – both men and materials, installing miles of barbed wire, sowing mines by the thousand, digging tank traps, burying lethal steel obstacles on beaches, placing flak batteries and flooding fields against air landings, positioning and repositioning troops then drilling them day and night until they dropped. And everywhere he went he drummed the same message home: don't let them get off the beaches. If you do it's over. There is no fallback plan.

And yet, unknown to all but a trusted few, there was.

*

How do I know? Because, at the request of his family, I'm sitting at *his* desk in *his* study wading through *his* personal papers. And that's a peculiar thing for a lowly British medic and no question.

Tonight is my second session. Having returned to Erik with the startling news that the good burghers of Ulm are looking to us for safety and salvation – at which his jaw duly drops – I hastily wolf down the slop they call supper, wash and smarten myself up, and, remembering to take my English–German dictionary, descend the stairs to await the Herrlingen car. Prien has gone off duty, Vorst we haven't seen in days, so one of the guards signs me out. He does so without a glance, and it's obvious that he doesn't care if I never come back. That I could slip out right now and simply wander off. But wander off where, is the question. Germany's in chaos, with desperate and bloody fighting going on in all directions, and bombs falling hourly by the thousand. Order is breaking down, as is transportation and information; there's no food, no cover and no obvious route to safety. Wandering off would be madness. *Bide your time,* Stalag 357's CO, McKenzie, preached to my irritation back in November. *Keep your head down and we'll all be home before we know it.* He may have been wrong then, but not these days. How things have changed in five months.

I'm wondering if Rommel might have suffered some sort of breakdown in his final months. As I read through his papers I can't help but reflect on his state of mind from a medical perspective. There are frequent references to illnesses, doctors, stress and exhaustion, hospitals and sanatoria over the years. And as D-Day loomed, his writings suggest increasing inner turmoil. On the one hand there's no question he threw himself into his duties wholeheartedly and without question, as he always did. On the other he's clearly conflicted. 'I'll be sending brave boys to a needless death,' he confides in one letter to Lucie. 'Knowing our leadership for what it is, can this be justified morally?' Furthermore he'd been waging war for years with no respite and unremitting pressure from above. God knows the cumulative cost of this to his mental equilibrium. I search further, burrowing down through the boxes, then come to a manila envelope containing a dozen or so typed sheets headed '*Fall Grün*' or 'Case Green'. And as I translate them, thumbing the dictionary at my side, my blood begins to run cold.

'*Herr Doktor Garland?*' Manfred Rommel appears round the door. 'Would you like a cup of tea? I made it myself.'

'Well, yes, I would. How very kind.'

'It is not your British tea, and rather old, nor do we have milk or sugar.'

'No matter, Manfred, please come in.'

He sidles cautiously forward and places the cup beside me. I take a sip and taste something bitter and non-tea-like. 'Delicious,' I say, wondering briefly if he might be trying to poison me. 'When do you have to report for duty?'

'Tomorrow. I leave early.'

'Where to?'

'Riedlingen. My unit forms part of the defence force there.'

'Will you please be careful, Manfred?'

He looks surprised. 'Yes.'

'For your mother's sake. Because if anything happened to you...'

'I understand.' He stands beside me, his eyes scanning the papers atop the desk.

'It must be a little odd,' I say, discreetly covering them,

'having someone, a stranger, an enemy in fact, sit here reading your father's papers.'

'A little. But Gertrud says we can trust you. Mother too.'

'You can.'

'Yes.' He hesitates, his fingers brushing the desk. 'It was here...'

'Here?'

'The last time I saw him. Alive, I mean. He called me in here to explain what was happening. Less than an hour before...' His voice fades.

'You must miss him terribly.'

'Yes.'

'Have you talked to anyone about it? About that day?'

He shakes his head.

'Would you like to?'

'I don't know.'

'It doesn't matter. I've no wish to intrude.'

'Sorry.' His young brow is deeply furrowed, and his lower lip none too steady.

'Look here.' I give him a nudge. 'It's his diary for last autumn. He writes of you nearly every day, and with great pride and pleasure, describing all the walks and talks you had together.'

'It was some of the best times. Although he was different.'

'Different?'

'Following his injury, in France. It changed him.'

A few weeks after D-Day. The fighting is intense, the Allies pushing hard to break out from the Normandy bridgehead. Rommel's in his staff car, racing from one defensive position to another, when he gets bounced by a Spitfire, strafed by machine guns and crashes. His skull is smashed; he isn't expected to live.

'Well, it was a very serious injury.'

'He was blinded for a while and suffered fits, and very bad headaches and blackouts. At first he was bedridden, and I would come and read to him, but his moods would change often and he could become upset or enraged. Then as the weeks passed and he slowly recovered, he became more calm, more happy – you know, playful even. As though his troubles were over. As though he was a youth again, and more like a brother to me than a father. It was quite special.'

Dusk is falling, the clock ticks on the mantel, and the soft hiss of spring rain drifts through the window. Beyond in the garden birds are roosting, flowers budding and the trees bursting into leaf, while somewhere in the distance a lone dog barks. War seems very remote; the setting, the house, Rommel's study are so peaceful that I can almost sense his presence. A family photo sits on his desk, one of those folding travel ones of leather. It is considerably battered, testament to its many years campaigning. Three figures smile out at him: Lucie, Gertrud and Manfred.

He suddenly draws a breath.

'Two officers came to the house,' he begins, as though reciting a prepared text, 'while a third man waited in the car. My father warned us there might be visitors that day but did not say what the visit was about. The officers arrived at about twelve. He didn't know them but received them politely and brought them into his study. I waited upstairs with Mother, who was becoming agitated. Gertrud was at work. About half an hour later the men came out and my father went upstairs and asked me to wait in his study while he spoke to my mother. In a while he returned here and told me he had just said goodbye to her, and now must say goodbye to me, because Adolf Hitler had given him the choice of taking his life, or being brought before the People's Court for his part in the twentieth of July plot to assassinate him. My father told me he'd known about the plot but had taken no part because he believed it would not solve Germany's problems and only make a martyr of Hitler. But three of his close friends had spoken his name under torture, which was enough to implicate him. The two officers told my father if he chose suicide then his family would be protected and provided for, and that he would be buried a hero. If he chose the People's Court, however, there was no such protection.'

His gaze in the twilight is fixed, and his voice determined, but I can see he's struggling. 'Manfred, old chap, you don't have to—'

'I begged him to choose the People's Court, saying if he told the truth then surely he would be found innocent. But he said the People's Court was a sham, set up only to convict people, innocent or guilty, and nobody was ever found innocent. I pleaded again, and became upset, and he told me his mind was made up and I must be brave and take on the role of man of the family. He then told me to say goodbye and we embraced. After that he went to his dressing room and changed into his field marshal's uniform with cap and baton, before descending to the hall where he said goodbye to the staff and Gertrud, who had returned. He then went out to the car where the two officers were waiting, and got into the back. The car drove off, and about an hour later we received a telephone call to say my father had suffered a heart attack, and a doctor had been called from Ulm Hospital, but he had died.'

A long silence follows. The mantel clock ticks on. Then, still standing at my side, he bows his head, and a single tear plops on the desk. I raise my arm and pat him gently on the back.

'Well done, Manfred. Very well done.'

'Will you...' He hesitates. 'Will you make sure people know?'

'I'll do my best. But you should write it down also. Like a sworn affidavit. And keep it safe. In case.'

'Will you help me?'

'Of course I'll help you.'

Back at the *Revier*, Prien's once more on the desk. As I enter he holds a finger to his lips and gestures at Vorst's door, beneath which a light glows. I nod, then tread softly up to the second floor. Where I need to speak to Theo Trickey.

He's awake, lying on his cot staring at the ceiling. He's down to one walking stick these days, able to hobble gamely about on it, and, though still weak and lame and confused, making reasonable if slow progress.

'Hello, Theo.' I squat beside him. 'How are we doing this evening?'

'Fine, thank you, Doctor. I didn't think I was asleep. But then I had a dream and woke up.'

A typical Trickey non sequitur. 'Jolly good. But listen, I wondered if you were up to a few questions.'

'Of course.' He hoists himself on to an elbow. 'What about?'

'Well, ultimately, I suppose, it's about Erwin Rommel.'

'I met him, you know. More than once, so I believe.'

'Yes. In fact you once told me he was your mentor.'

'Did I?' He looks perplexed. 'I don't remember that.'

'No. But well... anyway, do the German words *Fall Grün* mean anything to you?'

'*Fall Grün*?'

'Yes. As in Case Green or Plan Green or something.'

He considers, absently scratching the scar on his head. 'I don't think so.'

'Take your time, Theo.'

He ponders further. 'Wasn't there a *Fall Gelb* once?'

'Case Yellow? I don't know. I doubt it. This one was a plan, or project or something, that Rommel put together, last May or June…'

His head shakes some more.

'Concerning contact with the Allies.'

'I don't think…'

'That I believe you were involved in.'

He narrows his eyes, straining for recall. I wait, breath held.

But then he just shrugs. 'No, Doctor. Sorry.'

'Then who the hell's Horatio!'

'What?'

'Horatio, damn it! Is that you?'

'I… I don't know.'

'Or Andreas Ladurner. Is that you too?'

This is working. Shock treatment, and I can see it's getting through. But I'm making too much noise, figures are stirring on cots, someone grumbles 'put a sock in it' and downstairs I'm sure I hear footsteps.

'They *are* you, aren't they?'

'No. I… Horatio's dead.'

'For God's sake!' I rock back in despair. Then something comes to me. One more name. Mentioned by Gerhardt Brandt on the night of Rommel's post-mortem.

'Then who's Aurelia?'

He cocks his head, like an attentive bird. 'Who?'

The footsteps are coming up the stairs, and I know now whom they belong to. 'Aurelia, Theo. She's at a prison camp. Outside of Munich. Who is she?'

And then something clicks. 'Which camp?'

Vorst enters behind me. '*Was ist los!*'

'It's called Dachau, Theo, she's being held in a women's section—'

'*STEHEN SIE AUF, GARLAND!*'

He's drunk. Even in the semi-darkness I can see he's badly drunk, glassy-eyed, puce-cheeked, swaying and stinking of the stuff. This is dangerous. He leans forward, one hand resting on the holster of his pistol. 'What the hell do you think you are doing?'

'Attending to my patient, *Herr Oberstabsarzt.*'

'Insolence! I meant what are you doing creeping in at this late hour?'

'Oh. That. I was visiting Frau Rommel, *Herr Oberstabsarzt.* In Herrlingen. Her family, that is. She sent a car and returned me straight here. The guard signed for me.'

'Rommel was a damned traitor!'

'Yes, well...'

'He led the plot to assassinate our beloved Führer!'

Movement behind him. Erik appears on the landing, followed by Prien, both looking anxious.

'You repeatedly absent yourself to consort with traitors!' Vorst's hand twitches on the holster. 'Do you deny it?'

'I know nothing of these things, *Herr Oberstabsarzt.* Frau Rommel is a patient—'

'LIAR!'

'Actually I'm not sure he did.' Trickey, hauling himself to his feet, is speaking in fluent German.

Vorst looks thrown. '*Was sagst du?*'

'Another man was the leader. I met him, somewhere, in a tent, I think. He had a book. Dickens.'

'Are you mad?'

'*Herr Oberstabsarzt?*' Prien steps forward. 'Your supper awaits you downstairs. I've managed to find some gherkin. And that Mosel you like…'

'You!' The gun is out suddenly, a Luger, wobbling at me, one finger hovering inexpertly on the trigger. 'You will report to me for punishment tomorrow!'

Erik nods eagerly. 'I… yes of course, *Herr Oberstabsarzt.*'

'And you!' The gun wobbles at Theo. 'Will report for work duty!'

'But, *Herr Oberstabsarzt*, I really must object, he is in no fit state to—'

'I don't mind,' Theo says genially. 'I'm happy to go out and work.'

The next day Vorst's nowhere to be found. 'Home nursing a hangover,' Erik predicts, and Prien later confirms it. So I'm off the hook, it seems, at least for now. But Theo isn't, and despite my protestations Prien's adamant. 'His name's on the list,' he says. 'There's nothing I can do!'

And anyway Theo still seems unconcerned about it, determined even, to go out and spend all day shovelling rubble.

'It's a nice day, Doctor,' he says, tottering downstairs on his stick. Wearing an odd assortment of clothes over the battledress I found him in at Oosterbeek, a battered forage cap of Italian origin and ancient sand-coloured desert boots, he's certainly dressed for any weather.

'Now, don't you go overdoing it, Private. And that's an order.'

'No, sir.' Then to my surprise he comes and shakes me by the hand. 'I want to thank you for all you've done for me, these past months, Doctor, um...'

'Garland.'

'Garland, yes.' Then he smiles his guileless half-smile. 'I'll try and remember that.'

With that he holds my gaze a moment, nods and shuffles out into the sunlight.

And I never see him again.

CHAPTER 4

'Everything set here, Private?' Lieutenant Brotheridge moved along the line, checking men's kit.

'Fine, thank you, sir,' Theo replied.

'This must be old hat for you.'

'It never seems like it.'

'Well, we're glad to have you along. Even if the lads don't show it!'

Brotheridge moved on, leaving Theo to contemplate the moonlit scene – and the dew-covered aeroplane standing before him. Of all the aerial conveyances he had flown in, he decided, the one he was now waiting to board, together with twenty-seven other heavily laden airborne troops, was without doubt the oddest. The list, he conceded, was short. First was the training balloon at Ringway, swaying and tugging on its tether like a stubborn cow, while he and Percy Burns clung on in sickly terror. Then there was the Whitley bomber and its infamous kiss. Next the Dakota, a significant advance, big and comfortable, but vulnerable without weapons or armour. Finally the cramped little Bisley, speeding him over the pearl-pink Atlas Mountains before he dived through its floor to the desert.

With Antoine. The man who'd befriended him, shared his room in Algiers, showed him the city, and jumped with him into Gabès. The man whom Clare had deployed with into France. *I'm not certain he's entirely trustworthy,* she'd said at the Café de Paris. Now she was missing.

He checked his watch, forcing the thought from his mind. It was 10.45 p.m., the June air mild and calm after the previous days' storms. Though this was the second attempt at the mission, tonight the forecast was good and everyone felt confident. Especially General Gale, who'd been round to wish everyone luck.

'Jerry's like the June bride,' he'd quipped. 'She knows she's going to get it, she just doesn't know how big it is!'

The waiting went on. A fitful breeze sprang up, rocking the aeroplane which creaked on its wheels. Called a Horsa, it was one of six on the mission, each carrying twenty-eight men plus two pilots. Squatting there in the moonlight, it had a rather flimsy appearance, quite unlike the Dakota or Whitley. Nor was it especially streamlined or elegant. In fact it looked like something a schoolboy might build out of balsa wood and throw like a toy.

Major Howard appeared from the darkness. 'Right, lads.' He rubbed his hands. 'We're all set!' And with that Operation Deadstick began.

Albeit slowly, for the Horsa's ladder was steep, the doorway narrow and the men more heavily encumbered than Theo had ever seen. Quite apart from personal kit and rations, they were festooned with rifles, Stens, Brens, PIATs, grenades, mortars, explosives, radios and enough ammunition to supply a battalion. Shuffling forward, each man had to be propelled bodily up the ladder, and even as he watched, one stumbled and fell with an indignant yelp. Lying there like a stranded beetle, it took two others to haul him to his feet. The queue moved on; Corporal Parr went up, and Doctor Vaughan, then it was Theo's turn, until eventually all twenty-eight were safely aboard, wedged on to bench seats down either side of the cabin, which was cramped and dark and smelled of wood resin. Sandwiched between Parr and Vaughan, Theo fastened his lap strap, adjusted his back and chest packs and tried to get comfortable, uneasily aware suddenly that despite their loads, he like everyone was missing one vital piece of Para paraphernalia. A parachute.

The door clumped shut, the pilots checked their controls and Major Howard took position behind them, watching intently through the windscreen. Nerves were taut, the cabin oppressive – and dim, with just one light in the cockpit illuminating a paltry cluster of instruments. Then somewhere out ahead heavy engines rumbled to life. 'Here we go!' Howard called, and the rumble rose to a roar, only to fade as the aeroplane in front pulled away. The Horsa shook in its slipstream and suddenly there was a stout jerk and it lurched into motion. It gathered speed, pitching and swaying like a boat on a sea while the pilots wrestled for control. It began to bounce and lurch more violently; it left the ground only to thump back down again, trundle on, then after one final bone-jarring bounce the jolting stopped and it was airborne, rising in a series of drunken jerks into the still night air.

Theo patted his pocket again, checking for Clare's letter, lowered his head to his chest and tried to rest.

Everything had happened bewilderingly fast. Somewhere between his parents' reunion at the hospital, Grant's outburst in Baker Street, meeting the Atkins woman and learning of Clare's predicament, and the oddly poignant talk with John Frost at Susanna and Albert's wedding, he had somehow agreed, at least in principle, to meet the mysterious Major Howard and hear what he had to say. Possibly, he later acknowledged, because it might get him to France. The very next morning he was shaken awake by Eleni with the news that a car was waiting outside, and the 'corporal driver chappie' was getting impatient. The car then conveyed him, still wearing his wedding clothes, some hours westwards to a village near Salisbury, where it pulled up outside a handsome Georgian rectory.

'Where are we?' he asked the driver.

'6th Airborne HQ. Windy Gale's place. We call it the madhouse!'

Inside his identity was checked and his clothes searched before he was shown into a panelled sitting room, where the door was locked behind him. Plushly furnished with sofas and armchairs, by the window something box-like lay on a table covered by a sheet. A few minutes later, just as he was about to peek under the sheet, the door opened and two officers strode in, one a major and the other a major general, both tall and lean and both wearing Para insignia. The major was unknown to him, but the general he recognized from 2nd Battalion's early days at Hardwick Hall. Unsure whether to salute or not, he straightened from the table and shuffled to attention.

'So you're the elusive Trickey,' Gale said, locking the door shut again.

'Yes, sir.'

'Welcome to the madhouse. Thank you for coming at such short notice.'

'Yes, sir.' Not that he'd had much choice.

'Now, this won't take long. Depending on what happens, that is.'

'Sir.'

'This is Major John Howard, the man in charge of the op. He's going to show you something, and we want you to look at it very carefully. Understood?'

Op? Theo glanced towards the sheet-covered box. 'I think so, sir.'

It wasn't the box. Not at first. Howard stepped forward and pulled something from an envelope, a photograph, and thrust it under Theo's nose.

'Recognize this?'

'Yes, sir.'

'What is it?'

'It's a bridge.'

Gale snorted. 'Isn't it always?'

Howard seemed unamused. 'Which bridge?'

'It's the lifting bridge over the Caen Canal at Bénouville in Normandy.'

'And you know this how?'

'Because I was stationed there in 1940.'

Another photo appeared. 'Who's this?'

'Madame Thérèse Gondrée. She runs the café by the bridge.'

Another grunt from Gale. 'And that's not all.'

'How well do you know her?' Howard snapped.

'Quite well. She was very kind, and helpful to me.'

More questions followed, to do with his guard duties, the size and composition of his platoon, his commanding officer with the East Surreys, and several about the surrounding terrain. Then, seemingly satisfied, Howard finally led him to the table by the window and peeled back the sheet. Beneath it stood a beautifully crafted model of the bridge in a glass case, complete with little ships and cars, trees and vegetation, tracks and paths, road markings, surrounding buildings and even tiny people standing about on street corners. Theo bent lower, fascinated by the workmanship, which seemed perfect in every detail. Almost.

'Study it,' Howard ordered gruffly. Then he replaced the sheet. 'Notice anything?'

'It's the wrong way round.'

'What is?'

'The whole bridge. The balance, the bascule thing. It opens the other way.'

'Correct. Anything else?'

'The approach road's narrower, the café's nearer the bridge, there's a barn missing, and that pillbox wasn't there in 1940.'

'Correct again. Could you work the bridge mechanism if necessary?'

'Yes, the operator showed me.'

'Do you know the town of Bénouville?'

'Quite well, yes.'

'Is it true you speak German and French fluently?'

'German yes, French a little less.'

'Good.' Howard glanced at Gale. 'He's in.'

Details followed. The operation was codenamed Deadstick. Its objective was to seize and hold the canal bridge, and another bridge five hundred yards east over the River Orne. The mission was to take place the night before the main invasion: Caen was a key objective for the first day; the bridges were essential to achieving it. Secrecy was paramount; therefore Theo was to be taken immediately to an undercover location in Dorset where the rest of the team were assembled. Further briefings and training would follow there, and a uniform would be issued in the rank of second lieutenant, plus full kit and weaponry. Finally, he would not be allowed off base, nor permitted to contact anyone, including next of kin, until the mission was over.

'What happens then?' he asked.

'We relieve you,' Gale said. '6th Airborne. The following morning.'

'I mean after that, sir.'

Gale shrugged. 'We liberate France.'

'And me?'

'You return with the pilots – they're urgently needed here. You're then free to rejoin your unit.'

Theo stared at the model.

'So,' Howard said at length. 'Everything clear?'

'No.'

'What?'

'There are conditions, sir.'

'There bloody well aren't!'

'Then I refuse to go.'

'You'll do as ordered! Or—'

'A moment, John,' Gale interrupted. 'Frost mentioned this. Now, Trickey – er, Theodor, I mean – it's all right, just tell us what's on your mind.'

So he told them. He wouldn't fight, he wouldn't bear arms, nor would he wear the uniform of a lieutenant – or any officer. He would gladly go, as a private, and do whatever he could to assist the mission, but those were his conditions and they were not negotiable.

Gale listened, nodding slowly. 'John?'

'Christ.' Howard exhaled. 'Well, I suppose it is liaison I need him for, mainly, that's true, that and his local knowledge, radio ops, message running, questioning Jerry prisoners: all that sort of thing. Operating the bridge too, if needed. And he can do medical back-up for Vaughan.'

'I've done quite a bit of that, sir.'

'But everyone's a combatant if it comes to it. I've no room for conchies and cowards.'

'I am not—'

'Major,' Gale soothed. 'This young man was on Colossus. He fought at Oudna. And Tamera. He's a renowned partisan leader, one of SOE's best. You've seen his record, and heard what Frost has to say. Christ, he practically took that Sicilian bridge single-handed! Nobody's calling him a coward.'

'No. Of course not,' Howard mumbled. 'That's not what I meant. I just don't want anyone, you know, going peculiar if things get lively.'

Fleeing tanks in a French forest. Scots boys sprinting down a lane. A picture of camels crossing a desert. A red beret floating into mist.

He allowed himself a wry smile. 'I'll do my best not to, sir.'

The ride in the Horsa glider was the worst he'd ever experienced. Yanked along behind its tug like a wayward dog, the motion was awful, as nauseating as it was unnerving. 'Like being tossed about in a cardboard tube,' as Corporal Parr put it. Tightly gripping their bench seats, bumping and swaying like mannequins in a lorry, barely had they left ground before men were turning pale. Minutes more and the first was doubling over to retch; others soon joined in, some stoically producing paper bags in anticipation. The stench of vomit then mingled with the tang of wood resin and engine fumes from the tug, further compounding everyone's misery.

Theo clung bleakly to his seat. 'Is it always like this?' he asked Parr.

'Worse, sometimes. I expect you'd rather be jumping for it!'

'I expect I would. Do you ever get used to it?'

'Never. Mind you, it's better when we drop the tow.'

'Better?'

'Smoother. Exciting too, like a toboggan ride. Loads of fun, you'll see!'

The 'toboggan ride', he'd already learned, was the climax of a Horsa's flight – and its main *raison d'être*, which was to deliver men and equipment to the target. Six or seven minutes of free gliding, slipping silently through the darkness like an owl, it concluded with what was jokingly referred to as a 'controlled crash' in a field.

The field in question, he'd also learned, was the narrow strip of pasture between the Caen Canal and the Orne River, with trees at one end and a raised embankment at the other. Three of the gliders were to land there and seize the canal bridge, while the other three landed in another field to seize the river bridge. Surprise – and therefore an accurate landing – was everything, and everyone knew the demands on the pilots were formidable. Precisely timed to land at one-minute intervals, the approach had to be made in pitch darkness and at ninety miles an hour. Come in too short and they'd hit woodland, too long and they'd crash into the embankment, while to either side stood buildings and other obstructions. Any error, however slight, was likely to be disastrous. Then, just to add to the tension, three days before the mission, fresh reconnaissance photos had arrived, and nearly put paid to everything.

'Get the hell in here!' Howard had bellowed, summoning him to his office. Two weeks they'd all been waiting, locked into their compound like fractious hounds. Tempers were fraying, arguments and bickering flared, and now suddenly everything hung in the balance. Studying the photos with Howard was the lead pilot, Jim Wallwork.

'Do you know what this is?' Wallwork asked.

Theo looked. 'It's the landing field.'

'It's Rommel's fucking asparagus!' Howard fumed.

'Rommel's…'

'Those marks in the ground. They weren't there last week!'

Theo looked again, and saw a faint grid-like pattern of darker dots.

'It's one of his great inventions! Big bloody posts sunk in the ground braced with wires. Designed to scupper landings. Boffins call it Rommel's asparagus.'

'The point is,' Wallwork went on calmly, 'it looks like the holes have been dug, but the posts aren't in yet. And even if they get them in, everything depends on the firmness of the ground. Soft ground and we should be all right, hard ground and we're in trouble.'

'It's soft, sir. Rather boggy, in fact, as I remember.'

'Are you sure?'

He thought back. Training exercises with Kenny Rollings and the others. Crawling over the field on their bellies to simulate attacks on the bridge. The watching girls were impressed, but the boys got soaked to the skin. 'Yes, I'm sure. It was waterlogged.'

Wallwork nodded. 'It'll be OK, John, helpful in fact. If we do snag any, they'll tear out of the ground and slow us down.'

Howard looked doubtful. 'As long as we don't hit any head on.'

The gliders flew on. Despite their discomfort the men's morale seemed high, Theo noted. A sing-song had started, led by Wally Parr, which even the airsick men joined with. Jokes and laughter were breaking out, and someone began blowing on a harmonica. He looked on, wondering at the resilience of the British Tommy. 'They're keen as mustard,' Gale had told him privately at the madhouse, 'but few have seen action, which is why I want you there.' And minutes before take-off, one man from the next glider had thrown down his weapon and run off into the night.

'Five minutes!' Wallwork's shout came from the cockpit.

Instantly the jocularity stopped and the men swung into the ritual of preparation: stowing kit, tightening webbing, donning helmets, loading, checking and rechecking their weapons.

'Red light on, eh, Trickey?' Parr quipped, buckling his helmet. And across the cabin Lieutenant Brotheridge winked encouragingly. Another man opened and latched the door, allowing a chilly blast to clear the foetid air. Through it, white-topped surf could be glimpsed far below. He turned forward, watching the dark silhouette of their bomber tug rise and fall in the moonlight. Beyond it flak flashes lit the sky, star shells too and the glow of a distant bombing raid. As he stared, Wallwork's hand rose to a lever in the roof.

'Stand by!'

The next six minutes were unlike anything he'd ever experienced. Wallwork's co-pilot, stopwatch in hand, suddenly shouted, 'Release!' and Wallwork pulled the lever. A sharp jerk followed and the glider broke free from its tug. Immediately, exactly as Wally Parr said, the ride became smooth, and eerily quiet as the engine noises faded, leaving only the whistling slipstream and the creaking of the Horsa's wooden wings. The men too fell into practised silence, allowing the pilots to concentrate undistracted on their task. The nose went down, steeply, to keep up flying speed, while Wallwork, following the clipped instructions of his co-pilot, put the glider through a precisely timed sequence of manoeuvres designed to bring it over Bénouville, then down on to the field by the bridge. Several of the moves were alarmingly steep, with Wallwork tipping the Horsa on to one wing, then right over on to the other, or dropping the nose almost to vertical, before levelling off once more. Major Howard, meanwhile, still crouching between them, followed progress intently through the windscreen. Suddenly he pointed: 'There it is.'

Wallwork nodded. 'And no asparagus.'

'One minute!' the co-pilot called. 'Brace, everyone!'

Legs tucked, chins down, arms tightly linked like dancers in a chorus, the men made ready. Then the Horsa began to shake as Wallwork lowered flaps to reduce its speed. Theo stole glances through the open door. Shadowy houses and trees flashed by; he glimpsed a road, and the glint of water, a lorry, then a shout came from the cockpit: 'Chute!' and with a jerk the pilots released a drag parachute in the tail. A sinking sensation, trees and bushes flew by terrifyingly fast, then came a stupefying crash and the Horsa hit ground. Seconds of stunned silence followed as it bounced into the air; he felt a lightness as his body rose, felt Wally's arm tightening on his, then came a second violent crash, followed by a series of splintering impacts as the Horsa careered across the field, tearing itself to pieces as it went. Finally, still travelling fast, there was a shocking collision, everyone hurtled forward and the world went black.

He awoke amid a jumbled heap of bodies. The Horsa was motionless, the night uncannily quiet. From far in the distance drifted the crump of falling bombs, while dogs howled nearby.

Muttered curses and pained groans rose from the bodies as stunned men sought to disentangle themselves and their equipment. Theo followed them blindly outside, staggering from the wreckage into the moonlight, where the first thing he saw was the Horsa's smashed cockpit lying drunkenly askew. Two bodies were protruding from beneath it, with a third lying nearby. The next thing he saw, as though from a vividly remembered dream, was the canal bridge, rising stark and angular against the night sky, and so near he could smell its lifting mechanism. Other men too seemed transfixed, staring at the bridge in dazed awe. After weeks training for something existing only in imagination, Jim Wallwork, in an astonishing feat of flying, had just delivered them to within a stone's throw of it.

Furthermore, the enemy seemed unaware.

Howard appeared, a finger to his lips. 'See what you can do,' he whispered to Theo, gesturing at the pilots' bodies. 'Vaughan's down too, went through the windscreen.' Theo nodded, watching as Howard and the rest set off for the bridge. In seconds they'd reached it and begun fanning out along the embankment. A moment later a rumbling noise behind heralded the arrival of the second glider.

Both pilots were alive, he quickly discovered, and conscious, but pinned beneath wreckage. Following muffled instructions, he heaved and hauled at the woodwork until Wallwork wriggled free, his face running with blood from a head wound; then the two of them freed the co-pilot, whose leg was broken. Theo tended their injuries as best he could, before seeing to Doctor Vaughan, who appeared badly concussed.

'Thank you, waiter,' Vaughan said groggily, 'I'll try the turbot now.'

'Leave him with us,' Wallwork suggested. 'You join the others.' Just then a single shot rang out from the bridge. Theo gathered his bags and sprinted up the bank. By now all three gliders had arrived, with seventy men or more spread out along the embankment. Above them the road ran left on to the canal bridge, or right towards the river bridge, some five hundred yards away. To one side stood an unmanned anti-tank gun, while directly across the road, squat and solid in the moonlight, sat the pillbox he'd seen on the model.

'We heard a shot,' he murmured to Howard.

'Bloody sentry at the other end.' Howard squinted through binoculars. 'Must have spotted us, loosed off a round and run away. Jerry'll wake up now all right. How are the injured?'

'Pilots are hurt but OK; Doctor Vaughan's badly stunned.'

'Right, then you're MO until he comes round. Meanwhile, we need to take the far end – and fast.'

Whispered orders were then passed along the bank and men busied themselves moving into position; with an undeniable thrill he heard the familiar click of weapons loading and bayonets being fixed.

'You 2nd Battalion buggers think you know it all,' Howard murmured in the darkness. 'But this is how we do it in the Ox and Bucks!'

'Go!' he hissed, and two figures rose from the bank and scampered across the road. Pressing their backs to the pillbox, they reached round and dropped grenades through its slit windows. A final moment of silence followed, then the grenades exploded and the entire force leaped up and charged as one, bellowing like animals. Everyone had a role, he saw, with each move carefully choreographed. Some stormed the pillbox, kicking the door in and shouting furiously; some made for bunkers on the canal bank; others set up supporting mortar and machine-gun positions, while sappers scrambled into the girders beneath the bridge. Howard and the main group, meanwhile, sprinted across it, swiftly reaching the far end unchallenged. Theo followed, his boots ringing familiarly on the old ironwork, his eyes on the café, with its windows dark and shuttered. Around him men were already setting up firing positions, while others spread out in search of the enemy. Efforts at fortification were in evidence everywhere, with fresh trenches and bunkers dug along the canal bank, machine-gun positions and the anti-tank gun emplacement as well as the pillbox. Barbed wire surrounded the bridge, and across from the café stacks of sharpened stakes lay ready for planting – Rommel's asparagus, he presumed. Fifty yards further on was a T-junction where the road turned left for Caen or right to the coast at Ouistreham. Then shouts were rising along the canal, followed by the clatter of Stens and the crack of a grenade. '*Schiesse mir nicht!*' someone shouted in terror. Scattered shooting broke out, figures appeared, running in panic, some wearing only their underclothes. Other fearsome figures chased them, brandishing weapons, their faces blackened with cork, their teeth grinning in the moonlight.

Within minutes the bridge was secure at both ends. Some valuable equipment had been captured too, including rifles, machine pistols and much ammunition. The bridge defenders turned out to be few in number and comprised mostly of reluctant foreign conscripts, plus their German NCOs, who seemed nonplussed by the sudden appearance of Tommies. Little resistance was offered; they were corralled into a corner and ordered to behave. Theo, meanwhile, set up an aid post in a bunker and attended to the casualties, which numbered two Germans injured, plus Wallwork and the co-pilot, a platoon commander called Wood with leg wounds and, to everyone's shock, Lieutenant Brotheridge, who had been hit in the neck by a stray bullet.

'How is he?' Howard asked.

'I don't know. Unconscious. And losing blood. I could do with Doctor Vaughan.'

'And I could do with you questioning the prisoners.'

Vaughan duly arrived, limping unsteadily into the bunker. 'An entire army will hit French soil today,' he announced. 'But I hit it first!'

Theo handed over the wounded and went in search of the prisoners. As he emerged from the bunker he heard the drone of aircraft and saw searchlights scouring the sky to the north.

'6th Airborne!' Wally Parr trotted by, hefting a Bren. 'Dropping in to reinforce us!'

It was soon obvious that the prisoners, shivering and shrugging miserably, knew little of the bridge's defence arrangements. But one German NCO had recovered sufficiently to muster contempt.

'You boys will be blown to bits!' he sneered. 'There's a battalion of stormtroopers billeted up the road. Tanks too, and artillery!'

'Where?'

'You'll find out soon enough!'

'He may be right,' Howard said when Theo reported. He checked his watch. 'And we can expect no relief from the Paras for some hours yet.'

'Any word from the river bridge, sir?'

'Nothing. Nor can we raise anyone on the radio.'

Better news was that the sappers had found wiring and detonators under the bridge, although the charges themselves had not been placed. But having successfully seized and secured his target, Howard now had to redeploy his men to defend it, which was a completely different prospect. Lightly armed and equipped as always, they had little to fight off tanks and artillery.

'Fact of the matter is, Trickey, I need better gen.'

Theo nodded at the café. 'Shall I try in there?'

He had to shoulder his way through the door. Stumbling inside, the memories immediately flooded back: the smell of French cigarettes, beer and hot chocolate; listening to Maurice Chevalier on the wireless; thawing his feet and reading *Le Journal* by the fire; playing with the baby on the floor with Jeanette. '*Madame Gondrée?*' he called hesitantly in French, then remembering her Alsatian lineage tried again in German: '*Ist hier jemand?*' He stood for a moment, head cocked, but the house was silent, dark and cold. He checked in the main salon and kitchen, then went upstairs where he found the beds tidy but empty. Descending the stair once more he remembered the basement, a cellar Georges Gondrée used for storing wine, accessed through a trapdoor in the salon.

They were all there. Huddled on a mattress in a corner, lit by a single flickering candle. Georges was shielding the girls, their faces round with fear. Thérèse, meanwhile, was levelling a shotgun at his chest.

'Come no nearer,' she said calmly in German.

'*Madame? Monsieur?* It is me, Theodor Trickey.'

'Theodor…' A pause. Then a sigh. 'My God, we thought you were Boche looters.'

'Sorry.'

'The invasion. Tell us it's happening?'

'It is, madame. Tonight. As we speak.'

'Then the heavens be praised.'

They returned upstairs, and there in the salon she turned and embraced him, tightly, before standing him back for damp-eyed inspection.

'The war has aged you.'

'I am well enough, madame.'

'The bridge?'

'In our hands.'

'It's what we hoped but dared not believe. Then we heard shooting.'

'There will be more. You should consider evacuating, at least until it's over.'

Thérèse lit more candles. 'The Boche are here four years, and we never evacuate once. Now they're going and you want us to leave?'

She was the same as of memory: dark, petite, full of bustling energy. Georges too, although showing the strain of long occupation. The girls had grown, and the baby he'd played with was now a strapping five-year-old. They exchanged brief news; then he asked her about the garrison.

'But this information was already sent!'

'Madame?'

'The latest update was four days ago.'

'But, ah, could you repeat it to me?'

She rolled her eyes. '736th Grenadiers, based in Ranville, a mile east. About fifty in all, useless troops, foreigners, poorly trained with lazy officers who've been in France too long. A Major Schmidt's in charge; you should have no trouble dealing with them.'

'Is that all?'

'No! Don't your people read? 21st Panzer, two battalions, arrived in Caen three weeks ago. Hardened boys, Theodor,

Afrika Korps veterans, and well equipped with tanks, armoured cars and so on. A Colonel von Luck in command. He's experienced and tough, one of Rommel's best.'

'How soon could they get here?'

'As soon as ordered.'

'Then I'd better inform Major Howard.'

'Yes, you had.'

He turned to leave. 'So, you…'

'Yes, Theodor. I am the Resistance co-ordinator for this sector. Our operatives in the field gather the intelligence; I pass it to the Allies.'

'All along? When I was here in 1940?'

She patted his arm. 'I gave them your name. I said you were resourceful, brave and trustworthy, with valuable skills that were wasted guarding bridges. I told them they should strongly consider recruiting you.'

Shouts came from outside, then the distant rattle of a machine gun, followed by the nearer crump of explosion.

'That's a mortar,' he said.

'Then they're already here.'

CHAPTER 5

He emerged from the café into the moonlight in time to glimpse a German lorry race across the T-junction, bristling with troops. At the same moment a second mortar shell crashed into the pile of wooden stakes, flinging a hail of splinters in all directions. Then machine-gun bullets began pinging off the bridge's ironwork.

'And where's that coming from?' Howard demanded.

'There, I'd say.' Theo pointed. 'Bénouville, possibly the water tower.'

'Well, they're shooting blind, at least until it gets light. Right now our problem is reinforcing this bloody junction.' He nodded at the café. 'Any news?'

'Ranville direction shouldn't be the problem. Serious opposition will come this side of the canal.'

'Tanks? Armour?'

'Both, sir, probably.'

'As I thought.' He hesitated. 'Den Brotheridge died a few minutes ago.'

'Oh...'

'Vaughan said nothing could save him.'

'I'm very sorry.'

'Not your fault. But with Wood down too I'm out of

81

platoon commanders. And I still don't know what's going on at the river bridge.'

'Do you want me to find out?'

'What I want, Lieutenant...'

'Perhaps the bridge party could spare some men, if not too pressed.'

'... is to get the perimeter strengthened, and to do that—' Both men ducked as a third mortar round crashed in.

'That was closer!'

'Yes it was.' Howard straightened. 'All right, yes, go. Tell Priday to send any spare men he can, Gammons and a two-inch mortar. Also our PIAT got damaged in the crash; see if they can lend us theirs.'

Theo set off at a jog, recrossing the canal and out along the darkened Ranville road. The sporadic sounds of gunfire and mortar faded behind, above him poplar leaves rustled in the breeze, and soon the River Orne loomed into view, together with its road bridge. The good news, he quickly learned from the men there, was that it had been swiftly taken against little opposition; furthermore, a weapons cache, including grenades and a mortar, had also been seized. The less good news was that Howard's second-in-command, Captain Priday, together with an entire platoon, was missing.

'His glider never arrived,' a lieutenant told him. 'We fear it crashed.'

'Major Howard's under fire, and expecting enemy in strength. Can you spare some men and equipment?'

'But what if we get attacked?'

'His need is greater just now, don't you think?'

'I don't know...'

A discussion ensued, Theo prevailed and the arrangements

were made; then, just as the relief party was about to set off, an open-topped staff car careered into view from the Ranville direction and sped on to the bridge. A furious barrage of small-arms fire greeted it, whereupon it swerved and crashed into the barrier. Its driver, they discovered, injured but alive, was none other than Major Schmidt, officer in charge of the Ranville garrison.

'Some idiot said there are British *Fallschirmjäger* on my bridge!' he bellowed drunkenly in German. Theo checked the vehicle for weapons but saw only empty bottles and women's clothing.

'Yes, there are, Major.'

'This is an outrage! I'll have you all arrested and shot!'

A few minutes later the relief party, together with extra weapons and the injured Schmidt, arrived back at the canal. Howard was visibly relieved, especially when informed the river bridge was secure.

'Ham and Jam!' he gave his radio operator the code words for double success. 'Start sending them and don't stop till you get a reply!'

'What's his story?' he then asked, nodding at Schmidt.

'Apparently he was entertaining a lady friend when he heard of our arrival. He tried to phone for confirmation but the lines have been cut.'

'Thanks to your Resistance chums. So he hasn't called up reinforcements?'

'It seems he decided to investigate first.'

'Good. Right, you'd better get him to Vaughan—'

They broke off, heads cocked to an ominous new sound. The growl of heavy motors, followed by the unmistakable clatter and squeal of tank tracks. Then, before their eyes and with exaggerated slowness, a single machine rumbled ponderously into view at the T-junction, as though on to a stage, paused, and rumbled off again.

'Mark 4 Panzer,' someone commented.

'Big bastard too. Having a shufti, you think?'

'God knows,' Howard replied, 'but he'll be back for sure.'

Ten minutes later the battle for the bridge began in earnest.

First came a more intense mortar barrage, inaccurate but hazardous, the salvos crashing in at random to fling shrapnel, earth and stones at the crouching defenders. Gunfire was added, from several locations at once, including the emplacement on the water tower which hosed lethal arcs of machine-gun tracer. These softening-up tactics failed to dislodge the men but presaged the return of the tank, plus two more, which soon appeared from the Bénouville direction. Moving in line astern, each was followed by a gaggle of crouching infantrymen, in classic German style. Waiting to meet them was half a company of Ox and Bucks, inadequately armed with light weapons and grenades, but concealed along both sides of the approach road. Their orders were to stay down and hold fire, not waste ammunition on the tanks, but wait until the infantry drew close. As they crouched, and watched, the tanks reached the T-junction, paused, clattered into the turn and began advancing slowly towards them.

'You have to stop the front one,' Theo murmured to Wally Parr. They were crouching against a wall outside the café. Around them men lay prone, their weapons raised ready. 'He's the leader; if he stops the other two won't know what to do.'

Parr peered into the gloom. 'Wagger Thornton's up there somewhere with the PIAT. He may get one shot in before they spot him.'

Theo followed his gaze. The PIAT was an unreliable weapon, slow to load and notoriously inaccurate. You had to fire it standing up, and suicidally near the target to have any hope. Paras thought little of it. 'A Gammon might do better. If you could get close enough.'

Parr hefted a bag. 'Be my bloody guest!'

The clattering grew louder. The Mark 4 Panzer had a 75-millimetre gun, packing a punch almost as powerful as the dreaded 88. Three of them could probably wreck the bridge if so ordered, and the mission would then be lost. He eyed Parr's bag. Gammon grenades. Unscrew the cap, run at the tank, throw, and hope for the best. *Do it. Don't drop it*. The tanks ground on, turrets hunting left and right, their infantry bunched behind, and still no sign of a shot from the PIAT. Around him the men waited nervously, the ground now trembling beneath them as the monsters neared. Suddenly a flash lit the night and the PIAT went off, a metallic clang rang out, and everything vanished in a cloud of smoke. Everyone waited, darkness returned, nothing happened; then the engines rumbled, the smoke cleared and the tanks reappeared, rolling inexorably on. But as they watched, the front one jerked suddenly, lurched to a halt and yellow smoke began leaking from its turret like blood from a wound, then flames appeared, and with a blinding flash and ground-shaking explosion the whole tank blew up, flinging men, metal and debris high into the air.

'Jesus, he hit the bloody magazine!'

'Get down, everyone!'

A spectacular firework display ensued as the tank's ammunition exploded, shooting red-hot bullets and shrapnel in all directions. Men dived for cover as lethal shards hummed and whistled overhead; meanwhile, the wrecked tank burned like a beacon, flames roaring, bathing the scene in a sickly glow and thick choking smoke. Through it Howard's men saw the remaining tanks hesitate, then lurch into reverse, their infantry following like confused sheep. Within a minute they were gone and the attack was over, leaving only the flaming tank and a chorus of ragged cheers. Not one shot, save the single PIAT round from the amazed Corporal Thornton, had been fired.

Dawn came, tentative tendrils of grey creeping from the coal-black night. The angular shadow of the bridge solidified, the abandoned gliders materialized in their field, and faces, fatigued, stubbled, still streaked with burned cork, became recognizable as individual men. As an accompaniment to the dawn a new sound drifted, like very distant thunder sensed rather than heard as a vibration beneath the feet. As though the earth itself was shivering.

'Naval barrage.' Howard checked his watch. 'Bang on time too.'

Parr grinned. 'It's really happening then.'

'Yes it is. And God help any Jerry caught under it.'

Theo turned to listen. It was a sound he'd last heard with the San Felice partisans, high in the hills above Naples, the night the Allies landed at Salerno. The pulverizing of a shoreline by naval artillery of unimaginable strength. Scores of ships, hundreds of guns, all firing together at the land behind the sea, to smash the enemy's defences prior to sending men on to the beaches. And those men, some 160,000 strong, he'd heard, were at that moment wallowing in the grey waters of the Channel, cold, cramped and tense, waiting for the moment their landing craft charged the surf, and the ramps came down, and they ran ashore to meet the enemy.

Among them was a battalion of Royal Warwickshires, who were due to relieve the men at the bridge that evening. Before that, commandos from 1st Special Service Brigade were expected to arrive at around noon. Six hours or so after Paras from Gale's 6th Airborne Division, who'd been dropping throughout the night, turned up to help, theoretically, at any moment.

Until they did, Howard's one company must hold off an enemy growing stronger and more organized by the hour. The next German attack came with the daylight and consisted of a barrage of shelling from mortar and artillery positions around the T-junction. Heavy machine-gun and sniper fire too was added to the mix, from high vantage points further off, catching out the poorly concealed and forcing everyone to sprint from one position to another. To counter this, and wary of another infantry assault, Howard pushed men up to the T-junction, and even on towards Bénouville itself, probing the town's outer defences, until superior fire power and hidden snipers drove them back. Casualties inevitably followed, and Theo once more found himself helping them to Doctor Vaughan in his bunker.

'What have we got here?' Vaughan asked.

'This is Private Dixon. A sniper bullet went through his arm. I put a field dressing on and a tourniquet to stop the bleeding.'

'Sit him down here and let's take a look.' Vaughan cut away battledress to reveal the wound. 'It looks reasonably straightforward, Dixon old chap, hopefully the arm will be all right.'

'Thanks Doc. Bloody snipers.'

Vaughan set to work dressing the arm. 'So what's happening up top?'

Theo glanced at Schmidt, lying in a corner unconscious from alcohol and morphia. 'The enemy are waiting for reinforcements.'

'Before attacking again?'

'I'm afraid so.'

'No sign of Gale's boys then.'

'Not yet.'

'Trickey!' A shout from above. 'Where's that Trickey?'

He emerged into pale light to find Parr and Thornton crouching behind a tree, cupped cigarettes in hand.

'Know much about Jerry artillery?' Wally asked.

'I... A little. Not much.'

'See that?' He gestured towards a gun emplacement across the bridge.

'Yes, I did see it. After we landed. It's a PAK 38.'

'What's that when it's at home?'

'An anti-tank gun, 50-calibre. We came across them in Sicily. PAK stands for *Panzerabwehrkanon*—'

'Never mind that twaddle. Could it hit the water tower?'

Theo peered at the distant tower. 'It's not what it was designed for. But yes, I should imagine so.'

'Good. Do you know how to shoot it?'

'Well, no, but there's usually a button, on the left somewhere...'

'Right, let's go! And keep your bloody head down. Snipers everywhere.'

Tossing their cigarettes aside, the pair set off, Theo following, at a stooping run across the bridge. Bullets pursued them, ricocheting from the ironwork, but they made the eastern bank unscathed. There Howard had placed a

88

picket to guard the rear; otherwise it was quiet. The gun emplacement looked new; another Rommel innovation, he guessed, with a circular parapet and concrete chamber beneath for storage. 'Ammo galore!' Thornton announced after a search. Loading the gun took a while, but once the breech mechanism was worked out, the shell slid home with a promising clunk.

'Now for the button!' Parr rubbed his hands. 'Where is it...'

'I'd say it's that one.' Theo pointed. 'But watch out—'

An explosion, a gout of flame, the gun leaped and the spent shell case flew from the breech, narrowly missing Thornton's head, to lie smoking on the floor.

'... for the recoil.'

Parr coughed cordite. 'Bloody marvellous. Now for that bloody sniper!'

Theo left them to it, climbing from the pit to find the pilot Jim Wallwork struggling up the bank laden with supplies and ammunition.

'Lend us a hand, would you?' he puffed, his face streaked with dried blood. 'Howard wants everything from the gliders. I've done three trips already but he keeps shouting for more.'

'I suggest we wait a minute or two. It'll be safer.'

Parr's gun barked, and they turned to see a wooden shed beneath the tower explode into fragments.

'Up a bit, Wally!' Wallwork shouted.

They looked on as Parr elevated the gun. 'You're leaving,' Theo said. 'The pilots, I mean. After this.'

'Too right!' Wallwork patted his pocket. 'Special order, signed by Monty himself: all glider pilots get priority transport back to Blighty. You've got one too, haven't you?'

'Yes.'

'Then this time tomorrow we'll be on a destroyer back to Portsmouth.'

Parr's third shot struck the roof of the water tower, throwing up a cloud of dust and debris. Seconds later tiny figures atop the tower were seen scurrying for cover. Seizing the moment, Theo and Wallwork gathered the provisions and ran back across the bridge. Where a ferocious firefight was under way near the T-junction.

'Get the ammo forward!' Howard ordered. 'And tell them to hang on as long as possible. Once we start falling back we've had it.'

Stealing along the ditch he arrived at the T-junction to find a dozen men pinned behind a low wall. 'Sten clips and grenades,' he said, passing the bags to a corporal.

'For all the good they'll do!' And as he peered round the wall a long burst of machine-gun fire tore into it, demolishing brickwork and sending lethal shards flying. On and on it went, wild, undisciplined but deadly. Shooting back was out of the question, all they could do was hug the wall and wait for it to end.

Theo ducked low, eyes closed, holding his helmet to his head and thinking of a battered hillside in Tunisia, with Euan Charteris, Padre Egan and the others. Colonel Frost had known what to do then. And saved the day.

'This isn't a very good position,' he said when at last the shooting paused.

'Tell us about it!'

'But that gunner's wasting his ammunition. Do you know where he is?'

'House across the street.' The corporal pointed. 'First floor. We tried lobbing grenades but can't get near enough. There's snipers too in those houses on the left, and one up the church tower. Mortar's coming from further back in town. Jack Bailey's section across the road has a Bren, but they've got problems of their own.'

John Ross storming a machine-gun nest above Sedjenane. Captured intact and not a man lost. Do nothing and be beaten, or act and survive. From his great-grandfather, through Rommel, Frost, or a company of Highlanders at the bottom of a French field, if he'd learned it once he'd learned it a dozen times. Seizing the initiative invariably wins.

'We need to get into that house, then we'd have a three-way field of fire.'

'Brilliant, but how—'

'He's reloading now. I'll go speak with Bailey.'

'What!'

'Leave half your men on this side, Bailey does the same, wait for the next reload, then we storm the house together. Get ready.'

'Christ, but—'

'Do it fast, don't stop and we'll catch him by surprise. He's one, we're many, it'll work, I promise.'

'Well…'

'Give me covering fire while I cross. Wait, wait… Now!'

He leaped up and sprinted across. Bullets pecked at his feet as he ran, but in seconds he was tumbling into the opposite ditch.

'Blimey, where you sprung from?'

'Are you Bailey?'

'That's me.'

'I've brought ammunition for the Bren. Here's what I suggest we do…'

He laid out the plan, Bailey and his men made ready, signals were exchanged across the road, and then they were set.

Bailey picked up a Sten. 'Don't you want this?'

'No. Are you ready?'

'As I'll ever be.'

'Right, on my word—'

'I say!' A shout suddenly from behind. 'I say, just a moment!'

They hesitated.

'Who the hell are you?' Bailey demanded.

'If you hang on, we'll give you a hand!'

Theo stared. Figures were hurrying along the ditch towards them, many figures, in green, wearing camouflage jumping smocks with the tails hanging down. Led by a man brandishing a pistol. And wearing a red beret.

'Richard Archdale,' the man panted. '7th Battalion the Paras. Sorry we're late, had a spot of bother at the DZ.'

'You shouldn't really be out here,' Theo said to Thérèse twenty minutes later. 'It may be quiet at the moment but it's far from secure.'

'I'd not miss it for the world.' She smiled, inhaling the morning air.

'We're expecting a counter-attack any time.'

'Let them try. They're finished here and know it. As far as I'm concerned, ours is the first home liberated in the whole of France.'

'You're probably right.'

'And they're never having it back.'

They surveyed the scene together: smashed trees, cratered roads and the bullet-pocked masonry of her house. The burned-out tank, still smouldering where the PIAT had stopped it, blanket-covered bodies lying beside it. The three gliders askew in their field, Wally Parr's anti-tank gun roving left and right, the smoke-blackened windows of the pillbox, and the bridge itself, rusting, paint-flaked, dented but unbowed. And the men, sitting and standing, smoking and joking, the khaki of Howard's company mingling with the green-smocked Paras. Their commanding officer, he'd discovered, now standing to one side chatting with Howard, was none other than Richard Pine-Coffin, legendary former commander of 3rd Battalion, the man who'd paraded his troops through Bône twice to confuse the enemy, and led them so bravely through the carnage of Tamera. Right now his men were setting up fresh firing positions, replenishing weapons and ammunition stocks, moving up and moving forward, pushing into Bénouville itself, going house-to-house to drive back the enemy. Doing what Paras do, *utrinque paratus* as the motto went. Ready for anything.

As they watched, Georges Gondrée appeared beside the two officers, bearing a tray with bottle and glasses.

'Is that champagne?'

Thérèse chuckled. 'He buried it in the yard the afternoon you left, Theodor. A case of the best vintage. And he vowed never to dig it up until the day of liberation.'

'Four years. It seems much longer somehow.'

'Much has happened. To you especially, I sense.'

He nodded. 'There's something I need to ask you, Thérèse.'

'Your lady friend, and where she might be.'

'Yes.'

'You have anything to go on?'

He fumbled at his pocket. 'I've written down what is known, her network and code names, her contacts and areas of operation, details of her last transmissions. There's a photo too, here…'

93

She took the photograph. 'She's pretty. I assume Vera Atkins gave you these. A compassionate woman. Do you have anything else?'

'A letter. Undated, brought back to London by courier. It's personal.'

'Keep it.' She glanced through the notes. 'And I'll do what I can. But she was not of our network. And we have problems of our own.'

'I'm sorry.'

'Jeanette Bolpert is one of them. My waitress, you remember?'

'Of course. She brought me soup on the bridge.'

'She was quite enamoured of you. A talented operative too. Picked up three weeks ago on some trivial infringement, now she's in the municipal prison in Caen. Along with many others, including several women.'

'What will happen to them?'

'God knows.' Her eyes flickered. 'Especially now the invasion's begun. The Gestapo can act recklessly.'

'We must get to them somehow. Get to them all.'

'*Nacht und Nebel*, Theodor. You have heard of this?'

'No.'

'One of Hitler's personal directives. Night and fog. It's what happens to agents who get caught.'

CHAPTER 6

By late morning a form of stalemate was developing. The Germans held a half-mile perimeter around the T-junction; meanwhile, about a hundred 7th Battalion Paras had found their way to the bridge and were gradually replacing Howard's troops, who retreated to the eastern bank for a much-needed rest. Although rest seemed hard to come by. Firstly Wally Parr drove everyone mad banging away with his anti-tank gun. Next a lone Dornier rumbled overhead and they all had to dive for cover. The plane dropped one bomb, which missed the bridge, then flew away again. Barely had they sat down when shouts were heard and a German gunboat appeared, motoring up the canal from the sea and spraying the scene with machine-gun fire. Wally to his fury couldn't shoot because the bridge was in the way, so the trusty PIAT was brought up again. A well-aimed shot went straight through the boat's wheelhouse, whereupon it rammed the bank and burst into flames, its occupants scrambling ashore and hurrying away. Once more the Ox and Bucks men slumped down to rest, but the fighting at the T-junction was growing ominously louder, and sure enough, within minutes seemingly, they were being summoned forward to join the fray once more.

Theo went with them.

'We need better gen on Jerry,' Howard told him wearily.

'I'll go.'

'Strength, movements, intentions and so on. Here in town, but also nearer Caen.'

'There was a ferry crossing somewhere upstream. I'll try there.'

'Don't take any chances, Trickey, just learn what you can.'

Yet unknown to Howard the enemy knew little more than he did. Hamstrung by sabotaged communications, a muddled command structure and garbled rumours of mass invasion, Colonel von Luck of the Caen garrison had been waiting all night for permission to advance on the bridge in force. But 21st Panzer, as an elite unit, could only move on the direct orders of the Führer himself, and the Führer was holidaying in Berchtesgaden. Luck's superior, General Feuchtinger, was away in Paris, Feuchtinger's boss, Rommel, unusually, was nowhere to be found, and despite endless fruitless phone calls, Luck could find nobody in authority willing to override this order. Nor even show much interest in the seriousness of the situation: 'Call back in office hours,' being the typical response. Finally he got through to Berchtesgaden itself, only to be brusquely informed that the Führer was sleeping and certainly not to be disturbed over some trivial scuffle in Normandy. So in the end, hedging his bets and his orders, Luck had moved secondary units into the area to stem any breakout from the bridge, while holding his main force in reserve should Caen itself be threatened.

Theo set off, leaving the sounds of fighting behind, recrossing the bridge and stealing along the trees lining the eastern bank for a mile until he arrived at the crossing. Searching the bank for the rowing-boat ferry, he eventually spotted it—but moored on the far side. Scarcely pausing, he peeled off his battledress, tied it into a bundle and waded in.

The canal was cold but its waters still; he attained the far bank unobserved, re-dressed and set out once more. Crop fields and woodland lay between Bénouville and Caen and by sticking to tracks and paths he was able to close on the city, entering it from the east at Hérouville. All was eerily quiet, deserted of life both civilian and military, and soon he was edging down roads cratered by bombs and strewn with rubble. Water gushed from smashed mains, trees and telegraph poles lay drunkenly askew, some entire streets were impassable, their houses blasted to rubble, while smoke from a thousand fires rose and joined into a single giant pyre, blotting out the sunlight and enveloping the stricken city like fog.

'Psst, *rosbif!*' A hissed whisper came from a doorway. Theo stopped. An old man, leaning on a stick, was beckoning him closer. '*Vous êtes rosbif, n'est-ce pas?*'

'*Rosbif?*' Theo queried in French. 'You mean English?'

'*Anglais, oui.*'

'Ah... well, yes, I'm English.'

'We are liberated?'

'Not quite, but soon hopefully.'

'God be praised.' The old man planted stubbly kisses on his cheeks. 'It took you long enough.'

'Yes. Sorry.'

'But where is your tommy gun?'

'I don't... I'm on reconnaissance.'

'Oh. And what of your army? We heard it is in Ouistreham.'

'Yes, it landed this morning. It is coming. But where is everybody here? Where are all the people?'

The man shrugged. 'Left town. Or hiding in shelters, basements, their cellars.' He produced a crumpled leaflet. 'These fell in the night, by the thousand.'

Theo smoothed the page. *Citizens of Caen!* it read in French. *The Allies are coming; the hour of liberation is at hand. But first we must drive the enemy from your streets and destroy their warmongery. So stay indoors, under cover and in the shelters until the bombardments are over and the all-clear sounds. Vive la France, vive la liberté!*

'Tell them to stop,' the man said.

'What?'

'There are hardly any Germans in Caen; they know it's too dangerous. The main barracks are outside.'

'Outside where?'

'Colombelles and Vimont mainly. Some in Ranville. You must tell them to stop the bombing – you are killing innocent civilians and destroying our homes for no reason. Please tell them.'

'I'll try. Where's the prison?'

'West side. Long way. You'll never make it without getting spotted.'

Theo pushed on further, but the nearer he drew to the centre, the more people he saw, including armed militia and police patrolling for looters. Then a German half-track sped by followed by a lorry load of troops, and suddenly a lone British soldier skulking in the shadows was becoming conspicuous. And an object of interest.

'*Soldat anglais!*' A child shouted with excitement. 'Over there, *Tommy*, see!'

Two figures in grey turned to look. Theo ducked into a doorway.

'*Halt!*'

He leaped from the doorway and took off, sprinting back the way he had come. A single shot rang out and he felt the bullet hum by; he jinked into an alley and ran on. Then as he fled he heard a different sound, a distant throbbing, as though from hundreds of engines, and moments later a chorus of sirens began wailing around the city, and people outside began running in all directions, gathering their children and scurrying for shelter. The noise grew louder and he glanced up as he ran, glimpsing dozens, scores of tiny silver crosses filling the sky like stitches in a blanket. By the time he reached Hérouville, breathless and sweating, the bombs were already falling again.

He made his way back to the canal and paddled across in the rowing boat, but then had to make a detour to avoid a foot patrol approaching along the bank. Thirty minutes later, as he was jogging through woodland near Ranville, he was stopped in his tracks by a new sound. At first he thought he was imagining it, straining to hear above the rumble of far-off bombs and ack-ack guns, but then it came again: reedy, resonant, unmistakable. Bagpipes. Somewhere up ahead a Scots piper was playing. He hurried breathlessly on, emerging minutes later on to a road he recognized as the Orne River approach. And there, striding along towards the canal, tall, erect and in perfect time with one another, were three smartly dressed officers, led by a piper. One he immediately recognized as General Gale; the other two were brigadiers. Nobody else was anywhere to be seen.

'Is that a Trickey I spy in the bushes?' Gale swivelled his head as though on parade. 'Come along, Private, fall in there!'

So he fell in. He hadn't marched, not properly, for years, not since Eisenhower visited 1st Parachute Brigade back in Boufarik. At first it was a shambles; he felt flustered and clumsy, hopping along behind two brigadiers and a general, and struggling to keep time. But after a while, and with no sounds but the stirring song of the pipes and crisp crunch of boots, he began to find his stride, and his rhythm settled, and something long suppressed stirred within him, and as the canal bridge loomed into view he marched more erectly: his chin came up and he began to swing his arms and puff out his chest with the others. And when the men lounging at the bridge saw them, they got to their feet, gawping in disbelief, and began waving and cheering, and some even came to attention and saluted as they passed. Then Major Howard appeared ahead on the bridge, marching out alone to greet them. 'Parade!' one of the brigadiers bellowed like a sergeant major. 'Parade... halt!' And the five of them stamped smartly to a stop mid bridge, facing Howard who snapped to attention like a guardsman, threw up his hand and saluted.

'General, the bridges are yours.'

'Thank you, Major.' Gale smiled. 'You are hereby relieved.'

Howard grinned. 'You can say that again!'

Throughout the afternoon the transfer process went on. More and more troops arrived to bolster defences, the first motorized units appeared along with heavier weapons and artillery, the Germans drew back, content to hold their perimeter but advance no further, and at nightfall the Royal Warwickshires turned up to complete the handover. At which Operation Deadstick was over, mission accomplished, and some twenty-four hours after they'd climbed aboard their Horsas in Dorset, John Howard's men were at last stood down, fed and rested. Celebrations followed, further boosted by the surprise arrival of Captain Priday and his missing platoon, who'd been cut off after landing at the wrong river.

Yet the festivities were premature, for though the mission was a textbook success, the Bénouville bridgehead marked the furthest point in the Allied advance for weeks to come, and Caen itself, apart from Theo's one-man foray, did not see liberation for over a month, by which time it was a shattered ruin.

'Howard tells me you recced the place,' Gale said to him late that night. 'That was enterprising.'

'Yes, sir. I was on my way back when I met you.'

'So I gather.' They were inside the burned-out pillbox, which Gale had requisitioned as a temporary CP. Now furnished with radios, table and chairs and lit by a hurricane lamp, he had pinned a large map of Normandy on an easel. 'Learn anything useful?'

'Only that the main enemy forces are deployed outside the city.'

'21st Panzer, I hear, among others.'

'Yes. I believe they're at Vimont, here.'

'Anything else?'

'Anti-aircraft emplacements were firing around the perimeter. And there's a lot of damage within the city itself, from the bombing. And civilian casualties.'

'Not much we can do about that. 3rd Infantry was supposed to be taking Caen today; aerial bombardment was a necessary precursor. Hopefully it won't go on too long.' He paused, glancing at Theo. 'He wasn't that keen on you tagging along, you know. Howard, I mean.'

'I gathered that, sir.'

'But he tells me you've been a big help.'

'Thank you.'

'No, thank you. You seem to have a knack for blending in, you know, getting about unnoticed.'

'I've had rather a lot of practice.'

'Indeed. May I ask your intentions? I mean, you're free to return home with the pilots of course, rejoin Johnny Frost and your 2nd Battalion chums.'

'Yes, sir.'

'But between you and me, they're not going anywhere. Not for weeks probably.'

'I see.' *Get to her before the enemy do.*

Gale pointed at the map. '6th Airborne's to secure the area east of here and north to Sword Beach. My units are strung out, men and equipment scattered, communications to pot, and the enemy's pouring in reinforcements by the hour. I could dearly use you here for a while. On my intelligence staff.'

At dawn next morning, with the sound of renewed shelling and gunfire coming from the Bénouville direction, he threw his rucksack into the back of a truck and set off with Gale's entourage in the opposite direction. Progress was slow, hampered by traffic coming the other way, stockpiles of stores and equipment littering the roads, and endless columns of men wandering back and forth trying to find their units. The roads too were narrow and winding with tall hedges obscuring any field of view. 'Ideal ambush country,' the corporal beside him muttered darkly. After a while they arrived at a village north of Ranville, parked outside an empty house and began unloading. The rest of that day and the next was spent setting up Gale's HQ, and trying to establish contact with his many outlying units, and also with the main invasion force, currently strung out along the coast five miles to the north. The news from there was that rough seas and unusually high tides were hampering efforts to unload tanks, armoured cars and other heavy equipment, the beaches were severely clogged with vehicles and equipment, the Luftwaffe was bombing and strafing, casualties were mounting and the whole invasion plan was falling steadily behind schedule. Shelling could be heard in that direction, both from enemy artillery moving into the area, and answering fire from ships at sea, and as dusk fell in the evenings the northern sky was spectacularly lit by artillery flashes, star shells and tracer fire.

Two days went by, then on the third afternoon a harassed-looking aide gave him his first assignment.

'8th Parachute Battalion.'

'Yes.'

'It's missing.'

'Missing where?'

'If we knew that, Trickey, it wouldn't be missing!'

Further instructions revealed that the battalion had dropped with the rest of the division as scheduled, and was then supposed to position itself in a forested area four miles east of the bridges. But nothing had been heard from it.

'That's our flank they're protecting, Trickey, rough country with lots of cover, Jerry's flooding in from the east, and we've reports of heavy skirmishing. We need to find them, get a situation report and establish two-way contact. Got that?'

'Yes.'

'Good. And while you're at it, any gen on enemy strength and movements would be useful. Now, help yourself to kit, rations, a Webley and anything else you need. I'll get a driver to drop you in the vicinity.'

'No Webley, and I don't need a driver. But I'll take a bicycle if you have one.'

'Bicycle.'

'I've found them useful for this kind of thing.'

'Christ, as you please – I think there's one round the back. But for God's sake be careful, Jerry's popping up everywhere.'

'I will.'

'And, well, listen, Trickey, they're a pretty raw bunch the 8th, not exactly top notch when it comes to morale and discipline. Never seen action either. In fact Gale had to sack their CO and bring in a new one to knock them into shape.'

'Who's that?'

'Former CO of 1st Battalion. Tough nut called Pearson.'

He found the bicycle, one of the folding type carried by airborne units, loaded it up and set off, following his map towards the location which was a large forested area called Bois de Bavent. Though the rumble of shelling and gunfire on the coast never ceased, patrolling fighters thundered overhead and yet more bombs could be heard falling on distant Caen, the lanes and tracks around him were quiet. His bicycle clattered, birds sang in the hedge and a horse frolicked restlessly in a field; it was reminiscent of a young reservist pedalling in search of Scotsmen four years previously. At Blangy, less than a hundred miles away.

Then he heard a heavy engine revving. He braked to a stop and suddenly, not two hundred yards ahead, a lone German tank burst through the hedge. Wreathed in foliage and clouds of exhaust, the machine traversed a ditch and lumbered across the road. Caught in the open, Theo could only freeze and stare in shock. The tank was old and battered, and small like the French models; close behind it eight infantrymen walked, some resting their hands on its flanks, and staring straight ahead as though in a trance. Nobody saw him, no one even turned to look, and in seconds the entire apparition was vanishing back into the trees. Nothing followed, no more tanks came, the engine noise faded, and in a minute he was alone with the chirping birds and rustling leaves again.

Shakily noting the location on his map, he mounted up and pedalled on. Half an hour passed, the tracks grew narrower, and darker, and a dank canopy of green closed over his head like a dome. Rain began to fall, hissing through the trees and trickling down his neck; he smelled rotting leaves and damp serge. He pushed on, turning at random, until the map became sodden and meaningless and he knew he was lost. Dismounting once more to check his bearings, he continued on foot, senses heightened for signs of trouble, the bicycle clicking quietly at his side. When he detected movement in the bushes again he pretended to ignore it and kept moving, his body tensed for flight. Then he heard the unmistakable sliding of a German rifle bolt.

'*Nicht schiessen,*' he said quietly. '*Ich habe keine Pistole.*'

'Nicked cheese, my arse! Who the fuck are you?'

Four men, grimy, unshaven and mud-caked, emerged from the trees. 'Put your bloody hands up!'

He did as ordered. 'That's a German rifle. A K98. I thought you were—'

'Too right it is! One of your lot left it to me in his will!'

'I'm not German.'

'Bollocks! You're a fucking spy!'

'No.'

'Deserter then. All the same to me.' He raised the rifle.

'Not that either.'

'Then why you wandering around the woods speaking German and wearing a British battledress with no badges?'

'Because I'm looking for you. I'm Trickey...'

A guffaw. 'Fucking right you are!'

'... of 2nd Parachute Battalion.'

Another laugh, less fulsome. 'Don't be daft, where's your insignia?'

'I'm not wearing any.' The finger was flexing on the trigger, and more figures were emerging, standing in the lane to look on suspiciously. 'I've come from Divisional HQ, to find 8 Para. Is that you?'

'I ain't saying. I'm saying you're a spy and I'm shooting you!' The rifle waved menacingly.

'Your CO wouldn't approve. His name's Colonel Alastair Pearson. You call him Jock, but not to his face. He knows me; we fought together in Sicily. Tell him Lieutenant Trickey's here.'

'Bollocks! Why should—'

'And tell him this...'

'What?'

'*Waho Mohammed.*'

'They're keen but jumpy,' Pearson told him a while later. 'They thought they were coming to liberate Paris, not skulk about the woods getting sniped at. They'll get the hang of it.'

Theo sipped tea. They were sitting in the forest clearing that comprised Pearson's battalion HQ. The rain had faded to drizzle, the afternoon light grown dim. The camp consisted of two heavily camouflaged tents, one battered Jeep and scattered piles of weapons and stores. The radios weren't working, he'd learned, and neither was the Jeep; many of Pearson's men were still unaccounted for, as was much of his heavier equipment. Runners had been sent out twice to make contact with Division, but neither had returned. 'Ran into Jerry patrols probably,' Pearson said. For his part, Theo briefed him on the successful bridge mission and what he knew of the main invasion. Pearson explained that the battalion had to move constantly to avoid discovery. Sometimes, he said, the Germans shelled the forest at random, or raked it with machine-gun fire in the hope of hitting something. 'Unnerving for the lads.' As they talked, various junior officers approached and were introduced. They appeared very young, Theo thought, and wary of him, especially when Pearson recounted the Primosole story. One in particular, a subaltern called Farrar, listened in wide-eyed awe as Pearson described Theo's band of clerks storming the enemy bridge.

'That's amazing, sir,' he said to Theo. 'I can't imagine... Bravo.'

'It wasn't quite like that,' Theo replied modestly.

'Bloody was!' Pearson scoffed. 'I was there.'

'Well. It was a relief when you arrived. And the other COs.'

'A relief for us too. How is Johnny Frost by the way?'

'He's well. I saw him last month, at a wedding. He's not happy about 2nd Battalion being held in reserve.'

'I bet he isn't. But he'll get his chance.' Pearson drained his tea, glancing at Theo's clothing. 'No weapon, Lieutenant? No insignia or badges of rank?'

Theo explained as best he could. Half expecting rebuke or ridicule from the hard-bitten colonel, instead the Scotsman only listened.

'We all feel as you do, you know,' he replied eventually. 'Us older stagers especially: me, Johnny, the rest. We've been doing it too long. There's only so much one can take.'

Theo nodded. At twenty-nine Pearson was hardly an old stager, but the years of campaigning had aged him, even in the twelve months since Primosole, his black hair greying, his face lined and fatigued, and pallid from recurrent bouts of malaria. His posture too seemed hunched and weary.

'Look at this.' He held up a bandaged hand. 'Shot by one of my own men.'

'A Sten?' The Sten gun was notorious for misfires.

Pearson nodded, massaging his hand. 'Too excitable, these boys. Happened at the DZ. Damn careless but can't be helped.'

They were going out on patrol, he went on, that night. Deploying the battalion in daylight was too dangerous, and they weren't equipped for head-on confrontation, so he'd begun making night forays aimed at disrupting enemy movements, sabotaging communications and supplies, and generally spreading confusion.

'Hit-and-run stuff, useful recce and good training for the men. Care to tag along?'

'I should be getting back to Division.'

'It's all intelligence, Trickey. And Division will all be tucked up in bed!' He smiled. 'Anyway, there's something you should see.'

After a supper of bully-beef stew and tea laced with rum, they set out, one company making for the nearby town of Troarn, a second staking out the main road south, and the third in reserve guarding camp. Pearson led the first, setting off at speed along twisting woodland paths by the taped glow of a flashlight. His company followed behind, their hands on each others' backs in the darkness or clutching the toggled ropes Paras carry. Theo brought up the rear, using the ghostly flash of distant artillery for illumination, ears alert to sounds of pursuit. But excepting the distant rumble of shelling, the clicking of kit and the stamping of boots through undergrowth, all remained quiet. After twenty minutes a halt was ordered.

'Jerry stores dump.' The whispered word passed through the column. 'Small guard. We storm it on Jock's signal.'

Moments later a piercing whistle sounded and as one the Paras leaped up and charged, bellowing lustily. Theo followed, arriving at a clearing piled with crates, drums and boxes. Sten guns stuttered, shouts echoed and grenades cracked, lighting the scene like flashbulbs, capturing frozen images of Paras running with excitement, a German with his arms raised, another falling where he stood. In seconds it was over; the shooting died down and everyone stood around looking sheepish. Two bodies lay contorted on the ground, while two prisoners, both young and terrified, stood nearby. As sappers moved among the boxes placing charges, Theo took them aside.

'What's your unit?'

'709th Infantry. Medical reserve.'

'Medical?'

'Yes, I have epilepsy.'

'And I've a prosthetic foot, look.'

'Where are you based?'

'We don't know. The lorry only dumped us here this morning.'

Another blast on Pearson's whistle and the men moved off, prisoners in tow. A minute later they heard the crump of explosions as the charges blew behind.

They exited the forest, creeping along ditches either side of the road to Troarn. On the way they cut telephone wires, tore down direction signs and sabotaged a railway signal box. Reaching the town, the streets appeared quiet, the houses shuttered and the enemy unsuspecting. Pearson split the company and sent them in by platoon. Soon the sounds of shouts, gunfire and explosions were heard all over town; a guardhouse was stormed, military vehicles torched and a fuel dump set ablaze. Elsewhere an anti-aircraft gun had its breech spiked, a machine-gun emplacement was seized, and a parked half-track booby-trapped by the sappers. Little resistance was encountered, any return fire sporadic, and by the time the town defences realized what was happening the Paras were already moving on. Descending from town they gathered in the shadow of a steep bank. Beyond it a river flowed north to the coast, where artillery still flashed and rumbled. Pearson summoned Theo forward. Edging up the bank beside him, Theo saw the river meandering along the valley, with a single-span bridge crossing it. At the centre of the bridge German engineers were making repairs by shrouded floodlights.

'River Dives,' Pearson murmured. 'This crossing is Jerry's main road in from the Le Havre direction. Beyond those trees two armoured divisions are waiting to get across. When they do, they'll swing north, and God help the lads on the beaches.'

'What about the bridge?'

'We've already blown it twice. But they've placed heavy stuff around it, and now we can't get near. So tell Gale we need air strikes and armour. Also anti-tank—'

'Platoon charge!'

'What?'

Excited shouts along the bank, and before their eyes twenty men rose up and set off for the bridge led by a figure waving a pistol.

'Christ no, Farrar!' Pearson leaped to his feet. '2 platoon with me NOW!' He scrambled over the bank, his section following, and vanished from view.

While everyone else looked on in shocked silence.

'Covering fire!' Theo stood up. 'Fire on the bridge, now! Shoot the lights, shoot the enemy, keep shooting!'

Sporadically at first, then with gathering momentum, they opened up. Confusion followed. Pearson appeared, his section running along the river as a diversion, shooting at random. The first grenades went off, and a mortar shell thumped into the bank. Covering fire hit the bridge, sparks flew, the floodlights exploded and the German engineers dashed for cover. Farrar's section arrived to pursue them, but as they charged on to the bridge muzzle flashes sparkled across the river and a line of heavy machine guns opened up, flinging a storm of bullets at them. Some fell forwards, scythed to the ground; some staggered and whirled; some dived for cover; the rest turned and fled.

'Off! Get them off the bridge!' Theo leaped over the bank and scrambled down. He glimpsed Pearson's men angling in from the side, running, shooting, shouting. Mortars crumped, machine guns rattled, clods of earth spurted and rock shards flew, ripping into the ground all round. Smoke grenades began popping, enveloping the scene in acrid mist; he heard a zipping noise and felt a hot sting in his thigh, but kept running. He arrived at the bridge as the first of Farrar's men staggered from the fog. 'This way!' The next appeared, clutching his stomach, then more, singly, in pairs, some clinging to each other. 'Off the bridge, keep moving!' He ran forward to help them, choking on smoke. He saw a figure staggering in circles and dragged him back, then went forward again. His eyes burned; his thigh was wet and hot. He stumbled on something, knelt and glimpsed a figure on the ground.

Farrar, lying on his back. His eyes were staring, and blood welled from a wound in his chest.

'I'll help you.'

'Done it wrong.'

'Come on!' He hauled Farrar to a sitting position, bent and hoisted him like a sack on to his shoulder. Staggering back off the bridge he passed Pearson's men coming the other way. 'More back there, get them!' He reached the bank, bullets still thumping in all around. Aware now he was wounded he began struggling upwards. Halfway his leg buckled and a wave of giddiness swept over him. He heard Paras scrambling down, lifting Farrar from his back and gripping him under his arms. And as he reached safety and toppled over, he saw stars twinkling through the drifting smoke, and heard a voice saying Farrar was dead. And he tasted blood and the bitter sadness of loss; then giddiness overwhelmed him and he surrendered to the void.

CHAPTER 7

He spent three days with 8 Para. Apart from Farrar, two men died in the abortive assault on the bridge, with four injured. Theo's wound was superficial, uncomplicated but painful and bloody. The battalion MO cleaned, stitched and dressed it, and told him to rest it for forty-eight hours. After twelve he rose from his cot and limped outside, only to find the leg numb and useless. That afternoon the battalion moved again, northwards through the forest away from Troarn. Refusing to be carried, he hacked a crutch from a bough and hobbled along behind, only to incur the MO's wrath when his stitches tore. They encountered no Germans but heard gunfire, saw a motorized column rumbling past in the distance and a Messerschmitt that zoomed overhead but failed to spot them. Once settled in their new camp and with pickets set, Pearson sent another runner to Division with a report on the battalion's situation, strength, supplies and casualties. Theo appended a note for Gale, gave the runner his map and bicycle, plus what directions he could for Ranville.

On the third morning the runner was back. By then sensation had returned to his leg and Theo was moving gingerly about camp with a stick. Reading the runner's notes, Pearson beckoned him over.

'Something's up. Town called Bréville-les-Monts, couple of miles north of here. We're to reposition nearby. Heard of it?'

He had. Barely two miles from Gale's HQ, Bréville occupied the only high ground for miles around, and afforded commanding views in all directions. The Germans had been fighting hard to take it – and at considerable cost. So far Gale's men had held them off, but should it fall the whole sector would come under their guns, including the canal bridgehead. And Gale couldn't allow that. 'He said it was crucial they don't get it.'

'They already have, and in strength. Panzer Grenadiers, apparently. And Monty says we're to kick them off, come what may.'

'We?'

'6th Airborne presumably, although without armoured support, God knows.'

'I must get back.'

He set off, walking and cycling as the leg allowed. Staying off roads, he progressed slowly but invisibly; then, nearing Ranville, he heard heavy gunfire coming from the direction of Bréville, now visible on its ridge wreathed in drifting smoke. Arriving at HQ he found it unusually quiet, Gale and his brigade commanders absent, and only a skeleton staff of clerks and signallers, many of them busy packing up.

'Are we moving?'

'Hope it doesn't come to that,' an aide replied. 'Big push to retake Bréville this afternoon. It hasn't gone well – the general's there now.'

With instructions to help himself to food and await further orders, he clumped upstairs, found an empty bedroom and collapsed into sleep.

Hours later he was shaken awake. 'Trickey, the general wants you.'

Dawn light glowed at the window. Groggily he dressed and descended, found Gale's situation room, knocked and entered. The general was at his desk, surrounded by files and papers, a field telephone in one hand, his map on the wall and an aide at his side taking notes. His boots were muddy, tie loose, his Para smock flung carelessly over a chair. His face was gaunt, and drained, like someone who hasn't slept for days.

'Trickey.' He replaced the phone. 'Where's 8 Para?'

Theo pointed at the map. 'Here sir, covering the east as ordered.'

'Pearson?'

'He's fine, sir. The men too, they're doing pretty well.'

'Thank God. We may need them yet.'

Four of his parachute battalions, it emerged, had been trying to retake Bréville, all failing, and all suffering grave losses.

'12th and 1st Canadians took a terrible savaging yesterday. Most of the officers gone, barely a company of men left in each. 7th and 13th fared little better the day before.' He rose and approached the map. 'And we're running out of options...'

'Sir.'

'...but Monty says the enemy must be dislodged. That they're threatening the entire advance inland.'

Theo waited, as the general, swaying slightly, studied the map.

'It's as though Jerry knows how important this is,' Gale murmured. 'He's throwing everything at it. And without armoured support, it's killing us. He'll wipe out the whole division, do you see?'

'Yes, sir.'

'And I can't let that happen.'

'No…'

'So I phoned Browning. And said so.'

Theo froze. A divisional commander, going behind his commander-in-chief. Was he imagining it?

'And he said he'll do what he can.'

He made to reply, but Gale's aide shook his head. Moments later they were standing in the corridor.

'Stay nearby. We'll call you when needed.'

'Is he all right?

'He just needs sleep. I'll see to it.'

He spent the morning waiting. Messengers came and went, telephones rang, staff officers hurried, their expressions uniformly grave. Gale himself stayed at his desk, refusing to eat or rest until the matter was resolved. Reports from Bréville said pockets of Paras were hanging on, but barely, and the last reserve, 9th Battalion, under an officer called Otway, was being thrown into the breach. Pearson's 8th was engaging enemy reinforcements driving in from the east, commandos were trying to fight their way down from the beachhead, and a company of Devonshires was due from the canal. Other infantry support, possibly Scottish, was rumoured, but had yet to materialize. Apart from that there was nothing.

Then at noon came the longed-for breakthrough.

'Trickey.' Gale's door flew open. 'In here, now.'

Boy Browning had come through. Nobody knew how and nobody dared ask, but two armoured squadrons from the 13th/18th Hussars had been detached from the Caen offensive and were now standing by. Serious armour: Sherman tanks, self-propelled guns, towed artillery, mortar and heavy machine guns, plus a battalion of gunners to man them. The Hussars were at that moment forming up preparatory to moving out. All they needed were the necessary orders, and a guide.

'They're assembling here.' The aide jabbed the map. 'Saint-Aubin, about a mile north of Bénouville. Here's the paperwork. A major called Neave's their CO; a Jeep and driver are waiting outside; go like stink and don't let anyone hold you up.'

He set off, the driver crashing gears as they sped the short distance from Ranville, first to the Orne bridge, then on, weaving in and out of traffic until they reached the canal bridge.

Which was in the raised position.

He leaped out and ran along the line of waiting vehicles.

'What's happening?' he asked at the barrier.

'Supply barges coming upstream.'

'How long?'

'God knows. Took bloody hours yesterday.'

He stared around. The bridge area was barely recognizable, all but engulfed in the military circus. Checkpoints had been installed; queues of traffic waited to cross; stores and equipment lay everywhere; men marched; NCOs shouted while anti-aircraft guns scoured the sky for bombers. Through drifting fumes he could just make out the café across the canal, a Union flag hanging from one window, bunting fluttering in the eaves. The wrecked German patrol boat lay abandoned in the reeds, and in the landing field the three discarded gliders still remained, broken and forlorn like forgotten toys.

A cluster of metal dinghies was tied beneath the bridge. 'I've got to get across.'

117

'You and a thousand others.' The guard turned away. 'Now fuck off.'

He slithered down the bank, untied one of the dinghies and pushed into the stream. Angry oaths followed him as he sculled the short distance across, made it unscathed and ran to the café, pounding on the door.

'Theodor!' Georges appeared. 'Dear boy, Thérèse is not here but please come in and wait.'

'Can't,' he panted. 'Can't stop.'

'But she has word, and needs to speak—'

'No time! I'll come back. You have a bicycle?'

'The Boche looted it.'

'Saint-Aubin. How far?'

'That way.' Georges pointed. 'Less than a mile.'

He ran. A hot sun shone overhead; within minutes he was pouring sweat, his wound had reopened and blood was coursing down his thigh. He tied it off, found a stick and hobbled on; a while later he glimpsed farm buildings at the end of a long road, staggered on, crossed a stream, rounded a bend and there stood the column, a shimmering mirage of green steel, snaking through the village like a slumbering serpent. At the monster's head, sitting in a deckchair by his tank, was an officer reading a book.

'Major Neave?' Theo gasped.

'Good Lord. Where on earth did you spring from?'

It took an hour to coax the column back to the bridge, another hour to cross it, and a third to guide it to the Bréville rendezvous. Theo rode atop Neave's Sherman, headphones clamped to his ears, impressed by the shuddering power of the machine with its throbbing engine and roving turret, yet concerned at how ponderous an armoured column was, how unwieldy, how reptilian in its slowness. Just getting it into motion seemed to take an age: passing and receiving instructions, packing up, mounting up, starting motors, manoeuvring out and finally setting off. Like a procession of tortoises, everything seemed to happen in agonizing slow motion.

They finally arrived late in the afternoon, rumbling belatedly up the Bréville road to the weary cheers of the waiting Paras. Gale too was visibly relieved, hurrying from his command post to shake Neave's hand.

'Very glad to see you, Major.'

'Delighted to be of service.'

Within minutes he had called a commanders' briefing.

'Gentlemen. In view of the late hour, the plan now is to make a night assault. We will do this under cover of an artillery barrage laid down by our friends the Hussars. Who will then follow the infantry in with their tanks.'

Theo listened, feeling the painful throbbing in his thigh, and wondering why the British always sent infantry ahead of the tanks, while the Germans, more successfully, sent them in behind. He surveyed the gathered men, studying their faces. All, with the exception of Neave, looked battle-worn and weary. Under-strength too, with many units without leaders, so being commanded by junior officers or NCOs, some from different battalions. 12th Battalion had no original officers left, he'd learned, and 1st Canadian was being led by someone else's brigadier.

'Gen reports any civilians are long gone,' Gale was saying, 'so we hit the place hard. The enemy might be on top right now, but they've suffered badly and are as tired as we are.

Therefore we wait until twenty-two hundred, let them settle for the night, then give them everything we've got. With luck we'll catch them unawares and drive them out before they realize what's hit them.'

Afterwards he spoke to Theo. 'What about that leg?'

'Leg's fine, sir. Just needs a bandage.'

'And I need a runner. Up to one more job?'

Otway's 9th Battalion, or what was left of it, he explained, was holed up in a bombed-out chateau on the edge of town. Various attempts had been made to reach it, but all had failed. Gale needed to re-establish contact. 'Wait till it gets dark, take two men, load up with as much ammo as you can carry and see if you can get through. Then tell Otway to follow the barrage in with the rest of us. Got that?'

'Yes, sir.'

'And head for Jerry HQ. It's in the *mairie* behind the church. If we can knock that out everything else will follow.'

'Understood.'

'Good.' They gazed around. Everywhere groups of men sat or lounged, brewing tea, cooking rations or sharing a smoke. Others checked their weapons, filling their webbing pouches with grenades and ammunition, or wiping down their bayonets and daggers. Still more snatched sleep if they could, or simply stared ahead in dazed contemplation. Above them on the hill, small-arms fire was dying out as both sides drew apart to regroup. 'This has to work,' Gale murmured. 'We've nothing left if it doesn't.'

Daylight faded, and so too the fighting as exhausted men downed weapons to feed and rest. Bréville still burned, painting the skyline a smoky orange, flashes lit the northern horizon, and yet another air raid began over Caen. Stealing along a ditch, Theo and his bearers headed for the chateau. As they drew close a break in the overcast revealed a blackened façade, smashed windows and smoking roof.

'Looks quiet enough,' one murmured. 'Can't see our boys though.'

'And how do we stop them shooting us?'

Theo studied the approach. Fifty yards of lawn lay between them and the door. Enemy dug-outs could be anywhere, and the Paras inside would be understandably trigger-happy.

'All right.' He fumbled for a pouch. 'One each. We throw, shout and run. In that order. Ready?'

'Christ.'

'On my count. *One*. Pins out.'

Metallic pinging sounds. 'Jesus.'

'*Two. Three.*'

'*WAHO MOHAMMED!*'

Flashes lit the night as the grenades exploded, then three figures leaped from the bushes and ran, bellowing their battle cry. A flurry of panicked shooting came from one side, answering fire rattled from the chateau, the figures ran on, bent double with their loads, five seconds more and they were tumbling through the door.

'My.' A bandaged face grinned from the shadows. 'Look what the cat dragged in.'

The barrage began ten minutes later, the effect, as always, sudden, shocking and spectacular. Opening with the eerie shrieking noises overhead, lightning flashes and ground-shaking explosions followed as 25-pounders, 5½-inch field guns, and the 75-millimetre guns of the Shermans fired simultaneously, hurling red-hot steel into the approaches around Bréville. Sited just yards outside this ring of destruction, the effect on the men in the chateau was stupefying, the whole building quaking as walls shook, windows shattered and clods of ancient plaster rained on them from the ceiling.

'How long!' Otway shouted at Theo.

'Five minutes. Then we follow it up the hill.'

Theo hunched against the wall, feeling it shudder against his back as the shells crashed in. Dust fogged the air; through it barely fifty men sat waiting, all that remained of Otway's force. Several were too injured to carry on; Otway himself was bleeding from a head wound; all were hungry, exhausted and low on ammunition. Minutes ticked by, the barrage went on, mind-numbing and relentless, and then suddenly, as though from a change of wind, the noise altered and began imperceptibly to recede.

Theo scrambled up. 'Now would be good, sir.'

Otway led, hurrying down a corridor to a side door and out into the night. Where the barrage was even louder, the explosions blindingly bright as the shells crept ever upward. Fires burned everywhere, smoke rolling down the hill like fog, while overhead moonlight daubed the scene a ghostly grey. Otway set off, running through knee-deep crop towards a group of smashed farm buildings, his men in line behind. Mortar and artillery rounds still fell, craters and shell holes pocked the ground, the whole area was scorched and smoking. Surviving an enemy barrage was a lottery, Theo knew, yet also knew there would be survivors, crouching in their foxholes and dug-outs, their mortars and machine guns at the ready.

They reached the farm unscathed. Beyond it rose two hundred yards of open ground before the houses began. Crouching behind a wall, they watched as the barrage entered town, pummelling its outskirts to rubble like giant fists. Debris flew: masonry, earth, steel, trees, a whole German half-track tossed aloft like a toy. Otway waited, then drew his pistol. 'Forward the 9th!' And everyone charged from cover.

They were stopped before they'd gone thirty yards, a hail of machine-gun bullets hosing at them from the houses. With nowhere to run and nowhere to hide, men began dropping, cut down by the onslaught or throwing themselves to the ground. Theo too dived instinctively into a shell hole, surfacing in time to see Otway, his bandage like a turban, still running, still shouting and waving, then jerk and stumble over. Seconds passed, the shooting went on, he clapped his hands over his head, then a lull came, he looked up, the Germans were running, shifting their MG34s from one house to another. Some Paras rose, ready to go on, but the hailstorm resumed, stopping them in their tracks. The *mairie*, Gale had said, get to the *mairie* behind the church. He could see its battered spire through the smoke, tantalizingly near, yet hopelessly far. Then he heard a different sound above the guns, and turning in his shell hole glimpsed two squat shadows rumbling up the hill.

'Tanks!' he shouted. 'Get to the tanks!' Heads lifted, turning to see. 'There!' He pointed, rising to a knee. The leading machine drew near; he waited, timing his moment, then leaped up and ran. 'Come on!' Bullets followed him, spattering the ground, but he reached safety, ducking into the Sherman's lee. Others appeared; he grabbed them, pulling them in, then scrambled up behind the turret and bellowed through the slit. 'White house, right, one o'clock!' The turret swivelled, paused, then bucked and the house collapsed to dust. 'Now left, ten o'clock!' The turret bucked again; meanwhile, more men arrived, scurrying in from the sides. 'Stay behind, keep low!' The tanks rumbled on to a street, following the barrage, now stamping deeper into town, pounding whole areas to dust, exploding houses, shattering streets, incinerating vehicles to vapour. Debris fell on them as bullets pinged off the Sherman; it lurched over a crossroads, turret roving, and slewed to a stop. A pillbox loomed, gun flashes at its window; the turret jerked and the pillbox vanished. Then figures in grey ran from a house, charging at them through the smoke, screaming and shooting like madmen. The Paras stepped out and cleaved them to the ground. They moved on. The church was nearing; then Theo glimpsed a long muzzle poking through a wall; he shouted a warning, but the muzzle flashed, and a thunderous blow struck the Sherman, ramming it sideways and flinging him to the ground. He lay in the dust, deafened and gasping, then hands gripped his arms and a turbaned face swam before him. 'The church!' it shouted. 'This way!' He struggled up, lurching back to the tank, but it was stranded, one track hanging. Bullets were ricocheting from its flanks, mortar shells thumping all round, and a grenade landed at his feet, fizzing smoke. He kicked it away. 'Come on!' Otway shouted, and they set off, the others in tow. He glimpsed the church spire nearing, but more grey figures too, running, kneeling, shooting, and others rushing in from the side, pinning them in a crossfire. Twenty Paras trapped, backed up against the church wall, fighting for life. He glimpsed one, teeth bared, shooting a Vickers from his hip. Another stepped forward and calmly fired a PIAT into a house; others were fixing bayonets; one man, ammo gone, had his fighting knife drawn. The Germans were nearing; Otway dropped one with his pistol. Another grenade landed; Theo stooped and threw it back. Then a monstrous crash exploded behind them and they turned to see the church wall gone, demolished to rubble by a Sherman. Beyond it stood the *mairie*, squat and square, its swastika flag flying. Snipers fired from its windows, machine guns from the roof. The Sherman fired again, smashing the parapet; the Para with the PIAT fired into a window, then fell to a bullet. 'Come on!' Otway urged them forward again. They struggled on, clambering through rubble, moving, shooting, shouting. Another Sherman appeared, rumbling up from the opposite direction, a score of Paras in tow, then to Theo's astonishment he heard the pipes once again, wailing triumphantly above the tumult as though from a dream. And from out of nowhere they came, fifty strong, heads high, bayonets glinting, charging headlong into the fray, roaring their Highland war cry.

By dawn it was over, the fighting finished and Bréville secure. If ruined, with its streets unrecognizable, barely a house left standing, and the church and *mairie* razed to rubble. The swastika was gone too, replaced by a Union flag – and someone's blue and white flag of Scotland. Scores were dead on both sides, scores more wounded: orderlies and stretcher-bearers picked their way through the debris searching them out, tending those they could help, covering those they could not. German prisoners were rounded up, but surprisingly few, as it became clear most enemy combatants were either dead or injured. One senior survivor was a major of the Panzer Grenadiers. Theo, exhausted and giddy, was dozing in a bombed-out shop when Gale summoned him to interpret.

'Keeps muttering some claptrap about his regiment.' Gale scowled. 'See what he's on about, would you?'

Theo duly asked, while the major, his cheek bloody and one arm in a sling, stared back in bewilderment.

'He says his regiment is finished, sir. He says High Command ordered them to fight to the last, so that's what they did.'

'How touching.'

'He says many good men died here needlessly.'

'Then he should've bloody well surrendered,' Gale grunted and walked off.

'No surrender.' The major watched him go. '*Es ist verboten.*'

'You are part of 21st Panzer?'

'What's left of it. Berlin starves us of reinforcements, replacements, ammunition, food. Rest even.'

'Generalfeldmarschall Rommel?'

'He does what he can. But they don't listen to him.'

Later Theo limped back down the hill with the others. Fires still burned in the grass, tendrils of smoke drifting over the bodies like veils. Halfway down he missed his footing, slumped to one knee and found he couldn't get up.

'All right, laddie?' A voice from behind. *A-reet?*

'Could you help me up? My leg's numb.'

'That I could.' The Scotsman grinned. 'Here, put your arm round my shoulder.'

They moved on down the hill. The man had an unlit cigarette between his lips, his cheeks were soot-blackened, he smelled of tobacco and cordite. His tin hat clanked at his chest, his head now adorned with a green beret with scarlet hackle.

'You're Black Watch,' Theo said. 'That was you last night, wasn't it?'

'It was. Saved your Sassenach backsides too, I'd say.'

'Yes. Thank you. But what unit are you with? 1 Corps?'

'1 Corps be buggered, we're 51st Highland Division!'

'51st? But...'

'I know.' The Scotsman chuckled. 'It's taken us four years. But we're back!'

This time it was two weeks in the dressing station. The wound in his thigh, though originally minor, had become infected and was starting to poison him. The divisional MO debrided and cleaned it himself, but when after three days Theo's fever worsened he realized more drastic action was needed.

'It's called penicillin, Trickey. The new wonder drug everyone's talking about. Marvellous for treating infections, but in short supply so we dispense it sparingly.'

Theo turned away. 'Save it for the seriously injured.'

'You *are* seriously injured.'

The medication began, but the fever worsened, Theo tossing on sweat-soaked sheets suspended between reality and hallucination. Shivering and delirious, he dreamed of steel monsters pursuing him through a forest, the tortured screams of a boy strapped to a chair, and the pounding crash of artillery creeping ever nearer.

Later he dreamed of a woman's voice. 'Theodor?'

His eyes slowly opened, and a face swam into view. 'Grandmother?'

'No, Theodor, it is Thérèse.'

He struggled to rise. 'I must get to her, get to the bridge!'

'Be still.' A hand forced him back. 'And drink this. You have been ill.'

'Ill...' He tipped his head, the water cool and silky suddenly on his throat. Through a window he could see a summer dusk gathering outside. 'Where is this?'

'Ranville. They've set up a dressing station in the old convent. You've been here a week. But the new drug is working, the fever has broken and the doctor says you will recover soon.'

'A week?' He shook his head. 'But Georges... He said you... About Clare!'

'Clare is alive, Theodor. And secure.'

'But how—'

'No more for now.' She rose to leave. 'You must rest. I will return in the morning, when your head is clearer, and we will talk then.'

He passed the night in and out of a deep and dreamless sleep. Orderlies came and changed his dressing, helped him wash and fed him soup and bread. Through the convent windows drifted the sounds of distant gunfire, and artillery flashes flickered across the ceiling like far-away lightning. By dawn, however, all was quiet, and he lay listening to the twitter of birds mingling with the incongruous snores of patients.

Clare was in custody, Thérèse told him. She was being held in a special prison in Paris.

'Avenue Foch, it's in the sixteenth. It's, well, it's where they take captured agents.'

'She was arrested as a British agent.'

'I'm sorry, Theodor, but it appears so.'

'Please tell me everything you know.'

She told him. Deposited by fishing boat on to a moonlit shore west of Marseille, Clare and Antoine joined a Resistance network codenamed Stationer. Their orders were to expand the network northwards into the Loire region, Antoine by recruiting more operatives, Clare acting as a courier keeping everyone in contact, and also maintaining the radio link with SOE headquarters in London. The job meant they travelled a lot, sometimes together as a couple, increasingly alone, and on these occasions they depended on outside help for food and shelter. Not all helpers were what they seemed, however, and some time during the spring something had gone wrong.

'Nobody knows exactly.' Thérèse shrugged. 'Antoine vanished from sight. Clare was arrested boarding a train in Orléans.'

'When?'

'Late in March.'

While he was recovering on Rosa's farm. 'Then what happened?'

'She was imprisoned there for a while, then taken to Avenue Foch. It's the SS counter-intelligence headquarters.'

'For interrogation.'

'Yes.'

'Is she, will she be... tortured there?'

'Theodor.'

'Will she!'

'Most probably.' She touched his arm. 'But the fact she's still there, Theo, means she's still alive. Possibly held as a special case, seeing as she's a FANY officer.'

He shook his head. 'How could this have happened? Was it Antoine?'

'Who can say? He's not been heard from. But you know as well as I do networks become compromised. Even the best ones.'

'What do you mean?'

'Nothing.' She forced a wan smile. 'It's not your concern, Clare is. You must concentrate on her.'

'I... Yes.'

'And act, Theodor, if you can. Rumour is, as the Allies advance on Paris the SS will remove all prisoners to Germany. Or...'

'Caen.' He remembered then. The ferry crossing, the empty streets, the old man, the curious stares, and trying to reach the prison. 'That day I went into Caen. What happened?'

Her eyes flickered. 'They shot them.'

'What?'

'In the morning. When they heard the Allies had landed and were advancing on the town. They took the Resistance prisoners out one by one. And shot them.'

'My God. But... Jeanette too?'

'All of them.'

He stared at her, remembering. Warm soup on a cold bridge. Stolen kisses in the moonlight. Playing with a baby on the hearth. And a card. In Kingston, after Saint-Valery-en-Caux. 'These are bad days, Theo,' she'd written, 'think on me.'

'What...'

'Victory, Theodor, that's what. Crush the enemy and win. Only that can save Clare, only that can save us all. But the Allies must hurry. They must stop delaying, leave Normandy and free France. Quickly, before it's too late.'

But the Allies didn't seem capable. A week later, nearly a month after landing at the canal bridge, Theo was back at Gale's HQ, only to find the situation much as he'd left it. In stalemate. It scarcely seemed possible, yet despite steadily growing strength and a balance of power shifting daily in their favour, the British, Canadian and American troops had repeatedly failed to break out from Normandy. Indeed, most were still within a few miles of the beaches they had landed on. Worse still, nobody seemed to know why, although dogged German resistance was clearly a factor. Talking to worried-looking aides hurrying along corridors, he sensed the whiff of failure in the air, and with it a culture of blame. Poor air cover, some said, or poor tanks or poor armour, or reluctant British infantry, or undisciplined American GIs. Some said it was the terrain that was killing them, Normandy's infamous *bocage* of narrow lanes and tall hedgerows behind which enemy tanks and guns waited to annihilate the unsuspecting. Others cited a wariness among the troops, who, after five years of war and with the end in sight, saw no logic in rushing headlong to an unnecessary death. Even the generals were falling out, one aide confided, with Montgomery, Dempsey, Bradley and Patton all blaming each other for the lack of progress, and Eisenhower struggling to keep order. 'Work together, drive inland,' he repeatedly urged them. And they tried, launching operation after operation, but still the Germans repelled them. Meanwhile, casualties soared, Churchill fumed, the newspapers carped, the public looked on in bafflement, and the lines of advance on Gale's map remained stubbornly unmoving.

And yet, albeit invisibly to the men doing the fighting, Theo could sense the tide was turning. Days went by; temporarily deskbound, he spent them processing the scores of reports and signals that passed through Division. From these he learned of the overwhelming build-up of Allied forces, with thousands of tons of men and equipment arriving every day, while German reinforcements appeared to be dwindling. He learned that Allied fighters had all but beaten the Luftwaffe, which was now rarely seen, so they could strafe and bomb with impunity. He learned that rather than waste time, the Americans to the west had given up trying to take Cherbourg, and cut it off instead, advancing right across the peninsula to the coast. Now they were consolidating their position, and amassing in strength in preparation for a decisive strike south. And he learned the key to this, and indeed the whole Normandy breakout, was taking Caen. But Caen, a primary British objective since John Howard and his men seized its bridges on Day One, stubbornly refused to fall. Perch, Epsom, Windsor, Dauntless: the operations came and went like summer squalls, yet still somehow the beleaguered Germans held the town.

'How the hell do they do it?' Gale mused, gazing at his map. The hour was late; yet another air raid was under way over Caen, prelude to a major new offensive to take the town, codenamed Charnwood. Signals traffic was busy; Gale had asked his staff to stay on hand. 'I mean, we keep hitting them, strafing them, bombing and shelling them to buggery. We give them no rest and no quarter, we know they have no reserves, *they* know they're beaten, and yet still they fight on.' He turned to Theo. 'It defies all reason.'

Reason. He thought of von Stauffenberg: *War is a failure of reason.*

'Perhaps it's to do with fanaticism.'

'Hitler's, you mean?'

Theo shrugged. 'They've known nothing else for ten years.'

'Well, it's high time they did.'

A clerk appeared at the door. 'Car waiting outside, sir. From 2nd Army HQ.'

'Now what!' Gale picked up his cap. 'Yet another change of plan, no doubt.'

'It's not for you, sir.'

'What?'

'The car.' The clerk nodded at Theo. 'It's for him.'

CHAPTER 8

Theo Trickey's exit following his day out with the Ulm work party is a shock to us all. It also serves to highlight the shifting balance of power between captor and captive – and sets the scene on what will become the final act of my war. Even if I don't know it yet.

From the moment he walks out I sense something's wrong. I can't define it, but it's to do with his smile before hobbling away on his stick. As though we both know he isn't coming back. And the feeling of loss as I watch him go is profound, close to grief; we've been together so long that captivity without him seems unimaginable. And I keep remembering the Chinese proverb Arthur Marrable cautioned me about back at Apeldoorn: save a man's life and you're responsible for it for ever. And I do feel responsible, like a father for a son, and I worry that something I said or did prompted him to go. Consequently I spend the entire day fussing irritably about the place, inattentive with patients, updating the wrong records, misplacing stock and so on, with little care or attention to detail and one eye permanently on the clock. At lunchtime I'm grumpy with Erik, lose our postprandial chess game in five minutes, and to cap it all then cry off my shift at drop-in.

'Why, for God's sake?' he asks.

133

'So I can be here when he comes back.'

'What makes you think he won't?'

'I don't know. I'm just worried.'

Rightly so as it turns out, for as the hours pass and the afternoon wanes there's no sign of him. Work parties pack up with the setting of the sun; strict rules then require everyone to be back in their billet by dusk, and in due course those still living at the *Revier* start trickling in. I watch their arrivals closely, but by curfew there's still no Theo.

Erik gets back from drop-in and finally shows concern. 'What if he's had a seizure or something?'

'Or got lost. He barely knows what day it is.'

'Perhaps we should send out a search party.'

Evening roll call is usually a perfunctory affair. Corporal Prien wanders through the building ticking off names on a clipboard and that's about it. Tonight, though, we watch in trepidation as he goes by once, appears a second time looking perplexed, then goes round a third time before approaching us with a confused furrow on his brow.

'The patient Trickey...' He taps his clipboard.

'*Jawohl, Gefreiter?*'

'Is he not here?'

'He was sent out on a working party. Against medical advice.'

'I know this. Where is he now?'

'Is he not here?'

'I just said this.'

'Are you sure?' Erik and I exchange glances. 'The washroom perhaps.'

'*Nein.*'

'Or the latrine?'

'Nor there. Where is he, please?'

134

'Perhaps he's already in bed.'

'Not in bed, I checked. Where is he?'

'I haven't the slightest idea,' I say indignantly. 'But if you have lost one of our patients, Corporal, it will be on your head not ours.'

Pandemonium ensues. Prien, panicking, calls out the two guards and they go through the place at rifle-point, stamping and shouting angrily as they ransack rooms, overturning beds, emptying cupboards and the rest of it. We can only look on and wait. By now we've quizzed other work-party prisoners, none of whom recall seeing Theo, yet part of me still hopes he might yet reappear, wandering blithely through the door having lost his bearings, or simply gone for a stroll. But as the minutes tick by with nothing found – including his meagre belongings, which have also vanished – the truth finally dawns on everyone.

He's really gone.

Worse follows. Vorst is summoned, arriving from his girlfriend's pad an hour later in furious form. Stamping into his office the door slams and we hear him ranting at Prien for several minutes. Then the door opens again, and the ashen-faced corporal clumps upstairs to summon us.

'Please be tactful, Dan,' Erik pleads as we descend. Prudent advice as always, but I'm beyond prudence by now and 'tactful' no longer fits the bill. Theodor Victor Trickey, bless him, sick, lame, confused Theo, my friend, patient, albatross and fellow Para, has done what every POW is supposed to. And what *I've* been trying to do in my inept, dithering way ever since my capture back in September. He's escaped. Raised himself from his sick bed and walked off. And that changes everything. *Waho* bloody *Mohammed*.

The Vorst interview consequently is short.

'What is the meaning of this absence?' he demands.

Erik steps forward. 'Well, *Herr Oberstabsarzt*, we're sorry but—'

'You sent him out on work detail!' I interrupt.

'Be silent.'

'This despite knowing full well that he was not fit to work!'

'I said silence!'

'I will not be silent. You are guilty of gross medical misconduct. The Geneva—'

'SILENCE!'

And out comes the bloody Luger again, and suddenly he's on his feet pointing it at my head. But not drunk this time: he's sober and calculating and knows exactly what he's doing. 'Guard!' he shouts, with more than a hint of triumph, and Prien duly enters followed by the two privates. 'Hauptmann Garland is under arrest for threatening an officer of the Reich. You will escort him to the city police station on Hirschstrasse for imprisonment prior to processing. Go now. I will telephone to alert them of your arrival.'

And there it is. Checkmate, the moment he's been waiting for since the day I arrived. Handed to him on a plate. Before I know it I'm standing in the lobby with my armed escort wondering what just happened. Prien looks sheepish but businesslike, while *Revier* residents look on in bemusement. 'Good luck, Doc,' one offers helpfully.

Erik appears, hurrying downstairs with my greatcoat and beret. 'We'll try and get the rest to you tomorrow.'

'My notes…'

'Yes.' His eyes hold mine. 'And I'll do whatever else I can.'

'Thank you.' We clasp hands. 'I'm so sorry, Erik, for, you know…'

'It's all right. Keep strong. This isn't over.'

Then, because I can't think what else to do, I draw myself up and salute him. Vorst's door, meanwhile, squeaks open and the man himself appears, looking suitably satisfied. Nor can he resist one final dig.

'*Auf Wiedersehen, Gar-lant.*' He smirks. 'This is what you get for sympathizing with traitors.'

On the very eve of D-Day, just as Theo, John Howard *et al* were busy seizing the Caen bridges, the traitor in question, Erwin Rommel, was not stoically manning the barricades against the invading Allies, but some five hundred miles away down the road here in Herrlingen celebrating his wife's fiftieth birthday. For one normally so dedicated and astute, this seems an appalling lapse on his part – akin to Nero fiddling while Rome burned – but the documentation provides an astonishing explanation.

By the end of May 1944 the Germans were as ready for invasion as they'd ever be – largely thanks to Rommel. The Atlantic Wall defences had been greatly upgraded, divisions of extra troops brought in and deployed, formidable anti-ship, anti-tank and anti-aircraft measures installed, and plans drawn up to cover every possible contingency. As usual he was tireless in his labours: constantly on the go, inspecting, improving, training, exhorting, week-in week-out, and having toiled non-stop since his appointment in February was long overdue a break. Everyone knew invasion was imminent, but consulting his weather experts on 2 June he was assured nothing could possibly happen for at least two weeks, as firstly a series of stormy depressions were whipping through the Channel, and secondly the moon and tides were all wrong for landings. Rommel reported this to his superior in Paris,

General von Rundstedt, who thanked him for his work and approved a few days off, whereupon he bought Lucie a pair of expensive silk slippers and headed off to Ulm.

His homecoming, however, was not just about birthdays, or catching up on rest. For according to his diary and the 'Case Green' file, he had another vital reason for being in southern Germany.

Lobbying Hitler.

Following weeks of phone calls and behind-the-scenes machinating, Rommel had managed to secure a private audience with the Führer, then ensconced in his Bavarian retreat at Berchtesgaden. Obtaining such a meeting was no small feat; Hitler disliked one-to-one discourse and anyway his working days were planned to the minute. But Rommel was an old protégé and currently in favour following his defence efforts, so approval was eventually granted and an invitation issued.

'Stay there and await my phone call,' Hitler's secretary told him when he got to Herrlingen. 'Probably around the fifth or sixth of June. Can you tell me what this concerns?'

'A matter of great importance.'

And indeed it was. For Case Green was his master plan for making peace with the Allies.

'Germany's survival hinges on just one strategy,' he wrote in preparation. 'The European war as originally conceived is lost, and the war against Russia can never be won. So our efforts must be on saving the Fatherland.' This, he proposed, meant reaching an agreement with the western Allies *before* their invasion could take hold. Costly efforts to repel their advance up Italy should be abandoned therefore, he said, and should instead focus on stopping them at the Alpine passes of South Tyrol, which was a far easier prospect. This would release the extra divisions needed to repel the invasion of France. Once repelled and with Germany's southern and western flanks secure, attention could then turn eastwards, where a concerted effort would halt the Russian advance, at least temporarily. At that point diplomatic overtures would be made to the British and Americans, and an honourable ceasefire procured, followed by a peaceful transition to a post-war scenario, all the while keeping the Bolshevik horde at bay. Rommel spent days formulating the plan, and also discussing it with trusted aides and colleagues. All agreed it made perfect sense, but knew obtaining any form of approval depended on Hitler's frame of mind – and on Rommel putting it to him alone. Timing, everyone acknowledged, was crucial.

Lucie was delighted with the slippers, Manfred and Gertrud were home, a pleasant family weekend ensued. Then on Monday 5 June Rommel locked himself in his study to put the finishing touches to his proposal and await the summons from Berchtesgaden. No call came that day but in the early hours of the next morning confused messages began arriving from Normandy. Paratroops had been observed in the Carentan area, they said, or possibly to the east near Ouistreham. Enemy ships were shelling shore installations; Resistance fighters were cutting telephone wires; two bridges had been seized outside Caen. Rommel kept his nerve. Were these isolated events or part of something bigger? he demanded. Or were they simply a feint to divert attention from the Pas de Calais? The hours ticked by, the messages grew more panicked and more garbled. Still holding out for his meeting with Hitler, Rommel struggled to make sense of it. 'Stop gabbling,' he ordered one caller, 'and get me hard information!' Finally, mid-morning, his trusted chief of staff Hans Speidel got through. 'They are on the beaches,

Generalfeldmarschall,' Speidel said calmly. 'By the tens of thousands.'

'I'm on my way.'

By nightfall he was back in Normandy, striding into his headquarters in the chateau at La Roche-Guyon. En route he stopped twice to get updates and order counter-attacks, and what he learned didn't please him. Was 21st Panzer moving forward? Slowly, came the reply, but hampered by disrupted communications, conflicting orders and traffic chaos. What about the reserve divisions at Lisieux and Chartres? Being held back, he was told, on special orders from Berlin. And the infantry reinforcements at Le Havre? Yet to mobilize, was the reply.

He swung into action. Slow reactions by on-the-spot commanders had cost them dearly, and his greatest fear – that the enemy might secure a toehold on the coast – had already been realized. This meant Germany was now defending itself on three fronts, an impossible task, he knew, yet the die was cast. All that mattered now was every man doing his duty, and his was to hold Normandy. Heavy reinforcements in the form of four additional Panzer divisions were promised by Berlin; his plan, therefore, was to contain the Allies until the divisions arrived, then drive the enemy back into the sea.

And over the next few days, as he raced from one position to the next, he had reason to be optimistic, observing first-hand how slow the enemy was getting off the beaches, how they failed to connect up their various beachheads, and how little headway they made inland. This last thanks to his defence measures, and his men, who were performing magnificently. Using the Normandy *bocage* to best effect, tanks and artillery pinned the enemy down, while the infantry boys moved fast and hard to drive them back. Confidence was high, morale strong, supplies sufficient, and reinforcements on the way. 'Matters could be a lot worse!' he wrote to Lucie.

Days passed. Travelling by staff car he visited every inch of the front – a risky business with Spitfires roving overhead strafing anything that moved, and more than once his driver Daniel had to swerve into cover to dodge an attack. Ignoring these nuisances, Rommel soon concluded that his main strategic concerns – apart from delayed reinforcements and the disgraceful absence of the Luftwaffe – were the Cherbourg peninsula in the west, being contested by the Americans, and the Caen area in the east, under assault from the British and Canadians. A general called Bradley commanded the Yanks, while the Englishman Dempsey led the Tommies. He knew little about either, but soon learned that their boss, the man commanding all land forces in France, was none other than his old adversary, Bernard Montgomery, whose slow-but-steady methods he knew only too well. Monty wouldn't press forward until sure of favourable odds, he guessed, which allowed him time to manoeuvre and prepare. Once the reinforcements arrived, that is. In the meantime he needed to prioritize, and of the two sectors, the eastern one worried him most. Cherbourg might be an important port for the enemy to win, but they were fighting for it in the wrong direction, and anyway he'd blow it to rubble before letting them take it intact. Caen, however, was a different matter. Centrally located on the main routes east, Caen formed the 'hinge' of the whole Allied attack. And if he lost it, the door would swing open to the rest of France.

Caen therefore became his focus and he strove hard to hold it against repeated attacks from land and air. Allied mechanized units including tanks and artillery tried encircling moves from the west, and a British *Fallschirmjäger* division was dug in to its east. The encircling threat lacked vigour and he was able to repel it, but the airborne troops, which included battle-hardened veterans of the Tunisian and Sicilian campaigns, were fighting furiously and refused to give ground. They were also blocking vital supplies and reinforcements coming in from Rouen and Le Havre, including the much-needed 711th Infantry Division. If they prevailed, a pincer movement might yet close round Caen, with all that implied. One small hilltop town in particular was dominating matters, and coming to symbolize the struggle for the sector. Situated just east of Caen and repeatedly changing hands as the days passed, its name was Bréville-les-Monts.

The police station on Hirschstrasse is a modern brick-built affair, still amazingly intact despite much bomb damage to the buildings around it. Arriving there in the blackout with my escort, I'm handed over to an elderly *Polizeibeamter* who signs me in politely like a hotel receptionist before showing me to my cell. Prien, meanwhile, bids me a rather regretful farewell and heads back to the *Revier*. I see no sign of other guests; the cell is square and spartan with an iron bed and chair, folded blanket for bedding, a small window and single bulb for lighting. The policeman shows me in, apologizes for the cold and tells me to call if I need anything.

'*Etwas zu essen, bitte?*' I ask, pointing at my mouth.

'Sorry, but I have nothing.'

'Oh well…'

'You are the English doctor at the *Revier*, yes?'

'That's right.'

He nods. 'You are known as a compassionate man.'

142

And with that he leaves, quietly locking the door behind him. I pace up and down a little, the blanket about my shoulders, pondering this latest turn of events and rueing my impulsiveness yet again. Nor can I help wondering about Vorst's sinister term 'processing' and what that might mean. Some sort of sham trial, I presume, followed by a period of incarceration before being shipped to some Godforsaken POW camp in Poland. At least I hope that's what it means. Not for the first time my thoughts stray back to October, my day with Inge Brandt, and our visit to that dreadful camp outside Bergen. Then, since fretting's pointless, there's no food, no Erik to talk to, and nothing else to do, I stretch out on the bed to reflect on the folly of my ways.

It was around D-Day that my own military service stuttered into motion. In fact 6 June 1944 found me newly assigned to 11th Parachute Battalion as their regimental MO, although I actually joined up some months earlier. Why did I do this? A 26-year-old doctor with no military experience, little interest in the war and a perfectly good job in a top London hospital? It's a fair question – especially in view of my present predicament. And there are two answers. Firstly I was recruited. A major of the Royal Army Medical Corps came to the hospital and gave a talk on the urgent need for doctors in the army, particularly the airborne forces who were by now in the thick of it. We'd heard these talks before; one by an obviously drunk Royal Navy medic was particularly amusing. But unlike some colleagues, I'd never been tempted by the king's shilling, partly because of my ambivalence towards the war in general, and partly because I was engaged to be married, and running off would be selfish and uncaring – or so I told myself. But this RAMC major's talk was different from the others, because it struck a chord.

He was about forty, gently spoken, and clearly a man of insight and conscience. He talked quietly and honestly, and in a doctor's language we recognized and could relate to. And at the end he said something memorable.

'Battlefield medicine is counter-intuitive, you know, and contrary to so much we believe in as doctors. Our role, in effect, is to watch men try to kill each other, then repair the result so they can do it again. Prostitute ourselves, in other words. Like a vet at a cockfight, it is base and barbaric and an affront to our profession. And yet working in the midst of battle I have discovered humankind at its best. I have found compassion and charity, fellowship and humour. I have marvelled at the resilience of the human spirit, found solace amid great suffering, and drawn strength from the unique kinship of men at arms. Finally, to my surprise, I have found myself, my purpose, and who I really am. Which is, it turns out' – he smiled shyly – 'a servant of God.'

The second reason I joined up was because my fiancée ditched me for another man.

Who happened to be in uniform too, which only made things worse, so in a fit of self-pity, and in the pathetic hope she'd be impressed by this heroic gesture, I signed on the dotted line and waited for the summons. Of course she wasn't impressed, in fact probably didn't even notice, and subsequently sealed the break-up with a classic 'Dear John' letter which I carried next to my lovelorn heart until losing it, ironically, somewhere amid the carnage of Arnhem.

Which at that point was still some months away. Meanwhile, having received the call-up, I duly reported to Ringway to carry out the training course reserved for doctors, clerks, clergymen, bandsmen and so on. Disparagingly referred to as the 'vicars and tarts' course by regulars, this was an abbreviated version of the full Para training syllabus. We still had to do all the jumps, including two from the hated balloon, but we were excused some of the more extreme training: marching forty miles with full pack, swimming icy rivers, charging straw dummies with bayonets and so on. We did, however, spend much time in the classroom absorbing all we could about field medicine, learning about the triage system and the front-line-to-aid-post-to-dressing-station casualty movement process, typical battle injuries and how to handle them, and familiarizing ourselves with the rather basic equipment doctors use in the field. Nor were we excused twice-daily PT, dawn runs through the countryside, and hours of square-bashing round the parade ground. There was even some arms instruction: 'This here is the Webley service revolver,' a sergeant showed us grimly. 'Whatever you do don't fire it.' Ten weeks later, looking leaner and fitter than in years, we were duly commissioned as officers and passed out, marching inexpertly about in front of our families, before being awarded our insignia and red beret, which to my surprise meant more to me than almost anything – including my ex-fiancée. Two weeks' home leave followed, D-Day came, then finally the long-awaited envelope hit the mat.

My orders were to report to Colonel Lea at 11th Battalion, which was then based at Melton Mowbray in Leicestershire. In fact most of 1st Airborne Division was scattered about that county, some fifteen battalions of testosterone-charged Paras rampaging about the place, shattering the peace and clogging up the pubs, while impatiently following events in Normandy and chafing to go into action. New and untested, 11th Battalion was formed the previous year in Egypt, but since then had been something of a wallflower. Attached to 4th Parachute Brigade, most of its men had yet to fire a gun in anger, and so had a point to prove. I moved in to my hut with three other captains, introduced myself to Lea and his second-in-command Dickie Lonsdale, met Jack Bowyer and my batman Sykes, and settled down to wait for something to happen.

Unknown to Windy Gale and his men at the time, losing Bréville was a significant setback for Rommel. Not decisive in itself, it nevertheless signalled a turning of the German situation. Whereas before Rommel was exerting control, now he was losing it – mostly for want of proper support. The promised extra divisions didn't arrive, supplies of fuel and ammunition began to run low, devastating attacks from the air went unopposed, casualties soared, and his exhausted men – denied rest, respite or replacements – were fighting themselves to a standstill. Time was against him too, for as his situation weakened the Allies grew steadily stronger, with more tanks, more artillery, ammunition, vehicles, stores, fuel, and above all more men arriving on the beaches every day. Airfields sprang up, allowing them to ship goods in by air; they built artificial ports called Mulberry harbours to accommodate bigger ships, their beachheads linked up and their fronts stretched ever wider. And as their numbers swelled, their incursions inland at last began to gain traction.

Adding to Rommel's logistical difficulties were his orders from Berlin, which were ruthlessly inflexible. 'Give not one inch,' he was repeatedly warned, in a depressing echo of the African campaign. Nor was he allowed to act on his own initiative, with virtually every move requiring High Command approval. And the structure of that command was absurdly complicated. He could not move heavy armour without permission from Hitler himself. Sometimes that permission would take hours, or days; often it never came at all. Anti-aircraft units within his command would only take orders from Luftwaffe officers, and nearby SS Panzer units, well equipped and supplied, would only act on the direct orders of their leader, Heinrich Himmler, who seemed answerable to no one. Then there was Rommel's own superior, Gerd von Rundstedt, in charge of all France and holed up in his hotel suite in Paris. Rundstedt sympathized with Rommel's predicament but was elderly, weak and incapable of acting decisively. This left Rommel hamstrung, for if years of warring had taught him anything it was the importance of decisiveness, and speed, and flexibility. His commanders in the field understood this, even Rundstedt grasped it, in principle, but Germany's high commanders seemed in ignorance, and worse still, completely divorced from the reality of the situation. Hitler, Himmler, Goering and the rest, they weren't even there; they were hundreds of miles away, sticking pins in a map.

Then suddenly they weren't. A signal came through. In response to repeated requests, it said, the Führer was coming to France to see the situation for himself. Rommel was surprised but delighted, and immediately began preparing a front line tour, suitably protected of course, but designed to show his leader precisely what was what. At the same time, he hoped secretly, opportunity would finally arise to discuss Case Green. Two days passed in frantic preparation, then another message came. The visit would begin with a conference at the *Führerhauptquartier* in Margival. Rommel checked the map. Margival FHQ was a special bunker complex built for Hitler in 1940 for the invasion of England, but never used. It was in Champagne, over 170 miles from Normandy. 'Will the Führer still be touring the front?' he queried. 'That depends on the conference,' came the reply.

But the conference was a fiasco. Rommel attended with Rundstedt and their respective chiefs of staff, while Hitler's entourage included two High Command yes-men, Generals Jodl and Kluge. Rundstedt was invited to open proceedings with an overview of the situation, but soon became muddled and Rommel had to take over. Halfway through his report he became aware of sighing and tutting from Jodl and Kluge, while Hitler's attention appeared to be on the floor. Having politely waited for Rommel to finish however, he then ignored every word he'd said.

'Cherbourg is the key,' he announced bafflingly, 'and our efforts must focus on holding it at any cost. We must furthermore destroy the enemy's ability to bring in materiel, and I have therefore ordered the Luftwaffe and Kriegsmarine to open major new offensives in the air and on sea. These will become effective in the next two weeks whereupon the enemy will be strangled of supplies and their invasion attempt will founder.' When Rommel pointed out that the Luftwaffe hadn't been seen in weeks and the biggest naval force in history was currently patrolling – and shelling – the entire coastline, Hitler merely shrugged and said his decision was final, also chiding Rommel for his defeatism. Of the land war he made little mention except to repeat that retreat of any kind was utterly forbidden, and that supplies and reinforcements would be sent: 'as expediency dictates'. He then spoke expansively about incredible new wonder weapons that would turn the war in Germany's favour in a matter of weeks, Rommel made a swiftly rebuffed attempt to draw him into discussion about the war in general, and with that the conference closed. Nor, he was then told brusquely by Kluge, would the Führer have time to visit the troops at the front.

The mood on the journey back was sombre. Rundstedt made his own way by train, leaving Rommel alone with Hans Speidel to travel by car. For safety's sake they waited until nightfall before setting out; by the time they got back to La Roche-Guyon it was after midnight.

'This can't go on, Hans,' Rommel muttered darkly at one point. 'The lunacy, it must be stopped.'

'There are many who think as you, sir.'

'Case Green. If only he could be made to study it.'

'I fear it's too late. Something more radical is needed.'

'You are speaking of Stauffenberg and his madcap proposal.'

'It is more than a proposal, *Generalfeldmarschall*, it is a plan. It has widespread support; all that is needed are a few key people to be ready, including a senior field marshal to take command of the armed forces. When it is over.'

'You are in touch with him? Stauffenberg?'

'Indirectly.'

'Then tell him it's the wrong way. It will only create a martyr – and a dangerous vacuum of power. God knows who'd step in Hitler's place. Goebbels? Goering? That lunatic Himmler? No, Hans, the Führer must simply be made to see sense. He *must*.'

Theo kept a letter from a loved one close to his heart too, although his was rather better than mine. In fact his was the best love-letter I ever read.

Lying in my blacked-out prison cell, I can't help but wonder where he is and what he's doing. Rain has been falling heavily outside and I can hear the far-off rumble of thunder, which doesn't bode well for anyone camped out in the open. In any case Germany is no place for a confused British Tommy to be wandering. Although I admit he didn't look confused when he left this morning, he looked like someone waking from a dream. Like someone on a mission. Which is why I'm wondering about the letter.

Checking the pockets of those killed in battle is standard procedure, and one of the more melancholy chores of the medic. Although often surprising too. The stuff soldiers carry around beggars belief sometimes: books, food, games, clothes, musical instruments, lucky charms (lots of those), women's underwear, you name it – Jack Bowyer once found a pet mouse living in the pocket of one poor chap. These personal effects are noted down and placed in envelopes for return to next of kin – although the knickers and other dubious items such as contraband, condoms, dirty pictures, suspicious wads of cash and so on are tactfully omitted (mice too). Theo wasn't dead when we found him, but we still needed to know who he was, and since he couldn't tell us, we duly searched him. But there was nothing on him aside from the discs around his neck. No paybook, no identity card, no wallet or photos, nothing but the letter tucked into his chest pocket. I took it out that first night and skimmed through it looking for clues. It was well thumbed, grimy, bloodstained and obviously personal, so having learned only that his forename was Theo, I swiftly returned it to his pocket and forgot all about it.

For about five months. Then recently I decided it must be read properly. This was after the first session with the Rommel papers, when a Theo reference popped up in relation to Rome. Next day I wandered upstairs to question him. He was by then conscious and alert – more or less – but his memory was hopeless and as we spoke I learned little new, then remembered the letter and wondered if it might shed light on the whole mysterious business. Nor did I suffer misgivings about reading it, for by then I needed answers. Getting a peek was not so easy, and I had to wait for his allotted bath night when he went off to the washroom leaving his clothes on a chair. Fumbling through them, it took only seconds to find and read the letter. And again learn nothing useful. Except the power of true love.

Dearest Theo,

How I long for you, long to be with you and feel your arms around me. Our times together seem so distant, yet also so fresh and precious in memory. How they strengthen and sustain me these lonely days and nights. Remember the beach villa at Ténès? The power and tenderness of our lovemaking will remain with me always.

I am standing in a moonlit field in the countryside. A trusted friend is returning to London and has agreed to carry this letter. I have only a few moments to write it; I pray with all my soul that it reaches you, and finds you in good health and heart.

I love you, Theo, and think of you constantly. That we might be together after this war ends is my dearest wish and hope. Will you look for me? I pray so.

Take care and be strong, with all my love, C.

Dawn comes and still the rain falls. I'm lying on the bunk gloomily listening to it gurgle in the gutter when a key rattles in the door and the elderly police sergeant appears, bearing a tray. Black bread, cheese, a hunk of sausage and a steaming mug of ersatz coffee. Breakfast in bed, and suddenly prison life doesn't seem so bad!

'Good heavens,' I say, 'how marvellous, *vielen Dank*, Sergeant.'

He bobs his head. 'I'm sorry it cannot be more.'

'More? But this is wonderful.'

'The least we can do.'

I sip the coffee. 'We?'

'Like I said last night, you are known.'

'From the refuge for the destitute, you mean. At the old chapel?'

'Yes, but not just that.' He turns away. 'Now I must go.'

'Wait!' An idea comes. 'Wait, please.'

'Yes?'

'I wonder, do you happen to know the deputy *Bürgermeister*? No, not the deputy, he's the *acting Bürgermeister*, Herr... Oh, what's his name, Oden—'

'Adenauer. Yes, I know him, of course.'

'Good! So, I'm wondering, is there any chance a message could possibly get to him? About my, um, situation.'

He turns for the door. 'It is already done, Captain.'

More follows. After breakfast and a trip to the washroom, I return to my cell to find a bundle on the bed from the *Revier* – plus a note from Erik:

I send your clothes and shave bag and notebooks, will try and get food, etc. later. Hold on to there if you can! Wheels are rotating! Vorst gone early! Trickey still AWOL but we discover he stole money from Prien, food from kitchen and our map! We think he knows what he is doing! Be strong, Dan, your good friend Erik. PS did you hear it?!

His English foxes me as usual but I assume 'hold on to there' means 'stay put' (as if I have a choice) and wheels rotating means developments are afoot. But what's with the exclamation marks? And as for his PS... Did I hear what?

A tense morning ensues. Various comings and goings continue in reception, the telephone rings and voices are heard, but being stuck along the corridor it's impossible to know what's happening, if anything, so I stand, and pace, and sit, and stand again. The rain stops, planes drone overhead, noon comes, I hear children playing and the twitter of sparrows, and then I gradually become aware of a commotion in reception, of raised voices, men's and women's, angry exchanges, somebody banging on a desk, a piercing whistle, and finally another shout I recognize as Prien's, and suddenly all falls to silence.

A minute later the door unlocks and the police sergeant, head shaking, escorts me to reception where a dozen or so people are waiting. I recognize Adenauer, and several helpers from drop-in, and a civilian patient or two. In front of them all, faces set and rifles a-port, stand Prien and two guards.

'*Was ist los?*' I enquire.

Prien straightens. 'I am sorry, Hauptmann Garland, but Commandant Vorst has ordered your onward transportation. To Berlin.'

'For what purpose?'

'For questioning. We are to take you to the station. Guards will meet us there.'

'I object.'

'You what?'

'Excuse me.' Adenauer pushes forward. 'As acting *Bürgermeister* of the municipality of Ulm, it is my contention

153

that following recent developments, this city is now under civilian jurisdiction.'

'Bollocks. Says who?'

'Me.' He nods at the police sergeant. 'And him.'

The sergeant looks uncomfortable. Adenauer resolute. Prien dubious.

'No.' Prien shakes his head. 'Commandant Vorst—'

'Is not here. Where is he, by the way?'

'He… I believe he is away, on urgent business. He left strict instructions—'

'Away. So too are the officers of the garrison, leaving nothing but a few corporals and privates to protect the people and maintain the rule of law.'

'Not my problem!' Suddenly Prien grabs my arm. 'Let's go, Garland, I've had enough of this.'

'Einen Moment!' The door swings open and a small group enters. I spot Erik, and Gertrud Stemmer, and the chauffeur from Herrlingen; then to my surprise Trudi appears and gives a little wave. At their head, however, sweeping imperiously through the door in furs and hat, is Frau Lucie Rommel.

'Unhand the doctor, Corporal,' she demands.

'Yes, but, madam…'

'Right now, if you please. He is to return to his duties at the *Revier*.'

'On what authority?'

'This.' She hands him a paper. I glance over his shoulder and recognize the chit Pip Smith gave me back in Stalag XIB. 'It is his order from the medical services directorate transferring him to Ulm. Commandant Vorst does not have the authority to rescind it.'

Prien hems and haws, but knows he's beaten, and the upshot is he releases my arm and the whole thing fizzles out.

Formalities follow while they straighten out the paperwork; while this is ongoing I wander outside with Trudi and Erik.

'Thank you for coming,' I say to her. 'And, you know, supporting.'

'That's quite all right.'

'How did you know?'

'Doctor Henning telephoned my mother.'

Erik shrugs. 'I thought the young lady might want to say goodbye.'

'Ah. And the number?'

'Was in your notebook.'

'Of course. Although hopefully this isn't goodbye. At least for the moment.'

'Hopefully.' She smiles anxiously.

'So, Dan...' Erik rubs his hands. 'Did you hear it?'

'Hear what?'

'All that noise. Last night!'

'What... You mean the thunderstorm?'

'No, Dan, that was no thunder. That was shelling. The Allies are barely thirty miles away!'

'Good heavens. Which Allies?'

Trudi looks worried. Erik shrugs again. 'We'll have to wait and see.'

The date is 18 April 1945.

Ten months earlier, and following his disastrous Margival conference, Rommel, as ordered, went back to work, dutifully throwing himself into Normandy's defence. Though as diligent and hard-working as ever, close colleagues nevertheless noticed a change in him. He was less hands-on with the details, less emphatic with instructions, and less interfering, preferring to dispense advice and encouragement rather than criticism and orders. He began by making the front-line tour he'd planned so carefully for Hitler, driving from position to position talking to staff officers, field commanders, NCOs and the men themselves. All were buoyed up by his arrival, if disappointed their Führer couldn't make it. But from senior generals to the lowliest private, all told him the same story. Germany was losing in Normandy.

The statistics were staggering. Over a million men were now pitted against each other along a front barely eighty miles wide. Yet three-quarters of these were Allied troops. By late June 1944 Montgomery's 21st Army Group had assembled over forty divisions in Normandy, as opposed to the dozen or so in Rommel's Army Group B. And many of his were divisions in name only, so badly under-strength that they barely made a brigade. The 346th had been decimated at Bréville, and 21st Panzer was buckling under the onslaught. One of his divisions in the west, originally of ten thousand men, now comprised less than seven hundred.

Casualty figures everywhere were horrific, with an estimated hundred thousand Germans killed or injured thus far. Total dominance of sea and air meant every Allied move was preceded by devastating bombardments by fighters, bombers, rockets, artillery, even ships, which razed whole regiments before they could even engage the enemy. And when they did engage, overwhelming superiority in manpower, equipment and supplies ensured the defenders could never win. Nor fall back, with Hitler's 'stand or die' directive accounting for thousands more casualties, most of them pointless. And of his hundred thousand dead and injured, Rommel had received less than ten thousand replacements.

It could not go on, and he knew it. Nor was he alone in this assessment. Time and again senior colleagues pressed him to act before Army Group B was wiped from existence. Men like Leo Geyr of Panzer Group West, Hans Funck of 47th Panzer Corps up near Cherbourg, Carl Stülpnagel of 17th Army, even Nazi hard-liners like Sepp Dietrich, whose 1st SS Panzer Corps was struggling so desperately on the Orne. Many were former rivals of Rommel's, some had been his harshest of critics, yet as he drove from one to the next, all now looked to him to halt the madness.

'Your *Fall Grün* proposal, Erwin,' Geyr told him. 'You should proceed with it.'

'Without Führer approval? Impossible. I'd not get the support of the others.'

'They'll come round. Talk to them.'

'No. The order must come from the top.'

'He'll never agree. He'd rather everyone die.'

'I will try one more time. I will go to Berchtesgaden and insist he listen.'

'And if he doesn't?'

'Then God help us all.'

CHAPTER 9

The vehicle that collected Theo from General Gale's Normandy headquarters in July 1944 was not the usual truck or Jeep but a real car, a Citroën saloon with French number plates and steering wheel on the left. That was the first clue. The second was the driver, a corporal who said nothing the entire time but was wearing a 2nd Army flash on his shoulder, implying something unusual. The third was the drive itself, which was long and circuitous, perhaps thirty miles, and took him well outside 6th Airborne's operational zone. Hunched resignedly in the back, he stared through the window at the shadowy countryside, recalling other road trips to unknown destinations. Pushed to the floor of a partisan car in Rome; chauffeured to Gale's madhouse in Wiltshire; the long night drive to Salo with the Gestapo: these journeys in his experience rarely presaged anything good. Beyond the window the night was dark and the sky overcast, the Citroën's headlights were taped to thin slits, and he could tell only that they were travelling vaguely west. Passing successive small villages with names that meant nothing, they reached the larger town of Bayeux, drove right through and on another mile to a hamlet called Blay, followed a high stone wall and pulled up outside iron gates manned by guards. A muttered exchange followed, papers were scrutinized, a flashlight shone in his face, then the gates were opened and the Citroën crunched on to gravel. A large house loomed into shadowy relief at the end of a driveway, but before they reached it they turned down a bumpy track, lurched into woodland and stopped.

'Wait here.' The driver slammed the door and disappeared. Minutes passed, Theo heard the ticking of the engine as it cooled, and an owl hooting in the trees. To the north searchlights played over distant clouds, otherwise all was quiet.

'Ah-ha, there you are!'

A face grinned at the window. It took a moment to identify it in the darkness; the stubbled chin, the rumpled uniform, the red glow of the cigarette between the lips.

'Captain Grant? Is that you?'

'In the flesh.' Grant opened the door. 'Good to see you!'

They shook. 'You too, but…'

'Yes I know, they finally let me out, can you believe it!'

'Well, no, but that's good, sir, isn't it?'

'Absolutely. And call me Dennis. I hear you got a bullet in the bum.'

'Oh, yes, only a splinter though. In the thigh.'

'All healed?'

'It was infected but fine now.'

'Good to hear.' Grant took his arm, leading him along a path into the woods. As they went they passed pickets keeping guard. 'I got the call two days ago. Came over on a destroyer, by Jove. Then transferred to a patrol boat which brought me closer, then clambered into one of those amphibious six-wheeled truck things…'

'DUKW?'

'That's the one, and the damn thing drove me straight up the beach! Bloody marvellous, didn't even get my feet wet!'

'Marvellous, yes, er, Dennis. But can I ask why?'

Grant squeezed his arm. 'That's what we're here to find out.'

They entered a clearing. Ranged around it, dimly lit and heavily camouflaged with foliage, draped nets and branches, were several large tents, a scattering of small vehicles and motorcycles, and two lorries with large hut-like structures built on to them. Wires and aerials festooned the trees like decorations, and one truck had a large radio antenna turning on the roof.

'So listen, Theo, old chap.' Grant stopped by a tent. 'This is all a bit cloak and dagger, I know, but believe me it needs to be. Don't get put off, just be yourself, stand your ground, and listen carefully to what's said, OK?'

'Said about what?'

'You'll see.' With that he lifted the flap and ushered him inside.

About a dozen people waited within. Two were radio operators sitting at consoles with headphones about their ears; another, a major in American uniform, lounged by the entrance, while others lingered in shadow around the edges. A single woman, a FANY officer he noticed with a start, stood to one side with a notepad, and centre stage, leafing through a file, was a British army colonel.

'Is this him?' the colonel asked.

'Yes, sir. May I introduce Acting Lieutenant Theodor Trickey.'

The colonel turned pages. 'Then who is Andreas Ladurner?'

'That's him as well.'

'An alias?'

'Well not exactly, you see—'

'Can't the guy speak for himself?' the American quipped.

Theo turned and glanced, but didn't recognize him. *Stand your ground.*

'Yes I can. My full name is Andreas Theodor Josef Victor Ladurner-Trickey. It was shortened to Theodor Trickey for enrolment in the British army, whereas Andreas Ladurner is the name I used whilst in Italy.'

'Doing undercover work for Grant and the SOE,' the colonel said.

'Yes, sir.'

'And he gave you the codename Horatio.'

'I… Excuse me?'

'You heard. Did he?'

'No.'

'Then who did?'

An attentive hush had fallen. 'May I ask what this is about, sir?'

'Not yet. And I will ask once more. Who gave you that code name?'

'It wasn't a code name, not then, it was just a… a sort of nickname.'

'Don't fuck with me, Lieutenant. Who gave you the name!'

'Generalfeldmarschall Erwin Rommel.'

Some kind of contact had been made, he learned over the next ten minutes. The colonel's name was Matheson, he was with 2nd Army Field Intelligence, and he did most of the talking. The FANY woman wrote down everything on her pad; the rest watched and listened in silence. Apparently, Matheson explained, an American diplomat in Switzerland called Dulles had been maintaining low-level links with German resistance cells for some months. These groups aspired to much, but in reality delivered little; however Dulles kept contact in case something substantive developed. Lately it had, with growing rumours of overthrow and even assassination circulating; then out of the blue a startling new message had arrived from a different source.

'Dulles received it in person,' Matheson said, 'recognized it as significant and forwarded it to his superiors in Washington. They in turn sent it to London.'

'Where SOE got a copy,' Grant added, 'and spotted something.'

Matheson withdrew a sheet. 'You might as well read it yourself, Trickey. It's written in plain English.'

Theo took the page and scanned it. Then read again, his brow furrowing.

The killing can be stopped. Only desire and dialogue needed. And trust between two Norman foes. They bleed on both sides. Suggest the sayer be the bridge. Respond via Dulles.

'I... I don't understand.'

'Nor did we at first. Enlighten him, Grant.'

Grant took the sheet. 'Well, the first two sentences are obvious, as is the last. Then we guessed that "trust between two Norman foes" refers to the opposing commanders here in Normandy, that is to say, Monty—'

'Grant!'

'Sorry, sir, I mean Field Marshal Montgomery. And Field Marshal Rommel. Then we hit a stumbling block with "they bleed on both sides". At first we thought it was a reference to all the fighting, which I suppose it is, indirectly. But then one of our backroom boys spotted it's also a line from *Hamlet*.'

'Spoken by Horatio,' Matheson added pointedly.

'Exactly. Which means the next sentence: "suggest the *sayer* be the bridge" means they want Horatio, i.e. you, Theo, to be the bridge.'

'Bridge?'

'Intermediary. Liaison. Go-between.'

Pin-drop silence had fallen in the tent. Another man had entered too, he noted, standing with the others in the shadows. Older, tall, he wore a battered uniform cap and a woollen scarf tucked into his battledress.

'So, Trickey,' Matheson went on, 'the question is, based on your experience of the man, do you concur with this analysis? Or can you think of some other explanation?'

He couldn't. He took the sheet and reread it a third time. It bore all the hallmarks: *Here's what I propose*, Rommel seemed to be saying, *and here's how to do it*. Practical, direct and to the point, like the tip of a spear. Classic Rommel.

'No, sir, I can't.'

'Do you believe it originates from him?'

Goodbye, Horatio. Perhaps we shall meet once more. 'Most probably.'

'And do you see now why we had to be sure about the Horatio name?'

'Yes.'

'Splendid!' The scarf-wearing officer stirred from the shadows. 'So glad that's all settled. Thank you, Lieutenant, and thank *you*, Colonel Matheson, for all your hard work.'

'Always a pleasure, sir.'

A ripple of mirth circled the tent. Then: 'The only question remaining, therefore, is what's to be done.'

'General, I thought...'

'I take it we all agree Rommel's talking about some sort of local ceasefire.'

Heads nodded. The FANY's pen hovered.

'Well, that's out of the question. The Allies aren't interested in penny-packet ceasefires. We require total surrender of all Axis forces everywhere. Nothing less. General Eisenhower's very clear about that.'

'Rommel can't deliver that,' Matheson said. 'He hasn't the authority.'

'Indeed. Thus there's nothing to talk about. Officially.'

Another silence.

'Nonetheless...' The general patted his pockets.

'Sir?' Theo raised his hand.

'What is it?'

'Aren't the lives worth it?'

'I beg your pardon?'

'A ceasefire, here in Normandy, even a temporary one. The lives saved. It could be thousands, on both sides, and many civilian lives too.'

'You miss the point—'

'All I'm saying is shouldn't we at least find out what he wants?'

Everyone, he saw, was watching him, including the radio operators.

The general produced a note. 'Thank you, Lieutenant. If you'll allow me to finish, the answer to your question, seemingly, is yes. Ike doesn't think so, nor does Churchill, and Stalin certainly doesn't – not that we've told him. But Washington does.' He waved the note. 'And why? Because the American public are unhappy about the casualty figures here in Normandy. And since the American public are paying for most of this war, and their menfolk are fighting in it, *and* they have an election looming in November, it's considered politically expedient that we should at least look into the matter. So at Washington's request, we're sending you, Lieutenant Trickey, to find out what Rommel's on about. And you'd better be quick about it, because the mother of all offensives is gearing up to get under way here. And once it does, nothing on earth will stop it.'

Then he was outside once more, staring breathlessly up at the stars.

Grant appeared. 'Well done, old chap! That went swimmingly.'

'Who was that man?'

'Don't worry about Matheson, he's basically on side.'

'No, the other, the general at the end.'

'*That* was Freddie de Guingand, Theo. Monty's chief of staff!'

'Montgomery wants this?'

'He's about the only one. Says the lives saved warrants it. Like you.'

Two Norman foes. He inhaled damp night air. 'And the woman. The FANY?'

'She's SOE, but not with French ops.'

'Then—'

Grant pressed his arm. 'There's no more news, Theo. I checked with Vera Atkins before leaving. The gen Thérèse Gondrée gave you is the very latest. If we learn anything new you'll be the first to hear it, I promise.'

He was shown to a room in the main house, an attic garret with sloping roof, bare boards and a bed, and told to await further instructions. A plate of sandwiches had been left together with a bottle of English beer. Shedding boots and battledress he lay down and tried to rest, his head a-swirl with questions and implications. Later he fell into fitful sleep, dreaming of waves lapping on sand and a woman's cheek on his chest. The next day he was again told to stand by, so passed much of it restlessly wandering the house and gardens of the chateau, now serving as General Dempsey's 2nd Army HQ. A sizeable workforce filled it, more than a hundred figures in khaki, many with red Staff flashes, hurrying purposefully between rooms marked 'Maps', 'Meteo', 'Ops', 'Signals' and one marked 'Intel'. He saw no one he recognized from the night before, but from time to time a harassed-looking Grant hurried by in a cloud of smoke.

'Hello, Dennis. What's happening?'

'It's my first time, that's what!'

'What is?'

'This! Running an operation in the field.'

'Really?'

'Yes, really! It's one thing planning neat little ops from a cosy office in Baker Street, it's quite another fixing one from a field full of French cowpats!'

'Is there any news?'

A reply signal had been composed and sent to the American diplomat Dulles during the night, Grant said, which Dulles had duly acknowledged and passed on. But nothing since.

'It's a matter of waiting it out. And working on the nitty-gritty.'

'Nitty…'

'The who, the where, the when. Above all the *how*, Theo. These things don't happen by themselves!'

'No.'

'Think about it.' He lowered his voice. 'We're talking about squeezing a lone British officer through enemy lines, past half a million trigger-happy Jerries, and then somehow squeezing him back again – without getting him killed or captured. It's no simple matter, I can assure you.' He checked his watch. 'I'd better get going. And *you'd* better hope your chum Rommel comes up with something workable!'

'He's not my chum.'

But Grant had gone. Theo resumed his wanderings, sat in the garden, ate a NAAFI stew at lunchtime, then slumped into a library armchair and tried to read the English newspapers, most of which complained of poor Allied progress in Normandy. In other news he read of heavy fighting against the Japanese in the Philippines, a plan for a million Jewish people to settle in Palestine, and a sinister new German weapon called a 'pilotless flying bomb', one of which had killed six people in a house in Acton.

Which wasn't far from Kingston, he reflected, gazing through the window. Nor Hammersmith Hospital. Over a month he'd been in France, he realized, six weeks or more since he'd parted from his parents at Vic's bedside. And an aeon since he'd left Rosa and the twins at the farm. He tossed the newspaper aside and took to pacing the floor, then on a whim hurried off in search of writing paper, and sat down again, scrawling notes and stuffing them in envelopes. Slowly the afternoon waned. He spent an hour lost in thought by the lake, idly watching dragonflies dart above the mirrored water, then finally at dusk a clerk summoned him inside and led him to a side office where he found Grant sitting at a table.

'Hello, old chap.' He smiled. 'Do have a seat.' Bathed, shaved and cleanly dressed, his tie straight for once, his cigarettes and ashtray at his side, he looked refreshed, calm and in control again. Before him on the table lay a folder.

'This is quite a place, eh?' he began, studying the wood-panelled room. 'Eighteenth century. Some Norman count built it. Family been here two hundred years, then Jerry invaded and they had to flee. Lovely setting, no?'

'A clerk said it was Monty's camp we were in last night. Down in the woods. And that he sleeps in a caravan there.'

'It's true, though don't spread it around. After D-Day he was based in a chateau up at Creully, near the beaches. Then Churchill insisted on visiting, and the place was splashed all over the newspapers. Next day Jerry worked out where it was and shelled it to rubble. Fortunately Monty was away. Since then he prefers his woodland caravan.'

'I can see why.'

'He keeps a photo of Rommel on one wall, did you know? Has done since Africa. Says it helps him stay focused. Stops him worrying about home and family and so on.'

Theo nodded. 'I've been thinking about my father.'

Grant flicked a glance. 'He's poorly, Theo. We must get you home, soon as this palaver's over.'

Theo stared at the folder. 'He's replied, hasn't he? Rommel.'

'Yes.'

'With a plan?'

Grant opened the file. 'With a plan.'

Late the following afternoon he was driven back towards Caen, crossing the Orne at the canal bridge, passing 6th Airborne's positions, then on, skirting the city to the east. He sat in the back wedged beside Grant, while in front sat Colonel Matheson with the driver. Few words were exchanged, the July sun was hot, the weather close and heavy, and Theo fidgeted uncomfortably in his seat. Smartly attired in a new uniform, he felt constricted in shirt and tie, polished shoes, Sam Browne belt, overcoat, gloves and cap. Three captain's pips adorned his shoulder too, but when he queried this with Grant he was brusquely told it was to stop him getting killed – and wasn't negotiable. Tugging the shirt collar away from his neck, he sat in silence and stared through the window.

After the canal bridge the traffic began to slow as the military presence grew. They passed one checkpoint, then a second, complete with barrier, barbed wire and guards. 'Delays up ahead,' one told them. 'Jerry unusually twitchy this evening.'

They crept slowly onward, entering the battle-ravaged outskirts of a small town. Wreckage and rubble lay everywhere, craters pocked the streets, smoke drifted and several fires burned. Incoming artillery could also be seen and heard. 'Colombelles', the sign read; it lay on the eastern edge of Caen and right on the front line. As a third checkpoint loomed, Matheson wound down his window.

'Brigade's expecting us.' He passed out papers.

'Yes, sir. They're in the old police station, on the left there.'

Matheson got out. 'Wait here, you two.'

The door slammed. Theo felt the knot of tension tighten inside him. Grant, outwardly calm, lit up again.

'Shouldn't be long now.'

'What time's sunset?'

'An hour or so. Everything'll be fine.'

'I hope so.'

Grant blew smoke. 'It's rather droll really,' he mused. 'At first I thought we'd have to parachute you in behind enemy lines, or paddle you up the Seine in a rubber dinghy or something equally lethal. Then we considered using the Resistance to smuggle you through, but that was too complicated, and too slow to organize, and there just wasn't the time. Then came the reply from Dulles and, well, I must concede this way's simpler, and quicker. Safer too, so long as everyone follows instructions.'

'Yes.'

'Especially you. Got the documents?'

'Yes, Dennis.'

'Handkerchief?'

'Yes.'

'Mine, by the way. Password?'

'*Sternenlicht*.'

'Good. Who's the contact?'

'Hans von Luck. Colonel, officer commanding 21st Panzer Division.'

'*De facto* commander, Theo, remember, it may be important.'

Matheson reappeared, accompanied by an officer carrying helmets. 'Comms is all set up between here and 2nd Army HQ,' Matheson reported, 'and we've been approved to proceed. This is Major Ferguson – he's going to lead us forward. Tin hats on, let's go.'

With the crump of mortars and artillery still reverberating all round, the four set off into the town, making their way along narrow streets lined with tall buildings, dodging craters and rubble, gradually moving towards the sound of small-arms fire. Drawing along a cobbled alley, they came to a smashed wall behind which four Scotsmen were manning a machine gun. Beyond them lay the town square, deserted save for a single crumpled body lying beside a burning truck.

'All secure here, Corporal?' Ferguson asked.

'Aye, sir, pretty much.'

'Good.'

'Not that you'd know there's a ceasefire on!'

'Give it time. Where's the post office?'

'Over on the far side.' He pointed. 'Straight across, there with the flagpole.'

'And Jerry?'

'Everywhere beyond!'

They waited. Twenty minutes passed, the shadows in the square lengthened, the light began to fade, but still the shooting went on, albeit intermittently, sniper fire mixed with mortars and light artillery. Meanwhile, the evening air grew increasingly oppressive. Flushed and perspiring, Theo suddenly peeled off his overcoat and gloves and threw them to the ground. 'Not wearing them. And *that's* not negotiable!'

Matheson shrugged. Another twenty minutes passed. Still the shooting continued.

'Is that theirs or ours?' he muttered.

'Theirs.' Ferguson squinted through binoculars. 'Ours stopped at official sunset. As agreed.'

'Maybe sunset's different in Jerryland.' The gunner quipped.

'That'll do, Corporal.' Ferguson leaned towards Matheson. 'What if they don't stop?'

'We forget the whole blasted business and get on with winning the war.'

Ten minutes more. Darkness closed round the square like a veil. Somewhere in the distance a heavier bombardment started up. Matheson checked his watch again. 'That's it. Time's up. Let's get—'

'Listen!'

'I am listening, Trickey! That's heavy artillery, 88s probably, or—'

'Yes, but it's distant. In a different sector, on the other side of the city. There's no shooting round here.'

Grant fumbled a map. 'He's right. Look, according to the intel, 21st Panzer are holding this three-mile ring to the east

171

of Caen. Nothing else. And they've stopped. Ages ago. Exactly as agreed!'

He's reminded of two boys struggling across a village street carrying ammunition boxes another lifetime ago. And of walking over the stadium piazza towards a solitary German tank in Naples. That tingling feeling at the back of the neck, and the sensation of nakedness and vulnerability. And a form of detached resignation, like fatalism, as though watching someone else do it. Stepping out from behind the gunner's wall, holding his handkerchief aloft on a stick. Setting off across the deserted square, acutely aware that scores, perhaps hundreds of eyes are watching. Skirting the still-burning lorry and its lifeless driver, his shoes crunching on shattered glass. Reaching the post office, and pushing through the broken door, only to start with terror as it crashes to the ground behind him. On through the darkened shop with its empty shelves and abandoned counter. Groping along a dark passageway to the rear storeroom and the door to the outside. The *other* outside. Turning the handle to find the door jammed with rubble. Shoving at it doggedly with his shoulder until finally a crack opens and he stumbles out into the night.

'*Halt!*' a voice demands, and he halts. Then vehicle headlights burst to life, blasting him with harsh light. '*Heben Sie Ihre Hände!*'

He raises his hands, still clutching the flag.

'*Wie heissen Sie?*'

'*Horatio.*'

'*Passwort?*'

'Starlight... I mean *Sternenlicht.*'

A pause, then finally, and irritably, in English: 'You're late.'

CHAPTER 10

He awoke in the more comfortable bedroom of a different Norman chateau than the one he'd slept in twenty-four hours earlier. Blinking at bright sunlight slanting through shuttered windows, he could hear vehicles on the driveway outside, with voices and footsteps on the floors below, and sensed the hour was already late. Bleary and disorientated, he lay studying the ceiling plasterwork and trying to assemble his wits. Then he turned to the clothes hanging behind the door and knew he wasn't dreaming. Still the uniform of an army captain, they were no longer khaki, but field grey.

'Good morning, *Hauptmann*.' An orderly entered, speaking in German. 'I have brought hot water for shaving. There are toiletries on the washstand, and a late breakfast is in the salon downstairs.'

'I... *Vielen Dank*.'

'You're welcome. And Major Brandt requests that you report in thirty minutes.'

'Who is Major Brandt?'

'Aide to General Speidel. On the general staff.'

Speidel. Rommel's chief of staff. 'Where is the Generalfeldmarschall?'

'Not yet returned from Paris.'

'I should be with him.'

'He is expected later. May I ask, Captain, how long is your attachment here?'

'I'm not sure. A few days. What is the time now?'

'Noon. I detect your accent is Austrian.'

'Yes, well, I am from the south.'

'Thought so.' The orderly smiled. 'I too. Born in Salzburg.'

And with that he departed, leaving the door unlocked, Theo noted, thus confirming everything he could remember.

The night had been long and sleepless. Seven times he had shuttled back and forth across that debris-strewn square in Colombelles, endlessly relaying messages, demands and instructions like a runner in no man's land. His first meeting with the Germans, having stepped from the post office into the glare of headlights, had been with an aggressive artillery captain who spent minutes scrutinizing his papers before frogmarching him, still clutching his white flag, into a disused school building set up as a command post. There he met his contact, Colonel von Luck, a battle-hardened Panzer commander who, like his opposite number Matheson, was co-ordinating matters, but from the German side. Field telephones, Luck explained, connected him to Rommel's chief of staff Hans Speidel, who was waiting at Army Group B headquarters in La Roche-Guyon. Generalfeldmarschall Rommel, meanwhile, was at the end of a telephone in Paris, together with his superior Gerd von Rundstedt, chief of all forces in France. Luck would relay messages to Speidel who would then pass them to Rommel. The extreme sensitivity of the matter, he added, meant that communications had to be spoken in code, which would add time to the process. The first such message – that the 'bridging' materials had arrived and 'assembly instructions' were now awaited – duly went off shortly thereafter, then he and Luck sat down in a dusty schoolroom to wait.

'Been in Normandy long?' Luck enquired, like a stranger in a pub.

'Since the invasion. You?'

'Soon after.' He poured cups of bitter black coffee. 'Sent in to put a stop to it.'

'… Although I was also here in nineteen forty.'

'Me too! Junior officer in 7th Panzer!'

'The Gespensterdivision.'

'You know it?'

'I… was in Saint-Valery-en-Caux. At the end.'

'With all those thousands of Scotch boys! We sure kicked your arses that day!'

'Yes, I suppose you did.'

'And we'll do so again.' He produced a flask and tipped brandy into his coffee. 'You'll not break us, you know.'

'Then why am I here?'

Luck's eyes flickered, but he said no more. Thirty minutes later the first reply arrived from La Roche-Guyon and Theo was escorted back to the post office. Crossing the moonlit square once more, he handed the message to Matheson who promptly disappeared with it. Another hour passed; he spent it drinking tea in a bombed-out cobbler's shop with Grant. An aerial bombardment continued on the other side of Caen, searchlights scoured the sky and flak flashes lit the night, but the private ceasefire with 21st Panzer held.

'Your non-combat status…' Grant asked him at one point. 'You know, the no-shooting, no-killing, no-carrying-guns thing.'

'Yes.'

'How's that going?'

175

'It's difficult.'

'So I imagine.'

Eventually Matheson returned. 'He'll have to do better than that!'

'Rommel?'

'Of course Rommel!' Matheson waved a paper. 'He proposes arranging safe passage for the Allies through Normandy, or "opening the Caen door", as he calls it, but that's about all. Nothing about the surrender of Army Group B, nothing about German forces in the rest of France, nothing even about disarming the troops here. For all we know it could be a giant trap!'

'Allow us through the door, then pounce on us from behind.'

'Exactly, and Freddie de Guingand isn't having that! Right, Trickey, here's the reply, off you go and be smart about it.'

Gradually, through the long hours of night and repeated trips across the square, the terms were hammered out. Plodding back and forth from one camp to the other, Theo soon gleaned that Montgomery was being as wary as Rommel – and neither old foe was giving much away. The Allies were planning their Normandy breakout, but unknown to Rommel they needed more time to prepare; meanwhile, the Germans, weakened but dogged, were still inflicting great damage. Rommel's offer to open the door, even in some limited form, could catapult them across France and save weeks of bloody campaigning. Similarly, via increasingly frank conversations with Luck, Theo learned that Rommel had the backing of many of his officers, but by no means all, with some wavering and many still ignorant of the plan. Thus, unknown to the Allies, he too needed time to brief and win them over. Nor, crucially, Luck confided, was Rommel certain of Rundstedt's support.

'That dithering old goat!' he fumed. 'He should get off the fence or resign!'

Luck's tone was changing as the hours passed, Theo also noted, from cocky and disdainful to frustrated and morose.

'Only Rommel can save us now,' he murmured at one point.

'I believe he's trying to.'

Luck nodded. 'I've been with him since the beginning, you know, ever since 7th Panzer in forty. And you know where *they* are now?'

'No.'

'Being torn to pieces on the Russian Front, poor bastards.'

'Where were you after France?'

'With 21st Panzer in Africa. Not this 21st, the original one. Finest formation in the Afrika Korps. And do you know what happened to it?'

Theo shook his head.

'Decimated. Fed to the wolves during the final retreat to Tunisia, needlessly and pointlessly, all on the whim of that lunatic in Berlin.'

'I was in Tunisia. We fought against 10th Panzer.'

'10th! And you know what happened to *them* at the end!'

'No, we'd been withdrawn by then.'

'Wiped out. Driven into the sea at Tunis, when they could have been saved, *should* have been saved and brought home to fight again. But Hitler wouldn't have it and they went down, all killed or captured. And then he erased them from history, banning any mention of their name, because they had shamed *him*.'

Back at the cobbler's shop the mood was similarly sombre.

'We need this,' Grant muttered as the latest message went off with Matheson.

'This?'

'Rommel's plan. Nobody's admitting it but we need it. Everything's going to pot: the breakout, the advance across France, getting to Germany before the Russians – and that's crucial! There's infighting at the top, worse now that Patton's back on the scene. Churchill wants to sack Monty, Bradley and Dempsey don't get on, everyone hates Tedder and apparently Roosevelt's thinking of replacing Eisenhower as supreme commander. The wheels are falling off the wagon, Theo, yet this scheme of Rommel's could get everything moving again. We could roll up France in a matter of days, follow through into the Low Countries, and be in Berlin before Christmas. If only it can be made to work.'

And by dawn it appeared that it might, subject to certain conditions. Trudging wearily across the square, Theo delivered the final message to Luck. It agreed that Rommel had four days to arrange a cessation of all hostilities in France. No ground would be given during that time, the fighting would go on, and men would die, but the main Allied attack – beginning with the biggest air bombardment in history – was on hold for that period. Without specifying it, this four-day hiatus suited everyone, allowing the Allies to finish their preparations, and Rommel to consolidate support from his commanders in the field – and the wavering Rundstedt. Then, the agreement went on, once the ceasefire was in place, discussions about the future of Germany itself might begin, although their content was left undefined.

And as a final gesture of trust and good faith, to provide advice and clarification as needed, and as an objective observer, the liaison officer Trickey was to remain at Field Marshal Rommel's disposal, and under his protection, until the ceasefire was delivered.

'To make sure he doesn't try any tricks,' Matheson said.

'To ensure the Allies keep their damned word,' Luck said.

'To get you a step nearer Paris,' Grant said.

And as an orange sun rose above the smoking skyline, and he was driven away in the waiting staff car, the guns and mortars around Colombelles began shooting again.

'You find yourself in a curious situation, Captain.' Major Brandt smiled. Dark-haired, late thirties with an Iron Cross at his throat, General Staff collar patches, and the palm tree insignia of the Afrika Korps on his shoulder, he had introduced himself in clear English but then reverted to German. 'I trust the uniform fits?'

Theo tugged at the tunic, which was too small and smelled of carbolic. Equivalent in rank to his British uniform – now presumably locked in a cupboard somewhere – it too had green and silver Staff collar patches, but no other identifying emblems or insignia. Catching sight of himself in the bedroom mirror had been a chilling experience. 'A little tight.'

'Allied rations are more plentiful than ours. Anyway, it won't be for long.'

Four days, the first one already half gone. 'Where is the Generalfeldmarschall?'

'Carentan. Visiting 17th SS Panzer Grenadiers. He hopes to return tonight.'

'Hopes?'

'You understand he has little time to achieve what he must.'

'Yes. But I'm supposed to be observing…'

'You will. In the meantime, he requests that I escort you instead.'

'Escort me where?'

Brandt picked up his cap. 'You'll see.'

They set off, Brandt driving an open Jeep-like *Kübelwagen* laden with boxes and crates. The chateau at La Roche-Guyon lay on the Seine thirty miles northwest of Paris and over fifty inside German lines, and for an hour they drove west through pleasant countryside and a succession of small towns and villages showing little evidence of conflict. As they drew deeper into Normandy, however, Brandt became more watchful, repeatedly craning his neck around, and upwards to the sky. At one point he pulled in behind a barn as a flight of American fighters sped by a mile away. The detritus of war was more visible too, with baggage, discarded equipment and broken-down vehicles littering the verges, and columns of men and machines clogging the roads. At Lisieux he took the main street into town and drew up outside a bomb-scarred hotel. Retrieving the boxes, he piled their arms high and strode up the steps.

'What...?'

'Deliveries. Come on.'

It was a dressing station, hastily converted from the hotel and packed to the rafters with casualties. The smell hit him first, rank and nauseating in the July heat, an eye-smarting mix of disinfectant, putrefaction and sewage. Hefting his boxes, Theo followed Brandt up the steps and into a once-elegant foyer now crammed with injured men. Lying on stretchers, tables and chairs or simply head to toe on the stone floor like fish in a tin, many were bleeding from open wounds, some unconscious and one or two appeared dead. Sighs of pain, punctuated by cries of agony and delirious shouts echoed around the hall; orderlies worked among the wounded, tending and dressing as best they could, but from their expressions he could see they were overwhelmed. And even as he stared, stretcher-bearers barged him aside to carry in more.

'This way.' Brandt set off along a corridor. Picking his way past the casualties, Theo glanced into a room serving as operating theatre. In it a surgeon in a blood-soaked gown was sawing at a young victim's leg, while orderlies held him down. He was awake, Theo saw, his eyes delirious with terror.

'Don't they have ether?'

'Run out,' Brandt replied over his shoulder. 'We're trying to lay on hospital trains to get the boys home, and ship in extra supplies, but what with shortages – the Russian Front gets priority, you know – and the RAF attacks on the railways, not to mention the French Resistance blowing the lines, trains are hard to come by.'

Pushing through swing doors, they reached offices and storerooms at the rear of the hotel. 'In here.'

'Major!' A medical officer in a leather apron was sitting at a desk. 'Thank God. What have you got?'

'Some morphia, dressings, anaesthetics. Antiseptics, too, I think.'

'Wonderful. Any penicillin?'

'Sorry, impossible to get right now.'

'Never mind, any little helps. Thank you.'

'Thank the Generalfeldmarschall and his family. And he apologizes there couldn't be more.'

'No apology necessary, and please thank him when you see him.'

'I will. Is there anything else?'

'Well… Some blood perhaps. We're desperately short.'

'Of course. Captain Ladurner?'

'I… Pardon?'

'We shall give blood. What is your type?'

'Oh, er, type O, negative... that is, I think.'

'Excellent!' The doctor rubbed his hands. 'A universal donor. This way please.'

Thirty minutes later, arms bandaged, they were outside in the Jeep once more.

'The medical supplies,' Theo asked a little giddily. 'Rommel arranges them?'

'He buys them. Out of his own pocket. His wife then pays to ship them here.'

Grinding gears, he let out the clutch and sped off westward again, into the lowering sun. Once more he stuck to back roads and lanes, driving fast yet with an eye always on the sky. Soon they were entering the rearmost positions of the front line. Brandt stopped for directions at a crossroads; while waiting Theo saw machine-gun emplacements, camouflaged artillery, batteries of anti-aircraft guns, tanks, stores dumps, tents, vehicles, and men, everywhere, hurrying, resting, shouting, laughing, sitting at the roadside eating, or slumped asleep on the ground. None paid him, their sworn enemy, the slightest heed. But for the colour of the battledress, he reflected, it could be any army in the world. Brandt returned and they set off forwards again, passing a ruined village of dust and rubble and a field of bloated cattle corpses. A few refugees too, forlornly dragging their shattered lives away in a cart. They entered woodland, dark and pungent, the Jeep's engine echoing raucously, then at the end of an arched avenue they broke into open sunlight, rounded a bend and skidded to a stop.

An armoured column was blocking the road: two tanks, two half-tracks and two troop carriers. For a moment Theo thought it was parked, simply waiting to move off, then peering past the rearmost vehicle he glimpsed flames, and coils of black smoke, and the twisted bodies lying, and he knew what had happened. He'd seen it with the Sherwood Foresters four years previously, and countless times since. The terrifying suddenness of air attack, the noise and the speed of it, of running in panic as the attackers dived, cowering in ditches while the bombs shrieked and the guns stuttered. And the deathly stillness of the aftermath. Brandt shut off the motor and they dismounted; the lane was now silent but for the crackle of flames. Picking their way along the column, he saw not a single vehicle had escaped the onslaught; several were burning, one half-track lay tossed on its side, and bodies were strewn everywhere: in the road, in the verges, piled in the vehicles, many of them grotesquely mutilated. One was even hanging overhead, suspended in a tree like a scarecrow, his feet unaccountably bare, one arm waving, while another man, blackened by fire, slumped from his tank as though struggling from the flames. Further on they found a gathering of survivors, six or seven infantrymen clustered together like sheep, their eyes staring in shock, while another youth, his shattered arm hanging at his side, walked in dazed circles.

'Private, come.' Brandt steered the youth to the verge. 'Sit here. You others, take care of him. Are there any more?'

Heads shook.

'Make your way back.' He pointed. 'There's an aid post in about a mile. Keep moving, help each other.'

'Wait.' Fumbling at a pocket, Theo produced Grant's handkerchief and tied it around the youth's shoulder. 'Keep this tight, but loosen it every ten minutes or so.'

They watched them go, shuffling away like old men, then reboarded the Jeep, crawled slowly through the column and drove on. They passed more walking wounded coming the other way, then after another mile came to a copse of trees and pulled into a tented clearing. Once it had been a command post, but now there was no command in evidence: the clearing silent, the tents empty, a lone radio operator sitting at a lifeless console, a row of blanketed bodies to one side, and a few living ones standing aimlessly about like passengers on a railway platform.

'Who are you?' Brandt asked.

'39th Pioneer Reserves.'

'Where's Brigade?'

'We don't know. They pulled out.'

'Battalion?'

'That way.' A gesture through the trees.

'Christ.' Brandt drew his Luger and set off.

Theo followed. 'What is this?'

'The River Dives. 346th Infantry Division. Or was. Hurry, we're late.'

'The Dives? But...'

'Come on, stay low.'

Crouching, they hurried on westward into the trees. As the wood thinned they heard distant rifle fire and Brandt motioned for Theo to stay back, but something drew him on, something vaguely familiar in memory. They reached the edge of the copse and found a young officer leaning against a tree. He was holding binoculars in one hand, while his other hung in a sling. Theo followed his gaze, shielding his own eyes against the setting sun. Below the copse, a grassy meadow sloped down to a winding river, beyond which stood a small town. The grass was pale and golden in the evening light, but pockmarked with shell craters and dark stains where bodies lay. A single burned-out tank smouldered near a small bridge spanning the river. The same bridge, he then realized, that he'd last seen, and attacked, from the opposite side, with Jock Pearson and the men of 8 Para more than a month earlier.

'That's Troarn,' he said incredulously.

'Indeed,' Brandt replied. 'Taken by British *Fallschirmjäger* some time ago.'

'But—'

'And this is the remains of 346th Infantry. Tasked with taking it back.'

The young officer turned. 'Hello, Major. Any word?'

'Not yet.' He glanced at Theo. 'Lieutenant Schäfer, this is Captain Ladurner, newly assigned to our intelligence staff. He's… fact-finding.'

'Facts?' Schäfer forced a tired smile. 'The fact is, we're due to attack again at dusk. Unless the order changes.'

Theo looked around. Two mortar sections were set up just inside the trees; further along he glimpsed scattered handfuls of riflemen making ready. But that was all. 'Attack with what?'

'That is the question.' Schäfer shrugged. His face was exhausted, the bandage on his arm soiled and bloody, his tunic mud-caked and his boots split and sodden. Like the last man standing. 'We were a battalion a week ago, now we're barely a company. Our officers are dead, or injured, or transferred to other units. We're promised reinforcements every day – an armoured column is coming, they say, with field guns, Panther tanks and two companies of infantry…'

'They're not coming! Your reinforcements, they're all dead. In any case, what they're sending isn't enough, not nearly enough, believe me!'

'I know that, but the orders—'

'Damn the orders! That's open ground out there, you'll be cut to pieces.'

'Captain Ladurner,' Brandt interrupted. 'The lieutenant is well aware of the difficulties. As are his *men*.'

Theo glanced around. Several of the troops nearby were now listening, wide-eyed with concern. Many of them, he saw, were little more than boys.

'Can't we do anything?' he whispered. 'We can't just let them go.'

'The ceasefire negotiations. We've been waiting, and hoping, but time...'

'Anything?'

'Perhaps *you* can.' Brandt held his stare, then nodded. 'Captain Ladurner. I have a question.'

'What question?'

'As the ranking *intelligence* officer here, is it your considered assessment, in view of the absence of a senior *field* officer, that Lieutenant Schäfer should await clarification of the reinforcements situation, and up-to-date instructions from his divisional commander, before proceeding with his planned attack on Troarn?'

'What?'

'You heard.' Brandt's gaze was steady. 'Is it?'

'Well...' The penny dropped. 'Well, yes. Absolutely. He should definitely wait.'

And with that Theo had issued his first operational order.

He spent the second day frustratingly cooped up in the chateau at La Roche-Guyon. Brandt was away trying to organize hospital trains, Rommel's arrival was promised but repeatedly delayed, and no special arrangements had been made for Theo: no outings, no briefings and no meetings. As an 'observer' he was redundant – and ignored. Staff

186

hurried by with courteous urgency, but paid him no heed, and if he stopped to question them he was politely brushed off. Furthermore, guards ensured he was kept away from sensitive areas like the signals room; nor, he soon learned, was he allowed off chateau premises.

'You are our guest, Captain,' his orderly chided when he was caught near the gates. 'And as such you must remain here.'

'I was just going for a walk.'

'Once outside these grounds you are beyond our protection.'

'I'll take the risk.'

'Think about it,' the man went on more sternly. Theo was beginning to view him more as a gaoler than a servant. 'You are a British officer masquerading as a German one. That alone is a serious contravention of the rules of war. The identity discs around your neck are British, you have no German papers, discs or identity card, and you belong to no German regiment or unit. Nor are you wearing a weapon, which is against regulations. Your accent may fool the unwary but the most casual of inspections would expose you in seconds. If that happens, nothing can help you.'

'Am I under arrest?'

'It is a condition of the agreement that no harm comes to you. We will take whatever precautions necessary to ensure that.'

Duly chastened, he returned to the house. Later he was informed that Rommel's chief of staff General Speidel was holding an afternoon situation briefing in the ballroom, and to his surprise he was welcome to attend. Arriving there he found the room full of staff officers, clerks and aides of all ranks and disciplines, much as at Dempsey's chateau in Blay, and spotting an empty chair at the back sat down to wait.

Speidel arrived with a small entourage, strode through the room and stepped on to a platform with blackboards and a mounted map of Normandy. A diffident middle-aged man with wire-rimmed spectacles and thinning hair, he more resembled an academic or accountant than a military chief. In modest tones, he began by outlining the strategic situation in Normandy, pointing out the disposition of German forces along the front with the Allies, which appeared on the map as a black line meandering from the Cotentin coast in the west to Le Havre in the east. All along the line were the names of the dozen or so units defending it, with ominous bulges here and there where the Allies were driving forward. He saw '21 Pz' at Colombelles, which he knew was holding well, whereas '346 Inf' next door on the Dives was close to collapse. Interestingly, on the opposite side of the line were marked the various Allied units opposing them, including his own '6 Fall Div' which was still centred on Ranville. He wondered briefly about Gale, Howard, Pearson and the rest – chafing at the bit to break out, no doubt.

Having spoken of the local situation which he summed up as 'challenging but contained', Speidel widened his briefing, reporting that Army Group G under General Blaskowitz down in Provence was at full preparedness against the expected second invasion of France, Army Group C under Kesselring was holding the Allied advance up Italy at the Gothic Line, and finally Army Group Centre was manfully repelling Operation Bagration, the latest and to date largest Russian offensive against Germany. What he failed to mention was that Army Group G was in reality only half a group, the Gothic Line was Kesselring's last and most northerly line of retreat before the Alps, and Operation Bagration was storming westwards across Poland at a terrifying rate, with leading Russian units barely four hundred miles from the German border. Nor was any mention made of the dire shortages, crippling casualties, lack of replacements, absent air cover, or the divided and crumbling leadership. Instead Theo formed the impression of a situation that was tense and concerning, but basically under control.

Until the very end. Concluding his report, Speidel seemed to pause in mid flow and look around the room, studying the faces anew, before resuming in a quieter and more resigned tone.

'Gentlemen, as you know, the Generalfeldmarschall is hard at work visiting every unit in the Group. He apologizes for this absence but knows you will understand, for his efforts are of the utmost importance. A bold new initiative is at hand that could transform the situation for us, put an early and acceptable end to this campaign, and alter the outcome of the war in Germany's favour. Time is critical and discretion essential: there is much to put in place in a very short time, therefore he begs your continued patience and support.' Theo felt Speidel's gaze fall directly on him. 'And let us pray he is successful in his endeavours. Before it is too late.'

The orderly shook him awake well after midnight. 'Get dressed.'

'What?'

'Hurry, the field marshal's waiting.'

Struggling blearily into his clothes, he barely noticed that as well as uniform, cap and boots, the orderly was fastening a pistol belt around his waist.

'I don't need this.'

'Yes you do, you're going on a trip.'

'But…'

'It's empty, of course.'

Down in the moonlit driveway the car was waiting, a black Horch convertible with the roof up. A driver sat in front next to a guard hefting a Schmeisser; behind them both, lit by a map light and reading from a file, sat Erwin Rommel.

'*Junge,*' he grunted.

'Sir.'

'Apologies for waking you at this hour.'

'May I ask where we're going?'

'Paris.' Rommel leaned towards the driver. 'Let's go, Daniel, and we'd best be quick, the old man says it's urgent.'

Churning gravel, the car sped into motion; moments later it exited the gates and accelerated on to tarmac. Wide awake suddenly, Theo turned to Rommel. 'Whereabouts…'

'Not yet.' Rommel's eyes scanned the file. 'Let me finish.'

Theo sat back. Paris. Avenue Foch. Where was that? Could he get there, could he get in? Then what? A fortress prison and an empty gun? The questions rang in his head like bells. Outside the roads became wider, swiftly carrying them eastward towards a grey horizon. The Horch was warm and comfortable, the motion soporific; watching the nightscape he became aware of pressure on his shoulder and turned to see that Rommel, leaning sideways, had fallen asleep.

'Leave him,' the driver murmured. 'It's his third night without rest.'

In a while suburbs began to appear, then the car sped through a darkened forest, emerging on to a bridge over the Seine followed immediately by a second at Chatou. Suddenly they were entering Paris proper, bumping on to cobbled boulevards lined with trees and tall buildings. The hour was still early, the dawn dark, no lights showed and few people were in evidence. He searched for signposts but learned little of his whereabouts. Then Rommel awoke, blinking groggily.

'How long, Daniel?'

'About ten minutes, sir.'

'Good.' He passed a hand over his face, and Theo saw the lines etched in his cheek. 'So, *Junge*.' He yawned. 'These are curious times, no?'

'Very, sir, yes.'

'Yet momentous.' Rommel angled the map light at him. 'You've aged since last we met. But then so have we both. I trust you are in better health than then.'

Salo. The house above Lake Garda. After the Gestapo. 'I am, sir, thank you.'

'And spirits?'

'I am much recovered.'

'I rather assumed that when you gave my men the slip in Verona.'

Although they'd left him alone, car door unlocked, virtually inviting him to go.

'Now then, you'll be wanting an update on the bridge-construction project.'

'The bridge... Yes, I would.'

The car crossed the Seine a third time at Pont de Neuilly, and entered another wide tree-lined avenue at the very end of which, squat and shadowy in the gloom, stood the Arc de Triomphe.

'You're about to find out,' Rommel said. 'And I believe it will be significant.'

It was, but not in the way he expected.

The car pulled up outside the famous George V hotel, one whole floor of which had been taken over by Gerd von

Rundstedt as his personal apartment and headquarters. Clanking up in the lift, they were greeted by a grim-faced adjutant and shown straight into an ornate salon furnished in Louis XVI style. Rundstedt, grey-haired, approaching seventy, in shirtsleeves and braces behind a marble-topped desk, rose as soon as he saw them.

'He's sacked me, Erwin!'

Rommel gaped. 'What?'

'I'm to be sacked, for defeatism and lack of moral fibre! Here's the signal.'

Rommel scanned the sheet. 'But... that's impossible! When?'

'The next few days. It's all dressed up as retirement with full military honours and so on, but privately he's saying I'm no longer up to the job and must be replaced!'

'By who?'

'That fanatic Kluge!'

The facts emerged. Following their disastrous meeting with Hitler at Margival on 17 June, Rommel and Rundstedt had tried one final time to make their leader see sense, travelling to Berchtesgaden together to attend a conference on the French situation. During the conference Rommel tried twice to turn the conversation away from tactical matters and into a discussion about Germany's survival. The first time he was firmly rebuked by Hitler, the second he was ordered furiously from the room. Driving back to Normandy, both men agreed the Führer had lost all reason and intended nothing less than the total annihilation of Germany and its people, and that therefore they must take matters into their own hands by enacting *Fall Grün* immediately. Although Rundstedt was soon wavering, he agreed Rommel should press ahead with the first steps, which were to sound out their unit commanders for support, and establish contact with the Allies via an intermediary.

'Is this him?' Rundstedt gestured at Theo. 'The British liaison officer?'

'It is.'

'Well, he must leave the room! Immediately! We have much to discuss that the Allies mustn't know.'

'But he's—'

'No, I insist!'

Rommel saw him to the lobby. 'Wait here. He's just panicking.'

'What of the bridge project? Can it still go ahead?'

'If we hurry. We have a few days before Kluge takes over. But I know him, he's a pragmatist, and he'd come round to our thinking once he saw the situation for himself.'

'There isn't time. The Allied offensive...'

'I am aware of that! So we push ahead with or without Kluge. That means tackling Blaskowitz at Army Group G, then all the field commanders here in Normandy. Stay here, I'll call you back in when I can.'

He sank into a plush velvet armchair, but the moment Rundstedt's door closed he rose and went in search of the adjutant. 'The Generalfeldmarschall wants me to buy a few things.'

'You'll need a pass.' The adjutant produced a chit. 'And be careful walking about on your own, Parisians are jumpy as hell since the invasion.'

'Thanks. And how far's Avenue Foch?'

'What do you want there?'

'Nothing. Just sightseeing.'

'Ten minutes. Go back to the Arc and turn left, you can't miss it.'

He found the avenue swiftly enough, but soon saw that it was huge, nearly a mile in length and featuring a wide central carriageway flanked by two smaller avenues of imposingly tall buildings set back behind trees. With no idea of the house number, finding the right one would take hours, so he was reduced to asking directions.

'Which way is the police headquarters?' The hour was still early, with few people on the streets. He tried an old man walking his dog, but he merely scowled, while a cleaning woman swabbing steps looked at his uniform and spat on the pavement. With time growing short, and conscious that hostile eyes were watching him, he eventually approached two cruising *Feldgendarmerie* military policemen.

'*Papiere, bitte, Hauptmann!*' they immediately demanded, snapping their fingers.

Heart thumping, he handed over his only document, the chit signed by the adjutant on Rundstedt's paper.

'You are from the Field Marshal's office?'

'Yes. On an errand for him to SD headquarters.'

'On your own? That's not clever.'

'Sorry, it's a rush job.'

'Number eighty-four. Far end, right-hand side.'

'Thanks.'

'Nobody's there, mind you.'

'What?'

'Skeleton staff only. All packed up and headed back to Berlin.'

'What about the prisoners?'

'Fuck knows.'

He hurried to the building, a six-storey, stone-fronted block with tall windows and wrought-iron balconies. Hovering uncertainly by the entrance, he saw the driveway and garden was littered with boxes, crates and furniture. Eventually he spied a clerk staggering down the steps beneath a steel desk.

'Wait, let me help you with that.'

'Eh? Well, yes, OK, Captain, thanks. Just put it down there with the rest.'

'Going home?'

'Too right, thank Christ. France is finished.'

'Indeed.' He looked up at the building. 'So this is the place. Where they bring all the spies and insurgents and so on.'

'Next door actually. They had special connecting doors and tunnels built. To hide all the comings and goings.'

'Really? Where did they house them?'

'In the basement mostly. And see the barred windows on the third floor? Special cells muffled for sound. That's where all the *questioning* went on, if you know what I mean!'

A boy strapped to a chair. Blood-chilling screams as his fingernails tore out.

'I believe I do. Did you see much of that?'

'Me? Christ no, far too squeamish. But it went on round the clock – everyone knew. Horrific stuff too.'

'I don't doubt it. But all gone now. The prisoners, I mean.'

'Yes, sir, shipped home a week ago.'

'Where to?'

'The camps, I expect.'

'Camps?'

'Christ, Captain, where've you been!'

'Abroad. Italy mostly. Haven't been home in ages.'

'Well, there's camps. *Konzentrationslager*, where they dump all the undesirables. There's dozens: Natzweiler, Ravensbrück, Dachau...'

195

'What happens to them there?'

'The spies and so on? Tortured, tried and shot's my guess.' He turned for the steps. 'And good bloody riddance!'

The next forty-eight hours passed in a blur of rising tension and hyperactivity. Back at Rundstedt's HQ the waiting went on until mid-afternoon when Theo was suddenly summoned to the salon. There he learned that matters were proceeding, slowly, but that General Blaskowitz was insisting on a face-to-face meeting before agreeing to stand down Army Group G. Reluctant to let the erratic Rundstedt handle this, Rommel had no choice but to meet Blaskowitz himself. This meant a long drive south to a rendezvous in Burgundy, with Theo accompanying him to witness the exchange. In the meantime, most but not all of Rommel's field commanders had confirmed support; the rest would also need personal persuasion. Rundstedt's replacement Kluge had not yet surfaced, but might at any time, throwing the whole plan into question, while intelligence reports indicated Allied forces were amassing at key locations along the Normandy front, and Rommel feared they might be preparing to launch a pre-emptive attack before the deadline.

'Might they do that?' he asked as the Horch sped south.

'I wouldn't know.' Theo shrugged. 'I'm not in contact with them, though I'm supposed to report in daily. In any case they wouldn't tell me. But I do know not everyone was in favour of your proposal.'

'I can imagine.' Rommel grunted. 'We need to move fast. And you *have* reported in by the way.'

'What?'

'Your reports: they've been going off to the American diplomat in Bern each day as scheduled.'

'But saying what?'

'That everything's proceeding!' He glared. 'Which it is!'

The strain was telling, Theo realized, wringing the grit from the old warrior like water from a rag. Sick and spent, he'd been fighting this war for five years, virtually without pause, from France to Africa to Italy and back to France. Only to end up like this, crushed between an unstoppable Allied juggernaut and an insane despot. And as if to underline the point he was soon falling asleep again.

Blaskowitz hedged his bets. Since Army Group G wasn't yet fighting anyone, technically he had no need to order a ceasefire. And though a second Allied invasion of France was expected, it seemed unlikely in the coming few days, thus his was a simpler dilemma. Nevertheless, he spent over an hour whining to an increasingly frustrated Rommel, before finally giving in.

'All right, Erwin!' he said at last. 'You can count on my support, but *only* if I receive clear written orders from Rundstedt, or his successor, to cease hostilities, and also written assurances of safe conduct for me and my officers from the Allies.'

'Then you'll do it.'

'*And* immunity against any sort of, you know, criminal charges.'

'Understood. *Then* you'll do it?'

'Given those provisos, yes, the moment I receive confirmation of a ceasefire in the north, I will follow suit.'

'Slippery bastard!' Rommel muttered as they climbed back into the car. 'Won't stick his neck out either way.'

'Can you count on him?'

'He'll blow with the wind. If everything goes as planned, he'll issue the order.'

'And if not?'

'If not?' Rommel snorted. 'Then it won't matter anyway!'

They set off, the driver propelling the Horch swiftly northwards into the darkness. He too had been working days and nights with no rest, and somewhere near Auxerre, with everyone's heads nodding, he requested they pull in for an hour, bumped down a farm track and switched off beside a stream. Theo kept watch while they slept, listening to the peaceful murmur of water, and the leaves rustling in the trees. Only now did he appreciate the full implications of their mission. And its enormity. Less than thirty hours Rommel had, he calculated, to complete the negotiations, make the arrangements, and issue the order for all German forces in France to cease hostilities. How such news would be received in Berlin he could only imagine, but threats, denials, counterorders, arrest warrants and bitter denunciations would all surely follow. And the Allies? How would they respond? Were they functioning well enough to make best use of this opportunity? Would they race like mad across France, storm into Germany and end it all quickly? Before it was too late for Clare? The questions were endless, the answers unknown. *Will you look for me?* she'd written, as though foretelling her own arrest. *I pray so.* Somehow he must get word to her that he was. And that she must hold on, and stay alive, until he found her.

By breakfast they were back in La Roche-Guyon where, pausing only to eat, bathe and change, Rommel closeted himself in his office with Hans Speidel. Theo went too, soon learning that the chief of staff had not been idle during their absence, confirming that all but three field commanders were now in accord with Case Green, those three being die-hard Nazi waverers whom Rommel must convert personally. Meanwhile, a fourth, General Feuchtinger, Hans von Luck's superior at 21st Panzer, was nowhere to be found.

'What the hell does that mean?' Rommel fumed.

'Nobody knows. Rumour is he lives in a mansion on the Loire with his girlfriend and only shows up for parades and medal ceremonies.'

'Well, find him! And tell him to report. He's in command of the whole division!'

The matter was in hand, Speidel soothed. However, two other issues had arisen requiring the field marshal's attention. Firstly, Resistance contacts in Germany had tipped Speidel off that an attempt on Hitler's life was imminent.

'The Stauffenberg lunacy, you mean?'

'Well...' Speidel glanced at Theo.

'It's all right, the *Junge* met the man.'

'Good heavens. Well then, yes, most probably. And I wondered if we should perhaps consider pausing our plans until it happens. I mean, it could play to our advantage if the attempt is successful.'

'No! It will only create chaos and muddy the waters. In any case there's no time for pausing: the Allies are about to attack. We must ignore this nonsense and advance *Fall Grün* without delay. Stauffenberg's bound to mess it up anyway. What's the second thing?'

In a similar vein, Speidel went on, an intercepted enemy signal indicated that British special forces were preparing to enter France and carry out a 'capture or kill' mission on the field marshal.

'Well, well.' Rommel chuckled. 'This must be the fourth time! What have I done to upset these fellows so?'

'You should consider it a compliment,' Speidel said. 'But we suspect it is a back-up plan, in case *Fall Grün* should, you know…'

'Fail?'

'… become compromised in some way.'

Rommel waved the matter away and went on planning. And by late morning he and Theo, plus Sergeant Daniel the driver and their armed guard Holke, were back aboard the Horch heading west to the front line. The three wavering generals were Dietrich Kraiss of 352nd Infantry Division, Walter Harzer of 9th SS Panzer and Sepp Dietrich of 1st SS Panzer Corps. Dietrich had already given covert support to the scheme but wanted assurances, Harzer was hard-line SS and might take some convincing, whereas Kraiss sounded close to despair. His infantry division was deployed to the west near Saint-Lô, and speeding along in bright sunshine with the roof down, it was there they drove first.

In the event Kraiss's conversion proved foregone. Visibly moved to see Rommel striding into his bomb-ravaged HQ, Kraiss, his uniform grimy and plastered with dust, greeted him with a heartfelt clasp of hands. The 352nd, it emerged, once proud and strong, had been reduced to a battered shell following six weeks of bloody fighting against the Americans in the Bayeux sector. Now, with its strength down by half, its armour all but gone, and no rest or replacements in sight, total destruction loomed.

'The Führer promises supplies and reinforcements,' Kraiss lamented. 'At least he did at first, but now we hear nothing, and I fear we are to be sacrificed.'

Rommel nodded. 'As are we all, my friend.' Producing his cigarette case, he lit one for Kraiss and led him to a corner.

Theo stayed back, sensing what came next must pass between them alone. Drained and disillusioned though he was, Kraiss was nevertheless a loyal and long-serving officer, bound by sworn oath to his leader. Abandoning that allegiance would not come easily. Furthermore, Rommel could not pull the 352nd back, nor provide them with rest, or reinforcements; he could only offer sympathy and understanding. And Case Green.

A shell smashed into a nearby building. Theo turned to look. Dust clouds billowed, and debris fell like rain, while out in the smoke-filled street men were scurrying past hefting weapons and ammunition boxes, while others helped the injured. All inexorably rearwards, he realized, recalling Speidel's map, and the bulge south of Bayeux where the 352nd struggled to hold on. How much longer could it survive? In the corner of the room Kraiss's gaze was cast down, and as Theo watched, Rommel, murmuring softly, reached out and gripped his shoulder.

'He is agreed,' he said grimly as they returned to the car. 'I will say nothing more.' Five minutes later they were racing eastwards again, twenty miles to Thury where 9th SS Panzer Division, formerly a crack armoured unit, had been badly mauled in weeks of fighting south of Caen. These men wore the black uniform of the SS, and were answerable to no one but its leader, Heinrich Himmler. Having lost their commanding officer to injury, a replacement had just been appointed. Tough and experienced, Walter Harzer had refused point blank to discuss Case Green on the phone with Speidel, insisting it must be Rommel only, and in person. Pulling up outside the tents serving as Harzer's command post, Rommel leaped from the car and strode inside.

Ten minutes later he was back, Harzer at his side. Tall and fair with piercing eyes, Harzer's gaze fell on Theo.

'Is this him?'

'Yes.'

Harzer nodded. 'Then good luck, *Hauptmann*.' And with that he turned and left.

'Drive!' Rommel ordered, slamming the door.

Time passed; the car sped east.

'Sir?' Theo queried eventually.

'Incredible!' Rommel shook his head.

'He agrees?'

'Yes. He sees it as his duty to save what's left of his division, pull it back nearer to Germany and make a proper stand, to save the Fatherland. He agrees entirely with my analysis, says defending Normandy is a pointless waste of men and equipment and that High Command, including Himmler, must be made to see sense.'

'So he'll cease fire?'

'When I give the order. But he'll not surrender his division. He's going to try and get it out.'

Their final call was to Sepp Dietrich, commanding 1st SS Panzer Corps based twenty miles south of Thury near Argentan. The route took them through several rear echelons and Rommel stopped frequently to offer cheer and encouragement to the men, who grinned and waved at his passing. Thirty minutes more and they reached the *mairie* serving as Dietrich's HQ.

'Stay in the car,' he ordered. 'This shouldn't take long.'

But it was an hour before he emerged again. 'Sepp's old school,' he explained, settling beside Theo. 'It's the policeman in him. He wants every contingency covered, every last detail spelled out. It took a while.'

'But he's agreed?'

'Yes, thank God. What's more...' He produced a note. 'Feuchtinger's turned up. He's meeting us at Lisieux.'

'Will he consent?'

'Unless he wants to be shot for abandoning his command!' He checked his watch. 'If we hurry we'll be with him by sunset, and back at La Roche-Guyon by nightfall.'

'And then?'

'Then...' Rommel hesitated. 'Well, then we're all set. You send your message to the Allies, and I issue the order. To stop fighting at midnight.'

'My God, so it's really happening.'

'Yes. It's time for the madness to end. Before it kills us all.'

They set off, speeding along straight Roman roads across a flat plain of crop, the orange ball of the sun setting behind them. After the town of Trun they turned more northward and the way became wooded, plunging them into shade one moment and open fields of golden sunlight the next. The smell was of pine woods and ripening corn. Rommel, in reflective mood, stared out at the passing scenery.

'What will you do, *Junge*?' he asked after a while. 'When this matter is over.'

'I don't know. Return to my unit, I suppose. And await what happens. My original unit that is.'

'Ah, 2nd Battalion of the 1st *Fallschirmjäger* Brigade, isn't it?'

'That's right.'

'When did you last see them?'

He thought back. John Frost, Jock Pearson, Brigadier Lathbury, Vere Hodge and the *Newfoundland*. Swimming the river to take the bridge. Exactly a year ago. 'It was last July. In Sicily.'

'Hmm. Long time to be away.'

After Vimoutiers they drew near the village of Livarot, before which they passed a tiny hamlet called L'Angleterre.

'Angleterre, see, *Junge*!' Rommel nudged him. 'Ironic, wouldn't you—'

'LOOK OUT!'

The two Spitfires pounced at more than 300 mph. Diving from behind and out of the burning orb of the sun, there was no time to spot them, or take evasive action, or do anything but shout a strangled warning. And even as Daniel slammed his foot to the floor, their guns opened up, shredding the road behind and then tearing viciously into the car and its occupants. Daniel was immediately hit, and with the Horch travelling at more than sixty, it lost control, skidded off the road and crashed into a ditch, slamming everyone violently forward. Daniel and Holke smashed into the dashboard, while in the back Theo felt himself catapulted skywards, flying through the air like a flung doll, to crash into a stone wall beyond the ditch. Lying in a tangled heap, pain and giddiness overwhelming him, he raised his head briefly to see Rommel, still in the car, his bloody head thrown back, sliding lifelessly down the seat.

CHAPTER 11

The date of this is Monday 17 July 1944, at about five in the afternoon. According to the reports and notes I find in Rommel's files, a local pastor happens upon the scene about ten minutes later whilst cycling home from church. What he sees, he writes in a letter to Lucie, is the wrecked Horch nose down in the ditch, with both front occupants clearly dead (Daniel and Holke). Meanwhile, a young German officer with blood all down his face is trying to haul an older one from the back. The older officer has severe head wounds and also looks dead to the pastor, but the younger one screams that he isn't and begs him to get help, which he does, pedalling off to Livarot where there's a monastery with a doctor. A cart is quickly procured and the pastor returns with the doctor to find the young officer sitting in the road cradling the older one in his lap. The youth, seemingly delirious, insists again he isn't dead and exhorts them in various languages to save him *before it's too late* [my italics]. Both are then conveyed to Livarot where they're attended to by the doctor, who confirms the older one is indeed alive, although barely. An ambulance is then summoned from Bernay, twenty-five miles away, where there's a military hospital, and it's while waiting for it to arrive that the younger man, who has a broken arm, smashed ribs and wounds to his head, tells them that the unconscious officer is Field Marshal Erwin Rommel, on a mission of vital importance. He declines to give his own name, nor does he accompany the field marshal to Bernay, saying he will go to the dressing station at Lisieux which is much nearer. Later in the evening a farmer conveys him there in his van, and he's never heard from again. But according to the monastery doctor, so the pastor concludes in his letter, the youth's actions and insistence that the older man be saved were crucial to the field marshal's survival.

A peculiar and not altogether happy hiatus extends over Ulm in the days following my release from prison. As if the whole city is holding its breath or is in limbo or something. Everyone knows the end is at hand, yet the days tick by and nothing happens. Except that the rumble of distant artillery moves off, as though Ulm isn't important enough for the war to visit. Rumours abound as always, one being that it was American guns we heard, not Russian, which is a comfort to the citizenry; another that Stuttgart, some forty miles to the northwest, is now in Allied hands; a third outlandish one is that Hitler's preparing to flee Berlin and make a stand in the Bavarian Alps. But nothing can be checked or verified, newspapers don't exist, the radio only broadcasts old speeches and martial music, so all we can do is twiddle our thumbs and carry on waiting.

Back at the *Revier* work resumes, POWs continue to get sick and we continue to hold parades and clinics. The only difference is they now include German civilians who queue up in the misguided belief that we have the staff, skills and supplies to treat them too, which we don't. Indeed, basic essentials like food, fuel, medicines and raw materials are all running out, the water and electricity supplies are intermittent at best, as are the telephones, and even Ulm's wonderful tram system is close to collapse; all this because there are no spares or supplies, municipal workers aren't being paid, and the prisoner labour force has also downed tools, unsurprisingly. So nothing runs, nothing gets fixed, nobody comes and everyone's fed up.

On the plus side, I wander into Münsterplatz one day to find market stalls bearing unexpected treasure: radishes, spinach, cabbage and baby turnips, early spring vegetables bringing much-needed nutrition and variety to our meagre diets. Also, with Vorst gone, Prien and the guards cowed, and the town garrison reduced to boys and old men, we are effectively prisoners in name only, unshackled, answerable to no one, and free to come and go as we please, except during curfew. The bombings stop too, which is a relief, and even the weather perks up, with days turning mild and bright in the late April sunshine, such that a leisurely stroll through Ulm's rubble is almost a pleasure.

Which all just makes the waiting so much harder. Everyone feels it: prisoners, townsfolk, soldiers and civilians, young and old, the homeless and the destitute especially, friend and foe together. We've paid our dues, served our time and completed our sentence. Now we just want the whole ghastly nightmare to end.

Erik, to my surprise, more than anyone. Hitherto the voice of reason and calm, our roles seem to reverse such that he's the one stamping about losing his temper, while I, improbably, am preaching prudence and restraint.

'Five years, Dan!' he rants furiously one evening. 'Five years of my life that I will never get back, stolen by these bloody bastards!'

'Not for much longer now, old chap.'

'And for why? For nothing! For being a doctor in Dutch uniform! It bloody makes me want to kill someone!'

'I do understand. Another radish?'

My own mood at this time is oddly conflicted. Psychologically I've already packed my bags and left, my thoughts like Erik's turning repeatedly for home, London, family, friends, resuming ordinary life, my work and career and so on. And yet these seven months of captivity, and especially my time here in Ulm, have affected me deeply. I'm not the same man who leaped from that Dakota back in September; the battle, the frightful week at the Schoonoord, then Apeldoorn, Fallingbostel, Bergen and finally Ulm – even that bizarre interlude at Stalag 357 – these places, people and events have had a transformative effect. The regiment too, of course, has made an impact, its bravery in battle, its doggedness and pride, even in the face of defeat, stamping an indelible mark on my psyche. Colonel Lea, Arthur Marrable, Jack Bowyer, CSM Barrett on the Arnhem road, dear old Cliff Pountney, Pip Smith, Bill Alford, the young sapper Jenkins at 357: all these men taught me much about who I am, and how to be better at it.

And Theo Trickey, who in a way taught me more than anyone.

In seven months together we barely exchanged a single rational conversation, yet the most significant events of my journey happened because of Theo. Saving him at the Schoonoord, performing cranial surgery on the train, Stalag XIB, meeting Inge Brandt and seeing the Belsen camp, coming to Ulm, the drop-in centre, learning to be a proper doctor, standing up to Vorst, involvement with the Rommel family and so on: he had a hand in all these. And his quiet presence, his guileless smile, his refusal to give in to his injuries, his determination to recover and then simply walk off, well, it was educative.

Ulm. I'll be genuinely sad to leave it. For here in this battered old city I have found my purpose – as the recruiting officer described it back in London. I've become a general practitioner in the truest sense of the term, living and working among a community, trying to relieve suffering and heal its sick, often in far from easy circumstances. Two-minute consultations at sick parade, balancing the 10 per cent tightrope, slogging to French prisoners in a blizzard, visiting that dying old man in his freezing flat, Ditunka and the Slav women in the fields, homeless children queuing at the drop-in. And I too have marvelled at the resilience of their spirit, found solace amid their suffering and drawn strength from their kinship. General practice at its best, and surely no finer way to ply one's trade.

And in Ulm, too, I found Trudi Eichel.

We see quite a bit of each other these final days. Her job has ceased to exist, mine now allows me more freedom, and with the coming of fine weather people emerge, blinking into the sunshine like moles, to scratch among the debris, gossip over garden gates or simply wander restlessly about waiting for something to happen. We join them, going for walks together down by the river, to the university or what's left of the botanical gardens, where we sit on benches, hold hands and lay matters to rest. Our rapport, once awkward, is now accepting and truthful, which is a relief to us both. We know what we have is of its moment – a bond forged between two people in dire circumstances. Perfectly natural, honest and supportive, but fleeting and insubstantial. Like sandcastles built between tides. Never meant to last.

'Will we remain friends?' she asks at the end of one walk.

'I sincerely hope so. We may have other lives to resume, but there will always be this shared bond of experience between us.'

'Good.'

'I want to return to Ulm one day too, once it's had time, you know, to recover.'

She nods. Leaning on the old stone parapet, we stare out as the glassy waters of the Danube slide silently by.

'So.' She nudges me. 'What will you do?'

'I've been thinking of retraining as a general practitioner.'

'No, not that. I mean what will you do about the town meeting. At the minster on Sunday.'

My final visit to Herrlingen takes place next evening, some twelve weeks after the first. It scarcely seems possible, so much has happened in that time, so much come to light; I feel I know Erwin Rommel personally, intimately even, given the access I've had to his thoughts and words. I know all his foibles, his tics and quirks, the little anecdotes he puts in his letters to Lucie, his surprising skill at sketching, his interest in photography, the detail on his maps and plans, his meticulous notes and appendices. Immersing myself in his world, I've become confidant, critic and curator all in one. I don't believe every word he writes, and there are traits I dislike (blinkered vision, political naivety, hubris), but what I'm left with is an uncomplicated soul and loving family man, and a soldier of extraordinary talent, who dedicated his life to his country, only to have that loyalty betrayed.

It's all a far cry from that first fumbling foray into his life, when I tiptoed fearfully up to Lucie's bedroom back in

January. These days the butler greets me with a courteous nod, the maid takes my coat and beret, I stride across the flagstones, unlock Rommel's study as though my own, lay out my notebooks and pencils and set to work with barely a thought, freely poking into the most private corners of his life. Polite faces come and go, at some point a cup of tea appears, and Gertrud generally pops in if she's about. When I'm done I lock up and leave, nobody questions me, and no one interferes; mostly I'm left in peace to get on with my studies.

Which is just as well because with the end looming and some ground yet to cover, the question arises as to what I'm supposed to do with it all. Before that can be settled however, I must bring matters up to the present.

Rommel spent three weeks in hospital. His skull was cracked in four places, he had various internal injuries and at first he was not expected to live. Obviously he knew nothing of events during this period, thus I only have the notes he added subsequently, plus supporting evidence from other sources. For instance the very next day after the attack – attributed in a newspaper cutting to Canadian pilots of 412 Squadron – the British unleashed Operation Goodwood, their biggest operation since D-Day and aimed at kick-starting the much delayed Normandy breakout by blasting Caen's door clean off its hinges. I was with 11th Battalion at Melton Mowbray at the time so we all learned the details. Goodwood was massive, beginning it was said with the biggest aerial bombardment in history – bigger even than Great War barrages in terms of explosive mega-tonnage. And the numbers of troops and machines involved would also break records, as the Americans joined in, circling round from the west to close the net on the beleaguered Germans.

This circle eventually centred on the town of Falaise, twenty miles south of Caen, and it was here, in what became known as the 'Falaise pocket', that Army Group B was effectively wiped from the map.

But did the British jump the gun? It's hard to know; the timing is very close. Also they would have received intelligence of the attack on Rommel's car (initial reports said he was dead) in which case all ceasefire bets were off. Either way, with no word from him and the deadline expiring, it seems they had little faith he'd pull off his Case Green plan, and so went ahead with theirs. 'Besides,' Rommel pencils unsteadily in his notes, 'with the odds tipping daily in their favour, *warum die Mühe mit einem Waffenstillstand?* Why bother with a truce?'

Then, just two days after Goodwood began and with Rommel still unconscious, Claus von Stauffenberg planted his bomb under the conference table at Hitler's HQ in Poland. Standing outside when it exploded, he was certain no one had survived, hurried back to Berlin and activated his plan for a military coup. Within hours, however, it was clear Hitler had survived, Stauffenberg's plot collapsed and its principals were rounded up and shot that very same night. Then followed a lengthy, brutal and far-reaching investigation aimed at rooting out anyone with the slightest connection, tendrils from which would soon reach some of Rommel's closest allies, and eventually, as Manfred so painfully described, Rommel himself.

But not until later. Meanwhile, he came home to Herrlingen on 8 August, there to spend the last two months of his life in the protective bosom of his family. As both Manfred and Gertrud recounted, he was far from well: partially blinded, suffering fits and seizures, and plagued by crippling headaches. Yet he remained cheerful and active, taking short walks, listening to them read, entertaining old friends and shakily writing up his final notes. He also took close interest in the progress of the war, lamenting the destruction of German forces in France, following the rapid advance of the western Allies, their hesitation upon reaching Belgium, and of course, most interestingly for me, their failed attempt at ending matters quickly with Operation Market Garden. One related letter in particular stands out, being from Walter Harzer, commander of 9th SS Panzer Division whom Rommel had visited the day he was injured. True to his word, Harzer had managed to slip what was left of his division from the Falaise pocket and make a hurried retreat across France to safety. By September he'd reached the Netherlands where he was told to take up positions around Arnhem 'for rest and replenishment'. Only to have 1st Airborne drop into his lap.

'We were defending the bridge which appeared to be under attack from a single battalion of Fallschirmjäger,' he writes. 'This I learned from *sources* [my italics] was the 2nd Parachute Battalion you write of. Utter insanity them coming on against a whole Panzer division, even a badly depleted one, and doomed to fail of course, but they fought with great bravery...'

Rommel's chief of staff Hans Speidel was arrested at around this time in connection with the Hitler bomb plot. This came as a great shock to Rommel and I find several copies of letters he wrote to senior officials in Berlin pleading Speidel's innocence and good character. It's not known whether these were received, or even sent, but there are no replies on file. Nor, ominously, much mention of the matter in his final diary entries, which by now are dwindling to little more than two-line comments. As if he knows what's coming.

Sept 30th Walk with Manfred. I am sure the grounds are under surveillance. This can only mean SS or SD. We both carry weapons.

Oct 7th Letter from Keitel 'inviting' me to report to Berlin for discussions about 'future employment'. This without doubt a trap and I'd never reach Berlin alive. Sent polite response enclosing report from neurologist saying 'too sick to travel'.

Oct 11th Dinner at home with Otto Streicher whom I haven't seen for many years. We talked over the old days as students together at the military academy. How much simpler life was then!

Then the final entry of all:

Oct 13th Pleasant sunshine, walking with Manfred and Gertrud. Upon return was given telephone message. Generals Burgdof and Maisel travelling to see me tomorrow at noon.

And what of Theo? Apart from the letter from the pastor at Livarot, his name crops up twice during this final part of the archive. After Arnhem, Rommel asks for and is sent a copy of the Allied casualty list from Apeldoorn hospital. I remember it well; it was the first time the injured were together under one roof and thus the first time we could record their numbers and details properly. It took all day to complete the audit. Colonel Graeme Warrack supervised; then various copies were made and distributed. One went to the Red Cross to be sent back to England, one went to the German military, another to their medical directorate, Warrack kept one for the records and so on. Every casualty's name, rank and service number was recorded. Rommel's copy, presumably a duplicate of the one sent to the medical directorate, runs to several pages; many names are on it that I recognize, including Theo's. And beside his entry Rommel has pencilled an asterisk.

The second document is the movement order Lucie brought to prison. The one transferring Theo and me to Ulm from Möglich's clutches at Stalag XIB. This is the pivotal one, the one that confirms Rommel intervened personally to get Theo here. At least that's what I assume.

'Why was he so keen for this?' I ask Gertrud when she pops in.

'It was Frau Rommel,' she replies. 'Private Trickey had saved her husband's life. Hearing he too was severely injured she wanted to do everything to repay the debt.'

'But your father had already died by the time the order came though.'

'This changed nothing. It was *their* wish. We followed it through.' She glances round at the stacks of files and boxes. 'And now you are finished?'

'Ha! I doubt I'll ever be finished. His letters alone would take a year's work.'

'Then...'

'But I've done about all I can for the moment.'

'What does that mean?'

'I can't take this archive with me, it'd fill two trunks, and anyway it's too precious, it belongs here with you and Frau Rommel and Manfred. Have you heard from him, by the way?'

'His unit's still in Riedlingen, thirty miles west of here. He makes contact when he can. We tell him to be careful and take no risks.'

'Good. My advice is pack all this up and lock it out of sight, in a cellar or attic or something, so it's hidden and safe and can't fall into the wrong hands.'

'And your notes?'

'I'll take them home.' I tap my papers, now filling some half-dozen exercise books. 'When I get to England I'll make some enquiries – you know, publishers, historians and so on, show them what I've got and see what they propose.'

'Do you think there will be, you know, sufficient interest?'

'Having seen what I have? I'm sure of it. But I'm no writer and certainly no biographer. What's needed now is professional help.'

The door squeaks open and Lucie enters, tray in hand. She too has changed immeasurably since first I saw her. Still quiet, still slight and frail and sombrely dressed, she's nevertheless a different creature from the bed-bound husk I first encountered.

'I gather this might be your final visit, Herr Doctor.'

'It's hard to know. But I have reached a pause in the research.'

'Then you will take a glass of Mosel with us. Erwin's favourite.'

She pours, we toast and I taste delicious fruity tartness, also noting a wrapped package is sitting on the tray.

'And now I want you to have something. Of his. To remember him by.'

'That's not necessary, madam, really, I—'

'We noticed you both used it. Sitting here. To see things more clearly.'

216

She hands me the package and the penny drops. I unwrap tissue paper to reveal an elegant magnifying glass of the sort used for reading, in a silver frame with bone handle. It was on his desk among his letter openers and inkwells, and it's true I had often used it, to decipher tiny print, or examine a photo.

'Well, madam, I still feel it's unnecessary but thank you…'

'Good luck, Doctor.' A small hand takes mine; her gaze is locked and steady. 'We thank you for all you have done, and wish you a healthful and prosperous peacetime.'

Sunday comes, and with it another rumour. The Russians are in Berlin. As usual there's no way to verify this but since the news comes over state radio it bears the sobering hallmark of truth. And it throws the poor people of Ulm, whose nerves are already in tatters, into even greater paroxysms of anxiety. Berlin may be four hundred miles away, but it's still the nation's capital. If the Russians have it, won't the whole country come under their rule? Won't they be free to occupy our towns and villages, appropriate our farms and businesses, ship our menfolk to labour camps, abuse and rape our women?

God knows, but as eleven o'clock nears and Erik and I head towards the minster for what's billed as a 'town meeting with service of thanksgiving', an added and unwelcome frisson of tension fills the air.

The service is fine, however, a welcome breath of calm and tradition amid all the heat and uncertainty. The old church is packed, every available pew filled with townsfolk young and old, with many more standing in the aisles. Under their somewhat unnerving gaze we're shown to the front and seated alongside all the elders and dignitaries, which doesn't seem right. There, surrounded by cassocks and gowns, I spot the Rommel family off to one side, also the acting *Bürgermeister*, Adenauer, the old police sergeant in his best uniform, and various professors from the university in cloaks and floppy hats. Then, to a clatter of pigeon wings, the organ thunders to life, everyone stands and the clergy process up the nave, led by a choirboy bearing a cross.

The service is Lutheran, thus brisk and upbeat with plenty of music and singing. Erik, having never mentioned religion once during our time together, seems well at home and joins in with gusto, while I content myself gazing up at the minster's vaulted roof and ruminating on all that's passed. There's a sermon on the suitable themes of hope and reconciliation, and then the faithful are invited to partake of the holy sacrament. I sit this out, Erik goes up, and it's while he's gone and I'm idly watching the queues file past that, to my astonishment, I spot Wilhelm Vorst.

The shock is considerable. His bare head is bowed, his hands devoutly clasped, he's wearing a nondescript suit with spotted tie, and clutching a trilby hat. He looks shorter and more rotund than normal and for a moment I think I'm mistaken, but then he inclines his head to allow someone to pass and I know it's him. Following the other communicants, he processes solemnly up, receives his share, and heads off back across the church. Dumbfounded, I watch him go. Quite apart from the gall of it, and the barefaced hypocrisy, the shock of seeing him is enough to turn the stomach.

'Vorst!' I hiss furiously at Erik when he returns.

'What?'

'He's here! Didn't you see?'

'No.' He cranes his neck. 'Where? Are you sure?'

There's nothing to be done for the moment, as other matters are pressing. Soon the service concludes with a final rousing hymn, the clergy process out and there's a pause while furniture movements happen. Then the minister returns and announces that the meeting will begin shortly, once the formalities are completed.

Erik and I exchange glances. 'Formalities?'

These, it transpires, are the surrender of the city. To us.

Earlier in the week we had been asked to come to the meeting and say a few words of reassurance, and maybe answer some questions. That's all, nothing more, and so we'd politely agreed. Now, in front of the entire congregation, we find ourselves parading before a delegation of the good and great bent on giving us the city. Adenauer is among them, wearing his chain of office, and the dean of the university, the Lutheran minister, the police sergeant, a clutch of Girl Guides, and finally the garrison elder, an ancient Great War veteran in spiked helmet and spurs, clanking with medals and hefting a lethal-looking sabre. And before we know it, various items are being solemnly presented to us, including the town seal and scroll, a folded flag, a large and heavy register, a rusty iron key, and finally the sword, which the old man draws with a flourish and lays at our feet with a damp-eyed salute.

Silence falls.

Adenauer steps forward. 'A few words would be appropriate.'

'Erik!' I nudge. 'Your German's better.'

'Oh, ah, yes.' Erik stutters. 'Yes, well, indeed, we are very, honoured, to receive these, ah, historic and important artefacts. And we wish all the people of Ulm a safe and, er, orderly transition from war to peace. Thank you.'

We turn for our seats.

'Can you say a little about that?'

'Pardon?'

Adenauer beckons us back. 'There is much uncertainty. Can you say how you will be managing the handover of power to the Allies when they arrive? And also perhaps outline the interim arrangements for services, supplies and so on.'

No we can't, and suddenly I realize what's going on. With the city on its knees, its people starving and the enemy at the gates, the city elders, such as they are, are collectively washing their hands of civic responsibility, and passing the buck to us, who have no more comfort to offer than they do.

'Now just a minute...'

'What about food!' someone calls from the pews.

'Where's the Red Cross?'

'When's the water coming on?'

'Yes, and how will you protect us when the Russians arrive!'

This last raises a murmur of alarm and soon everyone's shouting.

'Protect us! Food and water! Law and order!'

'Stop!' We raise our hands. 'Stop please!' The elders too are calling for calm but the clamour's steadily rising. 'Be calm, please sit down!' Then I hear a familiar voice.

'Tell us, *Gar-lant*!'

A slight pause in the clamour. Somewhere across the nave a figure is on his feet. 'Yes, you! Captain *Gar-lant*! Tell us precisely how you will protect the people from rioting Allies bent on bloody revenge and reprisal!'

And off they all go again, louder than ever. The noise is atrocious, the anger growing. Erik and I exchange panicked stares, and I'm on the point of considering a hasty exit by a side door when suddenly the main doors bang open at the far end and sunlight floods in.

'Hullo!' a voice bellows in English, 'I said HULLO!'

He looks like a gunslinger in a western movie. Framed in the huge doorway in his scruffy clothes and boots, his pistol on his hip, ammo belts crossed across his chest, he strides inside, staring left and right.

A respectful hush falls.

'Who's the senior person here!'

About ten people, including Erik, point at me. 'Him!'

'You?'

'Well, yes, me, I suppose.'

'And you are?'

'Garland.' I stumble to attention. 'Captain Dan Garland. The Parachute Regiment.'

'You're a Brit?'

I nod, and then by God he's saluting *me*!

'Well, Captain, I'm Lieutenant Bill Phelps, Recon Company, 324th Battalion US 44th Infantry Division.'

'Recon... um, 324th... Infantry...'

'And you, buddy, may consider yourself liberated!'

CHAPTER 12

By the time he reached Lisieux, climbing painfully from the farmer's van some four hours after the Spitfire attack, Theo knew the *Fall Grün* plan was dying in the water. The field marshal was critically injured and might not survive. Yet only he could enact the plan. Rundstedt hadn't the courage, and no field commander would act alone. In short, with no Rommel there was no *Fall Grün*. And time was running out.

He wandered into the same dressing station he'd visited with Brandt. It was busier than ever, every inch of the hotel now crammed with injured men. Spotting his captain's uniform an orderly gave him aspirin, examined his arm and asked him to wait. But after ten minutes slumped restlessly against a wall he rose and left, limping outside into the gathering dusk. Men roamed everywhere, and military vehicles sped in all directions; eventually a *Kübelwagen* full of drunken officers offered him a lift. '346th?' They joked, 'Christ, what do you want to go there for?'

They dropped him in the woods near the burned-out armoured column. It remained exactly as he'd seen it days earlier, eerily still in the darkness. Only the bodies had moved, and were buried at the roadside, all except the one in the tree, with the bare feet and arm that waved macabrely in the breeze. He left it behind, walking on towards a horizon lit by artillery flashes and drifting star shells, and some time later, with the sound of gunfire nearing, he reached the abandoned command post, still occupied by the forgotten troop of pioneer reserves.

'Where's Lieutenant Schäfer?'

'Who's Lieutenant Schäfer?' they replied blankly.

He moved on through the trees, hugging his broken chest, and as he did so the gunfire and flashes fell silent, as if on a signal, so that all he could hear suddenly were his feet in the undergrowth and his own pained gasps. Then he came to the edge of the woods, and the tree where Schäfer had stood. Below him the grey meadow led down to the shadowy hump of the bridge; beyond it the outline of Troarn stood out in the darkness. Shrugging off his uniform jacket with difficulty he hung it on the tree; then unravelling his sling, he tied it to a stick and stepped from the woods into the open. No one saw him, no shots or shouting came as he trudged steadily down the slope, flag high, then up on to the bridge itself, still debris-strewn and cratered from battle. Then halfway across he heard the sliding of a rifle bolt.

'That's close enough, Fritz laddie.'

'I'm not Fritz, I'm British.'

'Bollocks. I just watched you come from their lines.'

'I know. I escaped.'

'Ha! Deserted, more like...'

'You're Scottish. 51st Highland Division. I fought with you in 1940. My name's Trickey, I'm a Para, attached to 6th Airborne Division under General Gale. He's based in Ranville, barely five miles from here. Arrest me, take me to his HQ and—'

'Will you shut your fucking gob!'

He was escorted to a CP in Troarn where he was searched and questioned by an intelligence officer from the Black Watch. With only his identity discs for proof, it was some time – and a radio call to Ranville – before his bona fides were finally verified. In the meantime a borrowed British battledress was found, and a medic stitched his scalp wound, bound his ribs and rebandaged his arm.

'You only just got here in time.'

'Why, what's happening?'

'We're pulling back.'

'What for?'

'Can't say. And this arm will need to be reset properly.'

'Can't you get me to General Gale? It's important.'

They couldn't, all troop movements were strictly controlled, and later he was withdrawn another mile to a dressing station in Bures. Here, semi-conscious from morphia and sleeplessness, he passed the remainder of the night tossing and turning in a tent full of wounded Scotsmen, until shortly before dawn when they were all shaken awake by the sound of approaching thunder.

'What the hell's that, Sarge?'

'Sounds like engines. Hundreds of 'em.'

'Aye, laddie, that's the RA-bloody-F!'

Minutes later the first bombs were falling, the prelude to Operation Goodwood, and more than a thousand bombers were raining high explosives on the German positions all along the front. Then the Allied guns were joining in, over seven hundred medium and heavy artillery, plus supporting fire from Royal Navy ships patrolling the coast. Lying in their canvas shelter a full two miles behind the lines, the effect was still shocking, and the noise deafening as shells screamed overhead and the ground shuddered as though in spasm.

'I guess that's why they pulled everyone back last night!' one Scotsman shouted above the din. And as daylight emerged from night, the barrage could be heard beginning to move slowly forwards, as the massed troops of five infantry and armoured divisions followed in its wake – including the Highlanders.

'There go the lads.'

'Forward the 51st!'

'Christ, I wish I was with them.'

'No you don't!'

Gradually the sounds of battle moved away as Goodwood advanced. Theo fell back into exhausted slumber, roused at stages during the day to be fed and have his dressings changed. At some point a doctor came, reset his arm and swathed it in plaster of Paris. Later in the afternoon he rose stiffly from his bed and hobbled outside into hazy sunshine, there to sit beneath a tree like a sickly octogenarian. A few minutes later a Jeep roared up and Dennis Grant jumped out.

'There you are at last! Been looking for you everywhere.'

'Hello, Dennis.'

'Bloody hell, what have you done now?'

'It's nothing. I was lucky.'

'One day, Trickey, that luck of yours is going to run out!' Grant shook his head. 'And what's happening is they're sending us home.'

'When?'

'Now. Today. By air no less, the full VIP treatment. Looks like we're surplus to requirements!'

'Then, Rommel's plan…'

'It's over, Theo. Here, look, I've brought the rest of your kit.' Grant helped him to his feet and over to the Jeep.

'Was it ever, Dennis, you know, taken seriously? *Fall Grün*?'

'We have to believe so, initially at least by some of the SHAEF people. But Rommel left it too late; his negotiating position was getting weaker by the hour. Also many doubted he really could deliver a ceasefire.'

'He could. Everything was ready.'

'I suppose we'll never know. Come on, we've a plane to catch.'

They were driven a few miles north to a temporary airfield ripped from French farmland by engineers in a hurry. From there they boarded a home-going Dakota laden with walking wounded. After an untroubled flight over the glittering waters of the Channel, in no time they were crossing the English coast, and gazing down on neatly hedged fields of ripening corn.

'It all looks very peaceful,' Theo murmured.

'Don't it just. How long since you left?'

Operation Deadstick, the night of the D-Day landings, John Howard and the men of the Ox and Bucks. 'Six weeks.'

'Quite long enough.'

'Clare's in Germany.'

'Oh?'

'The Gestapo moved their prisoners out of France.'

'To where?'

'I don't know. Special camps for captured agents.'

'I'll see what I can find out.'

Theo turned to him. 'And what do I do?'

'You need to go home, Theo. I'm afraid I have sad news.'

Vic had died while Theo was in Normandy with Rommel. Although expected, his final passing had been sudden, so neither his wife and daughter nor ex-wife Carla were with him at the end. Arriving back at Kingston that night, Theo, having first been scolded by Eleni for his battered physical condition, and then fed leftovers omelette using her egg ration and powdered milk, was given all the details, learning that in accordance with directions left by Vic, the hospital had arranged his cremation at Acton crematorium, with the ashes forwarded to Theo's address in Kingston – together with the bill. And instructions for a party.

Theo reread the note. 'What kind of party?'

'Lor' knows. Vic a bloody rascal all right, but he always know how to have damn good knees-up.'

'Who would we invite?'

Eleni shrugged. 'Everyone. Vi and the little girl, you mama and Abercrumble. Vic still has a mother somewhere, I think, and a sister up Willesden Junction; maybe they know cousins and whatnot. You could ask some your friends from school too, be nice chance to catch up. We could do it here, you know, bring-a-bottle and that.'

'Vic's mother? You mean I have a grandmother I know nothing about?'

'Think so, if she still alive.'

She was, although long since remarried – Vic's father had died when he was young. She arrived at Burton Street at noon the following Saturday, a prim, bustling old woman called Mrs Balsam, who studied Theo closely before sweeping inside with a muttered: 'Nothing like him.' Then there was a half-brother to Vic from Mrs Balsam's second marriage, plus his family, then Vic's sister Joan and her family including several cousins, Vi's parents plus brother and sister, and even some of Vic's former 'business associates' who seemed to materialize out of nowhere. 'How did you know?' he asked of one at the door. The man winked. 'Jungle telegraph!'

Some of Eleni's former lodgers came; then Nancy charged in, throwing herself at Theo with a delighted shriek, and the newlyweds Susanna and Albert Fitch plus several others from his grammar-school days. Carla arrived late, and looked ill at ease surrounded by her ex-husband's relatives, but Nicholas Abercrombie proved an animated guest, cheerfully escorting her from one group to the next. Crates of beer and sherry bottles appeared, Eleni fussed about with sardine sandwiches and semolina cake, the mood became relaxed and noisy; meanwhile, Theo looked on in bemusement, hosting as best he could.

Just one attendee arrived in uniform: Henry Winterbottom, Carla's erstwhile suitor, standing awkwardly on the front step fingering his cap. 'Sorry for intruding. Mrs Popodopoulos invited me.'

'It's quite all right. Won't you come in?'

'For a minute perhaps.'

Quieter and thinner than of memory, with nervous hands and wary eyes, Winterbottom said he was now a company commander with the East Surreys 1st Battalion, and recently home from overseas.

'Your neck of the woods, Theo. Italy. Monte Cassino, do you know it?'

'No.' But he knew of the fighting. Everyone did. 'I heard it was hard.'

'Yes. And long. Four months, on and off. We finally got pulled back in June.'

'That's a long time in the line.'

'Yes, and all for some blasted monastery on a hill. Bloody mess, we lost many good men.'

'I'm sorry.'

'No, I'm sorry.' He stared around the room. 'We did you an

injustice, Theo. After what happened to you in France back in forty. The regiment did.'

'The regiment?'

'Well, me then. And the colonel. Discharging you like that. That's why I'm here. To apologize.'

'There's no need.'

'There is, now I know something of what you've been through.' He produced an envelope. 'And your father did serve with the regiment. Briefly. As a private in the first war. I found his record.'

'Thank you.'

'It's rather short.' Winterbottom smiled. 'And not terribly, you know, edifying.'

'I can imagine.'

'He certainly had a nose for trouble!'

'Yes, he did. Speaking of which, have you met my mother's new husband?'

He handed him over to Abercrombie, busy entertaining Mrs Balsam, then went in search of Carla, who was in the kitchen quizzing one of Vic's prison friends.

'So you knew Victor was alive?' she was saying.

'Ah, well, yes, but, you see…'

'And not dead in skiing accident.'

'No. That's to say…'

'And yet you agree not to tell anyone.'

'Well, he made us swear, didn't he?'

'His landlady for instance. Or even his wife.'

'Er, yes, true, but—'

'Excuse me.' Theo smiled. 'Mama, may I speak with you?'

She allowed him to lead her aside. 'Incredible,' she muttered, 'these crooks and liars, not one with the courage to speak honestly.'

'No. Although we went over this with Father, in the hospital, remember?'

She studied him. 'Theodor dearest, you look so thin, and what happened with all these plaster and bandages!'

'I was in a traffic accident, Mama. It's nothing. Tell me, is everything well with you? How is Nicholas? And your work with PPS?'

She shrugged. 'All is as well as possible. Nicholas is a fine man, generous and kind, I'm very lucky.'

'I'm happy for you. And the Party?'

'The Party' – Carla sighed – 'is like an adolescent child, Theo. It grows bigger every week, and stronger and louder and more argumentative. Conflicted too, and riven by inner turmoil.'

'What turmoil?'

Factions, she explained. Since the fall of Mussolini, South Tyrol now came under OZAF governance – the Operational Zone of the Alpine Foothills. Superficially part of his puppet administration, in reality OZAF was entirely controlled by the Germans, who knew South Tyrol's strategic importance as a last line of defence. But not content with simply controlling the province, they also secretly wanted ownership of it, and so had begun reversing the Italianization programme instituted by Mussolini and Tolomei before the war.

'But isn't that good?'

'Changing a few road signs to German? Allowing Ladin to be spoken? Swapping Italian flags for Nazi ones? It's not independence, Theodor, it's oppression – worse oppression than before, if you ask me. Though many of my colleagues disagree.'

Partito Popolare Sudtirolese was split on the issue, she went on. Some in the party believed German rule was a significant improvement, others like Carla saw it as a backward step. Although one development was undoubtedly welcome.

'Your grandfather is to be released, Theodor. As an inducement by the Germans, you know, sweeten the people by releasing Tolomei's political prisoners.'

'Grandpa Josef? But that's marvellous! When?'

'Soon. Any day.'

'Will he come here?'

'Ha! I doubt it. You know your grandfather, he'll go straight back to Bolzano and make trouble!'

'I expect he will.' Theo nodded. 'And what about you, Mama? Will you go back too? After the war. With Nicholas.'

Her gaze flickered. 'He asks me the same question, you know. Once I knew the answer; now I'm not so sure. I feel I have a home here, and a job and purpose.'

'And a husband. A good one.'

'Yes.' She nodded. 'He is good.'

'I'm glad.'

'And you?' She brushed his cheek. 'Do you feel you have a home here?'

He squeezed her hand. 'I'm not sure I have a home anywhere.'

He spent a month in Kingston, resting, recuperating and building up his strength under Eleni's relentless feeding regime. Before he knew it she had him running errands and helping around the boarding house like days of yore. In his off-duty hours he scanned the newspapers for news of the Allied advance across France. One day he read a story about the liberation of Saint-Valery-en-Caux, and how Monty had insisted the men of 51st Highland Division were first into town, where they found cheering French people waving the blue and white flag of St Andrew. The next day, and in the unsettling absence of messages, orders or instructions, he rose early from bed, donned his borrowed battledress and caught the train to Lincolnshire. Arriving in Grantham he joined the queue for military buses, boarded one for Stoke Rochford and by lunchtime was back with his regiment.

'Hello.' A dark-haired officer he'd not seen before greeted him at 2nd Battalion's offices. 'And you are?'

'Private Trickey, sir. I was on Colonel Frost's staff, then got detached—'

'—to 6th Airborne, for the Caen bridge mission, yes, I heard!'

'You did?'

'Major David Wallis.' The officer rose. 'I'm Frost's new second-in-command. Very pleased to meet you.'

'You too, sir.'

'Your arm's in plaster.'

'It's nothing, a car accident. Another fortnight the doctor says, then it can come off. Is the colonel here?'

'He's at a brigade briefing.'

'Oh. I met Major Tatham-Warter last time...'

'Digby? He's there too, and Vic Dover and Doug Crawley, all three company commanders. Another week, another operation! They come and go so fast we can barely keep up.'

'What sort of operations?'

'Mostly dropping ahead of 2nd Army as it charges across France. Knocking out enemy defences, securing roads and bridges, the usual. Trouble is they're advancing so fast, by the time we're primed and ready they've already moved on.'

'Have there been many?'

'At least a dozen by my counting. Frankly it's driving the boys mad. Here we are, back to full strength at last, fit, trained and raring to go. Every week we come to readiness, get briefed, get packed and loaded, only to be stood down at the last minute. It's not good for the nerves. Or morale.'

'Sir, I need to report for duty. If the battalion will have me.'

'*Have* you?' Wallis looked surprised. 'For God's sake, you're one of the originals. You've been on every op this battalion's ever done. Of course we'll have you!'

'Thank—'

'But not with your arm in plaster.'

He was to go home, Wallis ordered, work on his personal fitness, lose the plaster, regain the strength of his arm and await orders.

'What if something happens?'

'Then we'll call you in, *if* it actually happens.'

'I see.'

'You'd want your old role, I presume. On the colonel's intelligence staff?'

'Yes.'

'As a combatant?' Wallis shuffled papers.

'I...'

'It's all right. Frost told me. And I do understand. But we need to know.'

Theo studied the floor. *It's time for the madness to end,* Rommel had said. *Before it kills us all.*

'We have to get this over with. That's all that matters now.'

'Agreed. Now go home, get fit and make ready. We'll be in touch soon enough.'

But it was four weeks, and another four cancelled missions, before he finally got the call.

CHAPTER 13

Sunday 17 September dawned clear, sunny and windless, perfect conditions for a massed parachute drop. Embarkation was set for ten in the morning; 2nd Battalion's buses began arriving at Saltby Aerodrome soon after nine. Theo's stick gathered beside their Dakota, smoking, chatting, studiously feigning the nonchalance none of them felt. Around the aerodrome, hundreds more were making ready, with yet more thousands assembling at other airfields all over eastern England. Always the worst time, Theo recalled, sensing the familiar hollowness in his stomach. Once aboard and airborne, Paras turn from passive passengers to eager soldiers and the nerves melt like the mist. But the waiting, the dallying about like overladen pack animals, so burdened you can't even stand properly, but only stoop, crack bad jokes, share a last smoke, and yearn for the order to emplane, that was the worst.

And yet he felt ready, calmer and more prepared than he could remember before any operation. Dressing himself that morning, performing the ritual of packing his kit and strapping it to his body, had felt natural and reassuring, like donning long-forgotten armour. After a wash, he began with a new battledress straight from stores, in the rank of private, no officer's stripes but with parachute wings on one arm, Airborne patch on the other, and 2nd Battalion's yellow lanyard looped around his shoulder. 'Army boots are cack!' someone once told him, so below his gaitered ankles he wore the battered but comfortable desert boots he'd bought off the LRDG in Gabès. Then on his head he positioned his red beret, the one issued for the Caen bridge mission. By now it felt well worn and familiar, and checking in the mirror he'd seen the half-smile on the face in the glass and found himself coming to attention, and saluting, as though to an old comrade. Then he'd returned to his kitbag, carefully packing everything needed for the mission. Forty-eight hours' food rations, including the dried fruit and biscuits secreted by Eleni. A full change of clothes, then his mess kit and mug, cooking and eating utensils, wash kit, medical kit, sewing kit, gas mask, gloves, waterproof cape, scrim scarf, compass, map folder, message pads and finally his blanket. Pressing them down, he tightened the drawstring and hefted the bag to his shoulder, finding it heavy but manageable – far more so than the overstuffed sacks many men burdened themselves with. For the drop it would dangle from his waist by a twenty-foot line. Some kitbags were so heavy they broke their lines and crashed to the ground, endangering other jumpers and scattering their contents like litter. Double-checking the knot on his, next he donned his webbing: canvas belts and straps criss-crossed over his body with sacks and pouches crammed with arms and equipment. Sten-gun clips, pistol ammunition, .303 rifle ammunition, grenades, flares, sheathed bayonet and the German binoculars he'd bought in Algiers. Hanging outside the webbing was his steel helmet, entrenching tool, Sten-gun stock, toggled rope and water bottle, while strapped to his thigh was a Fairbairn Sykes dagger, not just a fearsome weapon but a cutting tool if he landed in trees or had to hack through wire or undergrowth. The Denison jumping smock came next, green and brown camouflage, long and baggy; he shrugged it over everything, fastening it securely with zips, fasteners and the tail between his legs so that when he jumped nothing inside could foul the parachute. Next came the parachute harness, thick webbing straps passing around the shoulders and between the legs to join at the four-point release mechanism on his chest. The parachute itself would be issued at the airfield. Last of all came his weaponry. Looped through the harness on his chest was a Mark 5 Sten gun with the stock removed for the jump: light, compact and quick to get at. And holstered inside the smock, high against his chest, was a Webley service revolver. The Sten, the ammunition boxes and clips, the grenades and flares were for adding to battalion stocks after the drop. The Webley, as a compromise, was his.

One final item remained. His sole personal effect, Clare's letter, the one given to him at Grant's office by Vera Atkins. The one asking him to look for her. Rereading it one last time, he folded it carefully into his battledress pocket and clumped outside to await the bus.

Shouted orders and blown whistles sounded, and with that emplaning finally began. With his parachute now attached and his kitbag strapped to his leg, he queued up with the others of his stick, twenty men in all, flying in Major Wallis's Dakota as a duplicate command team of officers, senior NCOs, signals, medical and intelligence staff, ready to take charge of the battalion should anything happen to Colonel Frost's stick. Theo knew none of them except Wallis – and Padre Egan, who waved at him cheerily from across the fuselage. Soon they were all seated and strapped; the engines whined and coughed to life, then rose to a rumble as the Dakota bumped round the perimeter for take-off. Pausing only briefly, the rumble rose swiftly to a roar, everything shook, the brakes were released and the Dakota set off, slowly at first, then quicker, the tail rising, the wheels bouncing until with a final thump the shaking stopped and the machine laboured into the air. Craning his neck to a window, Theo glimpsed dozens, scores, seemingly hundreds of other aircraft, more than he'd ever seen, many towing gliders, circling near and far, clawing up into the clear Lincolnshire sky like flocking crows. Then as he watched, and as if on signal, the circling stopped, they rolled their wings level and set out on course for the target.

Which he knew little of, except that it was a bridge over a river in a town in Holland called Arnhem. Like Primosole, like Caen, the bridge itself was of secondary interest; what mattered was that the river it crossed was the Rhine, forty miles behind enemy lines, and less than a dozen from Germany. 1st Airborne Division, some eight parachute battalions, plus a Polish brigade and sundry engineering, reconnaissance, field artillery and field ambulance battalions were to land there in the biggest airborne operation ever mounted, then take and hold the bridge. Two American airborne divisions, meanwhile, were to land and take bridges further south, all so that Monty's 2nd Army, led by the tanks of 30 Corps, could charge up the road from Belgium, cross the Rhine at Arnhem, sweep into Germany and end the war.

And Theo intended being there when they did. He settled lower in his seat, his kitbag between his knees. Around him the men of Wallis's stick dozed or smoked, checked weapons, chewed NAAFI sandwiches and read the newspapers. Beside the gaping door Wallis studied maps, while across from him Padre Egan thumbed a paperback. Through the windows Dakotas were visible in all directions, near and far, silently rising and falling as though suspended on threads. Here and there flew their escorts, nimble Spitfires and Mustangs darting in and out like nervous sheepdogs. Yet all remained peaceful: the air warm, the sky clear, devoid of enemy flak or fighters, the sea below smooth and calm. Soon the yellow strip of the enemy coast was passing beneath, then an endless patchwork of dykes and fields, many of them flooded and glinting like mirrors. Twenty minutes more and the dispatcher appeared from the cockpit, casually holding up ten fingers, and without ado everyone rose and made ready: fussing with kitbags, helmets and harnesses, weapons and static lines, checking their own, checking the man in front's, feeling the tension mount as they shuffled towards the waiting doorway. Above it the red light glowed, while Wallis, helmet buckled, thrust his head into the buffeting gale. More taut waiting, then Theo glimpsed lines of parachutes sprouting above a plain of brown scrub and suddenly the green light flashed and Wallis was gone, followed by Egan, then the others hobbling hurriedly rearwards and out. Theo reached the door, clasped his arms across his chest and jumped, feeling the battering slipstream, the anxious tumble, and the blessed jerk and bounce of the canopy as it opened. Swinging wildly he looked up, tugging shrouds, and saw more parachutes than he could have imagined, clouds of them drifting thickly down like blossom, while the trumpeting of engines sounded overhead. Then the ground was rising and only seconds remained: he freed his lanyard, lowering his kitbag, smelled grass, heard shouts and glimpsed smoke, tussocky gorse rushed up, he swung forward, checked, tucked and with a crash was down.

Lying stunned on his back, he blinked up at the drifting blossom, then heard a different trumpet sound – the boisterous toot of a hunting horn. He raised his head, saw distant yellow smoke and knew his colonel was down. Banging the parachute release, he freed himself from the tangle of lines, hoisted his kitbag to his shoulder and set off, arriving at the rendezvous to find 2nd Battalion already busy gathering. Jeeps and Bren carriers, many towing trailers, drove up from the glider sites; motorcycles revved; bicycles were unfolded; men called out raucously to one another, pushing trolleys laden with weapons and equipment. It reminded him of exercises on Dartmoor: jokes and banter, everyone bustling, everyone knowing his job, while the sections, platoons and companies formed up like magic. Best of all there was no gunfire, no shelling, in fact no sign of the enemy at all – even though an entire division had just landed on its doorstep.

Half a division. Divesting himself of kitbag, stores, weapons and ammunition, he sought out Frost, finding him in a woodland CP, deep in conference over the bonnet of his Jeep. Wallis was there, so too the other company commanders, all poring over a map of Arnhem. Frost acknowledged him with a nod and went on with the briefing, from which Theo soon learned that Operation Market Garden, as it was called, might not be unfolding quite as originally envisaged.

'... so half stays behind here,' Frost was saying, 'to guard the DZ until the rest of the division gets here tomorrow.'

'Leaving what to attack the bridge with?' Wallis asked.

'Us. The three battalions of 1st Para Brigade. Plus some odds and sods.'

'But I thought everyone was arriving today.'

'That was the plan, but apparently there aren't enough pilots, or Dakotas, to lift the whole division in one go.'

'So we've only half a division, and half of *them* have to stay here.'

'Correct. Now—'

'Trickey!' Another Jeep roared up, the familiar figure of Brigadier Gerald Lathbury at the wheel. 'My God, it is you, isn't it?'

'Yes, sir, it's me.'

'Then we're saved!' Lathbury joked, jumping out. 'Last seen on that blasted bridge in Sicily. What a fiasco that was. Let's hope we don't need any battleships to rescue us this time. Johnny, there you are. Are we all set?'

'All set, sir.'

'Excellent, let's hear it.'

The three battalions of Lathbury's brigade were to advance on Arnhem, then continue through it to the bridge, which was some eight miles east of their present position. This long march was unfortunate, as it gave the enemy ample time to observe and respond, but the planners had insisted there was no alternative. So 1st and 3rd Battalions would take separate routes through the town centre, while 2nd Battalion followed the course of the river. Frost's orders were to advance swiftly to a railway bridge downstream from the road bridge, seize it, send a company across to the southern bank, then advance on the road bridge, taking it from both ends at once by *coup de main*. They were then to hold it until the other two battalions arrived. Speed was crucial, while opposition was expected to be light.

'Old men and boys, so we're told,' Lathbury said. 'But you never know, so for God's sake—' He broke off as shooting rang out across the drop zone. 'Sounds like they're waking up at last.' He grinned. 'Right, Johnny, off you go. I'll be following with Brigade HQ. Keep in touch on the radios, and move as fast as you can – we need that bridge secured before nightfall.'

'Yes, sir. Do we know when 30 Corps might arrive there?'

'Any time from noon tomorrow, apparently.'

And with that 2nd Battalion moved off. The time was 3.00 p.m.

From the DZ, they followed sandy woodland tracks for three miles, passing the occasional curious onlooker and scattered farms and houses from which enthusiastic Dutch people emerged cheering and waving flags. Theo spoke to a few who confirmed Germans were in the vicinity, but in unknown strength. Advancing in battalion order, he stayed in mid column among Frost's HQ Company, while Frost himself hurried back and forth in his Jeep. To his frustration the new portable walkie-talkie radios didn't seem to be working, so keeping tabs on his column meant old-fashioned legwork. And soon that column was spreading out over a mile or more as the lightly equipped A Company, led by Digby Tatham-Warter, scouted on ahead, leaving the rest to follow at a more measured pace. Digby's company were well-known 'thrusters' – nothing seemed to slow them – and twice early on Theo heard bursts of shooting up ahead, only to pass dead Germans at the roadside a while later. Apart from these, and some sporadic shooting further off, opposition still seemed light and the battalion made good progress.

For about another mile. As woody countryside gave way to Arnhem's western suburbs, the battalion entered the town of Oosterbeek, passing rows of trim houses with tidy gardens and picket fences. More locals hurried out to greet them, younger ones running alongside excitedly, the more elderly reaching out to clasp their hands. Several joined the column on bicycles, somewhat to Frost's consternation. Then he came to a crossroads with shops and a hotel called the Schoonoord where he turned the battalion to descend towards the river, now occasionally visible through trees to their right. Dappled sunlight bathed them in warmth; the smell was of dog rose and river meadow. Passing an old stone church, the trees thinned suddenly and the railway bridge hove into view, half a mile away across open fields. Sizing up the situation, Frost called a halt to regroup his battalion.

'Go and fetch Vic Dover,' he murmured to Theo, squinting through binoculars.

A few minutes later C Company's commander arrived.

'It's awfully open, Vic.'

'So it appears.'

'Can't see any sign of Jerry this side of the river, and the other side's too far to tell. Think you can manage it?'

'We'll be careful.'

'Good.' He pulled out a map. 'I'd stay and offer support, but time's short and we must crack on for the road bridge. All being well we'll meet in the middle of it in a couple of hours. If you can't get across here, then make your way to Brigade HQ which is earmarked for this building here, just north of the road bridge, and we'll rendezvous there. Clear?'

'Clear.'

'Good luck.' They saluted and Dover left.

'Theo.' Frost cupped his eyes to the setting sun. 'I hate to leave C Company like this, especially without proper radio contact, but we've only a couple of hours' daylight left and must get on. So I want you to stay here, observe what happens then catch up and report.'

'Yes, sir.'

'And be careful.' Frost folded his map. 'Something about this feels all wrong.'

As the battalion moved off, Theo waited, watching through his binoculars as C Company began its approach to the rail bridge. Still mostly comprised of Scotsmen, he couldn't help but recall its advance on the airfield at Depienne nearly two years previously. This time there were no bagpipes and no brazen marching; stealth was needed, and extreme caution, for with no cover save the occasional hedge or ditch, their progress was worryingly easy to follow. Worse still, to gain the railway itself required climbing a steep embankment, atop which there was no cover at all. Breath held, he saw Dover lead them steadily forward, then pause in a ditch short of the embankment, before sending one platoon ahead to reconnoitre. All went well as they scrambled up, but the moment they reached the top long bursts of machine-gun fire opened up from across the river, flinging a hail of bullets and lethal stone shards in all directions, injuring two men and sending the rest scurrying for cover. C Company immediately replied, furiously firing Vickers, Bren and two-inch mortar shells across the river, while laying down a smokescreen with grenades. As the smoke thickened the shooting stopped, and the recce platoon tried again, swiftly deploying up the embankment and along the rail tracks towards the bridge. Through the smoke Theo glimpsed tiny figures darting forward, using the girders for cover, until they gained the main structure itself. Then, just as they were setting out to cross it, a monstrous flash lit the sky, explosions boomed out like thunder and the entire bridge disappeared into clouds of black smoke. He fumbled his glasses, peering in disbelief as, to the tortured screech of twisting steel, the whole central span broke free and sank into the wide waters of the Rhine.

'One man dead, sir, four injured and two missing,' he reported breathlessly to Frost an hour later. 'And the bridge is completely out.'

'We heard the explosion. Where's Dover now?'

'Making for the town centre as ordered. He had to retrace his steps to the church at Oosterbeek. He's now trying to enter by one of the main roads.'

'And that won't be easy, judging from the shooting back there.'

'No, sir. And there's more. Major Dover and I met one of Brigadier Lathbury's runners while C Company was regrouping. He told us that 1st Battalion's making little headway against growing opposition, 3rd Battalion is being attacked from the rear and has laagered for the night, Brigadier Lathbury's held up with them, and no one's heard anything from Division.'

'No General Urquhart?'

'He hasn't been seen, and can't be reached.' Theo hesitated. 'Apparently their radios aren't working either.'

'Christ, what a cock-up. And we're not doing much better here.'

Still a mile short of their objective, 2nd Battalion, minus Dover's C Company, was pinned down at a bottleneck between the railway and the river. Sniper fire, mortars and machine guns were increasingly in evidence on high ground to their left, which provided a commanding field of fire for an enemy growing stronger by the minute. While the rest of the battalion sought cover where it could, the ever resourceful A Company was doing its best to mouse-hole a way forward through alleys, houses and gardens. Meanwhile, the light was fading.

'Might that not favour us?' Theo offered.

'As so often in the past, you mean.' Frost smiled. 'Let's hope so.'

Sure enough, as full darkness descended, the sniping died down. At the same time Digby's A Company reported a breakthrough, and the column began moving again. Advancing in silent order, they stole the final mile unseen, swiftly filing along narrow streets of tall houses, keeping to the shadows, pausing in doorways and ducking behind walls, until suddenly a towering semi-circle of steel loomed out of the night above them. 2nd Battalion had reached the bridge.

Frost wasted no time. The bridge was accessed via an approach road rising from the town on concrete columns. Deploying teams beneath and beside this ramp, he hurried back along it, noting that vehicles and cyclists still occasionally crossed over, suggesting 2nd Battalion's arrival was undetected. Positioning the rest of his men in buildings surrounding the approach, he selected a tall house with windows and balcony overlooking it, knocked on the door and politely requisitioned it from its bewildered owner. Battalion HQ was soon up and running, with men posted at every window, the roof and balcony set up as observation posts, and a mass of weapons, ammunition and stores swiftly manhandled upstairs. A bedroom was appropriated for a command post and Theo found himself setting up trestles and draping lengths of aerial out of the window in the hope of getting the radios to work. Brigade HQ arrived – albeit without Lathbury, who was stuck with 3rd Battalion – and moved into a building nearby, also sundry Reconnaissance Squadron, Royal Engineer, Royal Artillery and Service Corps units, who were all swiftly dragooned into service and deployed around the perimeter with the rest. With that, 'Bridge Force' was in place, the northern end of Arnhem road bridge secured, and barely a shot fired. The time was 10 p.m.; a while later Theo attended a rooftop conference at Frost's HQ.

Digby Tatham-Warter was adamant that A Company be allowed to attack the southern end of the bridge right away. Frost was tempted, but cautious. His plan was to send Doug Crawley's B Company back along the riverbank to where an old pontoon bridge was supposed to lie, send them across it under cover of darkness, then take the southern end from both directions at once.

'But that'll take hours!' Digby protested, waving his umbrella. 'Right now we've the element of surprise. I mean, Jerry doesn't even know we're here!'

'And we don't know what Jerry's got over there! Could be a few Home Guard on bicycles, or it could be half an armoured brigade!'

In the end a compromise was reached. The length and curvature of the bridge meant the German end couldn't be seen, but also meant a few men might advance unobserved to reconnoitre the situation. If it looked promising, a full-scale attack could then be organized. Meanwhile, B Company was despatched to investigate the pontoon bridge. Only one detail remained.

'Keep a close eye on *that*, Digby.' Frost pointed at the bridge. Squatting at the nearer end was a concrete pillbox, complete with camouflage paint and slit windows.

Digby studied it. 'Looks unmanned to me.'

He was wrong. Barely had his patrol gained the ramp when machine guns opened up from the pillbox, tearing into the road, injuring two men and sending the rest hurrying back. Cursing, Digby waited thirty minutes and then sent a two-man flame-thrower team up via an iron stairwell. Frost's party watched from the roof as the pair stole up on to the bridge, then ignited the thrower, spraying arcs of molten flame at the pillbox, to the audible cries of its occupants. But they also set fire to a wooden hut behind it which suddenly and spectacularly exploded, bathing the entire scene with yellow light. Fireworks followed as bullets, grenades and mortar shells blew up, flinging lead and shrapnel in all directions.

'They've hit a bloody ammo dump,' Frost said, his face lit by the glare. 'That'll shake things up all right.'

Theo pointed. 'What's that coming across the bridge?'

Four lorries packed with German troops were lumbering slowly over the rise.

'What are they doing?' Wallis said.

'Perhaps they don't realize we're here.'

'Then they're about to find out.'

It was quickly over. Illuminated by the blazing ammunition store, the lorries made ponderous and unmissable targets, and before even reaching halfway were engulfed in a storm of gunfire and flung grenades from the Paras. The drivers, panicking, had no time to accelerate, no space to turn and no chance to reverse their vehicles, and, trapped in the maelstrom, they were destroyed where they stood. Not one man made it across the bridge; only a few managed to scramble back into cover. Within minutes all that remained were four blazing wrecks and a dismal litter of dead and dying men.

'Think they got the message?' Digby said above the crackle of flames.

'Yes, the bloody idiots,' Wallis replied.

But Frost was scowling. 'Far too much ammunition expended. At this rate we'll run out in hours. See the word gets round.'

And with that he clumped inside. A few minutes later he stood Bridge Force down for the night. The men had achieved much in the ten hours since landing, and enough was enough. Despite unforeseen difficulties and a dire shortage of manpower, they'd advanced eight miles through enemy territory, reached, taken and secured their objective, and already repelled an attack on it. All without serious loss. But with no news from B Company at the pontoon, nor from the still-missing C Company, he didn't want to push his luck. What he wanted was everyone settled, fed and rested ready for whatever the morrow might bring.

Theo spent the night in the ops bedroom, dozing on the floor while radio operators tried in vain to make contact with the outside world. Apart from occasional bursts of shooting and the popping of flares and star shells overhead, all remained quiet and he was able to snatch sleep. Then at dawn he was shaken awake.

'Trickey, the colonel wants you.'

Hurriedly donning boots and beret he clattered downstairs past the humped shapes of sleeping Paras to the basement, where he found a stony-faced Frost glaring at two German prisoners.

'Patrol caught these two snooping about the perimeter,' Frost murmured. 'Surly buggers too – they put up quite a fight. And take a look at the uniforms, Theo, that's not Home Guard or Hitler Youth. That's SS. So find out what the hell they're doing here in Arnhem.'

It took a while. Both men had taken a bruising from their captors and were hostile and reluctant to converse, even with a German speaker. But then one, as he'd learned with the SS, couldn't resist bragging.

'You stupid Tommy fools!' he spat contemptuously. 'You have no idea who you're dealing with!'

'So tell me.'

'9th SS Panzer! And we're going to wipe the floor with you!'

'9th...' Theo could barely hide his shock. 'No, you're lying, 9th SS was caught at Falaise. Everyone knows that.'

'A few of us maybe, but most got away, thanks to the *Oberführer.*'

Harzer. Piercing blue eyes scrutinizing him in Rommel's car. *Good luck,* he'd said, before walking away. Now he was here, in Arnhem, with a whole battle-hardened Panzer division, where no such force was supposed to be.

'So much for boys and old men,' Frost sighed when Theo reported.

'They said they were pulled back here after France. To rest and re-equip. It's just bad luck they were still here when we arrived.'

'I'll say! And since we can't raise anyone on the radio, we must assume nobody else knows.'

'Would it change anything if they did?'

'Christ knows.' Frost shook his head. 'And you say you've met him. This Colonel Harzer.'

'Just once, sir, briefly.'

'What's he like?'

'He seemed very competent, and, well, sure of himself. Determined.'

A while later the day's first attack began.

To everyone's surprise it came from the town, not the bridge, a column of men and vehicles nosing its way warily up the road, as if unsure what it might find. What it found was half of 2nd Battalion, plus several brigade and support elements who had made it during the night, in all some five hundred men, well placed, well concealed and, for the moment, well armed and supplied. All were under strict instructions to stay hidden and hold fire until ordered. Crouching at the ops room window, Theo watched through his binoculars as the convoy drew near, while Frost's section waited above on the roof. A tense minute passed. Down in the road all was quiet save for boots crunching on cobbles, the jangle of kit and the grumble of motors as the Germans crept onward. Then came the blast on the hunting horn and a torrent of shouting.

'FIRE! Open fire! Shoot shoot shoot!'

Gunfire erupted like thunder, a withering hail of lead streaming at the Germans from all directions: rooftops, windows, doorways, behind walls and barricades, and upwards from foxholes in the ground. Rifles and Stens, Brens and Vickers, pistols, grenades, even the flame-thrower put in an appearance. The barrage was merciless, the crossfire deadly; with no cover and no chance to retaliate, the advance was swiftly routed, the besieged Germans throwing their engines into reverse and sprinting back for safety. A minute more and it was over, and the scene fell into an uneasy, smoke-drifting silence of burning vehicles and groaning victims, scattered about the road like dolls.

Then, as so often before, the jubilant Paras fell quiet and khaki-clad men wearing red cross armbands appeared among the casualties, kneeling beside them, tending and treating, and loading them on stretchers to carry them away.

The debrief was far from celebratory.

'Too much ammo expended,' Wallis declared. 'Again.'

'More to the point,' Digby demanded, 'where the hell did they come from?'

'North's my guess. Or west.'

'West? Then they're between us and Division!'

'And between us and C Company, don't forget.'

'Could you see anything, Theo?' Frost asked quietly.

'Not really, sir, although they seemed to pull out to the north.'

'Indeed. So my guess is, that was Harzer's way of sounding us out. Which means he'll be back, and in strength.'

But the next encounter was not from the town. A lull followed during which defences were fortified, and food and ammunition distributed. Morale was high, with coarse jokes and ribald shouts echoing round the perimeter, further boosted by the return of B Company, or half of it, from its abortive pontoon expedition. Whistles and insults welcomed them into the fold; then a triumphant yell was heard from a lookout.

'30 Corps! Look, 30 Corps is coming!'

All turned towards the bridge. Still obscured by smoke drifting from the night's burned-out lorries, at first nothing was seen. Then, picking its way carefully through the wreckage, emerged the squat profile of a Humber armoured car, closely followed by several others, including an armoured Bren carrier. Cheers rang out and berets flew; some men even ran out to greet the arrivals. Then they saw the black crosses on the trucks, and the grey uniforms of their occupants, and the Humber turned into a Daimler and the Bren carrier began shooting at everyone. The Paras dived for cover, yet even as they snatched up their weapons the leading vehicles accelerated down the ramp and sped away into town. Six disappeared unscathed in this way, including the Bren carrier or *Panzerkampfwagen* as it really was. Only the two rearmost trucks were caught and angrily despatched, adding their burned-out shells to the accumulating wreckage on the road.

'What was that about?' someone asked sheepishly.

'Who knows? Fucking tossers.'

Noon came and went, and with it another lull, which waned steadily as German infantry began closing in from the town. Squatting in the ops room, Theo allowed himself some of Eleni's fruit and biscuits, chewing methodically as the first mortars began thumping in, randomly at first, then more accurately as the gunners found range. Soon they were smashing walls and punching through roofs, pocking the perimeter's streets and alleyways with craters. Casualties inevitably followed: a Vickers section was killed by direct hit, two more men by a falling wall, several others wounded by flying shrapnel. Then the sniping began, and the casualties quickly mounted. Stealthily infiltrating nearby buildings, the Germans began picking off men where they stood, firing from a window and then swiftly moving to fire from another. The Paras replied, shooting back as best they could, but by late afternoon, with ammunition dwindling and opposition mounting, the perimeter had begun to shrink, and moving about in the open became a lethal lottery. Digby's A Company caught the brunt; holed up beneath the bridge with only a few houses for cover, they were repeatedly beset, and being furthest from the aid post had to manage their wounded too. Time and again Digby was seen scurrying between positions, his umbrella up, offering comfort and encouragement to his men.

'That brolly won't do you much good!' one joked as he arrived.

'But what if it rains?' he replied in all seriousness.

And despite the deteriorating situation, the shortages and the casualties, the Paras remained cheerful and steadfast, drawing on inbuilt reserves of strength and doggedness as so often before. Aggressive too – any enemy foolish enough to show himself or venture too close was ruthlessly despatched. And should they approach the bridge, or worse still attempt to gain it, the response was furious and deadly.

At dusk Frost made a tour of the perimeter, hurrying between positions checking his men and supplies. He found them in good spirits but low on supplies. Then he visited Brigade headquarters for a situation update, before returning to his own HQ to brief his team.

'Brigade managed to raise 30 Corps on the radio,' he began encouragingly.

Murmurs of approval. 'So where are they?'

'Held up south of Nijmegen, so it'll be another twenty-four hours at least before leading elements get here.'

'Ah.' Doug Crawley nodded. 'And, er, Division?'

Frost shook his head. 'Buggers' muddle. And General Urquhart's still missing.'

The second drop had taken place that afternoon, he explained, as planned, but late due to fog in England. However, it had immediately run into opposition on the DZ, and now its three battalions – 10th, 11th and 156th – were struggling to fight their way into town. All three were currently stalled for the night with several miles still to go.

'So we won't be seeing *them* for a while,' Wallis murmured. 'What about 1st and 3rd Battalions. Any word?'

'Having quite a time of it apparently. 9th SS Panzer, as we feared, seems to have driven a wedge between them and us. 9th Panzer also controls the high ground north of town, and have begun moving in armour and heavy artillery, including 88s. And tanks.'

'How tedious of them.' Digby tutted. 'But what of our missing chaps? C Company I mean, and the other half of Doug's B Company?'

'I don't know.' Frost's gaze flicked to Theo. 'But I need to.'

'I'll go.'

'I was hoping you would.' Frost turned to Wallis. 'There's more, David. Lathbury's been injured. I don't have the details but he's out of the picture. Brigade is being commanded by a Major Hibbert, fine chap, but with no Urquhart or Lathbury he feels out of his depth. And he feels as senior officer I should take over.'

'Good idea.'

'Which means you're in command of 2nd Battalion. Feel you can manage?'

'Absolutely, sir, without a doubt.'

CHAPTER 14

Theo waited until full darkness before setting out, by which time the worst of the shooting was dying down. Occasional bursts still rang out and several vehicles and buildings still burned, illuminating anyone caught in the open, so speed and stealth were essential for a safe getaway. Lightly encumbered for ease of movement, he timed his moment, ducked from cover and sprinted away into the shadows.

His orders were firstly to search for the remains of Crawley's B Company, cut off during fighting at the pontoon bridge, secondly find out about C Company, missing now for over twenty-four hours, and thirdly get word out that 2nd Battalion was alone at the bridge and badly in need of assistance. Anything else he might learn, concerning supplies or reinforcements for instance, or the whereabouts of 1st and 3rd Battalions, or indeed anyone from 1st Airborne Division, would, Frost said, be much appreciated.

But in contrast to a relatively clear picture at the bridge, the situation in town was confused and fluid. Small-arms fire crackled in all directions, occasionally accompanied by the rattle of machine guns and crump of heavier weapons. Many fires burned, filling the air with drifting smoke, discarded vehicles and equipment cluttered streets, and bodies too lay abandoned, both British and German. Heading westward, he made for the river, trying to retrace the battalion's route in, but the enemy's presence here was heavy, with armed patrols, snipers on roofs, street-corner gun emplacements and armoured vehicles roaming. Twice he heard boots marching on cobbles and had to dart away to avoid a passing patrol. Soon he became confused about his direction; he was lost. Pausing to check bearings in a doorway, he pulled out his compass, then started in shock as a hand gripped his arm.

'Not this way!' a shadowy figure hissed.

'I... What?'

'Too many *Mof*!'

'Mof...'

'Yes, Mof! Boche, Jerry, Kraut. You must go north.'

'North? But what about the river?'

'Mof everywhere there. Patrol boats too with machine guns and searchlights. Go north a quarter-mile. Find big church then go to Bakkerstraat, you find many British hiding there.'

Thanking his unknown guide, he set off again, one eye on the luminous dial of his compass, mind reeling at the speed of the German incursion. *Mof everywhere*. Yet this time yesterday there were barely any. Harzer's work, he guessed. Nor was the irony of British soldiers in Baker Street lost on him, even if locating them proved thorny. He found the church, large and Gothic-looking with a tall spire. Bakkerstraat emerged nearby to the north, a long cobbled road of shops and houses intersected by narrow alleys. Its buildings bore signs of fighting, with smashed windows, broken doorways and walls pocked by bullets. A haze of smoke hung in the air from smouldering fires. The street seemed deserted, but he sensed unseen eyes watching and knew venturing down it would be folly, so he circled behind, creeping through gardens and courtyards from one building to the next, pushing through gates and climbing fences as he went. Halfway along he dropped over a wall to be confronted by Paras pointing rifles.

'Who the fuck are you?'

'Trickey, 2nd Battalion.'

'Like hell. What's the password?'

'I've no idea. *Waho Mohammed*?'

'That'll do. Get inside before we're spotted.'

The speaker's name was Galt, an older corporal with a bandaged arm, part of a six-man recce section from 1st Battalion, he said, cut off during fighting that afternoon. When Theo asked about the rest of his battalion, Galt said he didn't know, but that other 'random sods' were sheltering in houses nearby.

'Which sods?'

'Service Corps bods, a REME section, a few South Staffordshire wankers, various others. Maybe thirty in all. Some of your lads too.'

'C Company?'

'B, I think. They're next door.'

'Any officers?'

'A Recce Squadron lieutenant, but he got killed by a sniper earlier.'

'Germans?'

'Everywhere.'

'So you're the ranking man.'

Galt shrugged. 'Suppose.'

Theo slipped outside, ducked through a gate and into the next house. There he found Crawley's men, a dozen unhappy survivors of a platoon once numbering thirty, sitting on the floor with their backs to the wall. They'd been cut off at the river, they told him, and their friends all killed or captured. 'Half-tracks with machine guns!' one said bitterly. 'What the hell use is a rifle against that?'

'Not much.'

'We thought we'd been forgotten,' another lamented.

'Not at all. Major Crawley's very worried. I'm here to guide you back.'

'Back where?'

'To Battalion. At the bridge.'

'We still hold the bridge?'

'Of course.'

'What about reinforcements?'

'Division's on its way, 30 Corps expected tomorrow. And you're needed too.'

The news brightened them, as did the prospect of purposeful action. Ten minutes later, having collected everyone he could find, Theo assembled them in the yard of the first house. Of assorted units and disciplines, as Galt said, they were variously armed too, mostly with rifles and Stens. And even as he spoke, two more hurried round the corner.

'Is this the bus for the bridge?' one quipped.

'Yes and it's just leaving, you dozy tossers,' Galt replied.

'All right, listen.' Theo drew his Webley. 'We're going now. I'll lead; Corporal Galt's section covers the rear. We move quickly and quietly, we don't stop, we keep moving and we all stay together. Clear?'

'Hold on,' someone asked. 'Who did you say you were?'

But he was already gone.

He led them the way he'd come, running at the crouch, sticking to side streets and hugging shadows until he arrived at the church with the tower. Here he gathered them beneath an arched window.

'Go that way.' He pointed. 'Carry on four hundred yards and you come to a road, then a piece of parkland with trees, then you'll see the bridge to your right. That's our perimeter. Pickets are expecting you; they'll guide you in.'

'Aren't you coming?'

'Work to do.'

'What work?'

But he'd gone again.

C Company was nowhere to be found. He returned to Bakkerstraat, then began working his way towards its last known position on Utrecht Street, the main road into town. Progress was slow; he had to retrace his steps often, doubling back and forth to find routes around obstructions, or lying in cover until dangers passed. And the further west he went the more exposed he felt, with gunfights raging all round, tracer bullets arcing overhead and exploding star shells bathing him in white light. He could even hear occasional shouting in German. After another hour he finally reached the bottleneck between railway and river where the battalion had stopped on Sunday. Pausing there to catch his breath, he glimpsed a flash at a window and ducked as a bullet smacked into the wall by his head. He sprinted away, bent low, skidding headlong round a corner only to confront a vehicle roadblock not twenty yards ahead. He froze, hemmed in by houses, standing in plain view with nowhere to go. Figures in grey guarded the vehicles; he could see them standing about smoking. Any second and they'd spot him. So he vaulted over a hedge, sprawling headlong on to damp grass, expecting shouts or running boots or the crack of a shot to follow. Seconds passed, minutes, and nothing happened. He rolled on to his back, and took stock. He was in the garden of a town house, once elegant, now battle-damaged, with broken windows and scarred walls. Although trapped, he was in cover and undiscovered. He checked his watch, realizing it was four hours since he'd left the bridge. Overcome with strain and fatigue suddenly, he crawled to the house, hauled himself through a window and collapsed to the floor.

He awoke at dawn to the unmistakable thump of artillery. Enemy artillery, a few miles west, he estimated, somewhere between the town and the DZ. The time was precisely six too, suggesting an organized offensive was under way. Sitting on the floor he listened as the barrage swelled, pitying the men beneath it and recalling Blangy, Tamera, Bréville and the others, the screaming shells, the spurting earth, the choking air and quaking ground. Then he rose and began searching the house. Since leaving the bridge he'd eaten nothing and drunk no water, but the kitchen supply was off and the only food was a solitary pear in a cupboard. He ate it gratefully, treading softly upstairs to reconnoitre the street. Pushing open a bedroom door, a cry of alarm sounded and to his astonishment he saw two figures in the gloom, an elderly man and woman lying side by side in bed, wide eyed with terror.

'Nicht schiessen!' the man whimpered.

'I won't.' Slowly he withdrew the Webley. 'It's all right, no gun, look.'

'You are British?'

'Yes.'

'Thank the Lord! We've been lying here all night thinking it was Boche downstairs.'

He was a retired tax inspector, his wife was ninety and deaf, they'd lived in the house forty years. When they heard British parachutists had landed they'd hurried into the street with the neighbours and cheered and draped flags from the windows like everyone. But then the battle began, the celebrating stopped, and they'd hurried indoors again.

'It was terrible. The fighting was so bad we could only hide up here and pray for it to end. Our windows got smashed by bullets, and there's a hole in the roof. I kept watch from up here. Your boys fought bravely but the Germans had tanks and rockets and machine guns and many were killed and wounded. Hundreds perhaps. I saw some of them carried over there to the hospital.'

'Hospital?'

'St Elizabeth. Across the road. Where all the vehicles are.'

He stole a look. The hospital was large and brick-built, with Red Cross flags hanging from windows and railings. How he'd missed it the night before he couldn't imagine. The vehicles outside it weren't a roadblock either, but parked or abandoned. Some were British, some Dutch or German, and as he watched a white ambulance pulled up and orderlies jumped out bearing stretchers. Orderlies in khaki.

'Who controls the hospital?'

'Who can say? Civilian staff work there, mostly Dutch doctors and nurses, but I also saw Germans, some with weapons. And I saw your doctors too, coming and going, treating wounded men from both sides. Sometimes right there in the street.'

Theo shed his Webley and fighting knife. 'Hide these and stay out of sight. Do you have provisions?'

'Under the bed.'

'Can you spare a little water?'

He drank greedily, then slipped downstairs through a back door, creeping onward until he arrived at an alley opposite the hospital. There he waited, crouching at the corner, unarmed, and his battledress sleeves rolled to the elbow like an orderly. Minutes passed, then another van pulled up with stretchers aboard. The back doors opened and a British medic jumped out. Glancing left and right, Theo stepped into the open and hurried over.

'Give you a hand,' he murmured, grasping one end of a stretcher.

'Put this on!' The medic fumbled a Red Cross armband. 'And lose the lanyard, for Christ's sake, you stand out like a dog's balls!'

Moments later they were clumping into the hospital.

Carrying an empty box as a prop, he toured its wards and corridors searching for C Company survivors. Injured men lay everywhere, both friend and foe; most of the staff appeared Dutch, although British field ambulance staff worked among them, all under the supervision of patrolling Germans. Everyone looked busy, nobody challenged him, and eventually he spotted three lone Scotsmen in a corner, clustered together on their stretchers as though for comfort. Kneeling beside them, he pretended to read their cards. Two were awake, he saw, but the third, an ashen-faced boy lying protected between them, looked close to death.

'Theo Trickey,' he murmured, 'HQ Company. Colonel Frost sent me.'

'Did we get the bridge?'

'Yes, and we're still holding it.' He hesitated. 'Can you tell me what happened?'

C Company was gone, it emerged. Wiped from existence like words from a blackboard. A few lucky ones may have escaped, they recounted, and many were missing, but the main bulk, a full company of over a hundred men, were either dead, injured or captured.

'Please tell me everything.'

So they told him. Following the failed attempt on the railway bridge, Major Dover had led them into town via the most direct route. By then a good two hours behind Frost, dusk was falling and he was anxious to catch up. But the further they went, the slower their progress, and they were increasingly harried by an enemy closing in from all sides. Then, long after dark, with everyone drooping from hunger and fatigue, they were suddenly caught in a storm of machine-gun fire.

'Blinding, it was,' one said, 'like rivers, you know, rivers of glowing fire, the tracer, humming down the road at us like sparks, bouncing off walls and that. It stopped us dead.'

'Lads up front caught it worst,' the other added, patting the third boy's arm. 'Cut down like ninepins they were. That's when the casualties really started.'

The column scattered, everyone running for cover into gardens and behind walls and garages. Further forward movement was impossible, so they lay low, then after a while the shooting died down and the order went round to dig in. A cheerless night followed with the Germans shooting off mortars and flares every few minutes to deny them sleep. Engines were heard too as their vehicles circled the streets around them. And casualties still rose as snipers who had infiltrated overlooking buildings picked off the unwary. The Scotsmen shot back with passion, and Dover sent patrols to flush them out, but the snipers always moved on before they could catch them. At dawn the scene was quiet. Dover roused everyone early and they made ready, grateful to be active and done with the night. With the road ahead barred, his plan now was to double back and find another route to the bridge. Stealthily if possible, and without alerting the enemy.

But the enemy was already alert, and the moment C Company moved off the killing began with a vengeance.

'They were all along the road, waiting in the houses and on the roofs, and in trucks following in the next street, so they could keep pace and pick us off at will, like one of those shooting stalls at a fair.'

'Aye, and we couldn't stop to fight them, that'd have been suicide. All we could do was keep moving, kneel, loose off a few rounds, get up, keep moving, kneel again. It was murder, like shooting fish in a barrel. You'd be crossing an alley with your mate and he'd fall down dead at your side. And that meant leaving him. Those that could walk we helped as best we could, them that couldn't we had to leave, and hope to God Dutch medics found them, or Jerry ones.'

The end came at a crossroads, near where they'd started the evening before. Low on ammunition, exposed on all sides, and with mortars and grenades now crashing in, as well as sniper and machine-gun fire, plus two Panzer tanks overseeing proceedings from an embankment, the Germans had prepared the perfect trap. There was no stopping, no escape, and no going back. Dover knew it, so did his remaining men, yet none were ready to give up. Using smoke grenades for cover, C Company's remnants rose up as one, bellowing their war cries, and stormed across the junction, shooting with everything they had. Then they flung themselves into a house on the other side. Fewer than thirty made it, and as the tanks rumbled up outside, and the machine-gun teams set up their tripods, and the first grenades came crashing through the windows, Dover bowed to the inevitable.

'He did what he had to. It was surrender or die.'

'What happened to him?'

'Got pulled to one side, being a major and that. Last we saw he was being led away to some SS colonel in a Jeep.'

'What about you?'

'Bought it trying to cross the junction.'

Theo looked at them. The unconscious boy had a blood-soaked dressing over a deep chest wound. His breathing was fast and shallow and his pallor deathly. His friends lay beside him, dabbing his brow and tucking his blanket in like doting parents. C Company, the wild men of Bruneval, the spear throwers of Sidi Bou, heroes of the Nefza Pimples and the bloody survivors of Primosole. Gone.

'I'm sorry.'

'No. We're the lucky ones.'

Still bearing his box and armband, he began making his way down to the street. On the way, a Royal Army Medical Corps officer stopped him.

'You there!' he hissed. 'You're not a bloody medic.'

'Ah, no, sir, you see—'

'In here.' He opened a storeroom door. 'Trickey, isn't it?'

'Yes, but how do—'

'How's the malaria?'

'Pardon?'

'Sedjenane, that blasted road in Tunisia, in all that bloody rain. You went down with malaria. We looked after you, don't you remember?'

'You're 16th Parachute Field Ambulance?'

'Ronnie Gordon, at your service. We were at Primosole too.'

'Yes, I remember.'

'And now we're here.' Gordon glanced around. 'Another cock-up.'

16th PFA had landed on the first day, he recounted, advancing with Lathbury's 1st Brigade as far as the hospital. Then the fighting began in earnest and the Germans drove everyone back, leaving Gordon and his team marooned.

'We were busy with casualties so it made little difference. The hospital changed hands a few times – we had it, they had it, and so on. Now it's theirs, probably for good. And they don't take kindly to combatants sneaking about so you should clear off and quick.'

'What about Division?'

'God knows. Radio problems evidently. Rumours are all bad though. Apparently Urquhart's starting to pull everyone back.'

'Back where?'

'A few miles west, some suburb towards the DZ.' He hesitated. 'Which rather leaves you chaps out on your own. Unless 30 Corps get there, and that seems unlikely.'

'But 1st Battalion. And 3rd...'

'I doubt they'll be coming. In fact by all accounts they don't exist as battalions any more, just bits and pieces scattered all over. We had a 1st Battalion major turn up here last night bringing a party of casualties. Company commander, he was, big chap name of Timothy.'

'John Timothy, yes, I know him.'

'He told me 1st Battalion got split up advancing on the bridge. He managed to keep his men together and moving forward, reckons they fought their way to within a thousand yards of you before being forced back. By that time he had less than fifty men left. 3rd Battalion fared even worse.'

'Are you in touch with them? Division, I mean. Or anyone...'

'Not for hours. The telephones were working, intermittently, and we keep trying on the radios. You never know.'

'Could you pass them this?' He produced a note. 'If you do make contact. It's from Colonel Frost – our location, situation, casualties and so on.'

'Of course.'

Gordon told him to wait in the storeroom until the coast was clear, but an hour later returned saying the streets outside were crawling with Germans. So he stayed, hunched on the floor, dozing when he could, listening to the muffled sounds of shooting and shelling outside. Nearer blasts set the stores rattling on their shelves. Gordon dropped by with occasional updates and what food he could spare, at one point a Dutch nurse in white uniform opened the door, collected supplies and left again without a word, but the hours passed and still Theo remained trapped. Finally, at sunset by his watch, a lull came in the shooting and he decided he must break out. As he opened the door a chink, Gordon reappeared with an orderly bearing a stretcher.

'Climb on. We'll carry you out.'

'Where to?'

'The mortuary. It's round the back. After that you're on your own, but I suggest you keep away from the street, follow the railway for a while then swing south and make for the bridge.'

'Thank you.'

'My pleasure. Good luck, and tell Frost we'll do our best to get his details to Division.'

He lay down, they covered him like a corpse, and he felt himself borne up. Stairs followed. He tried to lie still, German voices echoed, then he was outside, smelling rain-soaked streets and the tang of smoke. Moments later he was running for cover.

His Webley was unreachable, so too his fighting knife, but darkness and falling rain helped obscure his movements, and by keeping to the railway he made good time. Soon he was nearing 2nd Battalion's perimeter. Which seemed to have shrunk.

'Who goes there?'

'It's me, Trickey.'

'Jesus, Trick, I nearly shot your bloody arse off!'

He hurried on towards Battalion HQ, shocked by the change of scene in just twenty-four hours. As though the entire area had been struck by earthquake, barely a building stood undamaged: many were smoking hulks, and several had collapsed altogether. Fires burned everywhere, whipped by squally winds which sent flames dancing skyward and thick coils of smoke billowing along the road. The bridge itself, intermittently visible through the smog, was little more than a fire-blackened mess of steel and wrecked vehicles.

Frost was in the basement, lantern in hand, checking on the scores of injured men lying about the floor like victims of a shipwreck. Captain Logan, the battalion medical officer, was there too, and Padre Egan, kneeling beside an inert figure in one corner.

'Hello, Theo,' Frost said wearily. 'I was beginning to fear we'd lost you.'

'Sorry, got held up.'

'Things pretty hot in town?'

'Rather, sir.'

Frost nodded, his face tight-lipped as Theo delivered his report. On the situation in town, on what he knew of 1st and

3rd Battalions, on the rumours of a withdrawal by Division, and finally on the fate of C Company.

Frost listened. Scottish names on a list. His own pencilled at the top. Autumn 1941 and the birth of C Company. Now it was dead. 'God, what a mess. Poor Victor.'

'Yes.'

'Nothing on 30 Corps, I take it.'

'Sorry, sir.'

'Then we're on our own and that's that.'

'1st Battalion nearly made it. Some of them.'

'Yes, good old Tim. If anyone got through it would be him.' He hesitated. 'We lost David Wallis last night. Jerry was pushing in under the bridge, he went to see what could be done, got hit several times.'

'I'm sorry.'

'It's a bad blow – an old friend and terrific second-in-command. I've put Digby in charge of Battalion in his place. He's out there now somewhere, checking the perimeter, chivvying up the boys, waving his bloody brolly about.'

'How long can we hold out?'

'Ammo's practically gone. Food, water and medical supplies too. We've been reduced to fighting with bare hands, bayonets and petrol bombs, you know.' Frost managed a smile. 'We're Paras, Theo. We hold out as long as it takes.'

It took one more day. And it was the shelling that finished them. During the night pickets began reporting a repositioning of enemy forces, and hopes were raised of a German withdrawal, or even a retreat. But it was no retreat, merely a change of tactics by Harzer, abandoning costly infantry assaults in favour of bludgeoning the British into submission with artillery. Moving his guns up that night, his plan was the systematic destruction of every building in the vicinity, forcing the Paras into the open so the machine guns and snipers could do their work.

It began at first light with salvos of flak that hacked at buildings like axes. Soon larger-calibre pieces were added to the mix, including medium howitzers and the dreaded 88s which punched shells straight through walls with a noise like howling wind. Meanwhile, mortars and rockets fired incendiaries, starting scores of fires that filled buildings with flames and choking smoke. With the water mains cut, Paras were reduced to fighting fires with blankets and brooms, or fleeing burning houses altogether. And then, mid-morning, everyone paused to a new sound, a heavier thud that was felt rather than heard, like a punch to the stomach. Theo was on the battalion balcony spotting for a mortar crew when a house fifty yards away vanished in a pall of smoke.

'What the fuck was that?' the loader demanded.

Theo swung his binoculars. 'I don't know, but it came from across the river.'

Minutes later the next shell crashed in, blasting a lorry-sized crater in the road.

'Christ, Trick, they're ranging on us!'

'Time to move, come on.'

Grabbing the mortar they hurried for the stairs, already littered with rubble and debris from days of fighting. Halfway down they met Padre Egan puffing up.

'Theo! Colonel says we're to evacuate the—'

A blast of heat struck them, followed by a deafening explosion that flung Theo aside like a doll. Thunderous noise followed as walls collapsed, rafters splintered and an avalanche of debris came crashing down, while the whole building shuddered as though gripped by giant hands. The house was collapsing, he realized, clutching his arms over his head. But slowly the noise subsided, the floor stopped quaking, and the building swayed to a precarious standstill. Timbers creaked, lights flickered and a roof tile slid to the floor as, dazed and choking, he struggled to his senses. The ops room door was lying over him, and beyond it the bedroom was a roofless shambles. Smoke and dust swirled like fog, daylight showed where once a wall had stood, and a ragged hole in the floor now gaped in place of the stairwell. His legs were hurting and sticky with blood. Kicking the door off, he crawled to the hole in the floor and peered down. Sections of staircase were gone, he saw through the fog, so too the landing below, leaving a smoking void down to the hall.

'Come on,' he croaked.

'Christ.' The mortar section spluttered to life. 'What happened?'

'We must get down. The padre.'

'How, for God's sake?'

'This way. Keep to the side.'

He clambered unsteadily down until reaching the hall, where he found Egan buried in rubble. Bricks and timber surrounded him; his body was twisted like a broken dummy, and one leg was oddly angled.

'Padre!' He tore at the debris. 'Padre, can you hear me?'

Slowly Egan's head lifted, his face white with dust.

'... injured to Brigade HQ,' he gasped. 'Before it gets too dangerous in here!'

Their next hour was spent transferring men, equipment and casualties to the Brigade cellar, while Battalion HQ, once a graceful town house, was abandoned as a lethal ruin. Dodging bullets and mortar shells, he and the stretcher-bearers came and went until all were safely installed. Egan, protesting manfully, was dosed with the last of the morphia and placed among them. Limping stiffly, Theo surveyed the cellar: over a hundred injured men, he counted, once proud but now beaten. Yet not entirely beaten. Able finally to tend to himself, he began unbuttoning his trousers to inspect his legs. With predictable results.

'Look! Privates on parade!'

'Not now, Trickey dear, I've a headache.'

'Those knees! I'm in love.'

His legs were lacerated but not seriously, and he cleaned and dressed them himself. All the while the relentless crash and thump of the barrage kept on, fraying nerves and showering the basement with dust and debris. And every few minutes came the visceral punch as the huge field gun fired from across the river. Reporting for duty once more, Frost told him it must be silenced: '... before it blows us all to kingdom come. Any suggestions?'

'We could try with the mortar, sir. From up on the roof.'

'You'll get about three rounds off before he spots you.'

Theo smiled. 'Three's all we have left.'

Hurrying up through floors of offices, the mortar section following, he reached the roof and began scanning the far bank with his binoculars. Somewhere he heard a distant bell ringing, then a muzzle flash betrayed the gun's position half hidden in bushes. Gouts of smoke followed the flash; a moment later they all felt the thump as the shell exploded two streets away.

'It's on a limber,' he said, peering through the glasses. 'Like one of those old horse-drawn *Feldhaubitz* pieces. Slow to manoeuvre, and takes a big crew to operate.'

'Packs a hell of a punch though.'

272

'Can you hear a ringing noise?'

'Fuck knows, Trick, can we please get on with it before they see us?'

Their first shell was straight but short; he called the correction and their second, to their astonishment, landed right in the bushes with the gun. Theo watched as the smoke cleared. Figures appeared, scurrying in all directions, and moments later a tractor emerged pulling the gun away.

'Did we get it?'

'Well, we got it moved.'

'Good enough for me, let's get off this bloody roof!'

'What *is* that ringing noise?'

It was a telephone, in the room below, a clerk or secretary's office with filing cabinets, desk and shelves filled with ledgers. On the floor a phone was ringing. Gingerly Theo picked it up. Moments later he was running for the stairs.

'General Urquhart sends his compliments,' Frost began.

'Splendid,' Digby scoffed. 'Where did he get our number?'

'Looked it up in the directory,' Crawley offered.

'Aye, under "i" for idiots.'

It was mid-afternoon. Outside, as the buildings burned and crumbled around them, the Paras fought on, bravely and doggedly, but with growing desperation. The barrage had slackened, but then a new menace had threatened as Harzer's troops returned, stealthily, street by street, house by house, permeating the British like a rising tide, steadily corralling them into a shrinking ring of death. Yet the defenders kept going, sometimes with guns and grenades, increasingly with knives, clubs or whatever came to hand. Bricks and rubble were hurled from rooftops; petrol bombs engulfed the unwary; two Germans were crushed by a dropped wardrobe. Many fell to daggers and bayonets. But the enemy tide was inexorable, and as their numbers swelled and their position strengthened, the exhausted Paras fell inexorably back.

And then, to their dismay, they lost the bridge.

As the perimeter shrank, Harzer launched a pincer movement along the northern bank of the river. Stealing in from both directions at once, well armed and heavily supported, the SS men drove a wedge between defender and river, opened a gap under the bridge and thus completed their encirclement. More a symbolic setback than a strategic one, the loss was keenly felt by the Paras, and their determination to fight on inevitably wavered. An A Company lieutenant named Grayburn immediately gathered a scratch force and led a determined counter-attack, but was ruthlessly gunned to the ground with no survivors. A while later Harzer's men were seen setting up positions on the bridge itself, and with that the mission was lost.

An emergency meeting was called. One by one Bridge Force's senior surviving officers hurried into the battered Brigade building until all were assembled. Frost in command, Hibbert the brigade major, Digby Tatham-Warter now leading 2nd Battalion, Doug Crawley his second-in-command, a Recce Squadron major called Gough, and Logan the MO. Theo was there to record proceedings, which told him something momentous was coming. As the officers gathered, he studied them: haggard, filthy, all were exhausted, hungry and parched with thirst. Some carried injuries. And despite their attempts at humour, a sense of hopelessness filled the air.

'We've a decision to make,' Frost told them, 'and I'd be grateful for your thoughts.'

'What did Urquhart say?' Hibbert asked.

'He thanked us for our efforts. And apologized for not getting through.'

'So they've given up.'

'To be precise,' Frost sighed, 'he didn't know if they should come and rescue *us*, or we should go and rescue *them*.'

'How droll.'

The division was in tatters, Frost went on, and facing total annihilation, so Urquhart had decided his duty was to save what he could of it. 30 Corps might yet still arrive – it was desperately hoped it would – but in the meantime he was consolidating a position four miles west of the bridge in the town of Oosterbeek.

'Didn't we pass through there on the way in?' Crawley asked.

'Yes, we did. He's set up HQ in a hotel called the Hartenstein, with a mile wide perimeter around it. The division, what's left of it, is to fall back there and make a stand.'

'Christ.'

'Including us. If we so decide.'

A shocked silence was followed by expected replies.

'Fall back be buggered!'

'Over my dead body.'

'We're taking this bloody bridge back!'

Frost held up a hand. 'Commendable sentiments, and I agree with them, but we have to be realistic.'

'Sir.' Hibbert spoke. 'There's four miles of solid Jerry between us and Division. We'd never make it.'

'And we've very little left to fight them with,' Gough added.

'Well, I for one am not bloody surrendering!'

'All right, Digby. Anyone else?'

'What about the injured?' Logan said quietly. 'We can't just abandon them.'

With the decision deferred, everyone returned to their positions. Theo was sent round to tally up remaining ammunition, while Frost and Crawley set off to check the perimeter and count heads. Conferring in a doorway, a mortar round suddenly exploded beside them, blowing them off their feet.

It was the turning point. Both men were incapacitated, suffering blast wounds to legs and thighs. Bleeding and semi-conscious, Frost was carried in to lie with the other injured. Logan told him his wounds were serious; shortly afterwards Frost sent for Gough, the Recce Squadron officer.

'I'm sorry, Freddie,' he said hoarsely, 'but I'm out of it. As the most senior officer remaining, you must take command of Bridge Force.'

'Yes, sir. What are my orders?'

'To use your best judgement.'

Competent and resourceful, Gough saluted, left and immediately swung into action. Within an hour he had negotiated a ceasefire with the Germans to evacuate the wounded of both sides. Gradually, as dusk fell, an eerie silence descended on the scene, broken only by the crackle of fires and rumble of German motors. Trucks pulled up, and the injured were quietly loaded aboard under the enemy's watchful gaze. Doug Crawley was among them, so too Padre Bernard Egan, and lastly John Frost, his face grey with pain and anguish.

'Tell them!' he gasped, beckoning to Theo. 'Tell them what happened here.'

'They'll know, sir.' They clasped hands. 'Everyone will know.'

Afterwards the adversaries drew apart and resumed fighting as though nothing had happened. But the outcome was foregone and both sides knew it. Gough, playing for time, issued orders for remaining survivors, variously estimated at a hundred men, to wait until darkness then slip away in twos and threes and make for Oosterbeek as best they could. Digby Tatham-Warter wanted to stay and launch an attack on the bridge, but was dissuaded when enemy tanks were seen lumbering on to it. And as darkness fell, Bridge Force gradually dispersed, stealing away into the night like thieves. Soon all but a handful were gone. Theo, as a final act, was charged with despatching one last message to the world. Sitting at the worthless radio, he dutifully tapped out the words Gough dictated.

Out of ammo. God save the King.

Only the Germans heard it.

CHAPTER 15

'Good luck, Trickey.'

'You too, sir.'

And with that Gough was gone. He wouldn't make it. None of them would; Gough, Digby, Hibbert: they'd all be caught within a few hours, as would most of the survivors of Bridge Force, stopped, as Hibbert had predicted, by the wall of Germans between them and Oosterbeek.

An impenetrable wall, Theo had already learned, so instead of trying to cross it he stayed put, waiting alone in the Brigade basement for the wall to come to him. Hours passed, and the sounds of fighting died to silence. He rested a while; rain fell and he drank it from a gutter, scavenged for food, jotted notes in his pad, and rested some more. A while before dawn he awoke to the sounds of approaching boots and murmurs in German.

'In here.'

'Are you sure?'

'Yes, this was their HQ.'

'But there's no one.'

Then a flashlight beam appeared, scouring the cellar walls. Theo coughed and stood up, and the light blasted in his face.

'There's one! Fuck!'

'*Nicht schiessen.*'

'Put your bloody hands up!'

'They are up. Don't shoot.'

'Where are the others?'

'Gone. There's only me.'

They dragged him outside, and made him sit in the rubble-strewn street with his hands on his head while they continued searching. Rain still fell. A third man guarded him with a rifle while others searched buildings nearby; ten minutes later the first two returned.

'Where are they? *Die Roten Teufel*?'

'I told you. They've all gone.'

'Then why are you still here?'

'To speak to your commanding officer.'

'Ha! That's a joke!'

'It's no joke. Oberführer Harzer. Tell him the British liaison officer he met in Thury on 17 July is here and wishes to speak with him.'

'You were in Thury?'

'Yes. With Generalfeldmarschall Rommel. Go and tell him.'

It took another hour. As he waited, a grey dawn broke overhead, slowly revealing the full devastation of the bridge environs. Sprinting head down from one building to the next, he'd not appreciated how extensive it was, how cataclysmic, but now, sitting at gunpoint in the rain-puddled road, he could only stare in amazement. Not one building remained undamaged, and many were either gutted shells or smoking rubble. Fires burned everywhere, trees were blasted to white-limbed skeletons and the street was a cratered waste ground of wrecked vehicles and abandoned equipment. So entire was the destruction it seemed impossible anyone could have survived it. Two days, he mused, watching German soldiers pick cautiously through the debris, 2nd Battalion had been asked to hold out for two days at most. This, he realized wearily, was the morning of the fifth day.

A half-track appeared, grinding in and out of the wreckage towards him, then pulled up. Harzer, scowling, was sitting in the back.

'Get in.'

Weaving round obstacles, the vehicle then slowly drove, to Theo's astonishment, up the approach road and straight on to Arnhem Bridge. Though its steel girders and arched span had dominated his subconscious for days, he'd never been closer than a few hundred yards. Now for the first time he was actually upon it, the cause and focus of so much fighting and bloodshed. Wreckage lay everywhere, scattered from the burned-out pillbox, exploded ammunition shed and destroyed vehicles, while a forlorn line of blanket-covered corpses waited to one side. And yet work was already under way returning the bridge to service, with an army bulldozer busy clearing debris, fire teams damping down smouldering embers and engineers checking the structure for damage.

'Are there explosives?' Harzer demanded.

'I have no idea,' he replied truthfully. 'But it would seem sensible to check.'

'Out.' Harzer's glare was icy. He too looked exhausted, Theo noted, red-eyed and haggard, almost as bad as Frost, which was some consolation. Fighting for the bridge had evidently been as hard for the Germans. They disembarked the half-track, and Harzer led him to the centre of the span, out of view and earshot.

'Give me one reason why I shouldn't arrest you,' he said, lighting a cigarette. 'Or better yet, shoot you.'

'Because of *Fall Grün*.'

Harzer glanced round. 'One mention of that will get us both shot.'

'I know.'

'No, you don't. After Stauffenberg there's paranoia everywhere. And spies.'

'How is Generalfeldmarschall Rommel?'

'Alive. Recuperating slowly. I believe we owe you partly for that.'

'You owe me nothing. Please pass him my respectful good wishes.' He produced his pad and tore off a page. 'And this.'

Harzer glanced. 'Are you out of your mind?'

'She's a friend. Maybe he can do something.'

'You *are* out of your mind!'

'Can I go now?'

Harzer looked dazed. 'What?'

'We must be clear about our duty. The Generalfeldmarschall taught me that. But more importantly we must be loyal to our beliefs and convictions, and to what we know is right. He said we're nothing without that.'

'Very noble but—'

'I must rejoin my regiment, and fulfil my duty.'

'And you expect me to just let you?'

'Yes. It's the right thing. And he'd want you to.'

'Jesus.' Harzer ground out his cigarette. 'He said you were an intractable bastard.'

Moving in daylight meant certain capture or worse, so he stayed at the river's edge, found a timber pile covered in tarpaulins, crawled underneath and went to sleep. Slowly the long day passed. He heard rats foraging among the wood, patrol boats cruising, engineers at work on the bridge, and the thump of artillery to the west. Occasionally he emerged to survey the scene and check the water level on the shore, but mostly he stayed hidden. During the afternoon rain fell again; the tarpaulin kept him dry but stank of creosote and river mud. Huddled beneath it he gathered planks into a bundle and tied it with wire, ate crumbs scavenged from his pockets, redressed his legs with soiled bandages and waited for dusk to come. When finally it did he had to wait further, until the lapping waves stopped creeping up the shore, paused, then finally began to retreat. Only then, with the current flowing downstream, did he emerge into the darkness, carry his wooden bundle down to the water, and wade quietly in.

The Rhine was cold, wide, and smelled of diesel oil. Gripping his woodpile he paddled out to mid river and allowed himself to be carried, bobbing like a drifting bough, gently downstream. Passing Arnhem he saw fires still burned, painting the townscape with flickering orange shadows, and the tower of the church he'd paused at was gone, but the shelling had stopped and the sounds of shooting died down. He drifted on, the river following a wide loop, and Arnhem was lost from sight, then he rounded a bend and discerned a shadowy obstruction in the darkness ahead. Soon the obstruction grew wide and large like a dam, and he could hear water rushing through it, and he realized it was the collapsed span of the railway bridge, still lying where it had fallen days earlier. He kicked hard to swim round it, regained calmer waters with an effort and resumed drifting. Arnhem's docks and wharves lay far behind him now; here the riverbanks were grassy, the fields beyond them wide and flat and misty grey in the darkness. Once clear of the rail bridge, he released his bundle and swam quietly to shore, crawling from the water to lie, shivering with cold, on its muddy bank. He remained there a while, ears alert to the slightest sounds. By his estimate he was level with the small church where C Company had rallied after its attack on the rail bridge. The church was a quarter of a mile away across fields; behind him German artillery lay in strength across the river, while in front somewhere their infantry waited in their foxholes and dug-outs, feeding and resting, cleaning their weapons and counting the hours before attack. But he could hear nothing save the mournful piccolo call of a curlew, so he rose and set off for the church.

The first person he encountered was British, a sentry, slumped asleep at his post.

'Wake up.'

'I... Christ, who are you?'

'Trickey, 2nd Battalion. What's your name.'

'Stubbsy. Albert Stubbs, I mean. We heard 2nd Battalion was—'

'You were asleep, Albert. And there's Jerry everywhere.'

'I know, I'm sorry, we've been at it so long...'

'Who's your CO?'

'Brigadier Thompson, at least it was, but then he got injured so it was Major Cain. Then he got shot too, so now it's a Major Dickie somebody of 11th Battalion.'

'Lonsdale?'

'That's him. It's a scratch force see, there's us South Staffs lads, some Royal Artillery, a few Borderers and lots of Paras, all mixed up.'

'Where is he?'

'In the church. You won't tell him, will you?'

Theo patted his arm. 'Rest, Albert, you need it. But don't sleep.'

He found Lonsdale on a pew having a bloody head wound dressed by an orderly. One arm was in a sling; his other hand too was bandaged.

'Good Christ alive!' he exclaimed. 'It's…'

'Trickey, sir, hello.'

'That's right! Johnny Frost's intelligence bod. Where on earth did you spring from? You're soaking wet.'

'The river, sir. From Arnhem Bridge. I'm afraid it's all over there.'

He gave an abbreviated report, outlining events since 2nd Battalion's arrival on Sunday. Lonsdale, head shaking, listened in awe.

'Jesus. Poor Johnny. Is he badly hurt?'

'His legs caught the worst of it. Should I report to General Urquhart?'

'You could try, but I doubt you'll get near.'

Lonsdale Force, as it was called, was holding the southeastern corner of the Oosterbeek perimeter, but becoming increasingly isolated as the enemy closed in.

'We're also to keep a corridor open to the river,' Lonsdale confided. 'In case.'

Theo looked round the church. Shadowy humps on pews and floors indicated Paras trying to sleep, while glowing cigarettes betrayed those unable to. 'In case?'

'There's a brigade of Poles trying to reach us from the other side somewhere. And who knows, 30 Corps may yet turn up, the dozy sods.' He lowered his voice. 'But we can't hold out much longer and Urquhart knows it. There's talk of trying to evacuate the division across the river.'

'Should I stay here?'

'I could dearly use you. Some of these boys are very green.'

A blanket was found, and water and dried rations to chew on, then he sat himself on the steps of the wooden pulpit and waited for the dawn to come. Later he slept, and dreamed he was on a train. He was lying on a cot, something heavy was pressing on his head, and three men were looking down at him wearing unfamiliar uniforms: an American airman, a Royal Navy lieutenant, and an RAF fighter pilot. 'How is your war?' the navy officer asked. 'I've found it hard,' he croaked in reply.

At six precisely he was jerked from reverie by the earsplitting shriek of shells. Moments later the first explosions shook the ground. Fired from across the river, other guns soon joined in, until Oosterbeek was under assault from all sides. Inside the church the lights shivered on their wires, a framed painting crashed to the floor and a fog of dust fell from the ceiling. Pulling on damp boots he hurried out in time to see Lonsdale Force already deploying, with half-dressed men scattering to their positions hefting weapons and ammunition. Southeast, Lonsdale had said, which meant the enemy would come across open fields from the river, along the road Frost had taken into Arnhem, or both. He surveyed the lie, noting the rise of the road, the openness of the fields and the distant remains of the rail bridge; then, as he watched, a line of mortar blasts began stamping across the field towards him, exploding from the earth like giant flowers. Men scattered from their path, except one, who was standing transfixed by the road.

'Get down!' He sprinted across, tackling the youth to the ground. They fell heavily; Stubbs threw his rifle aside, kicking and struggling in panic.

'Albert, stop!'

'Let me go!'

A final shell exploded in a tree, cleaving it in two as though by axe.

'Stop. It's all right.'

'No!'

'It's over, listen, they've stopped.'

'What?'

'Where's your firing position?'

'It's… it's in the ditch in the field down there. Where those shells just landed!'

'Come on, let's go.'

'But I can't! You saw—'

'You're safer there. Come on, get your rifle, we'll go together.'

Gripping the youth's arm, he rose and led him into the first field, hurried across it, traversed a hedge, crossed a second field, found the ditch and leaped in. Helmeted heads could be seen at intervals along it, as though in a trench, twenty or more, he counted. Stubbs's section, six South Staffordshires led by a lance corporal, was holding one end. They greeted Stubbs with coarse jokes and insults, eyed Theo suspiciously, then went back to scanning the distant railway.

'They'll come from the river.' Theo pointed. 'That way.'

'Bollocks,' the corporal scoffed. 'They'll come from the railway.'

'Too much open ground. The river's much closer.'

'Is that so?'

'Yes. I was here before.'

The corporal turned. 'So, Stubbsy, who's this bloke you've brought us then?'

'He's from 2nd Battalion. Can't remember his name.'

'Well, tell him to fuck off, will you? We don't need his sort.'

'Yes, but he—'

'Back in a minute.' Theo set off, hurrying down the ditch, bent low, murmuring to the troops as he passed them. 'Hold your fire, wait for the word, hold your fire, wait for the word...'

'THERE!' someone shouted. 'Movement, on the embankment, see?'

All heads turned. Tiny figures were spreading out along the railway, with others following, pushing what looked like carts and trailers.

'There they are!'

'No, it's a feint. A diversion. Keep covering the river. And you should fix bayonets.'

By the time he returned to Stubbs's section, the troops on the railway had stopped moving, and appeared simply to be watching.

'What are they doing?'

Theo peered. 'I think they're engineers. Something to do with bridge repairs perhaps...'

'Mortars!' A tattoo of rapid thumps sounded from the river. Seconds later a hail of explosions was straddling the ditch.

'Fuck this!'

Quickly the barrage swelled, shell after shell blasting gouts of earth high in the air. Shrapnel flew; soil and stones pelted them, smoking holes appearing in the ground as though punched by a fist.

'Fall back!' someone shouted.

'No! Keep down, fix your bayonets!'

They stayed, hunching lower in the ditch, showered with dirt and debris, then smoke rounds crashed in, creating a drifting screen that blotted everything from sight.

'What now, for Christ's sake?'

'Hold your positions. Wait for the word!'

Then as suddenly as it began the barrage stopped. An eerie lull followed, silent but for the twitter of larks and hissing shell holes. Seconds ticked, then minutes, and still nothing happened. Smoke obscured everything; then came a glimpse of shadowy movement, and the clicking of kit, and suddenly the enemy was materializing before them like ghosts through mist.

'NOW! Charge, come on!'

He leaped up, the others following, hesitantly at first, then eagerly, rising like a tide from the ditch, surging forward, bayonets glinting, and bellowing like bulls. Shots rang out, and the clashing of steel, and confused shouts as both sides joined. Standing in the melee, Theo saw running shadows, two men fighting on the ground, another wielding his rifle like an axe, and a fourth falling from a bullet. And, as he'd seen so often before, the sheer unexpectedness of the rebuff, its fervour and ferocity, were enough to carry the day, and he saw the enemy falter, and hesitate, and panic, until in seconds their attack had foundered and they were running back into the smoke.

He found Lonsdale atop the church tower, scanning the scene with binoculars.

'They'll try again, no doubt,' he said.

'I expect so, sir. But without armour they're at a disadvantage.'

'Can we hold them?'

'A Vickers or two would help. And we're low on ammunition.'

'There's supposed to be air-drops.' Lonsdale peered at the sky. 'But the only planes I've seen are Jerry ones.'

'Any word from Division?'

Gunfire echoed from the town direction, both British and German, including the crackle of light weapons and grenades. 'Rumour is the Panzer Grenadiers are closing in, and if that happens we risk getting cut off. I've heard nothing for hours.'

'Do you want me to get through?'

'It may come to that.' Lonsdale paused. 'There's something else first.'

An artillery position was under fire along the Arnhem road, and Lonsdale feared for its survival. 'We've a 6-pounder either side of the road, and they've been doing a grand job holding Jerry off. But they need ammo, Trickey, and I need info. A Sergeant Baskeyfield's in charge. Find out what's happening and tell him to pull back if things get too hot.'

6-pounders were 1st Airborne's only field artillery. Flown in by glider, their ammunition came in heavy metal boxes loaded on to hand carts. Theo found the cart and set off, dragging it up the same road 2nd Battalion had used on the first day – quiet, tree-lined, with trim white houses to one side and the distant river to the other. The road sloped upward, bright sunlight now shone overhead, the day was warm and he was soon sweating. Gradually Oosterbeek fell behind, and with it the raucous clatter of battle, punctuated now by a new sound up ahead, the percussive 'stonk' of a 6-pounder firing.

He found the guns a quarter of a mile further on. The road became lined with shops and houses, then rose to a crest; the 6-pounders were positioned at the bottom, one in a garden, the other across the road behind a low brick wall. Well sited, they had a commanding field of fire to the top of the road, but there was no infantry support, no machine-gun or mortar emplacements, just the two field guns. As he drew breathlessly near he saw one had the name 'Hilda' painted on its barrel.

'Watch out!' Two men ran forward and pulled Theo and the cart into cover. As they did so a salvo of bullets tore into the road behind them. 'Missed us, you bastard!'

Baskeyfield introduced himself. 'Thanks for coming, we were getting anxious.'

'Major Lonsdale's a bit concerned too.' He looked around. 'How many are you?'

'Was seven but two got injured. They're in the house behind. Me and Billy Balfour are here on Hilda, Terry Smith and his boys over the other side.'

Polite waves were exchanged. 'Was it snipers that injured your men?'

'It was a mortar, mounted on a half-track. We blew it to bits. But snipers, yes, there's a machine gun hidden up the hill somewhere. Long range. It's OK if you keep your head down. It's the heavy stuff we've to watch out for.'

The heavy stuff appeared a few minutes later. Two tanks, with infantrymen clustered behind in classic fashion. Turning on to the road several hundred yards ahead, they slowly began making their way downhill.

'Wait for it, Terry!' A wave came in response. Then the lead tank's muzzle flashed and a shell smashed into a house nearby, showering them with brick dust and debris.

'Shoot!' A thunderous crash as both 6-pounders fired, reloaded with a clang and fired again. Four shells exploded up near the tanks; one seemingly scored a hit, sending smoke and wreckage high into the air. Both tanks lurched to a stop, the men behind crouching hesitantly, but then one fired a second shell which exploded in the road, flinging rock, rubble and white-hot shrapnel in all directions. The sniper joined in, from much closer this time, pouring machine-gun bullets at them. 'Get down!' someone roared and Theo dived for cover. Bullets pecked the cobbles around him, a deafening explosion shook the ground, a 6-pounder barked in reply, then came a lull and a hoarse cry: 'We got the bastard!'

He raised his head. Clouds of dust filled the air; the house behind him was completely blown out, with the entire front wall crumpled to rubble. A thirty-foot poplar had splintered to matchwood ten yards away and a line of telegraph poles hung from their wires, drunkenly askew. Meanwhile, up the hill the lead tank was on fire, oily smoke belching from its turret, and the second was reversing away, with its infantry still huddled behind.

'Christ, Terry!'

Theo raised himself higher. Hilda's loader, Balfour, was pointing a bloody arm across the road. The second 6-pounder, wreathed in smoke, was lying on its side, destroyed by a direct hit. Three bodies were scattered about it, none of them moving.

'I'll go.'

He leaped across the road, the sniper's gun spitting bullets at his heels. He made it to cover, but as he reached the crew and knelt at their side, he knew from their shattered bodies they were dead.

'They're coming again!' Baskeyfield shouted.

The second tank was returning, nosing its way past the first, now furiously ablaze. Baskeyfield's gun fired but missed, and Theo could see he and the injured Balfour were struggling to reload it. Then a shell from the tank screamed in, smashing a nearby shop to rubble. Smoke and dust obscured all vision again. Theo started to cross the road but was stopped by a burst from the sniper. He ducked behind the wrecked gun, hearing bullets pinging from its steel plating. A rifle was propped against the wall, one of the gunner's. 'Trickey!' An urgent cry came from over the road. He picked up the rifle, leaped up, fired three rounds at the sniper's window and sprinted across. Balfour, staggering, was trying to load Hilda one-handed, while Baskeyfield was crouched behind its sights cranking a wheel. 'Hurry, lads!' Theo tore open a tin and fumbled a shell into the breech, Balfour slammed it shut and without waiting hit the firing lever. Hilda barked and debris spurted from a building above the tank. 'Again, boys, quick as you can!' Theo groped for another shell, the tank fired again and everything went black.

He came to lying on his back. All sound was gone save for a shrill ringing in his ears. Opening one eye he could see blurry blue sky and watery sunshine above a veil of drifting smoke. Through the other eye he could see nothing, because blood was dribbling into it from a wound on his brow. Much of his body seemed numb; the back of his head throbbed and felt hot and wet with blood.

'Push, Billy!'

Someone was shouting. Groggily he raised his head.

Hilda was lying askew, thrown bodily sideways by a blast from the tank, which he could see was motionless on the hill. Fighting waves of nausea and giddiness, he staggered to his feet. Jack Baskeyfield, his teeth gritted behind a mask of blood, had his back against the gun's wheel, and was trying to shoulder it straight by brute force. Billy Balfour, shattered arm hanging limply, was pushing feebly on the barrel with the other.

'She's fucked, Jack,' he was saying.

'No she ain't, she can still shoot. Push!'

'She's fucked.'

'Stop saying that! Trickey! Give us a hand before that bastard tank starts again.'

'She's fucked,' Balfour repeated, like a mantra.

Between them they manhandled the gun half straight. But then Balfour, checking his arm, face ashen, sank to the ground in a faint. Baskeyfield too sat wearily down, gasping for breath. Theo gave him water, and did what he could for the mumbling Balfour.

'I think perhaps you've done all you can here, Jack,' he said to Baskeyfield.

'You could be right.'

Theo nodded at the tank. 'They're waiting for reinforcements, and then they'll come at you, in strength.'

'Expect so.'

'Major Lonsdale wants you to come back. While you still can.'

'Fair enough.'

Baskeyfield hauled himself to his feet and crunched into the house. A minute later he returned, half carrying an unconscious crewman.

'Nichols has died,' he said. 'This is Ted Fletcher, got hit in the guts.'

They lifted Fletcher on to the hand cart, roused the groaning Balfour and set off. Theo removed the soiled bandages from his legs, tying one round his bleeding head and the other as a tourniquet on Balfour's arm. Then they crept away towards Oosterbeek, the air silent but for the clatter of cartwheels and the never-ending sounds of far-off fighting. As they went, the pounding in Theo's head grew worse, as did the ringing in his ears. Then halfway up an incline he heard a rumbling of heavy motors far behind.

'That's a Tiger,' Balfour muttered.

'They're bringing in the big guns then,' Baskeyfield replied wryly.

They walked on, pushing the cart to the crest of the incline, where they paused for breath. Half a mile ahead the squat tower of Lonsdale's church could be seen poking through trees.

'Manage from here?' Baskeyfield went on.

'What?'

'I'm going back.'

'But you can't...'

'See Fletcher gets help. It's all downhill from here, should be a doddle.'

And with that he turned and walked back down the hill.

'Mad fucker,' Balfour said, watching him go. 'We all are.' And without another word he too released the cart and stumbled after his friend.

Theo stared as the two limping figures descended from view. Halfway down, one placed a hand on the shoulder of the other. Not until they were gone from sight did he turn and continue for the church. And long before he made it, pushing the unwieldy cart over rutted cobbles, he heard the unmistakable stonk of a 6-pounder firing.

'Here's the lists, and here's my report.' Lonsdale handed him the sheets. 'Tell Urquhart we'll go down fighting if he wants, but without ammo that'll be soon. Probably within twenty-four hours.'

'Yes, sir.'

'Although I expect it's the same for everyone.' He glanced at Theo. 'You all right, Trickey? You look a bit pasty.'

'I'm fine, sir.' Theo fingered the back of his head, still sticky with blood. 'A little giddy, that's all.'

'Well, get it seen to. There's a dressing station in a hotel up there somewhere.'

'I will. Soon as I've reported to General Urquhart.'

'And thanks for your help.'

They saluted and he set off, roaming north through gardens and parkland. But within minutes he'd lost his bearings and, overcome with giddiness, had to lean against a tree. Blinding pain was spreading across his head. His neck hurt too, his vision was blurring and he felt nauseous and leaden with fatigue. Struggling onward he realized his left arm was becoming numb. After a while the trees thinned and he came to an avenue of chalet-style houses. Gunfire was nearby now, with hoarse shouts and small-arms fire sounding all round. He ignored it, stumbled through a squeaking gate, and something bee-like thrummed past his ear. 'Get out of it, you idiot!' someone shouted, so he pushed through a door into a dim hallway smelling of autumn roses. 'I will,' he said. 'I just need to sit down.' A door led from the hall, he opened it, hoping for chairs or even a bed. Instead a German soldier gaped at him from a window.

'*Vede a cësa,*' Theo said in Ladin. 'I'm going home.'

Everything happened slowly. The German, recovering, swung his rifle from the window to the room. Theo, legs buckling, sank to his knees. A shot rang out and the German staggered back, clutching his shoulder. Then the grenade appeared, rolling on to the floor through the open window.

The two men stared at it. Then at each other. Theo managed a shrug.

Then it went off.

The rest were fragments, real and remembered, floating by like pages in a book.

A bright flash followed by a long interval of nothing.

Running feet and muttered oaths.

Grandma Ellie cooking strudel.

Another interval of nothing.

Being lifted on to a stretcher.

A girl's head resting on his chest.

Water trickling between his lips.

Pain and blackness.

Scots boys charging down a lane.

Cold evening air and the shrill shriek of swifts.

'He's had it, lads, put him down there.'

Stars glimpsed through clouds.

A camel train in the desert.

A man waving a flag on a broomstick.

His own hand rising, like a puppet's.

The men on the train.

CHAPTER 16

And so the circle closes. A Dutch nurse spots Theo's body lying among the dead, and the next morning he and I begin our seven-month journey together. Both a literal journey – Arnhem, Apeldoorn, Fallingbostel, Bergen and finally Ulm – but also a figurative one, in which we exist, adapt and evolve, travelling through life and captivity as interdependent strangers.

Like a spiritual symbiosis.

Within forty-eight hours of the Allies arriving in Ulm, I'm on a plane heading for England. Everything happens with dizzying speed. American forces appear in strength throughout that Sunday, including a sizeable medical contingent who take over at the *Revier*, swiftly sorting and assessing our remaining patients for evacuation. After a slow start, 44th Infantry Division's advance across Germany has been swift, Ulm is of trivial significance and they aren't going to linger there, the priority being to cross the Danube and mop up the enemy's southern flank. The sheer scale and speed of their coming is bewildering after so long, and I find myself entering a state of trance-like awe, like a child at a circus. Allied POWs are to be repatriated right away, and sick ones go to the head of the queue, together with their medics, thus early next morning I find myself assembling on the street outside the *Revier* beside a fleet of American lorries and ambulances. Our orderlies Fenton and Pugh are coming too, while Erik elects to stay and oversee remaining departures. Parting from him so suddenly, and after so long together, is a poignant moment.

'Good luck, Daniel my friend,' he says, clasping my hand.

'You too. I hope you find your family well and hear good news of your brother.'

'Thank you.' He hesitates. 'Remember "Garland & Henning"?'

'Of course.' The grandly labelled package we received from Lucie Rommel, and how we'd joked about setting up in practice together. 'You know where to find me!'

'Yes.' He glances away, and I glimpse the damage five years' oppression has wrought on his kindly soul. He seems so vulnerable suddenly, so desolate and alone that I want to comfort him. Hug him actually, but that would seem excessive, so I grasp his hand again instead.

'I could never have done this,' I say rather belatedly, 'got through it, I mean, without you. That's a fact. And it's also a fact that I'm a cussed bugger and not easy to get on with. So I'd like to thank you – for your patience, your humour, your kindness and your wonderful company these past months.'

There's one more goodbye and this time hugging is included. Trudi has been waiting patiently to one side, a slight figure lost in all the bustle. I go to her and we cling on for quite a time, while American GIs look on disapprovingly. I don't care. This isn't about fraternizing with the enemy, it's about souls brought together by conflict. There's so much to say and yet no words come; my earlier reassurances now seem hollow and trite as I realize just how much I shall miss her. We kiss, she sheds tears on my lapel, then, amid much slamming of doors and honking of horns, we take our leave, and I clamber into the cab of the leading truck. The last we see of each other is a cheerless wave through the grimy glass of the windscreen.

We're driven forty miles to an airfield outside Stuttgart where there's a delay and we end up camping for a night. The Americans are wonderful hosts and ply us with far more food and drink than we're accustomed to, consequently the flight home is a sickly blur. I do remember the plane is a Dakota and I deliberately sit in the same position that I flew to Arnhem in – one place from the door – which brings it all back with a noisy jolt. We land a few hours later at RAF Cottesmore, which is barely ten miles from our starting point the previous September, and with that my Arnhem round-trip is complete. Still badly hungover, I mark the occasion by throwing up on the tarmac.

After a few days' processing we're finally sent on leave. A welcome period of respite follows at home with my parents, a time of much-needed solitude and reflection during which I sleep a lot, take long walks in the countryside, enjoy home-cooked food and generally revel in my new-found liberty. Then May comes, the war in Europe duly ends and it's time to make decisions about my future.

11th Battalion no longer exists, I've already learned, disbanded after its annihilation at Arnhem, so in effect I'm MO of nothing, which seems appropriate. Various postings are offered, including to airborne units overseas, but I'm done with soldiery and get myself demobbed at the earliest opportunity. My old job at St Thomas' is available and I slip back into the routine easily enough. But not for long, because my resolve to take up general practice remains firm, so having made the necessary enquiries, I fill in the paperwork and begin the process of requalification, most of which entails burying my nose in textbooks.

At the same time, which is about six months after returning from Ulm, I take out the diaries, notes and papers written whilst there and begin assembling them into some sort of order. First task is to transcribe them from tiny handwritten scrawl to neatly typed sheets, a painstaking if revelatory process which brings the memories flooding back, and makes good use of Rommel's magnifying glass, but also prompts me to contact old cohorts to fill in missing gaps. Erik's memory of events is more reliable than mine and we exchange several letters, one of which tells me of the death of his brother, Doctor Pieter Henning, at the hands of his Japanese captors in Burma. I know how devastating this is to Erik, and how the hope of seeing Pieter again had sustained him through his own captivity. Finding words to express proper sympathy seems impossible.

I also re-establish contact with many key Arnhem connections: Arthur Marrable and Pip Smith of the RAMC, George Lea and Dickie Lonsdale of 11th Battalion, who in turn put me in touch with others who knew Theo. These include Majors Ross and Timothy of 2nd Battalion, Jock Pearson of 1st and 8th Battalions and of course John Frost who writes at length, both of Theo and also rather bitterly of the costly fiasco that was Operation Market Garden, blame for which, somewhat surprisingly, he lays squarely at Boy Browning's feet.

'Many factors had a bearing,' he writes, 'failed radio communications, DZ too far from the objective, not lifting the whole division on Day One, slow 30 Corps, poor intelligence, unforeseen Panzer divisions, etc., but by far the worst mistake was the lack of priority given to the capture of Nijmegen Bridge.'

General Gavin, it transpires, commander of 82nd US Airborne, was the man tasked with taking Nijmegen Bridge, which is just eight miles south of Arnhem and 30 Corps's final obstacle before reaching us. But jumping in as planned on Day One, Gavin was suddenly ordered to prioritize his forces on a woodland area nearby called Groesbeek Heights where, coincidentally, Browning was setting up his personal HQ. Thirty-six hours was lost on this pointless diversion, and when attention belatedly returned to Nijmegen Bridge, the Germans were there in strength, Gavin had a terrible time taking it, and by then it was too late anyway – the fate of Frost's battalion, and arguably the whole of 1st Airborne Division, was sealed.

Some time later I have a pub lunch with Theo's Special Ops handler, Dennis Grant. By now SOE has been disbanded by the new Attlee government, with some staff transferring into what will become MI6, but many simply cast adrift, or sidelined into jobs in insurance or banking. Dennis is one of these and clearly irked by this shoddy brush-off, so perhaps talks more freely than he should, aided by the beer, of his work, his relationship with Theo, and especially the whole *Fall Grün* affair.

'Case Green never stood a chance,' he recounts, puffing on a cigarette. 'Too many chiefs were opposed to it.'

'Military or political chiefs?'

'Both. By then it was all about marching triumphantly into Berlin before the Russians got there, and certainly not doing grubby private deals with Nazi generals. Yet the irony is, if we'd gone along with *Fall Grün* we'd have been in

Berlin months before Stalin, and wouldn't be in the mess we are now.'

The 'mess' he refers to is Russia currently occupying all of Nazi-held Eastern Europe and still creeping westwards, something he says we should have thought of before embracing our 'glorious new ally' in 1941. He continues in this vein, becoming louder and more agitated, until heads are turning, so I buy him another beer and steer the conversation back to Theo, who was regarded highly by Dennis, but cautiously by SOE top brass.

'It was the Rommel connection. The fact that they had a relationship, a rapport even, it made the bosses suspicious. They thought he might be a double agent.'

'What do you think?'

'I never considered it for a moment. I trusted him completely. Still do.'

Tentatively I ask if he has any up-to-date information, but he just shrugs.

'I'm off the payroll, remember. The last time I saw him was on our return from Normandy, a few days after Rommel was injured, in July forty-four. At that point he ceased being my operative and resumed being a Para with 2nd Battalion. That was the end of it.'

'Nothing since?'

He sips beer, and I sense he's choosing his words. 'We lost many agents over the years, Doctor, brave men and women sent into the field never to return. You don't get used to that, nor can I begin to describe how it feels. The guilt, I mean, and the burden of responsibility. Those captured inevitably suffer torture and execution. Many vanish without a trace; only a few survive to tell the tale.'

'Like Theo.'

'Yes, although he was a changed man. But the point is, a good many are still listed as missing, and in my book it falls to us, therefore, their handlers, to find out what happened. So a small group, I'm told, is at work trying to track them down.'

'And you're in contact with this group?'

He smiles. 'I couldn't possibly say.'

Dennis gives me a contact number for Theo's next of kin and I duly ring it. The man answering turns out to be his mother's new husband, Nicholas Abercrombie. Carla is in the Hague, he says, leading a delegation promoting South Tyrolean autonomy. When I ask him about Theo he confirms they knew he was alive and a POW but that was all.

'His mother has had to grow accustomed to hearing nothing from Theodor for long periods,' he adds a little stiffly.

'Do you mean they're estranged?'

'To a great extent, regrettably.'

He promises to pass her my details and we hang up. Meanwhile, 'The Rommel Papers', as I've begun calling them, are taking shape, and growing rapidly in size and scope, and the question arises as to what on earth to do with them. The originals, it transpires, were secreted in various hiding places around Herrlingen in an effort to save them both from retreating Nazis and advancing Allies. Most survived, although some were lost or looted, and the Americans confiscated all Rommel's letters before reluctantly returning them later. I learn this from Gertrud Stemmer, who keeps in touch, and also from Manfred, who writes a touchingly polite letter telling me how he survived the war and is now home with his mother. One of his first acts, he recounts, having surrendered himself to the Allies at Riedlingen, was to hand over the affidavit he and I composed together recounting his father's death.

By now various academic papers and articles are starting to appear in the press about military strategies of the war, and I read them with interest. One in particular catches my eye, a newspaper excerpt from a forthcoming book by the eminent historian B. H. Liddell Hart called *The Other Side of the Hill*. To research it, Liddell Hart was given exclusive access to several imprisoned German generals, including Guderian, von Manstein and even the ageing von Rundstedt, from who he gained a unique and top-level insight into Germany's military thinking. The excerpt makes fascinating reading: *... but one eternal regret,* Liddell Hart writes intriguingly, *is that I shall never have the opportunity to interview Erwin Rommel, arguably the most important general of them all.*

One telephone call to his publishers later and a meeting is fixed. I approach this with some trepidation, for like it or not I am custodian of an important archive, and the prospect of handing it over to this renowned if controversial historian is not without risk. However, Liddell Hart is charming, complimentary and extremely knowledgeable and I'm quickly won over. Similarly his publisher, Mr Bonham-Carter of Collins, reassures me that a serious job will be done if a book does go ahead. Lean and bespectacled, Liddell Hart talks expertly of Rommel's achievements, failures and reputation, questions me enviously about my dealings with the family, and describes his ideas for said book, which he suggests might just consist of the papers, edited into date order and little else. 'Let the man speak for himself!' he enthuses, going on to suggest we make a joint trip to Germany together to interview Rommel's relatives and colleagues.

An attractive notion for more than one reason, but before anything can happen, approval must be sought from the family to hand over the archive. He entirely agrees, we part on good terms, and there's then a pause of some weeks while letters are exchanged between me and Herrlingen.

During which I receive a note from someone called Atkins.

This is by now December 1945, the first peacetime Christmas for six years, and suitably festive despite ongoing rationing and unusually cold weather. However, I don't feel particularly festive. I'm knee-deep in studies, temporarily housed in a threadbare student's room at St Thomas'. Damp and cell-like, the room consists of bed, chair and desk, a lukewarm pipe for heating, and windows running with condensation. Unsurprisingly I go down with a bronchial infection, as does much of London, and apart from a few days wheezing at my parents' house over Christmas, spend most of the holidays shivering in the room pretending to study. One day I return from the pub to find a note under the door.

'A former colleague of Dennis Grant's has information. Could you meet somewhere to discuss? Atkins.' Plus a phone number in Bayswater.

I call the number, a plummy-sounding woman answers and after some confusion I realize she is Atkins. We arrange to meet somewhere public next day – she suggests St James's Church in Piccadilly – I arrive early, and hang about outside coughing into my handkerchief. Piccadilly is swirling with shoppers and sightseers, many of them still in the military, so when a dark-haired woman in the uniform of the Women's Auxiliary Air Force detaches herself from the crowd and heads my way I'm caught unawares.

'Doctor Garland?' She holds out a gloved hand. 'Vera Atkins.'

'What? Oh, yes, sorry, I didn't see you.'

She offers a tight smile. 'I suppose that is the idea.'

We enter the church and take a pew near the back. The building was badly damaged in the Blitz but is now open again. A temporary roof has been erected, much of the remaining structure shows fire damage, but the church is busy with visitors, and someone's playing carols on the organ. I sit there sniffing, watching the comings and goings, and waiting for Vera to open proceedings. Which she eventually does.

'I gather you knew one of Dennis's Italian agents. Codenamed Horatio,' she says in cultured English.

'Who?' Then I remember Case Green. 'Oh, you mean Theo Trickey.'

'No.' Her tone hardens. 'That is not correct.'

She's testing me, I realize, making sure she's got the right person. 'Oh, no, wait, it was André someone... Lad... er, Ladurner. That's it, Andreas Ladurner.'

'That is the name on file, yes.'

'You know him?'

'I met him once, briefly, here in London in May of last year.'

'Have you heard from him?'

'I have had no dealings with him at all. I worked for the French section.'

'Oh. Then, what's...'

'My job was to recruit and train agents to work in occupied France. Both men and women.'

'So what's the connection with Theo, I mean Andreas—'

'I'm attempting to tell you!'

Her dark eyes are afire suddenly. And something about the tightness of voice and stiffness of posture suggests suppressed emotions. So I shut up. 'Sorry.'

'As I said, our section ran agents to work in occupied France, and over the course of the war some hundreds were sent there to do essential but dangerous work. Unfortunately, inevitably you might say, some were betrayed or were caught. And I'm sure *you*, as a former POW, don't need me to describe their subsequent treatment.'

'No.'

'Of those captured agents, fifty-one were unaccounted for at the war's end, including fifteen women. They were my responsibility and it is therefore my duty to find out what happened to them, obtain justice for any ill treatment suffered, and seek proper recognition for the priceless work they undertook. And if necessary I will make this my life's work.'

'I see.'

'To this end I made a preliminary visit to Germany last month, and will be returning there again in the spring to continue my investigations.'

She pauses, so I venture a question. 'What did you find?'

'Of the fifteen, at least three have survived, and four remain unaccounted for.'

'Oh.'

'While eight are known to have been executed.'

'Christ.'

'Indeed, Doctor, but he couldn't help them. The methods of their murders were barbaric, and include lethal injections of air or phenol followed by cremation whilst still alive, guns fired into the back of the neck, and asphyxiation in gas chambers.'

A long silence follows. She leans forward in the pew, elbows on knees, as though in prayer. Eventually she shakes her head. 'I'm sorry. This isn't your concern.'

'Isn't it everyone's?'

'I intend to make it so.' She turns, and manages a small smile. 'In the meantime, Doctor, do the initials C, CT or AAB mean anything?'

'No.'

'The names Clare Taylor, or Aurélie Anne Bujold?'

'I don't think...' Something pricks at my subconscious. Theo's letter, his one personal effect, was signed with a C. And on the night of Rommel's exhumation, when we found the cyanide capsule in his throat, Gerhard Brandt spoke to me about a message from his wife, Inge. She'd been posted to some camp as punishment for supplying medicines to POWs. A camp like the one at Belsen she showed me. *Tell him not to worry*, her message said. *Tell him Aurelia's here.*

Atkins is waiting, and watching me closely. So I take a chance. 'Oh, yes. Aurélie, now I remember.'

'Remember what?'

'That, er, she was in a camp.'

'Which camp?'

'Oh, um, what was it...'

Afterwards. A week or so after the exhumation. Back at the *Revier*, I go upstairs to question Theo. The day before he vanishes. Who the hell's Horatio, I demand. And while you're at it, who's Andreas Ladurner? And he stonewalls me, pursing his lips and frowning and saying he can't remember. And then I lose my temper. 'Then who's Aurelia!' I shout. And he cocks his head like a bird.

Who?

Aurelia, Theo. She's at a prison camp. Outside of Munich.

Which camp?

'Which camp, Doctor?' Atkins repeats.

Dachau!

And the next day he's gone.

*

We part outside the church, where she hands me the envelope, and apologizes.

'I'm sorry, Doctor. Force of habit. We never pass information without being absolutely sure it's going to the right person.'

'That's quite all right,' I reply, somewhat giddily.

'It's a copy of course, and a translation, and only an extract, for obvious reasons.'

'I understand. Good luck with your mission.'

We shake hands. 'And you with yours.'

I don't read it then, I walk through to St James's Park, cross Westminster Bridge to the hospital, climb wearily to my freezing garret and slump on to the bed, fully dressed in overcoat, boots and scarf, and feeling like I'm the one that just endured interrogation. Which in a way I have. Leaning to the bedside locker, I extract bottle and glass from among the flu remedies, slop in Scotch and pour it down my throat. Only then, fumbling at my coat pocket, do I pull out the envelope and open it.

In the autumn of 1944 I was transferred from my position as medical director at Bergen Hospital to a new position at the Dachau internment camp outside Munich. The circumstances of my transfer relate to regulations infringements on my part, and were a demotion. Dachau is a very large SS Konzentrationslager establishment spread over several sites and housing as many as 40,000 inmates and over 1,000 staff. It is not to be confused with camps further east used for mass killings; nevertheless, conditions were appalling for the inmates who were used as slave labour, and many died of maltreatment, disease and starvation.

Torture, hangings and shootings were also commonplace. My position was on the medical directorate, teaching at a medical school for military doctors and also working in the staff infirmary.

As one of the few female doctors on site, I also had access to the women prisoners' block, which was adjacent to the main camp. Part of this block included a special wing for female political prisoners, saboteurs and agents. Shortly after arriving at Dachau I became aware of four British women being held in this block and arranged to visit them. They were in very poor condition, having been arrested months previously and moved from one place to another on a regular basis. All had suffered torture and all were sick and severely malnourished. Their morale was high, nevertheless, and they spoke to me of the Allies winning the war and eventually being freed. About a week after I visited them, however, a rumour went round that they were to be executed. I tried to visit them again but this was denied, and the following night they were taken outside, made to kneel down and shot in the head. A guard later told me they held hands during this ordeal but made no sounds. Two of their names I since learned were Yolande Beekman and Elaine or Éliane Plewman, but I have been unable to learn the other two names so far. I will continue to investigate the matter, and hope this is of some help in your researches.

Some weeks later another female British prisoner was brought in and housed in the secure block, and as soon as possible I visited her. She told me her name was Aurelia Bujold, although later confided this was not her real name. She told me nothing of the reasons for her arrest and captivity but it was clear she was being treated as an agent or saboteur like the four earlier women. This meant her fate

310

was likely to be the same, so I began to make efforts to save her. This was by now early in 1945 and it was clear the war would soon be lost for Germany. Many staff at the camp knew this and had begun to make arrangements accordingly, and through contacts I was able to transfer Aurelia to my staff as a prisoner orderly and also get word out that she was alive. This would not save her if orders came through for her execution, but I was able to ensure she suffered no further maltreatment, received proper medical attention and better food.

Early in April 1945 rumours were strong of imminent German defeat and fears arose as to what the SS would do with the prisoners. One rumour was they would attempt to murder them all to erase evidence of the abuses. Then in the third week of April word went round that 'fitter' prisoners were to be marched south to the Tyrol as hostages of the SS, who were planning a last stand there. Few at the camp believed in such a stand; nevertheless, the arrangements were made and on the 23rd or possibly 24th of April the march began. I arranged to go as part of a medical contingent and Aurelia came too as one of my orderlies. Two days after our departure, I later learned, the order arrived at Dachau for her execution.

The march was long and hard and the prisoners suffered cruelly. In all an estimated 10,000 began the march, most of them suffering from diseases such as typhus and diphtheria as well as malnourishment and starvation. The pace was slow and the terrain increasingly difficult as we headed generally south towards Bad Tölz. SS guards followed the column, shooting prisoners that fell behind, there was no shelter at night, and no food except what could be scavenged at the roadside. The weather was unseasonably cold too,

*with temperatures below freezing at night and several days
of snow. By the third day about a quarter of the prisoners
had died or been left to die; the few medics in the column
could do nothing to help them and in any case were in little
better condition. On the fourth day I too began to suffer
a fever and had to be helped, and it was during this time
that Aurelia, who was ill with pneumonia, told me of her
real identity, speaking at length of her family, her travels in
the Maghreb and Europe and of a man she'd met in Algeria
and hoped to marry. Her real name she told me was Clare
Margaret Taylor. She wrote this down and asked in the event
of her death that this be passed on to you to notify her family.*

*On the sixth or seventh day the column had been reduced
by over half and was moving only extremely slowly. By
now we had passed Bad Tölz and were travelling southeast
towards the Tegernsee. It was also noted that many of the
guards had deserted and those remaining were unsure how
to proceed. During the afternoon we passed the town of
Reichersbeuern where we learned that Adolf Hitler had
committed suicide in Berlin. Many more guards fled then, in
effect abandoning the remains of the column. We proceeded
further, the suggestion being that we attempt to seek help
and shelter at the next town, which was Waakirchen. I
and a few others led an advance party towards the town;
Clare Taylor came too, as we were supporting each other.
Halfway along this road we came to a bridge crossing a
river, and on the bridge, walking slowly towards us with a
stick, was a man wrapped in coats and wearing distinctive
sand-coloured boots. This man was Clare Taylor's friend
Theodor Trickey whom I had treated in hospital in Bergen
and who had walked more than seventy miles from Ulm to
find her.*

I believe they are currently staying on a farm in Campania, Italy, but do not know the address. If I learn anything more of them or the other missing women, I will get in contact.

I hope this is of some help in your researches.

Inge Brandt MD

Nuremberg, November 1945

A letter from the publisher

We hope you enjoyed this book. We are an independent
publisher dedicated to discovering brilliant books, new
authors and great storytelling. If you want to hear more,
why not join our community of book-lovers at:

www.headofzeus.com

We'll keep you up-to-date with our latest books, author
blogs, tempting offers, chances to win signed editions,
events across the UK and much more.

If you have any questions, feedback or just want to say hi,
drop us a line on hello@headofzeus.com
or find us on social media:

@HoZ_Books

HeadofZeus

HEAD *of* ZEUS